With Love From

COLLECTION

January 2020
**With Love From
Las Vegas**

February 2020
**With Love From
Cape Town**

March 2020
**With Love From
Sydney**

April 2020
**With Love From
Florence**

May 2020
**With Love From
Athens**

June 2020
**With Love From
London**

With Love From Athens

CATHERINE SPENCER

SHARON KENDRICK

LUCY GORDON

MILLS & BOON

First Published in Great Britain 2020
By Mills & Boon, an imprint of HarperCollins*Publishers*
1 London Bridge Street, London, SE1 9GF

WITH LOVE FROM ATHENS © 2020 Harlequin Books S.A.

The Greek Millionaire's Secret Child © 2009 Catherine Spencer
Books Limited.
Constantine's Defiant Mistress © 2009 Sharon Kendrick
The Greek Tycoon's Achilles Heel © 2010 Lucy Gordon

ISBN: 978-0-263-28142-2

MIX
Paper from
responsible sources
FSC™ C007454

This book is produced from independently certified FSC™ paper to ensure responsible forest management.

For more information visit: www.harpercollins.co.uk/green

Printed and bound in Spain
by CPI, Barcelona

THE GREEK MILLIONAIRE'S SECRET CHILD

CATHERINE SPENCER

CHAPTER ONE

EMILY singled him out immediately, not because his father had described him so well that she couldn't miss him, but because even though he stood well back from everyone else, he dominated the throng waiting to meet passengers newly arrived at Athens's Venizelos Airport. At more than six feet of lean, toned masculinity blessed with the face of a fallen angel, he could hardly help it. One look at him was enough to tell her he was the kind of man other men envied, and women fought over.

As if on cue, his gaze locked with hers. Locked and lingered a small eternity, long enough for her insides to roll over in fascinated trepidation. Every instinct of self-preservation told her he was bad news; that she'd live to rue the day she met him. Then he nodded, as though he knew exactly the effect he'd had on her, and cutting a swath through the crowd, strode forward.

Given her first unobstructed view, she noted how his jeans emphasized his narrow hips and long legs, the way his black leather bomber jacket rode smoothly over his powerful shoulders, and the startling contrast of his throat rising strong and tanned against the open collar of his white shirt. As he drew closer, she saw, too, that his mouth and his jaw, the latter firm and faintly dusted with new beard shadow, betrayed the stubbornness his father had spoken of.

When he reached them, he asked in a voice as sinfully seductive as the rest of him, "So you beat the odds and made it back in one piece. How was the flight?"

"Long," Pavlos replied, sounding every bit as worn and weary as he surely must feel. Not even painkillers and the luxury of first-class air travel had been enough to cushion his discomfort. "Very long. But as you can see, I have my guardian angel at my side." He reached over his shoulder, groped for her hand and squeezed it affectionately. "Emily, my dear, I am pleased to introduce my son, Nikolaos. And this, Niko, is my nurse, Emily Tyler. What I would have done without her, I cannot imagine."

Again, Nikolaos Leonidas's gaze lingered, touring the length of her in insolent appraisal. Behind his chiseled good looks lurked a certain arrogance. He was not a man to be crossed, she thought. "*Yiasu,* Emily Tyler," he said.

Even though her sweater and slacks pretty much covered all of her, she felt naked under that sweeping regard. His eyes were the problem, she thought dizzily. Not brown like his father's, as she'd expected, but a deep green reminiscent of fine jade, they added an arresting final touch to a face already possessed of more than its rightful share of dark beauty.

Swallowing, she managed an answering, *"Yiasu."*

"You speak a little Greek?"

"A very little," she said. "I just exhausted my entire vocabulary."

"That's what I thought."

The comment might have stung if he hadn't tempered it with a smile that assaulted her with such charm, it was all she could do not to buckle at the knees. For heaven's sake, what was the matter with her? She was twenty-seven, and if not exactly the most sexually experienced woman in the world, hardly in the first flush of innocent youth, either. She knew well enough that appearances counted for little. It was the person inside that mattered, and from everything she'd been told, Niko Leonidas fell sadly short in that respect.

His manner as he turned his attention again to Pavlos did nothing to persuade her otherwise. He made no effort to embrace his father, to reassure him with a touch to the shoulder or hand that the old man could count on his son for whatever support he might need during his convalescence. Instead he commandeered a porter to take care of the loaded luggage cart one of the flight attendants had brought, and with a terse, "Well, since we seem to have exhausted the formalities, let's get out of here," marched toward the exit, leaving Emily to follow with Pavlos.

Only when they arrived at the waiting Mercedes did he betray a hint of compassion. "Don't," he ordered, when she went to help her patient out of the wheelchair and with surprising tenderness, scooped his father into his arms, laid him carefully on the car's roomy back seat and draped a blanket over his legs. "You didn't have to do that," Pavlos snapped, trying unsuccessfully to mask a grimace of pain.

Noticing, Niko said, "Apparently I did. Or would you have preferred I stand idly by and watch you fall on your face?"

"I would prefer to be standing on my own two feet without needing assistance of any kind."

"Then you should have taken better care of yourself when you were away—or else had the good sense to stay home in the first place, instead of deciding you had to see Alaska before you die."

Emily was tempted to kick the man, hard, but made do with a glare. "Accidents happen, Mr. Leonidas."

"Especially to globe-trotting eighty-six-year-old men."

"It was hardly his fault that the cruise ship ran aground, nor was he the only passenger on board who was injured. All things considered, and given his age, your father's done amazingly well. In time, and with adequate follow-up physical therapy, he should make a reasonably good recovery."

"And if he doesn't?"

"Then I guess you're going to have to step up to the plate and start acting like a proper son."

He favored her with a slow blink made all the more disturbing by the sweep of his lashes, which were indecently long and silky. "Nurse and family counselor all rolled into one," he drawled. "How lucky is that?"

"Well, you did ask."

"And you told me." He tipped the porter, left him to return the airport's borrowed wheelchair, then slammed closed the car trunk and opened the front passenger door with a flourish. "Climb in. We can continue this conversation later."

As she might have expected, he drove with flair and expertise. Within half an hour of leaving the airport, they were cruising the leafy green streets of Vouliagmeni, the exclusive Athens suburb overlooking the Saronic Gulf on the east coast of the Attic Peninsula, which Pavlos had described to her so vividly. Soon after, at the end of a quiet road running parallel to the beach, Niko steered the car through a pair of ornate wrought-iron gates, which opened at the touch of a remote control button on the dash.

Emily had gathered Pavlos was a man of considerable wealth, but was hardly prepared for the rather frightening opulence confronting her as the Mercedes wound its way up a long curving driveway, and she caught her first sight of…what? His house? Villa? Mansion?

Set in spacious, exquisitely landscaped grounds and screened from local traffic by a stand of pines, the place defied such mundane description. Stucco walls, blindingly white, rose in elegant proportions to a tiled roof as blue as she'd always imagined the skies to be in Athens, even though, this late September afternoon, an approaching storm left them gray and threatening. Long windows opened to wide terraces shaded by pergolas draped in flowering vines. A huge fountain splashed in a central forecourt, peacocks preened and screeched on the lawns, and from somewhere on the seaward side of the property, a dog barked.

She had little time to marvel, though, because barely had the car come to a stop outside a set of double front doors than they opened, and a man in his late fifties or early sixties appeared with a wheelchair light years removed from the spartan model offered by the airport.

The devoted butler, Georgios, she presumed. Pavlos had spoken of him often and with great fondness. Behind him came a younger man, little more than a boy really, who went about unloading the luggage while

Niko and the butler lifted Pavlos from the car to the chair. By the time they were done, he was gray in the face and the grooves paralleling his mouth carved more deeply than usual.

Even Niko seemed concerned. "What can you do for him?" he muttered, cornering Emily near the front entrance as Georgios whisked his employer away down a wide, marble-floored hall.

"Give him something to manage the pain, and let him rest," she said. "The journey was very hard on him."

"He doesn't look to me as if he was fit to travel in the first place."

"He wasn't. Given his age and the severity of his osteoporosis, he really ought to have remained in the hospital another week, but he insisted on coming home, and when your father makes up his mind, there's no changing it."

"Tell me something I don't already know." Niko scowled and shucked off his jacket. "Shall I send for his doctor?"

"In the morning, yes. He'll need more medication than what I was able to bring with us. But I have enough to see him through tonight." Struggling to preserve a professional front despite the fact that Niko stood close enough for the warmth of his body to reach out and touch hers, she sidled past him and took her travel bag from the pile of luggage accumulating inside the front door. "If you'd show me to his room, I really should attend to him now."

He stepped away and led her to the back of the villa, to a large, sun-filled apartment on the main floor. Consisting of a sitting room and bedroom, both with

French doors that opened onto a low-walled patio, it overlooked the gardens and sea. Still in the wheelchair, stationed next to the window in the sitting room, Pavlos leaned forward, drinking in the view which, even swathed in floating mist as the storm closed in, held him transfixed.

"He had this part of the house converted into his private suite a few years ago when the stairs proved too much for him," Niko said in a low voice.

Glancing through to the bedroom, Emily asked, "And the hospital bed?"

"I had it brought in yesterday. He'll probably give me hell for removing the one he's used to, but this one seemed more practical, at least for now."

"You did the right thing. He'll be more comfortable in it, even if he won't be spending much time there except at night."

"Why not?"

"The more mobile he is, the better his chances of eventually walking again, although…"

Picking up on the reservation in her voice, Niko pounced on it. "Although what? You said earlier you expect him to make a reasonable recovery. Are you changing your mind now?"

"No, but…" Again, she hesitated, bound by patient confidentiality, yet aware that as his son, Niko had the right to some information, especially if her withholding it might have an adverse effect on Pavlos's future well-being. "How much do you know about your father's general health?"

"Only what he chooses to tell me, which isn't very much."

She should have guessed he'd say that. *There's no need to contact my son*, Pavlos had decreed, when the hospital had insisted on listing his next of kin. *He minds his business, and I mind mine.*

Niko pinned her in that unnerving green stare. "What aren't you telling me, Emily? Is he dying?"

"Aren't we all, to one extent or another?"

"Don't play mind games with me. I asked you a straightforward question. I'd like a straightforward answer."

"Okay. His age is against him. Although he'd never admit it, he's very frail. It wouldn't take much for him to suffer a relapse."

"I can pretty much figure that out for myself, so what else are you holding back?"

Pavlos spared her having to reply. "What the devil are the pair of you whispering about?" he inquired irascibly.

Casting Niko an apologetic glance, she said, "Your son was just explaining that you might not care for the new bed he ordered. He's afraid you'll think he was interfering."

"He was. I broke my hip, not my brain. I'll decide what I do and don't need."

"Not as long as I'm in charge."

"Don't boss me around, girl. I won't put up with it."

"Yes, you will," she said equably. "That's why you hired me."

"I can fire you just as easily, and have you on a flight back to Vancouver as early as tomorrow."

Recognizing the empty threat for what it really was, she hid a smile. Exhaustion and pain had taken their toll, but by morning he'd be in a better frame of mind. "Yes, sir,

Mr. Leonidas," she returned smartly, and swung the wheel-chair toward the bedroom. "Until then, let me do my job."

Niko had seized the first opportunity to vacate the premises, she noticed, and could have slapped herself for the pang of disappointment that sprouted despite her best efforts to quell it. The faithful Georgios, however, remained on the scene, anxious and willing to help wherever he could. Even so, by the time Pavlos had managed a light meal and was settled comfortably for the night, darkness had fallen.

Damaris, the housekeeper, showed Emily upstairs to the suite prepared for her. Decorated in subtle shades of ivory and slate-blue, it reminded her of her bedroom at home, although the furnishings here were far grander than anything she could afford. Marble floors, a Savonnerie rug and fine antiques polished to a soft gleam exemplified wealth, good taste and comfort.

A lady's writing desk occupied the space between double French doors leading to a balcony. In front of a small blue-tiled fireplace was a fainting couch, its brocade upholstery worn to satin softness, its once-vibrant colors faded by time. A glass-shaded lamp spilled mellow light, and a vase of lilies on a table filled the room with fragrance.

Most inviting of all, though, was the four-poster bed, dressed in finest linens. Almost ten thousand kilometers, and over sixteen hours of travel with its inevitable delays, plus the added stress of her patient's condition, had made serous inroads on her energy, and she wanted nothing more than to lay her head against those snowy-white pillows, pull the soft coverlet over her body and sleep through to morning.

A quick glance around showed that her luggage had been unpacked, her toiletries arranged in the bathroom and her robe and nightshirt laid out on the bench in front of the vanity. But so, to her dismay, was a change of underwear, and a freshly ironed cotton dress, one of the few she'd brought with her, hung in the dressing room connecting bathroom and bedroom. And if they weren't indication enough that the early night she craved was not to be, Damaris's parting remark drove home the point in no uncertain terms.

"I have drawn a bath for you, Despinis Tyler. Dinner will be served in the garden room at nine."

Clearly daily protocol in the Leonidas residence was as elegantly formal as the villa itself, and the sandwich in her room, which Emily had been about to request, clearly wasn't on the menu.

The main floor was deserted when she made her way downstairs just a few minutes past nine, but the faint sound of music and a sliver of golden light spilling from an open door halfway down the central hall indicated where she might find the garden room.

What she didn't expect when she stepped over the threshold was to find that she wouldn't be dining alone.

A round glass-topped table, tastefully set for two, stood in the middle of the floor. A silver ice bucket and two cut-crystal champagne flutes glinted in the almost ethereal glow of dozens, if not hundreds, of miniature white lights laced among the potted shrubs lining the perimeter of the area.

And the final touch? Niko Leonidas, disgracefully gorgeous in pale gray trousers and matching shirt, which together probably cost more than six months' mortgage payments on her town house, leaned against an ornately carved credenza.

She was sadly out of her element, and surely looked it. She supposed she should be grateful her dinner companion wasn't decked out in black tie.

"I wasn't aware you were joining me for dinner," she blurted out, the inner turmoil she thought she'd conquered raging all over again at the sight of him.

He plucked an open bottle of champagne from the ice bucket, filled the crystal flutes and handed one to her. "I wasn't aware I needed an invitation to sit at my father's table."

"I'm not suggesting you do. You have every right—"

"How kind of you to say so."

He'd perfected the art of withering pleasantries, she decided, desperately trying to rein in her swimming senses. The smile accompanying his reply hovered somewhere between derision and scorn, and left her feeling as gauche as she no doubt sounded. "I didn't mean to be rude, Mr. Leonidas," she said, her discomfiture increasing in direct proportion to his suave assurance. "I'm surprised, that's all. I assumed you'd left the house. I understand you have your own place in downtown Athens."

"I do—and we Greeks, by the way, aren't big on honorifics. Call me Niko. Everyone else does."

She didn't care what everyone else did. Finding herself alone with him left her barely able to string two words together without putting her foot in her mouth. Resort to calling him Niko, and she'd probably manage to stuff the other one in next to it.

"At a loss for words, Emily?" he inquired, evil

laughter shimmering in his beautiful green eyes. "Or is it the prospect of sharing a meal with me that has you so perturbed?"

"I'm not perturbed," she said with as much dignity as she could bring to bear. "Just curious about why you'd choose to be here, instead of in your own home. From all accounts, you and Pavlos don't usually spend much time together."

"Nevertheless, I *am* his son, and the last I heard, my choosing to spend an evening under his roof doesn't amount to trespassing. Indeed, given the present circumstances, I consider it my duty to make myself more available. Do you have a problem with that?"

Hardly about to admit that she found him a distraction she wasn't sure she could handle, she said, "Not at all, as long as you don't interfere with my reasons for being here."

"And exactly what are those reasons?"

She stared at him. His eyes weren't glimmering with laughter now; they were as cold and hard as bottle-green glass. "What kind of question is that? You know why I'm here."

"I know that my father has become extremely dependent on you. I know, too, that he's a very vulnerable old man who happens also to be very rich."

She sucked in an outraged breath at the implication in his words. "Are you suggesting I'm after his money?"

"Are you?"

"Certainly not," she snapped. "But that's why you're hanging around here, isn't it? Not because you're worried about your father, but to keep an eye on me and make sure I don't get my hooks into him or his bank account."

"Not quite. I'm 'hanging around' as you so delicately put it, to look out for my father because, in his present condition, he's in no shape to look out for himself. If you find my concern offensive—"

"I do!"

"Then that's a pity," he replied, with a singular lack of remorse. "But try looking at it from my point of view. My father arrives home with a very beautiful woman who happens to be a complete stranger and whom he appears to trust with his life. Not only that, she's come from half a world away and signed on to see him through what promises to be a long and arduous convalescence, even though there's no shortage of nurses here in Athens well qualified to undertake the job. So tell me this: if our situation was reversed, wouldn't you be a little suspicious?"

"No," she shot back heatedly. "Before I leaped to unwarranted conclusions or cast aspersions on her professional integrity, I'd ask to see the stranger's references, and if they didn't satisfy me, I'd contact her previous employers directly to verify that she's everything she purports to be."

"Well, no need to foam at the mouth, sweet thing. Your point is well taken and that being the case, I'm prepared to shelve my suspicions and propose we call a truce and enjoy this very fine champagne I filched from my father's cellar. It'd be a shame to waste it."

She plunked her glass on the table so abruptly that its contents surged over the rim with an indignation that almost matched her own. "If you think I'm about to share a drink with you, let alone a meal, think again! I'd rather starve."

She spun on her heel, bent on making as rapid an exit as possible, but had taken no more than two or three steps toward the door before he caught up with her and slammed it closed with the flat of his hand. "I regret that, in looking out for my father's best interests, I have offended you," he said smoothly. "Trust me, I take no pleasure in having done so."

"Really?" She flung him a glare designed to strip paint off a wall. "You could have fooled me. I'm not used to being treated like a petty criminal."

He shrugged. "If I've insulted you, I apologize, but better I err on the side of caution."

"Meaning what, exactly?"

"That my father's been targeted before by people interested only in taking advantage of him."

"He might not be quite so susceptible to outsiders if he felt more secure in his relationship with you."

"Possibly not, but ours has never been a typical father-son relationship."

"So I've been given to understand, but I suggest the time's come for you to bury your differences and stop butting heads. He needs to know you care."

"I wouldn't be here now, if I didn't care."

"Would it kill you to tell him that?"

He gave a snort of subdued laughter. "No, but the shock of hearing me say so might kill *him*."

What was it about the two of them, that they held each other at such a distance, she wondered. "Do either of you have the first idea of the pain that comes from waiting until it's too late to say 'I love you?' Because I do. More often than I care to remember, I've witnessed the grief and regret that tears families apart because time ran out on them before they said the things that needed to be said."

He paced to the windows at the other end of the aptly named garden room whose exotic flowering plants set in Chinese jardinieres must give it the feel of high summer even in the depths of winter. "We're not other people," he said.

"You're not immortal, either." She hesitated, conflicted once again by how much she could say, then decided to plunge in and disclose what she knew, because she wasn't sure she could live with herself if she didn't. "Look, Niko, he'll probably have my head for telling you this, but your father's not just battling a broken hip. His heart's not in very good shape, either."

"I'm not surprised. That's what comes from years of smoking and hard living, but nothing his doctor said was enough to make him change his ways. He's a stubborn old goat."

That much she knew to be true. Pavlos had discharged himself from Vancouver General against medical advice, and insisted on flying back to Greece even crippled as he was, because he refused to put up with the nursing staff's constant monitoring. *They don't let a man breathe,* he'd complained, when Emily tried to talk him into postponing the journey. *I'll be carried out feetfirst if I let them keep me here any longer.*

"Well, the apple doesn't fall far from the tree, Niko. Where this family's concerned, you're both pretty pigheaded."

He swung around and surveyed her across the width of the room; another long, searching gaze so thorough that a quiver shafted through her. He probed too deeply beneath the surface. Saw things she wasn't ready to acknowledge to herself. "Perhaps before *you* start leaping to unwarranted conclusions," he purred, advancing toward her with the lethal grace of a hunter preparing to move in for the kill, "you should hear my side of the story."

"You're not my patient, your father is," she said, backing away and almost hyperventilating at the determined gleam in his eye.

"But isn't modern medicine all about the holistic approach—curing the spirit in order to heal the body, and such? And isn't that exactly what you've been advocating ever since you walked into this room?"

"I suppose so, yes."

"How do you expect to do that, if you have only half the equation to work with? More to the point, what do you stand to lose by letting me fill in the blanks?"

My soul, and everything I am, she thought, filled with the terrible foreboding that unless she extricated herself now from the web of attraction threatening to engulf her, destiny in the shape of Nikolaos Leonidas would take control of her life, and never give it back again. Yet to scurry away like a frightened rabbit was as alien to her nature as taking advantage of Pavlos. So she stood her ground, pushed the irrational presentiment out of her thoughts and said with deceptive calm, "Absolutely nothing."

"Really?" He leaned toward her, dropped his voice another half octave and latched his fingers around her wrist. "Then why are you so afraid?"

She swallowed and ran her tongue over her dry lips. "I'm not," she said.

CHAPTER TWO

SHE was lying. The evidence was there in her hunted gaze, in her racing pulse, so easily and unobtrusively detected when he took her wrist. And he intended to find out why, because for all that he thought he'd remain unmoved by whatever he discovered when he went to meet their flight, the sight of the old man, so brittle and somehow diminished, had hit him with the force of a hammer blow to the heart. They spent little time together, had long ago agreed to disagree and shared nothing in common. But Pavlos was still his father, and Niko would be damned before he'd let some hot little foreign number take him to the cleaners.

Oh, she'd been full of righteous indignation at his suggestion that she wasn't quite the selfless angel of mercy she presented herself to be. He'd hardly expected otherwise. But he'd also seen how indispensable she'd made herself to Pavlos; how successfully she'd wormed her way into his affections. His father had never been a demonstrative man, at least not that Niko could remember. Which had made the way he'd clung to Emily's hand at the airport all the more telling.

If his assessment of her was correct, redirecting her attention would be simple enough. After all, a millionaire in his vigorous prime was surely preferable to one in his dotage. And if he was wrong…well, a harmless flirtation would hurt no one. Of course, when his father figured out what he was up to, he wouldn't like it, but when was the last time he'd approved of anything Niko did?

"You're very quiet suddenly," she said, interrupting the flow of his thoughts.

He looked deep into her dark blue eyes. "Because I'm beginning to think I've judged you too hastily," he answered, doing his utmost to sound convincingly repentant. "But I'm not entirely without conscience. Therefore, if one of us must leave, let me be the one to go."

Ignoring her whimper of protest, he released her, opened the door to leave the room and found himself face-to-face with Damaris. He could not have orchestrated a better exit. Timing, as he well knew in his line of work, was everything. "*Kali oreksi*, Emily," he said, standing back to allow Damaris to carry in a platter loaded with olives, calamari, dolmades, tzatziki and pita bread. "Enjoy your meal."

He was over the threshold before she burst out, "Oh, don't be so ridiculous!"

Suppressing a smile, he swung around. "There is a problem?"

"If having enough food to feed an army is a problem, then yes."

He shrugged. "What can I say? Greeks love to eat."

"Well, I can't possibly do justice to all this, and since I have no wish to offend your father's housekeeper when she's obviously gone to a great deal of trouble…"

"Yes, Emily?"

She grimaced, as if her next words gave her indigestion. "You might as well stay and help me eat it."

He stroked his jaw and made a show of weighing his options. "It would be a pity to let it go to waste," he eventually conceded, "especially as this is but the first of several courses."

For a moment, he thought he'd overplayed his hand. Skewering him with a glance that would have stopped the gods of Olympus in their tracks, she waited until Damaris mopped up her spilled drink, then took a seat at the table and said, "Try not to gloat, Niko. It's so unattractive."

He wasn't accustomed to female criticism. The women he associated with were so anxious to please, they'd have swallowed their own tongues before issuing such a blunt assessment of his shortcomings. That she suffered no such hesitation appealed to him in ways she couldn't begin to imagine. He devoted his entire life to challenging unfavorable odds. And took enormous pleasure in defeating them.

Collecting the wine bottle as he passed, he joined her and topped up their flutes. Nothing like dim lights and good champagne to set the scene for seduction. Raising his glass, he said, "Here's to getting to know one another all over again."

She responded with the merest tilt of one shoulder, took a dainty sip, then helped herself to a little tzatziki and bread.

"Have more," he urged, pushing the tray of mezedes closer.

She selected an olive, but ignored her champagne.

"You don't care for Greek food?"

"I'm not very familiar with it."

"There are no Greek restaurants in Vancouver?"

"Hundreds, and I'm told they're very good. I just don't eat out very often."

"Why is that? And please don't tell me you lack opportunity. Suitors must be lined up at your door, wanting to wine and dine you."

"I'm afraid not. Shift work tends to put a crimp in a nurse's social life."

Right. And you're such a dedicated professional that you never take a night off!

He shook his head in feigned mystification. "What's wrong with Canadian men, to be so easily discouraged? Are they all eunuchs?"

She almost choked on her olive. "Not as far as I know," she spluttered. "But then, I haven't bothered to ask."

"What about your colleagues? As I understand it, hospitals are a hotbed of romance between doctors and nurses."

"The idea that all nurses end up marrying doctors is a myth," she informed him starchily. "For a start, half the doctors these days are women, and even if they weren't, finding a husband isn't particularly high on my list of priorities."

"Why not? Don't most women want to settle down and have children? Or are you telling me you're the exception?"

"No." She nibbled a sliver of pita bread. "I'd love to get married and have children someday, but only if the right man comes along. I'm not willing to settle for just anyone."

"Define 'the right man,'" he said—a shade too abruptly, if her response was anything to go by.

She dropped her bread and stared at him. "I beg your pardon?"

"By what standards do you judge a prospective husband?"

She reached for her glass and took a sip while she considered the question. "He has to be decent and honorable," she finally declared.

"Tall, dark and handsome, too?"

"Not necessarily." She gave another delicate shrug, just enough to cause her dress to shift gently over her rather lovely breasts.

He wished he didn't find it so alluring. "Rich and successful, then?"

"Gainfully employed, certainly. If we had children, I'd want to be a stay-at-home mom."

"If you had to choose just one quality in this ideal man, what would it be?"

"The capacity to love," she said dreamily, her blue eyes soft, her sweet mouth curved in a smile. Outside, the wind tore at the palm trees with unusual strength for September. "I'd want love more than anything else, because a marriage without it is no marriage at all."

Annoyed to find his thoughts drifting dangerously far from their set course, he said flatly, "I disagree. I'd never let my heart get the better of my head."

"Why not? Don't you believe in love?"

"I might have once, very briefly, many years ago, but then she died of a blood clot to the brain. I was three months old at the time."

"You mean your *mother*?" She clapped a distressed hand to her cheek. Her eyes glistened suspiciously. "Oh, Niko, how very sad for you. I'm so sorry."

He wanted neither her sympathy nor her pity, and crushed both with brutal efficiency. "Don't be. It's not as if she was around long enough for me to miss her."

The way she cringed at his answer left him ashamed. "She gave you life," she said.

"And lost hers doing it, something I've been paying for ever since."

"Why? Her death wasn't your fault."

"According to my father, it was." Her glass remained almost untouched, but his was empty. Needing something to deaden a pain he seldom allowed to surface, he refilled it so hurriedly, the wine foamed up to the brim. "She was forty-one, and giving birth at her age to an infant weighing a strapping five kilos put her in her grave."

"A lot of women wait until their forties to have children."

"They don't all die because of it."

"True. But that's still no reason for you to think Pavlos holds you responsible for the tragedy that befell her. After all, she gave him a son and that's not a legacy any man takes lightly."

"You might be a hell of a fine nurse, Emily Tyler, but you're no spin doctor."

Puzzled, she said, "What do you mean?"

"That nothing you can say changes the fact that my father didn't care if he never had a child. All he ever wanted was my mother, and as far as he's concerned, I took her away from him."

"Then he should have seen to it he didn't get her pregnant in the first place—or are you to blame for that, as well?"

"After twenty-one years of marriage without any sign

of a baby, he probably didn't think precautions were necessary. Finish your wine, woman. I don't care to drink alone. It's a nasty habit to fall into."

She took another cautious sip. "I still can't believe that, once his initial grief subsided, having you didn't bring Pavlos some measure of comfort."

"Then you obviously don't know much about dysfunctional families. My father and I have never liked one another. He has always resented me, not just because I cost him his one true love, but because I remained wilfully unimpressed by his wealth and social status."

"I'd have thought he'd find that commendable."

"Don't let misplaced pity for the poor motherless baby cloud your judgment, my dear," Niko said wryly. "I rebelled every step of the way as a child, took great pleasure in embarrassing him by getting into trouble as a teenager and flat-out refused to be bought by his millions when I finally grew up. I was not a 'nice' boy, and I'm not a 'nice' man."

"That much, at least, I do believe," she shot back, leveling a scornful glance his way. "The only part I question is that you ever grew up. You strike me more as someone with a bad case of defiantly delayed adolescence."

This wasn't playing out the way he'd intended. She was supposed to be all willing, female compliance by now, ready to fall into his arms, if not his bed, not beating him at his own game. And his glass was empty again, damn it! "When you've walked in my shoes," he replied caustically, "feel free to criticize. Until then—"

"But I have," she interrupted. "Walked in your shoes, I mean. Except mine were twice as hard to wear.

Because, you see, I lost *both* my parents in a car accident when I was nine, and unlike you, I remember them enough to miss them very deeply. I remember what it was like to be loved unconditionally, then have that love snatched away in the blink of an eye. I remember the sound of their voices and their laughter—the scent of my mother's perfume and my father's Cuban cigars. And I know very well how it feels to be tolerated by relatives who make no secret of the fact that they've been saddled with a child they never wanted."

Flushed and more animated than Niko had yet seen her, she stopped to draw an irate breath before continuing, "I also learned what it's like to have to work for every cent, and to think twice before frittering away a dollar." She eyed his shirt and watch disdainfully. "You, on the other hand, obviously wouldn't know the meaning of deprivation if it jumped up and bit you in the face, and I don't for a moment buy the idea that your father never wanted you. So all in all, I'd say I come out the uncontested winner in this spontaneous pity party."

He let a beat of silence hang heavy in the air before he spoke again, then, "It's not often someone spells out my many shortcomings so succinctly," he said, "but you've managed to do it admirably. Is there anything else you'd like to tell me about myself before I slither behind the wheel of my car and disappear into the night?"

"Yes," she said. "Eat something. You've had too much to drink and are in no condition to drive. In fact, you should be spending the night here."

"Why, Emily, is that an invitation?"

"No," she said crushingly. "It's an order, and should

you be foolish enough to decide otherwise, I'll kick you where it'll hurt the most."

She probably weighed no more than fifty-four kilos to his eighty-five, but what she lacked in size, she more than made up for in spirit. He had no doubt that, given her knowledge of male anatomy, she was more than capable of inflicting serious injury. Which should have deterred him. Instead the thought of fending her off left him so suddenly and painfully aroused that, for the first time, he questioned the wisdom of his plan of attack. *She* was the one supposed to be at *his* mercy, not the other way around, but so far, she remained utterly indifferent to his charms. He, on the other hand, was anything but impervious to hers.

Damaris came back just then to serve spinach-stuffed breast of chicken and ziti, a welcome diversion, which allowed him to wrestle his wayward hormones into submission and redirect his energy into more productive channels. "Why did you allow my father to coerce you into letting him travel, when he's clearly not up to it?" he inquired casually, once they were alone again.

"I did my best to dissuade him," Emily said. "We all did. But the only thing he cared about was coming home to Greece, and nothing anyone said could convince him to wait. I think it's because he was afraid."

"Of dying?"

"No. Of *not* dying in Greece."

That Niko could well believe. Pavlos had always been fanatically patriotic. "So you volunteered to see him safely home?"

"It was more that he chose me. We got to know one another quite well during his hospital stay."

An hour ago, he'd have rated that little morsel of information as yet another sign of her ulterior motives. Now, he didn't have quite the same enthusiasm for the task. Emily the woman was proving a lot more intriguing than Emily the fortune hunter.

To buy himself enough time to reestablish his priorities, he switched to another subject. "What happened to you after your parents were killed?"

"I was sent to live with my father's sister. He was thirty-six when he died, and Aunt Alicia was eleven years older. She and Uncle Warren didn't have children, but they were the only family I had left, so they were more or less stuck with me. It wasn't a happy arrangement on either side."

"They mistreated you?"

"Not in the way you probably mean, but they never let me forget they'd done 'the right thing' by taking me in and would, I think, have found a reason to refuse if they hadn't been afraid it would reflect badly on them. Of course, the insurance settlement I brought with me sweetened the deal by defraying the cost of putting a roof over my head and keeping me fed and clothed for the next nine years."

"What happened then?"

"The summer I graduated high school, I applied to the faculty of nursing, was accepted and moved into a dorm on the university campus at the end of August. I never went 'home' again."

"But at least there was enough insurance settlement left to pay your tuition fees and other expenses."

She shook her head. "I scraped by on scholarships and student loans."

Caught in a swell of indignation he never saw coming, he stared at her. Whatever else his father's sins, he'd never tampered with Niko's inheritance from his mother. "Are you telling me they spent money on themselves, when it should have been held in trust for your education?"

"No, they were scrupulously honest." She started to add something else, then seemed to think better of it and made do with, "The settlement just wasn't very large to begin with, that's all."

Something about *that* answer didn't sit right, either. Wasn't the whole point of insurance to provide adequate recompense to beneficiaries, especially minors? But although the subject bore investigation, he decided now was not the time to pursue it and asked instead, "Do you keep in touch with your aunt and uncle?"

"A card at Christmas about covers it."

"So they have no idea you're here now?"

"No one has," she said. "My arrangement with Pavlos was strictly between the two of us. If my employer knew what I'd done, I'd probably be fired."

Which wouldn't matter one iota, if Niko's first impression of her was correct and she'd set her sights on a much more rewarding prize. What she earned in a year as a nurse wouldn't amount to pocket change if she married his father.

Wondering if she had any idea how potentially damaging her revelation was, he said, "Then why take the risk?"

"Because your father was alone in a foreign country without friends or family to look after him when he was released."

"He had a son. If you'd thought to contact me, I could have been there within twenty-four hours."

"Maybe," she said gently, "he didn't want to bother you."

"So he bothered a perfect stranger instead, even though doing so might end up costing her her job. Tell me, Emily, how do you propose to explain your absence from the hospital?"

"I won't have to. I took a three-month leave of absence and scheduled it to coincide with his discharge."

"A noble gesture on your part, giving up your holiday to look after my father."

"Well, why not? I had nothing else planned."

Except setting aside an hour a day to polish your halo! Struggling to hide his skepticism, Niko said, "All work and no play hardly seems fair. We'll have to see what we can do to change that."

A sudden gust of wind rattled the French doors, making her jump. "Just being here is change enough. If the weather ever clears up, I'm sure Pavlos won't begrudge me the odd day off to see the sights."

"Count on both," he said, recognizing opportunity when it presented itself. "And on my making myself available to act as tour guide."

"That's nice of you, Niko."

No, it's not, he could have told her. Because whatever *her* motives, *his* were anything but pure. And because he'd meant it when he said he wasn't a nice man.

They passed the remainder of the meal in idle conversation, interrupted only by intermittent bursts of rain at the windows, but before coffee was served, she'd run out of things to say and was wilting visibly. Even he, unscrupulous bastard though he undoubtedly was, felt sorry for her. The long transatlantic flight would have been tiring enough, without the added strain of looking after his father. So when she set aside her napkin and begged to be excused, he made no attempt to stop her, but left the table himself and walked her to the foot of the stairs.

"Good night," she murmured.

"*Kali nikhta,*" he returned. "Sleep well."

She was perhaps halfway to the upper landing when a brilliant flash of lightning arrowed through the night. Almost immediately, the electricity failed and plunged the house into darkness.

He heard her startled exclamation and the click of her high heel hitting the edge of the marble step as she stumbled to a halt. "Stay put," he ordered, well aware how treacherous the staircase could be to the unwary. Once, when he was still a boy, a new housemaid had slipped and broken her arm—and that had been in broad daylight. But he'd grown up in the villa; could quite literally have found his way blindfolded anywhere within its walls, and was at Emily's side before she, too, missed her footing.

Just as he reached her, a second bolt of lightning ripped through the night, bleaching her face of color, turning her hair to silver and her eyes into pools as huge and dark as those found in undersea caverns. "What happened?" she whispered, clutching the bannister with one hand as she teetered on the edge of the stair.

Instinctively he pulled her close with an arm around her shoulders. They felt slender, almost childlike to the touch, but the rest of her, pinned warm and sweet against him, was unmistakably all woman. "The lights went out," he said, resorting to the absurdly obvious in an attempt to deflect her attention from the fact that his body had responded to hers with elemental, albeit untimely vigor.

She choked on a laugh. "I pretty much figured that out for myself."

"I expect a power pole was struck."

"Oh," she said faintly, aware as she had to be of her effect on him. Blatant arousal was difficult to hide at such close quarters. "Does it happen often?"

Were they talking about the same thing, he wondered, as his mind fought a losing battle with his nether regions. "No, especially not at this time of year."

"I ought to make sure your father's all right."

"No need," he said, hearing footsteps and noticing the shadow of candle flames flickering over the walls at the rear of the downstairs hall. "Georgios is already on the job. But if it'll ease your mind any, I'll see you as far as your suite, then go check on him myself. Do you know which one you're in?"

"Only that it's blue and cream, with some gorgeous antique furniture, including a four-poster bed."

He nodded, recognizing her description, and keeping one arm looped around her waist, steered her the rest of the way up the stairs, turned right along the landing and felt his way along the wall on his left until he made contact with her door. Pushing it wide, he directed her inside.

The logs in the fireplace had burned down, but enough of a glow remained to fill the room with dim orange light. Enough that when she looked at him, their gazes locked, held prisoner by the sexual awareness, which had simmered between them from the moment they'd first set eyes on each other.

He hadn't meant to kiss her this early in the game, had planned a much more subtle attack, but when she turned within the circle of his arms and lifted her face to his, it was the most natural thing in the world for him to tighten his hold until she was once again pressed against him. The most natural thing in the world to bend his head and find her mouth with his.

CHAPTER THREE

EMILY had been kissed before, many times, but always with some part of her brain able to rate the experience objectively: too slobbery, too bland, too aggressive, too many teeth, too much heavy breathing, not enough tenderness. More often than not, kissing, she'd concluded, was a vastly overrated prelude to romance. Until Niko Leonidas came on the scene, that was, and felled her with a single blow.

Except "blow" was no more the right word to define his effect on her than "kiss" adequately described his action. What he did with his mouth transcended the ordinary and surpassed the divine. Cool and firm, it yet seared her with its heat. Though undemanding, it somehow stripped her of everything—her independence, her focus, her moral compass, even her sense of survival.

Apart from one rash, distinctly forgettable experience, she'd chosen to remain celibate because sex for its own sake held no appeal, and she'd never come close to being in love. But she'd have let him take her there on the floor, if only he'd asked. Would have let him hike up the skirt of her dress and touch her as no other man ever had. For as long as his kiss held her in its spell, she would have let him have his way with her however he wished.

Obviously he did not wish for a fraction of what she was willing to give. Because releasing her, he stepped back and said, rather hoarsely to be sure, "I'll go look in on my father and see about getting some candles up here."

Weak as water, she clutched the back of a nearby chair and nodded. She couldn't have spoken if her life depended on it. Although he'd put a respectable distance between them, she remained trapped in his aura. Her body still hummed. Her breasts ached. Moisture, warm and heavy, seeped between her thighs.

When he turned away, she wanted to cry out that she didn't need candles, she only needed him. But the words remained dammed in her throat and he was gone before she could free them. Dazed, she lowered herself to the chair and waited for him to return.

A brass carriage clock on the mantelpiece marked the passing minutes. Gradually its measured pace restored her racing pulse to near-normal and brought a sort of order to her scattered thoughts. What kind of madness had possessed her, that she'd been ready to give herself to someone she'd known less than a day? He spelled nothing but trouble.

I won't let him in when he comes back, she resolved. I'm out of my league with such a man and don't need the heartbreak an affair with him would bring.

But when a discreet tap at her door signaled his return, all logic fled. Heat shot through her, giving rise to a single exquisite throb of anticipation that electrified her. She couldn't get to him fast enough.

Pulling open the door, she began, "I was beginning to think you'd abandoned—!" then lapsed into mortified silence at the sight of Georgios standing there, a lighted silver candelabra in one hand, and a battery operated lantern in the other.

"Niko asked me to bring these, *thespinis*," he informed her politely, "and to tell you that Kirie Pavlos is sleeping soundly."

Rallying her pride, she stood back to let him pass into the room, and mumbled, "Thank you."

"Parakalo." He placed the candelabra on the dresser and handed her the lantern. "I am also to tell you that he has been called away."

"At this hour of the night?" She made no attempt to hide her disbelief.

He nodded. *"Ne, thespinis.* He received an urgent phone call and will most likely be gone for several days."

Oh, the louse! The cowardly, unmitigated rat! Swallowing the anger and humiliation threatening to choke her, she said scathingly, "It must have been some emergency to drag him out in the middle of a storm like this."

Georgios stopped on his way to the door and shrugged. "I cannot say. He did not explain the reasons."

"Never mind. It's not important." *He* wasn't important. She was there to look after the father, not chase after the son.

"Thank you for the candles and flashlight, Georgios. Good night."

"Kalispera, thespinis. Sleep well."

Surprisingly she did, and awoke the next day to clear skies and sunshine. Last night's storm was as much a part of the past as last night's kiss.

Pavlos was already up and dressed when she went

downstairs. He sat on the veranda outside his sitting room, gazing out at the garden. A small empty coffee cup and a phone sat on a table at his side. A pair of binoculars rested on his lap.

Catching sight of her, he pressed a finger to his lips, and gestured for her to join him. "Look," he whispered, pointing to a pair of fairly large birds. Pretty, with bluish-gray heads, pearly-pink breasts and brown wings mottled with black, they pecked at the ground some distance away. "Do you know what they are?"

"Pigeons?" she ventured.

He grunted disdainfully. "Turtle doves, girl! Timid and scarce, these days, but they come to my garden because they know they're safe. And those over there at the feeder are golden orioles. Didn't know I was a bird fancier, did you?"

"No," she said, noting the spark in his dark eyes and his improved color. "But I do know you look much better this morning. You must have had a good night."

"Nothing like being on his home turf to cure a man of whatever ails him. Not that that son of mine would agree. Where do you suppose he is, by the way? I thought he might at least stay over, my first night back."

"No. He was called away on some sort of emergency."

"Gone already, eh?" He squared his shoulders, and lifted his chin, a formidable old warrior not about to admit to weakness of any kind. "Off on another harebrained escapade, I suppose. Doesn't surprise me. Never really expected he'd stick around. Ah well, good riddance, I say. You had breakfast yet, girl?"

"No," she said, aching for him. He could protest all he liked, but she saw past his proud facade to the lonely parent underneath. "I wanted to see how you were doing, first."

"I'm hungry. Now that you're here, we'll eat together." He picked up the phone, pressed a button and spoke briefly with whoever answered. Shortly after, Georgios wheeled in a drop-leaf table set for breakfast for two, and equipped with everything required for what she soon realized was the almost sacred ritual of making coffee. It was prepared with great ceremony over an open flame, in a little copper pot called a *briki*, and immediately served in thick white demitasses with a glass of cold water on the side.

"No Greek worthy of the name would dream of starting the day without a *flitzani* of good *kafes*," Pavlos declared.

Possibly not, and she had to admit the aroma was heavenly, but the strong beverage with its layer of foam and residue of grounds took some getting used to. She found the fruit and yogurt salad topped with almonds and drizzled with honey and a sprinkling of cinnamon much more enjoyable.

In the days that followed, she also found out that Pavlos had little faith in doctors, rated physiotherapists as next to useless and had no qualms about saying so to their faces. He could be fractious as a child when forced to suffer through the regimen of exercises prescribed to strengthen his hip, and sweet as peach pie if he thought Emily was working too hard.

While he napped in the afternoons, she swam in the pool, walked along the beach or explored the neighborhood, taking particular pleasure in the shops. In the evenings, she played gin rummy or poker with him, even though he cheated at both.

One morning, she was wheeling him along the

terrace after his physiotherapy session when he asked, "Do you miss home?"

She looked out at the flowers in brilliant bloom, at the peacocks strutting across the lawns, the blue arc of the sky and the stunning turquoise sea. Soon the rainy season would come to Vancouver, its chilly southeasterly gales stripping the trees of leaves. People would be scurrying about under a forest of umbrellas where, just few weeks before, they'd been lying on the beaches taking in the last of summer's sunshine. "No," she said. "I'm happy to be here."

"Good. Then you have no excuse for wanting to leave early."

She thought not, either, until the beginning of her second week there, when Niko reappeared as suddenly as he'd left.

"So this is where you're hiding," he said, coming upon her as she sat reading in a wicker love seat on the patio—except they called it a veranda in Greece. "I've been looking everywhere for you."

Though startled, she managed to hang on to her composure enough to meet his glance coolly and reply with commendable indifference, "Why? What do you want?"

Uninvited, he sat down beside her on the sun-warmed cushions. "To ask you to have dinner with me tonight."

The nerve of him! "I don't think so," she said, projecting what she hoped was an air of cool amusement. "You're likely to take off at the last minute and leave me to foot the bill."

"The way I did the other night, you mean?" He grimaced. "Look, I'm sorry about that but—"

"Forget it, Niko. I have."

"No, you haven't. I haven't, either, and nor do I want to. Spend the evening with me, and I'll try to explain myself."

"Whatever makes you think I'm interested in anything you have to say?"

"Because if you weren't, you wouldn't be so ticked off with me. Come on, Emily," he wheedled, inching closer. "Be fair, and at least hear me out before you decide I'm not worth your time."

"I usually play cards with Pavlos in the evening."

"Then we'll make it a late dinner. How is my father, by the way? I stopped by his suite before I came to find you, but he was sleeping."

"He still tires easily, but he's better since he started physiotherapy."

"I'm glad he's on the mend." He glanced at her from beneath his outrageous lashes, stroked his finger down her arm and left a trail of shimmering sensation in its wake. "So what do you say, sweet thing? Do we have a date?"

Resisting him was like trying to trap mist between her hands. "If that's what it takes for you to leave me to read in peace now, I suppose we do. But I won't be free much before ten, after your father's settled for the night."

He edged closer still, a long, lean specimen of masculine grace, handsome as sin, dangerous as hell, and kissed her cheek. "I can wait that long," he said, "but I'm not saying it will be easy."

He took her to a restaurant on the water, about a fifteen-minute drive from the villa. She'd pinned up her hair in a sleek chignon, and wore a black dress she'd bought on sale in a boutique just a few days earlier, and high-heeled black sandals. Simple but beautifully cut, the dress had a narrow draped skirt, strapless bodice, and a shawl lushly embroidered with silver thread. Her only accessory was a pair of dangling vintage silver earrings studded with crystals.

All in all, a good choice, she decided, glancing at her surroundings. Unlike the bougainvillea-draped tavernas she'd seen in the neighborhood, with their paper table-cloths and simple, sometimes crudely constructed furniture, this place gave new meaning to the term stylish sophistication. Crisp linens, a single perfect gardenia at every place setting, deep, comfortable leather chairs, a small dance floor and soft music combined to create an ambience at once elegant and romantic.

They were shown to a window table overlooking a yacht basin. Tall masts rose black and slender against the night sky. Beyond the breakwater, moonlight carved an icy path across the sea to the horizon, but inside the room, candles cast a warm glow over the stark white walls.

Once they'd been served drinks and he'd chosen their meal—noting no prices were listed on the menu, she'd left him to decide what to order—Niko leaned back in his chair and remarked, "You look very lovely tonight, Emily. More like a fashion model than a nurse."

"Thank you. You look rather nice yourself."

Which had to be, she thought, mentally rolling her eyes, the understatement of the century. The superb fit of his charcoal-gray suit spoke of Italian tailoring at its best, and never mind the gorgeous body inside it.

He inclined his head and smiled. "I like your earrings."

"They were my mother's. She loved jewelry and pretty clothes." She touched her fingertip to one crystal pendant, memories of her mother, all dressed up for an evening out, as clear in her mind as if they'd taken place just yesterday. "I still have all her things—her dinner gowns and shoes and beaded handbags."

"Do you use them?"

"Not often. I don't have occasion to."

His gaze scoured her face, meandered down her throat to her shoulders, and it took all her self-control not to shrink into the concealing folds of her shawl. "What a waste," he murmured. "A woman as beautiful as you should always wear beautiful things."

"My mother was the beauty, not I."

"You think?"

"I know," she said, nodding thanks to the waiter as he presented a tray of appetizers. *Mezedes*, she'd learned, were as integral to the evening meal as the main course itself. "And my father was incredibly handsome. They made such a glamorous couple."

"Tell me about them," he said, resting his elbow on the arm of his chair, wineglass in hand. "What were they like—beyond their good looks, that is?"

"Crazy about one another. Happy."

"Socialites?"

"I suppose they were," she admitted, remembering the many times she'd watched, entranced, as her mother prepared for a gala evening on the town.

"What else?"

She stared out at the yachts rocking gently at their moorings. "They wrung every drop of enjoyment from life. They'd dance in the sitting room after dinner, go swimming at midnight in English Bay, dress up in fabulous costumes for Hallowe'en, decorate the biggest tree they could find at Christmas. They were on everyone's guest list, and everyone wanted to be on theirs. And they died much too soon."

Detecting the sadness infecting her memories, he framed his next question in quiet sympathy. "How did it happen?"

"They were on their way home from a party, driving along a road infamous for its hairpin bends. It was raining heavily, the visibility was poor. They were involved in a head-on collision and killed instantly."

Again, his voice grazed her with compassion. "Ah, Emily, I'm sorry."

Aware her emotions swam dangerously close to the surface, she gave herself a mental shake, sat a little straighter in her seat and firmly changed the subject. "Thank you, but it all happened a long time ago, and we're here to talk about you, not me. So tell me, Niko, exactly what frightened you off after that impulsive kiss last week? And please don't say you were too busy checking the main fuse box to find the cause of the power failure, because Georgios already told me you left after receiving a phone call. Had you forgotten you had a previous date, or was I so inept compared to the other women you know that you couldn't wait to escape me?"

"Neither," he said. "I had to go to work."

"You *work*?"

"Well, yes, Emily," he said, laughing. "Don't most men my age?"

"Yes, but you don't seem the corporate type."

"I'm not."

"And it was the middle of the night."

"Right, again."

"So?"

"So I had to prepare to leave Athens at first light, the next day."

"To go where?"

"Overseas."

"How tactfully vague. You'll be telling me next you're involved in smuggling."

"Sometimes I am."

It was neither the answer she was expecting nor one she wanted to hear. Tired of his stonewalling, she threw down her napkin, pushed back her chair and stood up. "If this is your idea of explaining yourself, I've had enough."

"Okay," he said, grabbing her hand before she could bolt, "I delivered some urgently needed supplies to a medical outpost in Africa."

Abruptly she sat down again, her annoyance fading as the implication of his reply hit home. "Are you talking about Doctors Without Borders?"

"In this particular case, yes."

Their waiter came back just then to whisk away the remains of the mezedes and deliver their main course. A dozen questions crowding her mind, she waited impatiently as he made a big production of serving grilled calamari and prawns on a bed of rice. "How did you get there?" she asked, when they were alone again.

"I flew," Niko said.

"Well, I didn't think you walked!"

His mouth twitched with amusement at her acerbic response. "I happen to own a small fleet of aircraft. It comes in handy on occasion."

"Are you telling me you piloted your own plane?"

"In a word, yes."

"Going into places like that can be dangerous, Niko."

He shrugged. "Perhaps, but someone has to do it."

She stared at him, her every preconceived notion of what he was all about undergoing a drastic change. "Where did you learn to fly?"

"After finishing my National Service, I spent five years as a Career Officer with the HAF—Hellenic Air Force. That's when I first became involved in rescue missions. It irked my father no end, of course, that I chose the military over seconding myself to him and his empire."

"Is that why you did it?"

"Not entirely. I loved the freedom of flying. And providing humanitarian aid wherever it's needed struck me as a more worthwhile undertaking than amassing more wealth. How's your calamari, Emily?"

"Delicious," she said, though in truth she'd hardly tasted it. What she was learning about him was far more interesting. "You said a while ago that you own a fleet of aircraft, which I assume means you have more than one."

"Ten in total, and a staff of fifteen. We're a private outfit, on call twenty-four hours a day, seven days a week, and go wherever we're needed, providing whatever kind of help is required. Last month, we joined forces with the Red Cross after an earthquake in northern Turkey left hundreds homeless. The month before, Oxfam International called on us."

"Well, if you care so little for money, how are you able to afford all that? Does Pavlos support you?"

"You ought to know better than to ask such a question," he scoffed. "Even if he'd offered, I'd have starved before I took a single euro from him. And for the record, I never said I didn't care about money. It's a very useful commodity. I just don't care about his."

"Then I don't understand."

"I inherited a sizable fortune from my mother which, to give credit where it's due, Pavlos invested for me. By the time I had access to it at twenty-one, it had grown to the point that I could do pretty much anything I wanted, without having to rely on sponsors. And I chose to use it benefiting those most in need of help." He glanced up and caught her staring. Again. "Why do you keep looking so surprised?"

"Because you told me last week that you're not a nice man, and I believed you. Now I realize nothing could be further from the truth."

"Don't get carried away, Emily," he warned. "Just because I'm not immune to human suffering doesn't make me a saint."

"But you are, I begin to think, a very good man."

Irritably he pushed aside his plate, most of the food untouched. "The wine must have gone to your head. Let's dance, before you say something you live to regret."

She'd have refused if he'd been in any mood to take no for an answer—and if the prospect of finding herself once more in his arms hadn't been more temptation than she could withstand. "All right," she said, and followed him onto the dance floor.

Weaving a path through the others already swaying to the music, he waited for her to catch up with him and extended his hands in invitation. "Come here, sweet thing," he said, and she went.

Whatever resentment she'd harbored toward him had melted away, and left her completely vulnerable to him, all over again. Who could blame her, when the plain fact of the matter was that with a single touch, a glance from those dark green bedroom eyes, he could make a woman forget everything she'd ever learned about self-preservation? That he also turned out to be so thoroughly *decent* merely added to his appeal and made him that much more irresistible.

CHAPTER FOUR

IT FELT good to hold a woman whose curves hadn't been ravaged by malnutrition. Whose bones, though delicate and fine, were not so brittle that he was afraid they'd break at his touch. Whose breasts hadn't withered from bearing too many children she hadn't been able to nourish properly. Who didn't shrink in fear when a man touched her. Who smelled of flowers, not poverty.

"Stop it," he said, inhaling the sweet fragrance of her hair.

"Stop what?"

"Thinking. I can hear your brain working overtime."

"Well, I can't help wondering—"

He pulled her closer, enough for her warmth to melt the block of ice he carried inside, and make him whole again. Whenever he returned from a particularly harrowing assignment, a woman's soothing voice and generous, vital body always helped erase the hopeless misery he never got used to witnessing; the wasted lives, the terror, the shocking evidence of man's inhumanity to man. "Don't wonder, Emily," he said, glad she'd left her shawl at the table, and loving the ivory smoothness of her skin above the top of her strapless dress. "Don't ask any more questions. Forget everything and just be with me in the moment."

"Not easy to do, Niko. You're not who I thought you were."

Sliding his hand down her spine to cup her hip, he pressed her closer still. "I know," he said.

He was worse. Much worse. Not at all the high-minded hero she was painting him to be, but a man on a mission that was far from laudable where she was concerned. Blatantly deceiving her as to his true motives for dating her, at the same time that he used her to assuage his personal torment.

She stirred in his arms and lifted her face so that her cheek rested against his. The whisper of silk against those parts of her he couldn't see or feel inflamed him. "I'm sorry I jumped to all the wrong conclusions about you."

"You didn't," he muttered, fire racing through his belly. "I'm every bit as bad as you first assumed."

"I don't believe you."

They weren't dancing anymore. Hadn't been for some time. While other couples dipped and glided around them in a slow foxtrot, they stood in the middle of the floor, bodies welded so close together that even if she weren't a nurse well acquainted with male anatomy, she had to know the state he was in.

"What I don't understand," she continued, so intent on her thoughts that nothing he said or did seemed able to derail them, "is how you can show such compassion toward strangers, and spare so little for your father."

"I didn't bring you here to talk about my father."

Her hips nudged against him, a fleeting touch that

stoked his arousal to disastrous heights. "And I wouldn't be here at all, were it not for him."

"Thanks for the reminder," he ground out, dancing her back to their table sedately enough for his rampant flesh to subside. "With that in mind, I'd better get you home if you're to be on the job bright and early in the morning."

"Actually I usually don't start work until nine. Pavlos prefers to have Georgios help him bathe and dress, and I join him for breakfast after that."

He picked up her shawl and flung it around her shoulders. The less he could see of her, the better. "Even so, it's growing late."

She nodded sympathetically. "And you're tired."

"Among other things," he replied ambiguously, gesturing to the waiter for the bill.

Outside, the temperature still hovered around twenty degrees Celsius, warm enough for the top to remain down on the BMW. "Rather than having to drive all the way back to Athens after you drop me off, why don't you stay at your father's house tonight?" she suggested, pulling the shawl more snugly around her as he started along the shore road to the villa.

"No," he said, surprising himself because, at the start of the evening, he'd planned to do exactly that. Had had every intention of seducing her; of using her soft loveliness to erase the heart-rending images he'd brought back with him from Africa and, at the same time, prove his original theory that she would sell herself to the highest bidder. After all, she now knew he had money to burn.

But much though he still desired her, he'd lost his taste for using her. And if she was as duplicitous as he'd first suspected, he was no longer sure he wanted to know.

* * *

It was well after one o'clock in the morning. Within its walls, the villa lay smothered in the thick silence of a household at sleep. Except for Emily, who should have been exhausted, but was instead wide-awake and so disappointed she could have cried.

Pacing to the French windows in her suite, she stepped out on the balcony and promptly wished she hadn't. The classical marble statuary in the garden, gleaming white under the moon, was too reminiscent of Niko's stern profile as he'd driven her home; the cool whisper of night air on her skin, too much a reminder of his lips brushing her cheek as he kissed her good-night.

What had happened, that the evening was covered with stardust promise one moment, and over the next? They'd been so close, so attuned to one another when they were dancing. She'd known how aroused he was, had felt an answering tug of desire for him.

She'd thought, when he announced they should leave the restaurant, that after the way he'd held her, he'd at least end the evening on a high note with a kiss to rival the one from the week before. She'd wanted him to, quite desperately in fact, and why not? He'd redeemed himself so completely in her eyes, she was willing to fan the spark of attraction between them and let it take them to the next level. But rather than setting her on fire as she'd hoped, he'd brought her straight back to the villa and walked her to his father's front door.

"Thank you for a lovely evening," she'd said woodenly, hardly able to contain her disappointment.

"My pleasure," he'd replied. "I'm glad you enjoyed it."

Then he'd bestowed that pale imitation of a kiss on her cheek, muttered, "Good night," and raced back to his idling car as if he was afraid, if he lingered, she might drag him into the shrubbery and insist he ravish her.

What a contradiction in terms he was, she decided, turning back into her room. On the one hand, he was all cool suspicion laced with lethal charm and passion when it suited him, and on the other side of the person-ality coin, a reluctant hero and considerate escort more concerned about keeping her out past her bedtime than catering to his own base needs. Either that, or he took masochistic pleasure in keeping the women he dated off balance. And if that was the case, she was better off without him. One temperamental Leonidas at a time was enough.

"Out on the town till all hours of the night with that no-good son of mine, were you?" Pavlos inquired, glaring at her across the breakfast table when she joined him the next morning. "What if I'd needed you?"

"If you had, Georgios knew how to reach me."

"That's beside the point."

"And exactly what point are you making, Pavlos? That I'm under house arrest and not allowed to leave the premises without your permission?"

Ignoring her sarcasm, he said baldly, "You're asking for trouble, getting involved with Niko. Women are nothing but toys to him, created solely for his entertain-ment and pleasure. He'll play with you for as long as you amuse him, then drop you for the next one who catches his fancy. He'll break your heart without a second thought and leave you to pick up the pieces, just like all the others who came before you."

Not about to admit she'd pretty much reached the

same conclusion herself, she said, "I'm a grown woman. I know how to take care of myself."

He scowled. "Not with a man like him, you don't. He's bad news, no matter how you look at it. Take my advice, girl. Stay away from him."

A shadow fell across the floor. "Talking about me again, old man?" Niko stepped through the open French doors.

No custom-tailored Italian suit this morning, she noted, but blue jeans again, and a short-sleeved blue shirt revealing strong, tanned forearms. Not that the packaging counted for much. It was the man inside and his sexy, hypnotic voice that set her heart to palpitating.

Annoyed that he so easily snagged her in his spell, Emily averted her gaze, but his father continued to look him straight in the eye and said, "Know anyone else who fits the description?"

"Can't think of a soul," Niko replied evenly.

"There you have it then." Pavlos thumped his coffee cup down on the table. "Why are you here anyway?"

"To have a word with Emily, and to see how you're coming along."

"You needn't have bothered."

"Obviously not. You're as cantankerous as ever, which I take to be a very good sign that you're recovering nicely."

"And Emily doesn't want to see you."

"Why don't you let her tell me that for herself? Or does the fact that you're paying her to be your nurse entitle you to act as her mouthpiece, as well?"

"Just stop it, both of you!" Emily cut in. "Pavlos, finish your toast and stop behaving badly. Niko, the physiotherapist should be here soon, and I'll be free to talk to you then."

He shook his head. "Afraid I can't wait that long. I have a meeting in the city—"

"Then don't let us keep you," his father growled, snapping open the morning paper and feigning great interest in the headlines. "And whatever you do, don't hurry back."

Niko's face closed, and spinning on his heel, he strode off down the hall. But not before Emily caught the flicker of pain in his eyes that he couldn't quite disguise.

"That," she told Pavlos, "was both cruel and unnecessary."

"Then chase after him and kiss him better."

"An excellent suggestion," she said, pushing away from the table. "Thank you for thinking of it."

Niko had already reached his car when she yanked open the villa's front door. "Niko, wait," she called, running across the forecourt.

He turned at the sound of her voice, but made no move toward her. "If you're here to apologize for my father, save your breath," he informed her curtly. "I'm used to him."

"Well, I'm not," she said. "Look, I don't know why he's in such a foul mood this morning, but for what it's worth, I want you to know that I don't let other people dictate whom I should or should not associate with."

"In this case, you might be better off if you did," he said, once again turning to get into the car. "After all, he's known me all my life which makes him some sort of expert on what I'm all about."

Stepping closer, she stopped him with a hand on his

arm. Although his skin felt warm, the flesh beneath was unresponsive as stone to her touch. Undeterred, she said, "Perhaps I'd have believed that yesterday at this time, but I know better now and it'll take more than your father's say-so to convince me otherwise. So if you're using the scene back there in the house as an excuse to end our friendship, it's not going to happen. Now, what did you want to talk to me about?"

He regarded her broodingly a moment. "Your time off," he eventually admitted.

"Why do you want to know?"

"Why do you think, Emily? I want to see more of you."

Again, the tell-tale lurch of her heart warned her how susceptible to him she was. "Then why the mixed messages last night, Niko?" she asked, deciding to lay her misgivings to rest once and for all. "Do you blow hot and cold with all the women you date, or have you singled me out for special attention?"

He didn't bother to dissemble. Was, indeed, shockingly, hilariously blunt in his reply. "In case you didn't notice, my dear, last night when we were dancing, I was sporting an erection that would have done a stallion proud. That ought to have told you something."

Smothering a burst of laughter, she said with equal candor, "At the time, I thought it did. But after hustling me outside, you either decided I wasn't quite your type after all, or else you lost your nerve."

A flush of indignation stained his finely chiseled cheekbones. "I neither lost my nerve, nor anything else."

"Then why the hasty brush-off?"

"There's a time and a place for everything, Emily, especially seduction. I'm not the sex-in-the-backseat-of-the-car type of guy—which isn't to say I didn't want to take you to bed. But you'd given no indication you'd have welcomed such an overture. Just the opposite, in fact. You never stopped talking."

"If you'd bothered to ask," she said, "I could have told you we weren't as far apart in our thinking as you seem to suppose. I just did a better job of hiding it."

He blinked. "Are you sure you know what you're saying?"

"Very sure. I realized the moment I set eyes on you that the chemistry between us could easily become explosive."

"This isn't the first time you've left me at a loss for words," he said, almost stumbling over his reply, "and I have a sneaking suspicion it won't be the last."

"Well, don't misunderstand me. I'm not saying I'm ready to jump into bed with you, but..."

"But you won't turn me down if I ask you out again?"

"I'll be disappointed if you don't."

He slid his arm around her waist and pulled her to him. "When's the next time you have a few hours off?"

"Later this afternoon, from about three until seven."

"I'll pick you up at three-thirty. Wear something casual—slacks and a light sweater in case you get cold, and bring a camera if you have one. Today, we play at being tourists in the city."

Then he kissed her. Hard and sweet. On the mouth. And made it last long enough that when he finally released her, she had to clutch the top of the car door to keep herself upright.

She'd read the travel brochures and thought she knew what to expect of Athens. Traffic congestion and noise and smog. Ancient, crumbling ruins sitting cheek by jowl with towering new apartment buildings. And overshadowing them all, the Acropolis and the Parthenon. But brochures didn't come close to preparing her for the real thing.

Niko showed up not in the BMW but on a candy-apple-red motor scooter. Helping her onto the passenger seat, he plunked a bright red helmet on her head, fastened the strap, then climbed aboard himself and said, "Hang on tight."

On that note, they were off, zooming through the outskirts of the city, weaving in and out of traffic, zipping up steep hills, along narrow streets and through tiny squares, until suddenly the famous landmarks were everywhere she looked. She should have been terrified at the speed with which they traveled. With anyone else, she undoubtedly would have been. But seated behind him, her front sandwiched against his spine, her arms wrapped around his waist, she felt fearless, confident.

She loved the wind in her face, the aromas drifting from the tavernas, the energy buzzing in the air. Loved the feel of him, all sleek muscle beneath his short-sleeved shirt, and the scent of his sun-kissed skin.

Finally he parked and locked the scooter, then led her through a pedestrian avenue lined with restaurants and cafés, and along a marble path to the top of the Acropolis. Up close, the sheer size and majesty of the Parthenon overwhelmed her. "I can't believe I'm really here, and seeing it for myself," she breathed. "It's amazing, Niko. Magnificent! And the view…!"

She lapsed into silence, at a loss for words. Athens

lay at her feet, a sprawling mass of concrete occasionally interspersed with the green of pine-covered hills.

"Gives a pretty good idea of the layout of the city," Niko agreed, "but if ever my father decides he can get through an evening without you, we'll come back another time, at sunset. Enjoying a bottle of wine and watching the lights come on is equally impressive."

"What surprises me is that it's not nearly as crowded as I thought it would be."

"Because most tourists have gone home and left Athens to those of us who choose to live here. The smart ones, though, know that October is one of the best times to visit."

They spent an idyllic few hours wandering among the ruins, stopping on the way down the hill for iced coffee at a sidewalk café, and visiting a beautiful little church tucked in a quiet square. But although everything she saw left Emily awestruck, it was what Niko brought to the afternoon that left the most indelible impression.

His lazy smile caressed her, hinting at untold pleasures to come. His voice reciting the history of the temples held her mesmerized. The way he took every opportunity to touch her—holding her hand to guide her over the uneven ground as if she were the most delicate, precious thing in the world to him, or looping an intimate arm around her shoulders as he pointed out some distant landmark—filled her with shimmering happiness.

With a casual endearment, a glance, he inspired in her an unsuspected passion and yearning. The blood seethed in her veins. She had never felt more alive; never known such an uprush of emotion.

Too soon it was six o'clock and time to head back to Vouliagmeni. The setting sun slanted across the lawns and the front door stood open when they arrived at the villa. "Are you coming in?" she asked, as he propped the scooter on its kickstand and swung her to the ground.

He shook his head. "No, *karthula*. Why spoil a perfect afternoon?"

"I wish it didn't have to be like that," she said, removing her helmet.

He took it from her, slung it over the handlebars and cupped her face between his hands. "It is what it is, Emily, and what it's always been."

"Well, I find it very sad. It's not—"

He silenced her with a lingering kiss that emptied her mind of everything but the heady delight of his mouth on hers. "Oh," she breathed, when at last it ended.

He lifted his head and stared past her, then, "I think we should try that again," he murmured, and drawing her to him, kissed her a second time at even greater length.

An exclamation—most likely an expletive, judging by its irate tone—shattered the moment, and spinning around, Emily found Pavlos leaning on his walker, silhouetted in the open doorway.

"Wouldn't you know it?" Niko said cheerfully, releasing her. "Caught in the act by my disapproving *patera*. I'd better make myself scarce before he comes after me with a shotgun. I'll call you, Emily. Soon."

A moment later, he was gone, disappearing down the long driveway in a candy-apple-red blur of speed, and taking with him all the joy the afternoon had brought. Because she knew without a shadow of doubt that the reason he'd kissed her a second time had nothing to do with her. He'd done it for the pure pleasure of stirring his father to anger.

Unbidden, and decidedly unwelcome, Pavlos's earlier warning came back to haunt her. *Women are nothing but toys to him, created solely for his entertainment. He'll break your heart and leave you to pick up the pieces, just like all the others who came before you....*

CHAPTER FIVE

PAVLOS wore such an unmistakable told-you-so expression that Emily knew she looked as let down as she felt. Shuffling along beside her as she stalked into the house, he crowed, "Lived down to my expectations, didn't he?"

"You don't know what you're talking about, Pavlos," she informed him curtly, rallying her pride. "I had a fabulous afternoon."

"And I ran a marathon while you were gone!" He elbowed her in the ribs. "Admit it, Emily. He disappointed you."

"If you must know, you both disappoint me. Father and son—grown men at that—taking potshots at each other isn't my idea of adult entertainment. Have you had dinner?"

"No. I waited for you."

"I'm not hungry."

"Ah, girl! Don't let him do this to you. He's not worth it."

The edge of compassion softening his tone caused serious inroads on her composure, and that he happened also to be right didn't make the advice any easier to swallow. "He's not 'doing' anything," she insisted.

Except play fast and loose with her emotions, which she wasn't about to admit to his father.

That night when he was preparing for bed, Pavlos slipped on the marble tiles in his bathroom and split his forehead open on the edge of the sink. Striving to maintain calm in the face of chaos—Georgios panicked at the sight of blood, was sure his beloved master was dying and blamed himself for the accident—Emily directed him to call for an ambulance while she attended to Pavlos who lay sprawled on the floor. Although somewhat disoriented, he swore irritably and smacked her hand away when she tried to prevent him from struggling to his feet.

Leaning against the tub, he scoffed, "I'm not dead yet, woman! It'll take more than a cracked skull to finish me off."

"It's not your head I'm worried about, it's your hip," she said, applying a folded facecloth to the superficial cut on his brow. In fact, the sink had broken his fall and that he was able to sit on the floor without showing much evidence of pain was a good sign, but she wanted more scientific proof that he was as fine as he claimed.

The paramedics arrived shortly after and transferred him to the hospital for X-rays. Fortunately he'd incurred no further damage to his hip, required only a couple of sutures to his cut and vetoed any recommendation that he stay there overnight. "I didn't bring you all this way to look after me so you could turn the job over to someone else," he reminded Emily.

By the next morning, he sported a black eye but was otherwise his usual self. "No reason to," he snapped, when she suggested letting his son know what had happened.

But, "He has a right to be kept informed," she insisted, and left a brief message on Niko's voice mail.

He didn't acknowledge it until three days later when he again showed up unannounced as they were finishing lunch. "Very colorful," he remarked, inspecting Pavlos's black eye which by then had taken on a distinctly greenish hue. "Tell me, old man, do you plan to make a habit of abusing your body?"

"Accidents happen," his father shot back. "You're living proof of that."

Emily winced, appalled by the stunning cruelty of his reply, but realized that although he'd rather die than admit it, Pavlos was hurt that Niko hadn't bothered to stop by sooner.

"We all have our crosses to bear, *Patero*," Niko said scornfully. "Yours isn't any heavier than mine."

"Don't call me *patero*. You're no more a son to me than a dog on the street."

After their last confrontation, Emily had made up her mind she was never again getting caught in the middle when these two went at each other, but the insults flying back and forth were more than she could tolerate. "How do you the pair of you live with yourselves?" she asked sharply.

"By having as little to do with each other as possible," Niko said, addressing her directly for the first time since he'd entered the room. "*Yiasu*, Emily. How have you been?"

"Very well, thank you. The same can't be said of your father, but I guess that didn't much matter to you, seeing that you waited three days to visit him after his accident."

"Don't waste your breath appealing to his sense of decency," Pavlos advised her. "He doesn't have one."

Niko regarded him with weary disdain. "Unlike you in your prime, my career involves more than sitting behind a desk while my minions do all the work. I was away on assignment and didn't get back to Athens until this morning."

"Racing off on another mercy mission to save the world, were you?" Pavlos sneered.

"As to *thialo, yarro!*"

"You hear that, Emily?" Pavlos flung her an injured glare. "He told me to go to hell!"

Emily glanced from one to the other. At the father, his iron-gray hair still thick and his eyes piercingly alive, but his once-powerful body decaying, its bones so brittle it was a miracle they hadn't crumbled when he fell. At the son, a modern-day Adonis, tall, strong and indomitable. And both so proud, they'd have walked barefoot through fire rather than admit they cared about each other.

"I can't imagine why he bothered," she said witheringly. "The way I see it, he's already there, and so are you."

On that note, she left them. They might be determined to tear one another apart, but she'd be damned if she'd stay around to pick up the pieces.

Exiting through the French doors, she marched along the terrace and around the side of the villa to the lodge behind the garages. The widowed gardener, Theo, and his son, Mihalis, whom she'd met the day she arrived, lived there. Snoozing on the step outside the back door was their dog, Zephyr, a big friendly creature of indeterminate breed who, when she approached, wriggled over to make room for her to sit beside him and planted his head on her lap.

Niko found her there a few minutes later. "Is there space down there for me, too?"

"No," she said. "I prefer civilized company and you don't qualify."

"But the dog does?"

"Definitely. I'll take him over you any day of the week."

He shoved his hands in the back pockets of his jeans and regarded her moodily. "For what it's worth, Emily, I take no pleasure in constantly doing battle with my father."

"Then why don't you put an end to it?"

"What would you have me do? Stand by and let him use me as a verbal punching bag?"

"If that's what it takes…"

"Sorry, *karthula*, I'm not the subservient type. And I'm not here now to carry on with you where I left off with him."

"Why are you here, then?"

"To ask if you'll have dinner with me again."

"What for? So you can flaunt me in your father's face, the way you did the other day?"

Ignoring Zephyr's warning growl, he hunkered down on the few inches of sun-warmed step beside her. "Would you believe because I can't stay away from you, though heaven knows I wish I could?"

"Why? Because you blame me for your father's accident?"

"Don't be absurd," he said. "Of course I don't."

"Perhaps you should. I'm supposed to be nursing him back to health, not exposing him to further injury.

It's a miracle he didn't do more damage to himself when he fell."

"The point is, he didn't, and I knew it within hours of the accident."

"How is that possible if, as you claim, you arrived back in town only this morning?"

"This might come as a surprise, Emily, but I'm not completely heartless. I admit I'm away more often than I'm here, but I maintain regular contact with Georgios or Damaris, and know practically to the minute if a problem arises. Judging from their glowing reports, not only are you a dedicated and skilled professional who's taking excellent care of Pavlos, but you're earmarked for sainthood when you die—which, I hasten to add, I hope won't be anytime soon."

"If you care enough about him to phone them for an update on how he's doing, would it hurt you to tell him so?"

"Why would I bother when he makes it patently clear it's not something he wants to hear?"

"He might surprise you."

"You're the only one to surprise me, Emily, and I can't say I'm enjoying the experience. I've got enough on my mind, without that."

At his gloomy tone, she ventured a glance at him. Noticed the grim set of his mouth, the frown puckering his brow and felt an unwelcome stab of sympathy. "You ran into problems when you were away?"

"Nothing unusual about that," he said, shrugging. "My business is all about solving problems, as long as they're other people's. But I learned a long time ago that the only way to deal effectively with them is to draw a firm line between my work and my personal life, the latter of which I make a point of keeping complication free." He paused, sketched a groove in the dust with the toe of his shoe as if to illustrate his point and laced his fingers through hers. "But somehow, you've become just that, Emily. A complication. One I can't ignore."

"I don't see how."

"I know you don't. That's half the trouble."

"Try explaining it, then."

"I can't," he said morosely. "That's the other half."

She sighed, exasperated, and pulled her fingers free. "I'm not a big fan of riddles, Niko, and you don't appear exactly overjoyed to be involved with me, so let me put us both out of our misery. Thanks, but no thanks. I don't want to have dinner with you again."

Bathing her in a molten-green gaze, he inched closer. Slid his hand around her nape. "Liar," he murmured, the tip of his tongue dallying insolently with the outer curve of her ear.

The last time a man had tried that, she'd barely managed to suppress a revolted *Eeuw!* before she shoved him away. What was so different about Niko Leonidas, that his every touch, every glance, left her panting for more?

"Just because I refuse to let you play games with me doesn't make me a liar," she insisted weakly, almost paralyzed by the throb of tension unwinding inside her to affect body parts she was beginning to wish she didn't have.

"It doesn't make you any easier to resist, either."

"Then I guess we've reached an impasse."

For a long moment, he stared at her as if trying to fathom the solution to a dilemma only he could resolve.

Then with a shrug that plainly said, *Ah, to hell with it,* he rose to his feet with indolent grace. "I guess we have," he replied, and sauntered away.

"Good riddance!" she muttered, crushing the wave of disappointment threatening to engulf her. "Other women might trip over themselves in their eagerness to fall in with your every whim and wish, but I'm made of sterner stuff."

She repeated her little mantra several times during the rest of the afternoon, because it was all that stood between her and the urge to call him and say she'd changed her mind about spending the evening with him. To make quite sure she didn't weaken at the last minute, she went for a long walk on the beach, and ate dinner at a taverna. Upon her return to the villa, she played checkers with Pavlos for an hour, then pleading a headache, escaped to her suite.

Night had long since fallen, and closing the door behind her, she surveyed her sanctuary with a mixture of relief and pleasure. Damaris had turned back the bed-covers and made a fire against the chill of mid-October. Flames danced in the hearth and cast burnished-gold reflections over the polished antique furniture. The pleasant scent of burning olive wood filled the air.

Yes, she'd definitely made the right decision, Emily thought, tossing her sweater on the foot of the bed and kicking off her shoes. Although she couldn't deny the magnetic attraction between her and Niko, she couldn't ignore her feminine intuition, either. From the start, it had warned her that giving in to her attraction to him would invite nothing but trouble. If she didn't step back now, she'd find herself hopelessly, helplessly entangled with a man so far out of her league that she'd be guaranteed nothing but misery. After all, he'd made it graphically clear that his interest in her was purely sexual, and realistically, what else could she expect? He had no room in his life for a serious relationship, and even if he had, her future lay half a world away.

Warding off the unavoidable but depressing truth of the matter, she went into the bathroom and while the whirlpool tub filled, stripped off the rest of her clothes, pinned up her hair and lit a scented candle. Solitude was preferable to heartache any day of the week, she told herself bracingly, as she sank up to her chin in the hot water and let the air jets massage the day's tension into oblivion.

With the candle finally burned down to nothing, she dried herself with a towel from the heated rack, applied a generous dollop of body lotion to her water-wrinkled skin and pulled on a clean nightshirt. Then feeling limp as cooked spaghetti and so relaxed it was all she could do to stand upright, she tottered back to her bedroom.

Surprisingly the fire still burned brightly as if it had recently been replenished. And her shoes stood neatly aligned next to the armchair which, she noticed in appalled disbelief, was occupied. By Niko.

"I was beginning to think you'd drowned," he remarked conversationally.

Horribly aware that she wore nothing but a nightshirt whose hem came only midway down her thighs, she tried ineffectually to tug it lower. A huge mistake because, when she let it go, it sprang up with alarming vigor and revealed heaven only knew what of her anatomy. "Don't look!" she squeaked, shock rendering her incapable of a more quelling response.

"If you insist," he said, and very politely turned his head aside.

"How did you get in here?"

"Through the door, Emily. It seemed the most logical route to take."

If she had an ounce of backbone, she'd have matched his sarcasm and told him to leave the same way, but curiosity got the better of her. "Why?"

"I decided I owe you an explanation. Again!"

Wishing the sight of him didn't fill her with such desperate yearning that she was practically melting inside, she said, "You don't owe me anything, Niko. And you have no business being in my room."

"But I'm here regardless, and I'm staying until I've had my say."

"It seems to me we've been through this routine before and it got us precisely nowhere."

"Please, Emily."

She gave a long suffering sigh. "Then make it quick. I'm tired and I want to go to bed."

He slewed an audacious glance at her bare legs. "Could you put on something a little less revealing first? I'm only human, and staring at the fire doesn't quite cut it compared to looking at you."

Annoyed at the burst of pleasure his words aroused, she stomped back into the bathroom, grabbed the full length robe hanging on the door and dived into it.

"That's better," he said, vacating the armchair when she returned with only her hands, feet and head open to his inspection. "Why don't you sit here?"

"No, thanks," she informed him starchily. "I don't anticipate this taking very long."

He'd convinced himself this would be easy. All he had to do was reiterate his initial reservations, explain he'd put them to rest and no longer had ulterior motives for pursuing her. But the sight of her when she first came out of the bathroom had wiped his mind clean of anything but the raging desire to touch her all over. To lift that absurd scrap of a nightgown and bury his mouth at the cluster of soft, silver-blond curls she'd so briefly and tantalizingly revealed in her attempt at modesty.

"I'm waiting, Niko," she reminded him, sounding like his high school math teacher.

Would that she looked like her, too—moustache and all! "I want to start afresh with you," he said.

"I'm not sure I understand what that means."

He swallowed, grasping for the words that persisted in eluding him. "We got off on the wrong foot, Emily. You're my father's nurse, and I'm his son...."

"To the best of my knowledge, the status quo hasn't changed. I'm still his nurse. You're still his son."

How could he do it? How cut to the chase and say bluntly, *Despite pretending I no longer believed it, I remained convinced you were out to take him for all he's worth and decided my only choice was to seduce you, but have now decided I was wrong,* and expect her to understand? He wouldn't, if their situation were reversed.

"But something else *has* changed," he said instead.

"What?"

He took a deep breath and plunged in, laundering the

truth in a way that made him cringe inside. "Can we just say I'm tired of playing games and leave it at that? I'm not interested in using you to score points off my father, or for any other reason. I want to be close to you not because it'll annoy him to see us together, but because I like you for yourself. So I guess the only questions still to be answered are, do you want the same thing, or have I misread the signs and the attraction I thought existed between us is just a figment of my imagination?"

"It's not a figment of your imagination," she admitted, "but I don't understand why you'd pursue it when you said just this afternoon that I was a complication you didn't need."

"Overanalyzing is second nature to me. It's saved my skin more often than I care to count. But in this case, I took it too far."

She shifted from one foot to the other, clearly weighing his words. "Maybe not," she said judiciously. "Maybe you simply realized there was no future in a relationship with me."

"Never counting on the future is another by-product of my job. The only certainty is the here and now."

He took a step toward her, then another, until he was close enough to inhale the scent of her skin. She'd pinned up her hair, but tendrils had escaped to curl damply against her neck. The robe was at least two sizes too large and gaped at the front, drawing his gaze to the faint swell of her cleavage just visible above the top of her nightshirt.

The urge to kiss her, to hold her, nearly blinded him. "What do you say, Emily?" he asked hoarsely. "Will you take a chance on it with me?"

CHAPTER SIX

THE persistent voice of caution warned her not to fall for his line of reasoning. What was he offering her, after all, but the pleasure of the moment?

On the other hand, what had she gained in the past by pinning all her hopes on a better tomorrow? A degree in nursing, a crippling mortgage on her town house, a secondhand car and a short-lived, disappointing relationship with a medical student. Even her circle of friends had dwindled as more and more of them exchanged the single life for marriage and babies. Not that they completely abandoned her, but their interests no longer coincided as they once had. Her schedule revolved around shift work and case histories; theirs, around spouses and midnight feedings.

"Emily?" Niko's voice flowed over her, sliding inside the bathrobe supposedly shielding her from his potent appeal, to caress every hidden inch of skin, every minute pore.

Why was she holding out for a future that might never dawn, when the man who epitomized her every waking fantasy was offering her the chance to fulfill them? Giving in to her heart instead of her head, she lifted her gaze to meet his and whispered, "Why don't you stop talking and just kiss me?"

He groaned and reached for her. Cupped her face between his hands and swept his lips over her eyelids, her cheekbones, her jaw. And finally, when she was quivering all over with anticipation, he buried his mouth against hers. Not as he had before, with calculated finesse, but in scalding, desperate greed.

For the first time in her life, her natural caution deserted her, annihilated by a yearning so painful, she was filled with the consuming need to satisfy it at any price. Barely aware that she'd anchored her arms around his waist, she tilted her hips so that they nudged boldly against him exactly where he was most evidently aroused. His hard, unabashed virility inflamed her, scorching any remnant of doubt to ashes.

Somehow, her robe fell undone and he was touching her, his clever seeking fingers tracing a path from her collarbone and inside her sleeveless nightshirt to shape the curve of her breast. But she wanted more and tried to tell him so, angling herself so that her nipple surged against his palm, and pleading with him not to stop.

But stop he did. "Not here," he ground out, a sheen of sweat glistening on his brow. "Not in my father's house."

"But I can't leave," she whimpered. "What if he needs me and I'm not here?"

"Emily, *I* need you. I need you now."

Without a twinge of shame, she lifted the hem of her nightshirt and guided his hand between her legs. "You think I don't need you just as badly?"

Chest heaving, he molded his hand against her and pressed, flexing his fingers just so. The ensuing jolt of sensation ricocheted through her body and almost brought her to her knees. Gasping, she sank against him.

Steering her backward, he lowered her to the bed and touched her again, teasing the pivotal nub of flesh at her core that marked the dividing line between cool reason and clamoring ecstasy. And when she tipped over the edge in explosive release, he smothered her high-pitched cry with his mouth and stroked her until the spasms racking her body faded to an echo.

How many languid minutes ticked by before he pushed himself upright and, in a belated attempt to restore her modesty, covered her limbs with the bathrobe? Not nearly enough, and she clung to him. "Stay," she begged.

He shook his head. "I can't."

"Don't you want me, Niko?"

"So badly I can taste it. But not with my father's shadow hanging over us."

"Then how...when...?"

"Tell him you're taking the weekend off. We'll go away to someplace where we can be completely alone."

"What if he won't agree?"

"He doesn't own you, *karthula*," he said. Then, searching her face, asked, "Or does he?"

"Of course not, but he *is* my patient and he *is* paying me to look after him. And whether or not you accept it, he isn't as far along the road to recovery as he'd have you believe. To expect Georgios to assume responsibility for him would be unprofessional and negligent on my part."

"All it takes to solve that problem is a phone call to a private nursing agency for someone to replace you.

We're talking three days at the most. He can manage without you for that short a time."

"I suppose," she acknowledged dubiously, not because she wasn't sure she wanted to spend the weekend with him, but because she knew she'd have to fight Pavlos to get it.

A muscle twitched in Niko's jaw. "You know, Emily, if I'm asking too much—"

"You're not!"

"Are you sure?"

"Yes." She pressed her lips together and nodded. For pity's sake, when had she turned into such a wimp? She'd been in Greece over three weeks and more or less at Pavlos's beck and call the entire time. It wasn't unreasonable for her to ask for a break. "I'll work something out, I promise."

He brushed a last kiss over her mouth. "Let me know when it's arranged."

In the hectic two days that followed, she alternated between euphoria and bouts of horror at how shamelessly she'd offered herself to Niko. How would she ever face him again? But her yearning outweighed her chagrin and overriding Pavlos's objections, she booked the weekend off.

"A bikini and lots of sunscreen," Niko said, when she called to tell him she'd be ready to leave on Friday evening at six and asked what she should pack.

"What else?"

She could almost hear his shrug. "Something warm for the evenings, maybe, although the weather's supposed to be good. Shorts, a couple of tops. Not enough to fill a suitcase, by any means. Just throw a few things in a carryall."

"In other words, travel light and keep it casual."

"That about covers it, yes."

Much he knew, she thought, scurrying out to shop late Thursday afternoon while Pavlos napped. The clothes she'd brought with her to Greece were, for the most part, serviceable and basic. She hadn't come on vacation, she'd come to work, and in her profession that meant easily laundered cotton slacks and tunic tops, and comfortable, soft-soled shoes. She certainly didn't have anything designed for a romantic weekend with the sexiest man on the planet.

After dinner that night, she laid out her purchases, setting aside the dark red velour jogging suit and white socks and runners for traveling, but stuffing racy new lingerie, sheer nightgown, sandals and silk caftan, as well as shampoo, toothbrush, cosmetics and all the other items he'd specified, into a canvas tote designed to hold far less. He had said they'd be completely alone, but clearly didn't understand that it wasn't looking the part for strangers that she cared about, it was looking her best for him.

Although Pavlos had allowed a nurse from an agency to fill in for her while she was gone, he'd made it plain he was doing so under duress. To drive home the point, he sulked all Friday morning and ignored Emily all afternoon.

The one thing he hadn't done was inquire where she was going, or with whom, although from his dire mutterings, he'd obviously concluded it somehow involved Niko. So with her replacement up to speed on her duties, and rather than starting the weekend on a sour note with a confrontation, Emily collected her bag and slipped out of the villa a few minutes before six, to wait for Niko at the foot of the driveway.

Right on time, he drew up in the BMW. "You made it," he greeted her, slinging his arm around her shoulders in a brief hug.

"Did you think I wouldn't?"

"Let's just say I wouldn't have been surprised if my father had thrown himself on the floor and started foaming at the mouth when you tried to leave. And the fact that you're lurking here, hidden from view by anyone in the villa, tells me you pretty much feared the same."

"If I admit you're right, can we agree that the subject of your father is off-limits for the duration of the weekend?"

"Gladly." He tossed her bag in the trunk and held open the passenger door. "Hop in, Emily. I want to get underway while we still have some daylight left."

"Underway," she discovered was not aboard an aircraft as she'd half expected, but a fifty-two-foot sloop moored at a private yacht club in Glyfada, a twenty-five minute drive north of Vouliagmeni. Sleek and elegant, with a dark blue hull and the name *Alcyone* painted in gold across her transom, she was, Niko told Emily, built for speed. But without any wind to fill her sails and sunset no more than a crimson memory on the horizon, he was forced to steer her under diesel power to the tiny island of Fleves, just off the east coast of the Attic peninsula.

It was a short trip only, but what made it magical for Emily was the rising moon, which laid down a path of silver to mark their passage, and the luminescence sparkling in their wake like a handful of tiny diamonds.

Niko, in blue jeans and a lightweight cream sweater wasn't too hard to take, either.

After they'd dropped anchor, he set a lantern over the companionway in the center cockpit, told her to stay put and disappeared below, returning a few minutes later with a bottle of chilled white wine, crystal glasses and a small tray of appetizers. "I'd toast you in champagne," he said, taking a seat across from her and pouring the wine, "but it doesn't travel well in a sailboat."

"I don't need champagne," she assured him. "I'm happy just to be here with you."

He tipped the rim of his glass against hers. "Then here's to us, *karthula*."

The wine dancing over her tongue, crisp and cold, lent her courage. "You've called me that before. What does it mean?"

"Sweetheart." He raised one dark brow questioningly. "Do you mind?"

"No," she said, and shivered with pleasure inside her cozy velour jogging suit.

Noticing, he gestured below deck. "Dinner's in the oven and should be ready soon, but we can sit in the cabin where it's warmer, if you like."

"I'd rather not," she said, shying away from the closed intimacy it presented. Now that the rush and excitement of getting away was over and it was at last just the two of them, she was gripped with an almost paralyzing shyness. "It's so peaceful and quiet on deck."

"But you're on edge. Why is that, Emily? Are you wishing you hadn't agreed to spend the weekend with me?"

"Not exactly. I'm just a little…uncomfortable."

He scrutinized her in silence a moment, tracking the conflicting emotions flitting over her face. At last, he said, "About us being here now, or about the other night?"

She blushed so fiercely, it was a miracle her hair didn't catch fire. "Do we have to talk about the other night?"

"Apparently we do," he said.

She fiddled with her glass, twirling it so that the lantern light glimmered over its surface. From the safety of distance, she'd been able to put her conduct on Wednesday down to a temporary madness *he'd* inspired. But now, with no means of escaping his probing gaze, how she'd responded to him left her feeling only shame-fully wanton and pitifully desperate.

What had possessed her to behave so completely out of character? Professionally she was ICU Nurse Tyler, capable, skilled and always in control. Socially, she was good friend Emily, affable, dependable—but again, always in control.

She did not rush headlong into affairs, she did not beg a man to make love to her and she most certainly did not brazenly invite him to explore her private parts. That she had done all three with Niko made her cringe. Yet, here she was, because embarrassed or not, she couldn't stay away from him. And that meant facing up to what had transpired between them.

"You must know how very difficult it was for me to leave you as I did," he said softly, divining so exactly the source of her discomfort that she wondered if she'd actually voiced her thoughts aloud. "I won't pretend I'm not eager to pick up where we left off, but only if you feel the same. We take this at your pace, Emily, or not at all."

She glanced around, at the velvet moonlit night; at the dark hulk of the island rising to her left. She listened to the silence, broken only by the gentle wash of the sea against the boat's hull. Finally she dared to look at the man staring at her so intently. "It's what I want, too," she admitted. "I'm just a little out of my element. This is all very new to me, Niko."

His posture changed from indolent relaxation to sudden vigilance. "Are you trying to tell me you're a virgin?"

She choked on her wine. "No."

"No, that's not what you're trying to tell me, or no, you're not a virgin?"

"That's not what I'm trying to tell you. I was referring to the setting—the boat, the glamour, the exotic location. As for whether or not I'm a virgin, does it really matter?"

"Yes, it does," he said soberly. "Not because I'll judge you one way or the other, but because if I'm your first lover, I want to know beforehand." He leaned across and touched her hand. "So?"

Another blush raced up her neck to stain her face, though she hoped it didn't show in the dim light. "I'm not."

Picking up on her discomfiture anyway, he burst out laughing. "Don't look so mortified," he said. "I'm not, either."

"But it was only once, and not exactly…a howling success. Contrary to the impression I might have given you the other night, I'm not very good at…well…*this*."

"I see," he said, making a visible effort to keep a straight face. "Well, now that you've got that off your chest, what do you say we have dinner and let the rest of the evening take care of itself?"

"I'd like to freshen up first." In reality, she'd like to put her head down the toilet and flush, or better yet, jump over the side of the boat and never resurface.

"Sure," he said easily. "I'll be a couple of minutes getting everything ready, so take your time. Our stuff's in the aft cabin, which has its own bathroom."

It had its own built-in king-size bed, too. Dressed in navy-blue linens, with a wide ledge and window at the head, and brass wall lamps on either side, it set the stage for seduction and sent a tremor of terrified anticipation fluttering in Emily's stomach.

Would she disappoint him? she wondered, unpacking her clothes and laying out her toiletries on the vanity in the bathroom. Make an even bigger fool of herself this time than she had before? Was she being too reckless, too naive, in straying so far out of her usual comfort zone? Or had she finally found the one man in the world who made all the risks of falling in love worthwhile?

Soft lights and music greeted her when she returned to the main cabin. The air was fragrant with the scent of oregano and rosemary. Navy-blue place mats and napkins, crystal, brushed stainless steel cutlery and white bone china graced the table. In the galley, on the counter above the refrigerator, were a basket of bread and a bowl containing olives, and chunks of tomato, cucumber and feta cheese drizzled with olive oil.

Long legs braced against the barely perceptible rise and fall of the boat, Niko stood beside the oven, arranging skewers of roasted lamb, eggplant and peppers over rice. "Not exactly a gourmet spread," he remarked, carrying the platter to the table. "Just plain, simple picnic fare."

"I'd hardly call it plain or simple," she said, thinking of the plastic forks and paper plates, which marked the picnics she usually attended. "How do you keep your dishes and glassware from breaking when you're under sail?"

"I had the boat custom built with cabinetry designed to keep everything safely in place. I'll show you later, if you're interested."

"Interested? Intrigued is more like it. At the risk of repeating myself, you're not at all the playboy I took you to be when I first met you."

Green eyes filled with amusement, he said, "You're an expert on playboys, are you?"

"No, but I'm willing to bet they don't put their lives on the line to help people in distress, and they don't cook."

"Don't let the meal fool you. I had it prepared at a local taverna. All I had to do was heat up the main course, which pretty much sums up my talents in the kitchen."

He brought the bread and salad to the table, poured more wine and clinked his glass against hers. "Here's to us again, *karthula*. Dig in before everything gets cold."

The food was delicious; conversation easy and uncomplicated as they discovered more about each other. They both enjoyed reading and agreed they could live without television as long as they had a supply of good books at hand, although he preferred nonfiction whereas she devoured novels. And neither could live without a daily newspaper.

Niko was an avid scuba diver and had explored a

number of wrecks off the Egyptian coast. The best Emily could manage was snorkeling in a protected lagoon and admitted to being nervous if she was too far away from the shore.

He'd seen parts of the world tourists never visited. She stayed on the safe and beaten track: other parts of Canada, Hawaii, the British Virgin Islands.

When they'd finished eating, she helped him clear the table. Dried the dishes he washed. Stacked the wineglasses in the cunning little rack designed to hold them. And loved the domesticity of it all. A man, a woman, a nest…

As ten o'clock inched toward eleven, he suggested they finish their wine on deck. The moon rode high by then, splashing the boat with cool light, but he took a blanket from a locker and wrapped them both in its fleecy warmth.

"I dream about places like this when I'm away," he said, pulling her into the curve of his arm. "It's what keeps me sane."

"What is it about your work that made you choose it? The thrill, the danger?"

"In part, yes. I'd never find satisfaction playing the corporate mogul sitting behind a mile-wide desk and counting my millions, despite my father's trying to buy my allegiance with more money than I could spend in a century of profligate living. To him, money's the ultimate weapon for bringing a man to heel, and it infuriated him that, in leaving me my own fortune, my mother stripped him of that power over me. It's the one thing she did that he resented."

"But there's another reason you decided on such an unconventional career?"

He shifted slightly, as if he suddenly found the luxuriously padded seat in the cockpit uncomfortable. "This isn't something I'd tell to just anyone, but yes, there's another reason. Using her money to help people in need eases my conscience at having killed her."

Aghast to think he'd carried such a heavy burden of guilt all his life, Emily burst out, "I know I've said this before, but her death was an unforeseen tragedy, Niko, and you're too intelligent a man to go on blaming yourself for something that wasn't your fault. That Pavlos let you grow up believing otherwise—"

"I thought we'd agreed not to talk about my father."

"We did, but you're the one who mentioned him first."

"Well, now I want to forget him, so let's talk about your parents instead, and satisfy my curiosity on a point that's puzzled me ever since you first mentioned it. You said they were killed in a car accident, so how is it that you were left with virtually no financial security? Usually in such cases, there's a substantial settlement, especially when a minor is left orphaned."

If she'd pressed him into confronting his own demons, his question very neatly forced her to address her own. "There was no settlement from the accident," she said. "At least, not in my favor."

"Why the devil not?"

She closed her eyes, as if that might make the facts more palatable. It didn't. It never had. "My father was at fault. He was speeding and he was drunk. Sadly he and my mother weren't the only victims. Four other people died as a result of his actions, and two more were left with crippling injuries. Because of the ensuing lawsuits, I was left with nothing but my mother's personal effects and a small insurance policy she'd taken out when I was born. And you already know how that was spent."

"They had nothing else of value? No stock portfolio or real estate?"

She shook her head. "We never owned a house, or even an apartment. Home was a top floor suite in a posh residential hotel overlooking English Bay in Vancouver. A place where they could entertain their socialite friends and host glamorous parties."

Niko muttered under his breath and she didn't have to understand Greek to know he swore. "So they could afford that, but never thought to provide for their only child's future?"

"They lived for the moment. Every day was an adventure, and money was meant to be spent. And why not? My father was hugely successful in the stock market."

"A pity he wasn't as committed to setting some aside for his daughter's future as he was to spending it on himself."

"He and my mother adored me," she flared. "They made me feel treasured and wanted. I led a charmed life, filled with warmth and laughter and love. You can't put a price on that."

"They were spoiled children playing at being adults," he countered harshly. "Even if they'd left you a fortune, it could never make up for what their fecklessness ended up costing you."

"Stop it!" she cried, not sure what angered her more: that he dared to criticize her family, or that he was right. "Just shut up!"

Throwing off the blanket, she climbed onto the side

deck and went to stand at the bow of the boat. It was the most distance she could put between them.

He came up behind her. Put his arms around her. "Hey," he said. "Listen to me."

"No. You've said enough."

"Not quite. Not until I tell you I'm sorry."

"What is it about 'shut up' that you don't understand? I'm not interested in your apology."

"And I'm not very good at taking orders. Also, I'm the last person qualified to comment on flawed relationships." He nuzzled the side of her neck, his jaw scraping lightly, erotically against her skin. "Forgive me?"

She wanted to refuse. To end things with him while she still could, and save herself more heartache down the road. Because that annoying voice of caution was whispering in her head again, warning her that this was just another in a long list of differences. They disagreed on too many critical issues ever to remain in harmony for very long. He didn't care about family. Didn't believe in love. Wasn't interested in marriage or commitment.

But the starch of her resistance was softening, leaving her body pliant to his touch, her heart susceptible to his seduction. A lot of men said the same things he had—until the right woman came along and changed their minds. Why couldn't she be the one to change his?

"Emily? Please say something. I know I've made you angry, hurt you, but please don't shut me out."

"Yes, I'm angry," she admitted miserably, "because you had no right trying to strip me of my illusions. And I'm hurt, because you succeeded." She spun around, dazzled by tears. "I've spent the last eighteen years wilfully ignoring the truth about the parents I so badly wanted to preserve as perfect in my memory. Thanks to you, I won't be able to do that anymore."

He swore again, so softly it turned into an endearment, and buried her face at his shoulder. She started to cry in earnest then, for lost dreams and fate's cruel indifference to human pain.

"Let me make it better, angel," Niko murmured, stringing kisses over her hair. "Let me love you as you deserve to be loved."

And because she wanted him more than she wanted to stay safe, she lifted her tearstained face to his and surrendered. "Yes," she said.

CHAPTER SEVEN

THE lover's grand romantic gesture—sweeping her into his arms and carrying her to bed—didn't work on a sailboat. Slender though she was, the companionway just wasn't big enough for them both at the same time. The best he could do was precede her into the main cabin and guide her as she backed down the four steps leading below deck.

Not exactly a hardship, he decided, steadying her with a hand on either side of her hips as she descended. She wasn't very tall, a little over one and a half meters, and weighed no more than about forty-six kilos, but as her slim, elegant legs crossed his line of vision, the prospect of laying them bare to his renewed inspection left him hard and aching.

Unfortunately, by the time he'd led her into the aft sleeping quarters, her eyes were enormous in her pale face, she was trembling and hyperventilating. Some men might have interpreted that as an eagerness that matched their own, but he'd seen too many refugees huddled in war zones with bombs exploding around them, to be so easily taken in.

Virgin or not, and for all that she'd seemed willing

enough when he'd asked her to let him make love to her, now that the moment lay at hand, she was afraid. And in his book, that meant ignoring the raging demands of his libido, because the day had yet to dawn that he satisfied his own needs at the expense of a woman's.

Instead he flicked on the wall lamps, and slipped a CD into the built-in sound system. With the soothing sound of a Chopin nocturne filling the silence, he drew her down to sit beside him on the edge of the bed and wiped away the remains of her tears. "You are so incredibly beautiful," he told her.

She managed a shaky laugh. "I doubt it. I never learned to cry daintily. But thank you for saying so. Most men hate it when a woman resorts to tears."

"I'm not most men," he said, running his fingers idly through her hair. It reminded him of cool satin. So did her skin when, grazing his knuckles along her jaw to her throat, he extended his slow exploration. "And you very definitely are not most women."

He touched her mouth next, teasing her lips with his thumb. Not until they parted of their own volition did he lean forward and kiss them softly.

Her eyes fell shut as if the weight of her lashes was too much to bear. She sighed. And when she did, all her pent-up tension escaped, leaving her flexible as a willow against him.

Still he did not try to rush her, but cupped his hand around her nape and touched his mouth to hers again. She tasted of wine and innocence, and only when the subtle flavor of desire entered the mix did he deepen the kiss.

Gradually she grew bolder. Her hands crept under his sweater and up his bare chest, deft and sure. She murmured, little inarticulate pleadings that said the fear was gone and she was ready. More than ready. Her hunger matched his.

Suppressing the urgency threatening his control, he undressed her at leisure, discarding her shoes and socks first, then her jogging suit. A practical outfit and attractive enough in its way, it did not merit lingering attention. But underneath, she wore peach-colored lace; a bra so delicate and fine, her nipples glowed pink through the fabric, and panties so minuscule they defied gravity.

Clinging provocatively to her body, they were so blatantly designed to stir a man to passion that he had to turn away from the sight before he embarrassed himself. Had to rip down the zippered fly of his jeans or suffer permanent injury from their confinement. Kicking them off, he yanked his sweater over his head, flung it across the cabin, and sent his briefs sailing after it.

Misunderstanding his abrupt change of pace, she stroked a tentative hand down his back and whispered, "Are you angry? Did I do something wrong?"

"You're the nurse here," he ground out roughly, spinning around so that there was no way she could miss the state he was in. "Does it look to you as if you did something wrong?"

She blinked. And blushed.

If he hadn't been such a seething mass of sexual hunger that the functioning part of his brain was concerned only with how soon he could satisfy it, he'd have told her how her shy modesty charmed him. But his stamina was nearing its limits and wanting his dwindling endurance to be focused on bringing her pleasure, he drew back the bedcovers and pulled her down to lie next to him.

Willing his obdurate flesh to patience, he undid the clasp of her bra. Slid the outrageous panties down her legs. And when at last she lay naked before him, feasted his eyes on her. Dazzled by her blond perfection, her delicate symmetry of form, and perhaps most of all by the sultry heat in her eyes, he shaped her every curve and hollow with his hands, and followed them with his mouth.

She undulated on the mattress, offering herself to him without reserve. Clutching his shoulders in swift bursts of tactile delight when he found her most sensitive spots. Arching, taut as a high-tension wire, as he brought her to the brink of orgasm. And collapsing in a puddle of heat as she surrendered to it.

That she was so responsive to his seduction gratified him, but it inflamed him, as well. He wasn't made of stone, and knew he couldn't go on indefinitely denying himself the same pleasure he afforded her.

She knew it, too, and reaching down, she closed her hand around him. With another of her engaging little sighs, she traced her fingers over his erection, glorying in its strength, cherishing its vulnerability. Did so with such reverence that she somehow managed to touch him elsewhere, in places he kept separate from other people. In his heart, in his soul.

The emotional onslaught, as singular as it was powerful, blinded him to the encroaching danger. Responsibility, finesse, all the vital prerequisites by which he defined his sexual liaisons, deserted him. He was consumed with the overwhelming need to possess and be possessed. Seeming to sense the latter, she angled her body closer and cradled him snugly between her smooth, beautiful thighs.

Her daring lured him past all caution. The blood pulsed through his loins. He could feel her damp warmth beckoning him, knew of his own near-capitulation, and with only nanoseconds to spare, he dragged himself back from the brink of insanity and sheathed himself in a condom. Then and only then did he bury himself fully within her.

Tilting her hips, she rose up to meet him, caught in his relentless rhythm, absorbing his every urgent thrust. She was sleek, hot, tight. Irresistible. She took his body hostage. Held him fast within her and rendered him mindless to everything but the rampant, inexorable surge of passion rising to a climax that threatened to destroy him.

It caught her in its fury, too. He felt her contract around him. Was dimly conscious of her muffled cries, her nails raking down his back, and then the tide crashed over him. Stripped him of power and tumbled him into helpless submission. With a groan dragged up from the depths of his soul, he flooded free.

Spent, but aware he must be crushing her with his weight, he fought to regain his breath, to regulate his racing heart. Finally, with a mighty effort, he rolled onto his side and took her with him. Glancing down, he found her watching him, her eyes soft, her lovely face flushed. A world removed from the trembling creature she'd been half an hour before.

Curious as to the reason, he said, "You were nervous when I first brought you down here, weren't you?"

"I still am."

It wasn't the answer he expected, but remembering her comment about her previous experience, he thought he knew what prompted it. "If you're thinking you disappointed me as a partner, *karthula*, be assured I could not ask for better."

"It's not that at all," she said. "Before we made love, I was afraid I'd end up liking you too much. Now I'm afraid because I know I was right."

Her admission splintered his heart a little, as if she'd driven a needle into it and caused a tiny wound. He was not accustomed to such quiet honesty from his partners. "Is that such a bad thing?" he asked her.

"Not necessarily bad. I knew making love with you meant taking a risk. I just didn't realize how big a risk."

Then don't think of it as making love, he wanted to tell her. Be like the other women I take to bed, and see it as enjoyable sex. But she was so aglow that he couldn't bring himself to disillusion her. Which, in itself, gave rise to another troubling stab to his hitherto impregnable heart. She brought out a protective tenderness in him that he found as frightening as it was unacceptable.

Reading his thoughts with daunting insight, she said, "Don't worry, Niko. I'm not so naive that I think this weekend is the prelude to a long-term relationship. I'm not expecting it to end with a proposal of marriage or a ring."

Why not?

The question so nearly escaped him that he had to bite his tongue to contain it. "I'm in no position to offer either, even if I wanted to," he said, when he recovered himself. "My career doesn't lend itself to that sort of commitment, and I doubt there are many women who'd put up with a husband who's away more often than he's at home."

"Exactly. Realistically, neither of us is in the market

for anything but a casual fling. I'm just not very good at 'casual.' "

"There's nothing wrong with liking the person you're in bed with, Emily, and if I haven't already made it clear, let me say now that I like you very much. I wouldn't have asked you to come away with me if I didn't."

Her smile turned into a thinly disguised yawn. "That's good," she said. "I'll sleep much better knowing that, but I need to brush my teeth first."

"Of course. I'll use the head—bathroom in nautical terms, in case you're wondering—in the forward cabin."

She slithered off the bed and disappeared, a too-fleeting vision of slender, lamplit femininity that stirred him to fresh arousal. But he had his own rituals to attend to, not the least of which was making sure the anchor was well set for the night. Nothing like having a sailboat run aground to ruin the romantic ambience.

When he rejoined her in the bed some fifteen minutes later, she lay on her side facing away from him and was sound asleep. Just as well, really. She made it too easy for him to forget the rules he'd long ago set for himself. To those he rescued—the orphans, the widows, the elderly—he gave everything of himself because they didn't trespass into his personal life. Those he associated with the rest of the time he'd learned to keep at a safe distance.

Even though he wasn't touching her, he lay close enough that the heat of his body coiled around her. She knew that if she turned, if she made the slightest overture, he'd take her in his arms and they'd make love again. And she couldn't do it. She was too terrified of his power over her. Terrified that as the pleasure he gave her built to an unbearable peak, she might utter the three words guaranteed to put an end to what she had rightly termed a fling.

He might like her very much, but that was light years removed from his wanting to hear her say "I love you." Not that she did love him. In fact, she knew very well that she did not. *Could* not. Because anyone with half a brain knew that blissful, incredible sex didn't equal love.

Men have a one-track mind, she once overheard an embittered nursing colleague say. *They want a woman between the sheets, and they achieve it by making you feel as if they don't want to be anywhere else but with you—until the next day or the next week, when they move on to someone else, and you're left feeling slightly shopworn and incredibly stupid. The only way to gain the upper hand is either to fool them into thinking you don't care if you never see them again, or else swear off sex altogether.*

Apart from her one dismal experience with the third-year medical resident whose ego had surpassed anything else he had to offer, Emily had subscribed to the latter. She would not risk her self-respect or her reputation for the sake of a tawdry one-night stand. What was best, she'd decided in what she now recognized as pathetic naiveté on her part, was to settle for nothing less than complete commitment before leaping into intimacy with a man. But that prudent argument was before Niko Leonidas swept into her life, and swept out all her pre-conceived notions of what was best.

Sharing the same bed with him now, and so graphi-cally conscious of him that her skin vibrated with awareness, she forced herself to remain completely still as she waited for his breathing to settle into the deep, even rhythm that signaled sleep.

Seconds passed. Spun into long, painful minutes. Nothing broke the silence but the whisper of the sea and the equally subdued sound of his breathing. He was a very quiet sleeper, unlike his father who snored lustily when he nodded off.

Cautiously she shifted her foot; tucked her hand beneath her pillow. And waited for a sign that he was as wide-awake as she was. He did not stir. Convinced it was now safe to do so, she stopped pretending, opened her eyes and admitted to the moon-splashed night the awful truth.

She *was* in love with him. She had been for days. She'd committed the ultimate folly and laid on the line everything she had to give, in exchange for what she'd always known could never be more than a passing affair. And now she was paying the price.

The painful enormity of what she'd allowed to happen overwhelmed her. Tears seeped onto her pillow and silent sobs shook her body. All at once she was a child again, left with a heart full of love and no one to give it to. She wanted Niko to look at her as her father used to look at her mother, as if she was the most beautiful, fascinating creature ever to grace the earth. She wanted the magic and passion and permanence they'd known. She wanted it all, and she wanted it with Niko.

In short, she wanted what he couldn't give her.

"Emily?" His voice swam softly out of the gloom. "Are you asleep?"

"No," she muttered thickly, "but I thought you were."

She heard the rustle of the bed linen, felt his hand glide over her silky nightgown and come to rest at her hip. "Anything but," he said, his voice sinking to a husky growl. "I'm lying here thinking about you…and wanting you again."

He inched the hem of her gown up past her knees. Past her waist. His hand ventured, warm and possessive, between her thighs. "Emily?" he said again.

Any woman with an ounce of self-preservation to her name would have slapped his hand away, but not Emily Anne Tyler. No, she melted at his touch. Rolled onto her back, let her legs fall slackly apart and advertised the fact that she was more than willing to accommodate him. Well, why not, some distant part of her brain rationalized. At this point, she had nothing left to lose and might as well hoard as many precious memories as possible of this brief enchanted interlude.

He kissed the side of her neck. Murmured in her ear all the words men were supposed to murmur to a woman they planned to seduce. Words calculated to break down her resistance, to make her compliant to his every wish. Eventually he lowered himself on top of her and, pulling her legs up around his waist, eased himself smoothly inside her. As if, she thought, struggling to retain a grip on reality, God had designed them specifically for each other.

He loved her slowly this time, transporting her in leisurely increments of sensual delight until she could hold back no longer, then supporting himself on his forearms to watch her as she climaxed. When he came, she watched him, too. Saw the grim line of his mouth as he fought a battle he hadn't a hope of winning. Saw how, at the last moment, he closed his eyes and groaned as his body shuddered in helpless surrender. The unguarded honesty of it all made her cry again.

"What is it?" he asked, clearly appalled. "Did I hurt you? Tell me, *mana mou*."

"No," she said, because confessing the truth—that with every touch, every word, every glance, he made her love him all the more—wasn't an option. "Making love again was so beautiful, that's all."

A weak excuse, but thankfully he accepted it. Cradling her so that her head rested on his shoulder and his arm kept her close, he said, "It was magnificent. It will be the next time, too."

She was able to fall asleep on that promise, comforted by the steady beat of his heart beneath her hand and lulled by the gentle rise and fall of the sea beneath the boat.

They didn't wake up until almost nine o'clock. After a simple breakfast of yogurt and fruit, they took their coffee up on deck. Although summer's intense heat was long past, it was still a shorts-and-tank-top kind of day.

"By noon," he told Emily, pulling her into the curve of his arm, "you'll be lying on the foredeck, stripped down to your bikini."

"Mmm." She lifted her face to the sun. "Lolling in a bikini on a sailboat in October. Not too tough to take, I have to admit."

"Happy you decided to come away with me?"

"Who wouldn't be? It's lovely here."

Right answer, but it didn't quite ring true. Something was bothering her. "Are you sure?"

"Of course," she said, and promptly changed the

subject. "Will the water be too cold for swimming, do you think?"

"We can find out later, if you like, but it's a bit too early yet. Emily, is there something—?"

"Early! Heavens, Niko, it's after ten already. Do you always sleep in so late?"

"Only when I'm away on the boat. It's my one, sure outlet of escape from the everyday routine." He didn't add that the constant danger inherent in his work, the risks involved, took a toll. He left that part of his life behind the second he cast off from the yacht club and took to the sea.

"Burn-out, you mean? I know what that's like. It's one reason I agreed to come to Greece and nurse Pavlos back to health. I needed a change of scene."

"And the other reason?"

She chewed her lip thoughtfully. "I'd grown very fond of him during the time he was hospitalized. In a way, we'd become more like father and daughter than nurse and patient, and I didn't feel I could abandon him."

"More like grandfather and granddaughter, surely?"

"When you don't have any other family, you don't quibble about little things like that."

A month ago, he'd have taken that remark and found any number of hidden messages in it. Now, he took it at face value.

"Even after all these years, you still miss your parents, don't you?"

"Yes. Very much."

"And I made it worse with my comments last night," he muttered, cursing himself. "I tarnished your perfect memories of them."

"Not really, because nobody's perfect, not even my parents, for all that I tried so hard to idealize them. The truth is, I've sometimes thought it was as well they died young and together. They wouldn't have dealt well with old age or being alone. And I would never have filled the emptiness left behind if only one of them had been killed in the accident."

She captivated him with her honesty, which was pretty ironic considering his first impression of her had been that she wasn't to be trusted. "They might not have been perfect, Emily, but they came close to it when they made you. I'm sure they loved you very much."

"Oh, they loved me," she said, moving away from him and gazing mistily at the blue horizon, "but they never really needed me. If you must know, that's why I decided to become a nurse. I wanted to be needed. You don't, though, do you?"

Her question threw him. "Why else do you think I put my life on the line to help other people?"

"Because they're strangers who invade your professional life for just a little while. But your personal life...well, that's different. It's off-limits. A person only has to look at your relationship with your father, to see that."

She saw too much, and he wouldn't sink so low as to deny it. "Having him join the party isn't my idea of a good time, Emily."

She made a face. "My fault. I'm the one who mentioned him."

"Then I suggest we make a concerted effort to get rid of him. What do you say we take the dinghy ashore and go for a walk on the island?"

"I'd love to," she said with alacrity. "Let me get my camera."

Her relief was palpable. Because she didn't want his father hanging around, either, Niko wondered, or because she wanted to put distance between the two of them?

He shouldn't have cared, one way or the other. Annoyingly he did.

CHAPTER EIGHT

A GREAT suggestion, Emily concluded, watching as Niko tilted the outboard engine clear of the water and the bottom of the dinghy scraped onto the narrow strip of gravelly beach edging the island. Luxuriously comfortable though it might be, the yacht's big drawback was that it offered no means of escape when the conversation got out of hand. And it had, dangerously so, straying close to disastrous when she foolishly brought up the business of wanting to be needed. Another few minutes and her feelings for Niko, which she was so desperately trying to suppress, would have spilled out.

Hiding behind her camera gave her the chance to regroup. She took pictures of flowers enjoying a riotous last bloom before winter: wild geraniums and gaudy poppies; daisies and ice plant in shades of mauve and white. She snapped the yacht riding peacefully at anchor in the sheltered bay. And when he least expected it, she captured images of Niko; of his dazzling smile, his chiseled profile, his lashes lowered to half-mast as he squinted against the brightness of the sparkling sea.

The atmosphere on the island was different, she realized. Freer, less soberly intense. Here, she could breathe and not have to worry about keeping up her guard. If necessary, she could put distance between her and Niko. Contrarily, because she could, she felt no need to do so.

Sensing her change of mood, he matched it with a lighthearted teasing of his own. "If you didn't have a camera slung around your wrist, you'd be up to your neck in trouble," he growled with mock ferocity, grabbing her before she could escape after she'd caught him unaware at the water's edge and splashed him.

That kind of trouble she could handle. "I wish I could say I'm sorry, and mean it," she returned cheekily, and splashed him again.

Suddenly his laughter faded and twining her hands in his, he regarded her searchingly. "*I* wish I could take you away for a month, instead of a weekend," he said. "Being around you is good for me, Emily. You remind me that there's more to living than burying myself in work. I'm a happy man when I'm with you."

Her spirit soared at that. Could he possibly be falling for her, too?

Well, why not? Wasn't she forever telling her patients and their families that they should never give up hope? And hadn't she seen for herself, time and time again, that miracles did happen? Why couldn't one come her way for a change?

"Keep looking at me like that," he went on, his voice lowering to a thrilling purr, "and I won't be held liable for what I might do, which would be a mistake on two counts. This beach isn't designed for comfortable seduction, and even if it were, I didn't bring a contraceptive with me."

Flirting shamelessly, she glanced up at him in her

best imitation of a siren bent on luring him to destruction. "Then why don't we go back to the yacht?"

His eyes darkened, turned a deep forest-green. "Race you to the dinghy, angel."

Love in the afternoon was different, she discovered. Sunlight pouring through the window above the bed and casting dancing reflections of the sea on the cabin ceiling brought an openness to intimacy that, at first, dismayed her because it left her with no place to hide.

He soon put paid to that nonsense. He examined her all over, from the soles of her feet to the top of her head. He found the tiny scar on her bottom where she'd fallen on broken glass at the beach when she was little, and he kissed it as if it were new and still hurting.

He paid attention to every inch of her, sometimes with his hands, sometimes with his mouth and tongue, pausing every now and then to murmur, "Do you like it when I do this?"

Like? She'd never before felt such slow, rolling awareness of herself as a woman. He made her quiver with anticipation. He brought her body to electrifying life and made it yearn and ache and throb. He made her scream softly and beg for more.

Until him, she'd never climaxed. With him, she came so quickly and with such fury that she couldn't catch her breath.

His touch sent her flying so high, she could almost touch the heavens, and he knew it because he watched her the entire time. Knew to the second when she hovered on the brink, and tipped her over the edge into a glorious, sparkling free-fall she wished might never end.

Then, when she was dazed with exhausted pleasure and sure she didn't have the strength to lift a finger, let alone peak again, he buried himself in her hot, sleek folds and taught her otherwise. Caught in his urgent, driving rhythm, she swooped and soared with him again to a magnificent crashing finale.

At two in the afternoon or thereabouts, they put together a snack of fruit and cheese and ate it in the shade of the canvas bimini in the cockpit. They drank a little wine, and they talked, mostly about Niko as it turned out, which inevitably meant Pavlos crept back into the conversation, too.

"Was he cruel to you?" Emily asked, when Niko spoke briefly of his unhappy childhood.

"Not in the way you're thinking," he said. "Far from it. I never lacked for a thing. Clothes, toys, tutors, whatever I needed, he provided. When it came to my later education, there was no limit to how far he'd go to make sure I had the best. He sent me to the most prestigious boarding school in Europe—more than one in fact, since I managed to get myself kicked out of several."

"Then why the estrangement?"

"He didn't understand that there was more to being a father than spending money."

"Or else he didn't understand that you were crying out for his love."

"It was never about love with him. It was about power. And from his point of view, money and power are one and the same. Which is another bone of contention between us because to me, money's merely the means to an end. If I end up without any, I'll find a way to make more, but I'll never let it rule my life the way it rules his."

"Why do you think he sets such store by it?"

"Probably because he grew up without any. He was the by-product of an affair between a housemaid and the son of her millionaire employer who abandoned her when he learned she was pregnant. If you asked him what his most driving ambition had been when he was a boy, I guarantee he'd say it was to end up one of the wealthiest men in Greece, able to pick and choose his friends, his associates and, eventually, his wife."

"He appears to have succeeded."

Niko inclined his head in agreement. "Yes, but it took him years. He didn't marry my mother until he was thirty-one which, back then, was considered pretty old. She was just twenty, and the only daughter of one of his biggest business rivals."

"Is that why he married her—to score points over her father?"

"No," he said. "He really loved her. I have to give him credit for that much."

"What a shame he could never see you as her most lasting legacy to him."

"I was too much the rebel, refusing to toe the Leonidas line, determined to go my own way and to hell with anyone who tried to stop me."

He'd never been so open with her before. Was it the lazy afternoon heat or their lovemaking that made it easier for him to share his life story with her now? Whatever the reason, Emily was hungry to know everything about him and prepared to listen for as long as he was willing to talk. "Did he want you to go to university?"

"In the worst way, and was pretty convinced he could make it happen since I wouldn't have any money of my own until I turned twenty-one. He saw a business degree as the next logical step to my joining his empire. But I got out from under his control when I joined the air force, and there wasn't a damned thing he could do about it. After I left the service, I spent a year in England with a former UN pilot who taught me everything he knew about mercy missions, and introduced me to the finer points of the English language. After that, I came back to Greece, took over my inheritance and set up my own operation."

"And the rest, as they say, is history?"

He stood up and stretched. "*Ne*—and pretty dull at that, if you ask me, not to mention a criminal waste of a beautiful afternoon. What do you say to a swim?"

He was finished baring his soul and, for now at least, she realized she'd gain nothing by pressing for more. "Okay, if you're sure the water's warm enough."

"Only one way to find out, Emily," he said, dragging her to her feet. "You coming in of your own free will, or do I throw you in?"

"At least let me change into my bikini."

"What for?" He dropped his shorts and briefs, pulled off his T-shirt and climbed onto the swim grid in all his beautiful naked glory. "Nothing like going au naturel, as they say in polite society, especially as neither of us has anything to show that the other hasn't already seen."

"Once a rebel, always a rebel," she muttered self-consciously as she peeled off her clothes.

He favored her with a lascivious grin. "I hardly expected a nurse to be so modest, my dear. Even your bottom's blushing."

There was only one response to that remark and she

wasted no time delivering it. Bracing both hands against his chest, she shoved him into the water. He landed with a mighty splash and she followed suit before he had the chance to climb back on board and exact his revenge.

After the first chilling shock, the sea was deliciously refreshing. Heaven had never seemed so close, Emily decided, floating on her back with her hair streaming out behind her and the big blue bowl of the sky arcing overhead.

Niko, whom she'd last seen swimming in a powerful crawl toward the mouth of the bay, suddenly bobbed to the surface next to her. "You look like a mermaid," he said. "A particularly delectable mermaid."

And he looked like a sea god, she thought, her heart turning over at the sight of his broad, tanned shoulders, his brilliant smile and the thick lashes spiking in clumps around his remarkable green eyes. Small wonder she'd fallen in love with him. What woman in her right mind could resist him?

They climbed back on board and lay down on the foredeck to dry in the sun's benign warmth. He'd swum farther than he intended, a strenuous workout that left him pleasantly tired and happy just to lie next to her, his limbs touching hers, his fingers brushing lightly against her arm. Not moving, not speaking, just looking into her dark blue eyes and letting utter contentment sweep over him.

Was he falling in love?

He couldn't be. It was completely out of the question. A misguided romantic fantasy brought on by brain fatigue or some other disorder of the mind, because he absolutely refused to entertain the possibility that it might have something to do with his heart. Yet if it was so impossible, why did he suddenly hate the man who'd taken her virginity? She belonged to no one but him, and should have waited until he found her.

"What dark thoughts are chasing through your mind?" she murmured drowsily, peering at him from half-closed eyes.

The unpalatable truth rose in his throat, bitter as bile. Scowling, he said, "I have a confession to make. More than one, in fact."

"Oh?" A shadow flitted over her face. "Such as?"

"For a start, I'm jealous of my predecessor."

Clearly at a loss, she said, "What are you talking about?"

"I'm jealous of whoever it was that you slept with before you met me."

"I see." She pushed herself up on one elbow, propped her head on her hand and regarded him thoughtfully. "Should I be flattered?"

"I don't know. I've never found myself in this kind of situation before."

And that, he thought, was the whole problem in a nutshell.

Before he met her, sex had been all about mutual pleasure with no strings attached. He never lied to his willing partners, never made promises he couldn't keep, was never intentionally cruel. But sometimes he hurt them anyway because they wanted more than he could give.

Until now. Until Emily, when his initial plan had somehow gone terribly wrong and he found himself in danger of wanting to give much more than he could ever afford.

"That doesn't sit well with you, does it?" she said.

"No. I prefer to stick to the rules."

"What rules?"

"Those I've set for myself."

"And you're breaking them with me?"

"Yes," he said grimly, uncertain whether it was self-preservation or self-destruction that drove him to bare his soul so brutally. "When I first started seeing you, all I ever intended was to act as a decoy."

"A decoy?"

He heard the wariness in her voice edging closer to outright dismay, and wished he'd kept his mouth shut. But palming her off with half-truths left him feeling dirty and unworthy of her. And even if it didn't, he'd said too much to stop now. "Yes," he said. "To keep you away from my father. There being no fool like an old fool, I decided to step in and save him from himself— and you—by diverting your attention from an ailing old man to one who could better please you."

Dazed, she glanced away and focused her attention on the boat, appearing fascinated by its sleek lines, gleaming fiberglass deck and oiled teak. "So this weekend is all about proving a point?"

"No. That's the trouble. Now it's about you and me, and feelings I never bargained for. I tried to tell you this the other night, but I lost my nerve."

She wasn't listening. Instead she was scrambling to her feet and swinging her head wildly from side to side, a wounded creature desperate to escape her tormentor.

Springing to her side, he trapped her in his arms. She

lashed out at him, catching him a glancing blow on the jaw. "Let me go!" she spat. "Don't ever touch me again!"

"You're not hearing me, Emily," he told her urgently. "Everything's different now."

"Sure it is." She was sobbing. The sound drove splinters through his heart. "You've finally shown your true colors."

"No, Emily. I made a stupid mistake."

"So you decided to make it up to me by giving me a weekend to remember? How tedious you must have found it, pretending you wanted to have sex with me."

"I wasn't pretending! For God's sake, Emily, you of all people know a man can't pretend."

"So how did you manage? By closing your eyes and imagining I was someone else?"

He crushed her to him, shocked. "Never. It was always you. Only you, right from the start. I just didn't realize it at the time."

"And here I thought we'd put to rest that whole ludicrous notion that I was some sort of fortune hunter out to fleece your poor father." She wasn't crying now. She was encased in ice.

"We have," he protested. "You are what you've always been, as beautiful on the inside as you are on the surface."

"I don't feel beautiful," she said tonelessly. "I feel stupid and pathetic, because I let myself fall in love with you."

"Then I guess we're both stupid and pathetic, because that's what I'm trying to say. I'm falling in love with you, too, and the damnable thing is, I don't know what the hell to do about it."

"Then I'll tell you," she said. "You get over it. We both do."

* * *

The look on his face told her it wasn't the answer he wanted to hear. "Why should we?" he whispered against her mouth.

But the damage was done and nothing he said or did could put things right again. "Because there's no future in it for either of us." She pulled away just far enough to look him in the eye, then added pointedly, "Is there?"

"If you're asking me to predict what might happen tomorrow, I can't, Emily. All any of us ever has is today. Can't you let that be enough?"

Temporary bliss, in exchange for long-term misery? Not a chance! She was in enough pain already, and prolonging the inevitable would merely increase the agony. "No. I made up my mind long before I met you that relationships heading nowhere are a waste of time."

"I could change your mind, if you'd let me."

She was terribly afraid that he could, and knew she had to get away from him before he succeeded. He was kissing her eyes, her hair, her throat. Stroking his hands down her arms and up her bare back with killing tenderness. Sabotaging her with caresses when words failed to get him what he wanted, and already her resistance was dissolving under the attack.

"I don't want to be here with you anymore," she said, clinging to her vanishing resolve with the desperation of a drowning woman. "Take me back to the mainland."

"I will," he murmured. "Tomorrow."

"Tonight."

"*Ohi*…no." He lifted her off her feet and set her down in the cockpit. Traced his lips over her cheek and brought his mouth to hers and kissed her softly.

He made her legs shake, her insides quiver. He made her heart yearn. "Please," she whimpered helplessly.

"Give me one last night, my Emily."

"I can't."

He touched her fleetingly between the legs. "Tell me why not, when I know you want me as much as I want you."

She shuddered, caught in the clenching grip of rising passion. "Tell me why I'm inexplicably drawn to a man who isn't at all my kind of man," she countered.

"And what kind of man is that?"

"The kind who's not afraid of love. Who's happy with a nine-to-five job and a mortgage," she said, grasping at a truth she'd refused to acknowledge until now. "The safe kind who doesn't need to flirt with danger all the time in order to find fulfillment."

"Then you're right. I'm definitely not your kind of man."

But he pulled her closer, and the way her body tilted to meet his, welcoming the questing nudge of his erection, proclaimed otherwise. As if she'd finally found what she'd always been looking for. As if he was exactly her kind of man.

She was lost, and she knew it. The irrepressible pulse of his flesh against hers enthralled her. Lured her into forgetting how he had deceived and used her. Nothing mattered except to know again the pleasure only he could give. If, the next day or the next week, he reneged on his protestations of love, at least she'd have this weekend to remember him by.

The hunger, rapacious, insatiable, spiraled to unbearable heights. Casting aside all pretense at dignity, she sprawled on the cockpit cushions. At once, he was on top of her. Thrusting inside her, hot, heavy, demanding.

Perfectly attuned, they rose and sank together, pausing at just the right moment to drown in each other's gaze. There was no need for words to justify a decision that went against everything they'd just said to each other. They had come together because they could not stay apart. It was as simple as that.

CHAPTER NINE

WHEN they finally stirred and she mentioned that she'd like to freshen up, Niko ran a critical hand over his jaw, said he could use a shower and shave himself and told her not to rush. "We have all the time in the world," he said. "We'll have mezedes and wine and watch the moon rise, then eat dinner when the mood takes us."

So she indulged herself in a leisurely bath, and shampooed the saltwater out of her hair. After toweling herself dry, she massaged lotion into her sun-kissed skin, spritzed a little cologne at her elbows and behind her knees and put on the silk caftan, glad she'd had the good sense to smuggle it aboard. He'd said he was in love with her, but she sensed he'd made the admission reluctantly, and pinned little hope on his feeling the same way in the morning. If so, and if this turned out to be their last night together, she intended it to be one neither of them would soon forget.

Nor did they, but not for the reasons she'd supposed. The very second she joined him in the main cabin, she knew their plans had changed. He'd showered—his damp hair attested to that—but he hadn't shaved. There was no sign of the appetizers he'd mentioned, no tempting aromas drifting from the oven, no wine chilling. All that lay on the table was his cell phone, and one look at his face told her it had been the bearer of bad news. "Something's happened," she said, a sinking feeling in the pit of her stomach.

"Yes. I'm afraid we have to head back right away."

"Is it Pavlos?"

He shook his head. "I just got word from my director of operations that we've lost contact with one of our pilots in north Africa. He was scheduled to pick up an injured Red Cross worker from a refugee camp. He never showed up."

"What can you do about it?"

He stared at her as if she wasn't in command of all her faculties. "Go find him. What did you think—that I'd sit back and leave him stranded in the desert?"

"No, of course not." She swallowed, stung by his brusque tone. "Is there any way that I can help?"

"Change into something warmer, for a start. That thing you've got on won't do. Quite a stiff onshore breeze has sprung up. It'll be a chilly trip back to the mainland."

She must have looked as forlorn as she felt because when he spoke again, his voice softened. "I know you're disappointed, Emily. I am, too. This isn't how I'd foreseen the evening playing out. But when situations like this come up, I'm afraid everything else has to go on hold. A man's life could be at stake."

"I understand," she said. And she did. Completely. But what about *his* life? How safe would he be, rushing off to the rescue without knowing the danger he might be facing? "Will it be risky, your going looking for him?"

"It's possible, but so what? Risks come with the job. You get used to it."

You, maybe, but not me, she thought, the harsh reality of his vocation hitting home with a vengeance for the first time and filling her with apprehension. "How will you know where to start looking for him?"

"If he's turned on his epurb—electronic positioning beacon, that is—it'll lead me straight to him. If not, I'm familiar with the area, I know where he was headed and his coordinates before he lost contact."

"What if you still don't find him?"

"That's not an option," he said flatly. "He's just a kid of twenty-three, the eldest of four children and the only son of a widow. It's my job to locate him and bring him home to his family. They need him."

"But what if—?"

He silenced her with a swift, hard kiss. "No 'what ifs.' It's not the first time I've had to do this, and it won't be the last. I'll be back before you know it—by tomorrow night at the latest, but we really need to get going now if I'm to be ready to set out at first light in the morning."

Set out to where? Some vast arid region miles from civilization? Some rebel stronghold where human life didn't count for a thing? "Then I'd better get organized," she said, and turned away before he saw the desolation in her eyes.

"At least my father will be glad to have you back earlier than expected."

"I suppose."

He came up behind her and wound his arms around

her waist. "Did I mention how lovely you look, Emily?" he said softly against her hair.

On the outside, maybe. But inside, she was falling apart.

The nurse who'd replaced her was so happy to be relieved of her job, she practically flew out of the villa before Emily stepped in. "Is impossible!" she screeched, indignation fracturing her English almost past recognition. "He die, then *me niazi*! I do not care. One day more, I break his neck. *Adio*. Please not call me again. *Apokliete!*"

"Have a nice night," Emily said wearily, as the front door slammed shut in her face.

Pavlos didn't even pretend to hide his glee when she appeared at breakfast the next morning. "Didn't take you long to come to your senses, did it, girl?" he crowed.

"Try to behave yourself for a change, Pavlos," she snapped. "I'm in no mood for your shenanigans."

He smirked into his coffee cup. "That bad, was it? Could have told you it would be."

"For your information, I had a wonderful time. The only reason I came back early is that your son has gone searching for a young pilot lost somewhere over the Sahara."

His derision faded into something approaching concern, but he covered it quickly. "Damned fool! Serve him right if he got himself killed."

"I'll pretend I didn't hear you say that."

"Why not?" he retorted. "Ignoring the facts isn't going to change them. Wherever the latest hotbed of unrest shows up, you can bet he'll be there, and one of these days he'll push his luck too far."

Ill-timed though it might be, the truth of his answer could not be denied, and how she got through the rest of the day she didn't know. The minutes dragged, the hours lasted a small eternity. Morning became afternoon, then evening and, all too soon, night. Every time the phone rang, her heart plummeted. And sank lower still when the call brought no news of Niko.

"Better get used to this if you plan on sticking with him," Pavlos advised her, as the dinner hour came and went without any word.

"The same way you have?" she shot back. "You talk a good line, Pavlos, but you're as worried about him as I am."

"Not me," he huffed, but there was no real conviction in his tone and his gaze wandered to the clock on the wall every bit as often as hers did. "Where did you say he'd gone?"

"North Africa—the desert—I'm not sure exactly."

"Hmm." He drummed his arthritic old fingers on the edge of the table. "That's a lot of ground for one man to cover."

She closed her eyes. Fear beat a tattoo in her blood.

"Go to bed, Emily," Pavlos said with uncommon gentleness. "I'll wait up and let you know if we hear anything."

As if she could sleep! "I'm not tired. You should rest, though."

But neither made any move. Anxiety thick as molasses held them paralyzed.

Just after eleven o'clock, the phone shrieked into the silence one last time. Hands shaking, she grabbed it on the first ring. "Niko?"

She heard his smile. "Who else were you expecting at this hour?"

"No one...you...but it grew so late and you hadn't called—"

"You're going to have to learn to believe what I tell you, Emily," he said. "I promised I'd be back today, and I am."

"Yes." Giddy with relief, she reached for Pavlos's hand and squeezed it. "Where are you now?"

"At the office. I'll be heading home as soon as I've filed my report."

"And the man you went to find?"

"Had a fire in his control panel that knocked out his communications system. He made an emergency landing on a deserted Second World War airstrip. There are dozens of them, hundreds even, all over the Sahara. The one he chose lay nearly two hundred kilometers from where he was supposed to be, but his epurb was still working and led me straight to him."

"And he's okay?"

"He's fine, though I wish I could say the same for the aircraft. But the good news is, we picked up the man he was supposed to bring back and got him to a hospital, albeit twenty-four hours later than expected."

"You've put in a long day and must be exhausted."

"Nothing an early night won't fix. I'll see you tomorrow?"

"I can't wait," she said. "I missed you."

"Same here, *karthula*." His yawn echoed down the line. "I'd come over now, but—"

"Don't even think about it. Go home and catch up on your sleep."

"Will do. *Kali nikhta*, my sweet Emily."

"Kali nikhta," she replied. "Good night."

* * *

In the days following, she should have been completely happy. Although he vetoed any suggestion that he should terminate her employment, Pavlos was on the road to recovery and didn't need her as he once had. Accepting that she and his son were an item, he compromised by letting her take the weekends off.

She lived for the sheer heaven of those two days and nights. Niko's spacious penthouse in Kolonaki was their retreat. The living and dining rooms and en suite guest room opened onto a terrace. A small library and starkly modern kitchen comprised the rest of the main floor, with a gorgeous master suite upstairs. The decor was as spare and elegant as he himself, lacking any of the usual personal touches like photographs, but the huge collection of books and CDs told her much about his tastes and hinted at a man content with his own company.

He did his best to please her during their time together; to make it seem they were like any other couple in love. Working around his erratic schedule, they explored the countryside, going by scooter if the weather allowed but, with the cooler temperatures of November, more often by car.

They hiked in the pine-covered hills behind the town, took a picnic hamper and sailed down the coast of the Attic peninsula. Sometimes, they drove to out-of-the-way villages where they sampled wonderful local dishes in quaint, unpretentious tavernas whose walls were lined with wine barrels. Other times, they went into Athens and dined in fine style on the best the city had to offer. They danced cheek to cheek in the Grande Bretagne Hotel; made passionate love in his king-size bed.

If he had to break a date—and he did, often—he sent

her flowers, or texted messages to her in the night so that she found them on waking. In return, she tried to keep her anxiety under control when he was away, but never knew a moment's real peace until he returned. She couldn't sleep and walked the floor half the night. She couldn't eat because anxiety robbed her of her appetite. Noticing, Pavlos never missed the chance to tell her she was making the biggest mistake of her life.

She learned to live with all of it because the alternative—to put an end to it—was unthinkable.

Once, when Niko discovered he'd left his cell phone on his desk at work and had to go back to get it, he took her with him and showed her around the private airfield that served as his base of operations. The flat-roofed office building had only four rooms but was equipped with the latest in electronic equipment. Probably the aircraft sitting on the tarmac were, too, but when Emily first saw them, what struck her most forcibly was how flimsy they seemed.

"Are they what you use to fly overseas?" she asked, trying to mask her dismay.

Discerning it anyway, Niko laughed and said, "Were you expecting hot air balloons, my darling?"

"No, but these things are so small and...old-fashioned."

"Old-fashioned?" He regarded her in mock horror over the top of his aviator sunglasses.

"Well, yes. They've each got two sets of those spider-leg propellor things stuck on the front."

"I know," he said dryly. "They're what get them off the ground and keep them in the air."

"But why wouldn't you use jets? Surely they're faster?"

"Faster, but not nearly as versatile or fuel-efficient.

Twin-engine piston aircraft like these don't require nearly as long a runway as a jet, can land just about anywhere and fly at a much lower altitude." He eyed her mischievously. "Would you like me to take you up in one and show you what it can do?"

"No, thanks," she said hurriedly. "I'll take your word for it."

As they were leaving, they ran into Dinos Melettis, Niko's second-in-command. "Bring her to dinner," he insisted, after the introductions were made. "Come today. We have nothing on the board until later in the week, which makes it a good night to relax with friends, and Toula would love to meet the lady in your life. Toula," he added to Emily in an aside, "is my wife."

They accepted the invitation and had a delightful evening. "Never before has Niko brought a ladyfriend to our home," Toula confided to Emily in her careful English. "He is very enamored of you, I think."

The way he pressed his knee against hers under cover of the table and muttered between courses that he couldn't wait to get her alone again, Emily thought so, too. Yet for all that the passion between them burned brighter by the day, not once in all those weeks did they talk about the future. To do so would have shattered a present made forever uncertain by the demands of his job.

Although Emily did her best to live with that, what she couldn't get over, what terrified her, was the nature of the work that took him away from her, and the fact he always assigned himself to the most dangerous missions.

When she dared to ask him why, he said, "Because I have the most experience and the least to lose."

"But what about Vassili?" she pressed, referring to another colleague they'd bumped into one day at a kafenion in Athens. "You told me he's one of the most skilled pilots you've ever come across."

"He also has a wife and two-year-old son at home," Niko replied.

His answer and all it implied chilled her to the bone.

One Sunday evening in mid November, they stood on the terrace outside his penthouse, sipping cognac and admiring the night view of Athens spread out below. But even though Niko appeared perfectly relaxed and content, a shimmering tension emanated from him, one Emily now recognized all too well, and she braced herself for what she knew was coming.

He didn't leave her in suspense very long. "I'm off again tomorrow," he said, as deceptively casual as if he were planning to play golf, but then added guardedly, "I might be gone a bit longer than usual."

In other words, this undertaking was riskier than most. "How much longer?"

"Three days, possibly four, but you can count on my being home by the weekend."

"Where to this time?"

"Africa again."

A typically ambiguous reply. He never elaborated about his exact itinerary, was always deliberately vague about why he had to go. *Delivering food and clothing to an orphanage...survival kits to a village cut off by a landslide...a medivac rescue...supplies to a field hospital,* he'd say offhandedly when she questioned him, then quickly change the subject.

But she knew it was never as straightforward or simple as he made it sound. If it were, he wouldn't come back looking so drawn. He wouldn't wake up bathed in sweat from a nightmare he refused to talk about. He wouldn't reach for her in the night as if she was all that stood between him and an abyss of utter despair.

"Where in Africa?" she persisted now.

"Does it matter?"

"Yes, it matters."

He hesitated and she hung on tenterhooks, waiting for his answer. When he told her, it was so much worse than anything she'd let herself contemplate, was such a hellhole of violence, devastation and peril, that she felt sick to her stomach.

She knew how she was supposed to respond. Calmly. With acceptance. And she couldn't do it. Not this time. Instead she started to cry.

"Ah, Emily," he murmured and held her close. "Don't do this. We still have tonight."

But she'd broken the rules and commited the cardinal sin of wanting tomorrow, and tonight was no longer enough.

Her tears caught him off guard. Angry with himself for distressing her, and with her, too, because she'd known from the first the career he'd chosen for himself, he said, "This is why, until now, I've avoided serious involvement with a woman. When I take off on assignment, my attention has to focus on people whose lives, for one reason or another, are in jeopardy. Worrying about you is a distraction I neither need nor can afford."

"I know." She swiped at her tears and attempted a valiant smile. "I'm being selfish and unreasonable. Sorry. I don't know what came over me. I'm not usually so emotional."

She hadn't been during the early days of their affair, he had to admit. Lately, though, the smallest thing seemed to upset her. Just last week, he'd gone to pick her up at the villa and found her all teary-eyed over a bird that had flown into a window and broken its neck. He wasn't very happy about the poor thing's untimely end, either, but she knew every bit as well as he did that death was part of life and didn't differentiate between old and young, guilty or innocent.

"If this is harder than you thought it would be and want out," he said now, "just say so. I'll understand."

She closed her eyes against another bright gleam of tears and shook her head. "More than anything else, I want you."

"Even with all the baggage I bring with me?"

"Even then."

He wanted her, too. Enough that he'd willfully overstepped the limitations he'd imposed on his personal life prior to knowing her. And at that moment, with her body haloed in the nimbus of light from the city, and her beautiful face upturned to his in vulnerable despair, he had never wanted her more. "Then come with me now," he whispered, drawing her inside and up the spiral staircase to the bedroom. "Let's not waste the few hours remaining before I have to leave you."

That night, unlike some when his desire for her overrode any attempt at finesse, he loved her at leisure. Caring only about pleasing her and driving the demons of fear from her mind, he kissed her all over. He seduced her with his hands, with his tongue. He hoarded the scent and texture of her skin. He watched the slow, hot flush of passion steal over her, tasted the honeyed warmth between her thighs. He commited to memory the tight rosy buds of her nipples and the little cry she made when she came.

When at last he entered her, he did so slowly. Wished he could remain forever locked within her tight, silken warmth. And when his body betrayed him, as it always did, he surrendered all that he was or ever wanted to be. *"S'agapo, chrisi mou kardhia,"* he groaned. "I love you, Emily."

He awoke just after dawn, left the bed quietly and in order not to disturb her, took his clothes and went to the guest bathroom to shower and prepare for the day ahead. When he was done, he returned to the master suite and stood a moment, watching her sleep.

Early sunlight caught the sweep of her eyelashes. Cast a pearly shadow along the line of her collarbone. Her hair fell in captivating disorder over the pillow. Her arm reached across to his side of the bed as if seeking him.

He wanted to touch her. Put his mouth on hers and whisper her name. And knew he could not, because doing so would make it impossible for him to leave her.

Turning away, he picked up his bag and quietly let himself out of the penthouse.

CHAPTER TEN

COMPULSIVE worry took over her life and gnawed at it until it was full of holes. Holes that tormented her every waking hour and haunted her dreams.

Niko had willingly flown into an area where none of the rules of the civilized world applied. Every day, news reports of unspeakable atrocities made the headlines. Murder, banditry and torture were commonplace; starvation and disease had reached epic proportions.

Intellectually Emily recognized that helpless men, women and children desperately needed the kind of humanitarian relief people like Niko dedicated themselves to providing. But the Geneva Convention had no meaning for the perpetrators of the crimes being committed, and those trying to help were finding themselves subjected to increasing violence, some of it so extreme they were being evacuated for their own safety. Others had lost their lives for the principles they believed in.

What if he became one of them?

Self-fulfilling prophecies were dangerous in themselves, she realized, and in an effort to divert her mind into other channels, she turned to anger. Why had he left without saying goodbye? To spare them both the pain of a farewell, or because he cared more about strangers than he did about her?

But that line of reasoning merely shamed her. How could any thinking person, let alone a woman who'd made caring for those unable to care for themselves her vocation, be so blindly selfish? His compassion for others was one of the main reasons she loved him so desperately.

She then turned to optimism, telling herself that he was the best at what he did. He'd never lost a pilot and to make sure he never did, insisted every man involved in his operation, himself included, constantly hone his skills to remain at the top of his game. "Emergencies aren't the exception," he'd once told her, "they're the rule, and we're always prepared."

How could she not support such heroic measures? How could she resent his taking a few days away from her to make a difference in the lives of those so much less fortunate? By Saturday, she'd be in his arms again and the nightmare would have passed.

But the weekend came and went with no word from him. By Monday morning she couldn't hold herself together any longer and broke down in front of Pavlos. "I'm worried sick about him," she sobbed.

"That's what happens when you get involved with a man like him."

"You make it sound as if I had a choice about falling in love with him, but that's not how it works. It happened despite my better judgment."

"What can I say? I tried to warn you, girl, but you wouldn't listen and now you're caught in a trap with no way out."

"You're not helping," she wailed, swabbing at her tears.

He looked at her sadly. "Because I can't help. I learned a long time ago that where my son is concerned, worrying's a waste of time. He's going to do what he wants to do, and to hell with anyone or anything that stands in his way."

"How do you sleep at night, Pavlos?" she cried bitterly. "How do you turn your back on your only child and not give a damn whether he lives or dies?"

"Years of practice at being unpleasant, girl. The way I see it, if I make him dislike me enough, he'll survive just to annoy me. My advice to you is the same as it's always been: forget you ever met him. You're better off not knowing what he's up to."

But she'd passed that point of no return weeks ago, and the uncertainty of not knowing was killing her. Another endless night of pacing the floor, and she'd lose her mind, so that afternoon while Pavlos napped, she took a taxi to the airfield. Better to learn the worst than be held hostage to the horrors her imagination so willingly conjured up.

The big hangar stood empty and only five aircraft waited on the tarmac, but several cars were parked outside the flat-roofed office. Not bothering to knock, she opened the door and stepped inside.

Huddled around a chart spread out on the desk in the reception area, three men and a woman talked quietly. She recognized Dinos and Toula; the other two were strangers. On hearing the door open, all four looked up and at the sight of her, their conversation subsided into a ghastly silence that fairly screamed of disaster.

"Emily." Dinos came forward with a smile. But it was a poor, pitiful effort that soon faded.

"You know something," she said, every fear she'd entertained over the last week crystalizing into certainty. "Tell me."

He didn't pretend not to understand what she was talking about. "We know nothing," he told her quietly. "We are waiting—"

"Waiting for what? To learn he's been taken captive? That he's dead?"

"There is no reason to assume either. He is a little overdue, that is all."

"Overdue?" She heard the shrill edge of hysteria climbing in her voice and could do nothing to control it. "He's *missing*, Dinos!"

At that, Toula came forward and grasped her hands. *"Ohi.* Do not distress yourself, Emily. He will return. He always does."

"How do you know that? When was the last time anyone heard from him?"

Again that awful silence descended, so thick it caused a tightness in her chest. She'd experienced the same suffocating sensation once before, the day she learned her parents had been killed.

"Thursday," Dinos finally said. "But in itself, that is not necessarily significant. Sometimes it is safer to remain incommunicado in hostile territory than risk giving away one's whereabouts."

He was lying and doing it badly. "You don't have the foggiest idea where he is or what's happened to him, do you?"

His gaze faltered and he shrugged miserably. "No."

She felt the tears pressing hot behind her eyes and fought to control them. "When were you planning to tell me? Or aren't I entitled to be kept informed?"

"Today I come to you," Toula interrupted. "That is why I am here first. To learn what is latest news and hope it will be good."

Hollow with despair, Emily said, "How do you do it, Toula? If Dinos doesn't show up when he's supposed to, how do hold on to your sanity?"

"I believe," she said, her dark eyes filled with pity. "I pray to God, and I wait. It is all I can do. It is what you must do also. You must not lose faith."

"Toula's right, Emily." Dinos touched her shoulder gently. "You must believe that whatever has happened, Niko will find his way back to you."

"*Neh*...yes." The other two men nodded vigorously.

"There is nothing you can do here," Dinos continued, guiding her to the door. "Go back to the villa and wait for him there. I will call you the very second I have anything to report. Where did you leave your car?"

"I came by taxi."

"Then Toula will drive you home."

Dinos didn't call. No one did. Instead as she was passing through the foyer late on Tuesday afternoon, she heard the sound of a vehicle departing down the driveway. A moment later, the doorbell rang. Fearing the worst, she rushed to answer and came face-to-face with Niko.

Bathed in the orange glow cast by the setting sun, he leaned against the wall, his left arm held close to his chest. "I hear you've been inquiring about me," he said.

She'd prayed for just such a miracle so often in the

last few days. Had rehearsed exactly what she'd say, what she'd do. But now that it had come to pass, she was at a loss for words and simply stared at him.

In one respect, he looked much as he had that long-ago day they'd met at the airport. Same blue jeans, open-necked shirt and black leather bomber jacket. Same rangy height, black hair and mesmerizing green eyes. But that man had been the picture of health. So strong and invincible, he could have taken on the world single-handed and emerged victorious. Had picked up his father as if Pavlos weighed no more than an infant.

This one looked ill. Gaunt, hollow-eyed and barely able to support his own weight, let alone anyone else's. The sight paralyzed Emily. Left her speechless with dismay.

"Well, Emily?"

Collecting herself with a mighty effort, she said, "You haven't shaved in days."

The ghost of a smile touched his mouth. "Somehow, I'd expected a warmer welcome. Perhaps I should have stayed away longer."

"Perhaps you should have," she said, shock giving way to irrational anger. "Perhaps you shouldn't have come back at all."

His gaze drifted over her and came to rest on her face that she knew was ravaged with pent-up misery. "Emily, *karthula*," he murmured, a wealth of regret in his tone.

Her insides sagged. Melted into tears that flooded her eyes and washed her aching heart clean of everything but the burning need to touch him. To feel the tensile strength of muscle and bone beneath his clothing, the steady beat of the pulse at the corner of his jaw. To prove once and for all that she wasn't dreaming and he wasn't a ghost, he was real. "I didn't mean that," she cried, launching herself at him.

He grimaced and fended her off with an involuntary grunt of pain, reinforcing her initial impression that something was terribly wrong. His eyes, she noticed belatedly, held a feverish glint and a film of sweat beaded his upper lip.

"What happened to you?" she whispered.

His careless shrug turned into a flinch. "Just a minor scratch to my shoulder. Nothing to get excited about."

"I'll be the judge of that," she said, drawing him over the threshold.

He stepped inside, but staggered against a table just inside the door, sending it and the vase of flowers it held crashing to the marble floor. The noise brought Damaris and Giorgios running from the kitchen.

"I need a hand here," Emily panted, buckling under Niko's weight as she struggled to hold him upright. "Help me get him upstairs to a bed."

From the rear of the house, Pavlos spoke. "My room is closer. Bring him this way."

Between the three of them, they half-led, half-dragged Niko the length of the central hall and into the suite. As they eased him onto the bed, the front of his jacket fell open to reveal a spreading bloodstain on the upper left corner of his shirt.

The housekeeper gasped faintly but Emily immediately went into professional mode. "Pass me my scissors, Damaris," she ordered calmly, peeling off his jacket. "I'll have to cut away his shirt. Giorgios, I need clean towels, disinfectant and hot water."

Under the shirt she found a blood-soaked dressing covering a ragged puncture wound slightly to the right of his shoulder joint and just below his collarbone. "I'd say being shot amounts to a bit more than a minor scratch, Niko," she said, hoping nothing of her inner panic showed in her voice.

"What makes you think I've been shot?"

"I'm a nurse. I know a bullet injury when I see it, and this one's infected. A doctor needs to look at it."

"A doctor already has. Who do you think patched me up?"

"Someone in too much of a hurry from the looks of it. I'm taking you to the hospital."

He closed his eyes, weariness etched in every line of his face. "You'll do nothing of the sort. If I wanted to spend another night in a hospital, I wouldn't have had Dinos bring me here."

"I'm not Dinos, and I'm not taking any chances with your health."

"And I'm not a child."

"Then stop behaving like one and do as I ask."

"Forget it. I didn't just escape one hell to be thrown into another."

She looked for support from Pavlos who stood impassively at the foot of the bed, his gnarled old fingers gripping its rail. "For heaven's sake, will you talk some sense into your son, Pavlos?"

He shook his head. "No point trying, girl. His mind's made up."

Frustrated, she swung her attention back to Niko. "Fine. Have it your way. But don't blame me if you end up dead."

He opened his eyes a slit. "As if you'd let that happen, *karthula*. You're my angel of mercy."

"Let's see if you still think so after I'm finished with you."

She put on a pair of surgical gloves and began her task. As far as she could tell, he'd sustained no permanent damage. She found no sign of an exit point when she rolled him over on his side, which meant the bullet had lodged in his flesh and hopefully been removed by the doctor who'd treated him.

"Yeah," he mumbled, when she asked. "I told him he could hang it on his key chain."

He'd been lucky. As gunshot injuries went, she'd seen much worse, with major organs and bones damaged beyond repair. Nonetheless, the point where the bullet had entered his shoulder was ugly, with swelling around the sutures and angry red lines radiating from the wound site. And therein lay the reason for her alarm. "When did this happen, Niko?"

"A few days ago."

Typical vague answer, she thought, exasperated. "Were you hospitalized?"

"Overnight."

"Did you receive a tetanus shot?"

"*Neh*. In my other arm."

"Are you sure?"

"I was shot in the shoulder, Emily, not the brain. Yes, I'm sure. I can still feel where they shoved the needle in."

One piece of good news at least. "You'll be feeling this, as well," she warned, knowing she was going to hurt him. But he'd left her no choice. Bits of debris from the dressing and heaven only knew what else were adhered to his sutures and had to be removed. "It isn't going to be pleasant."

"Do what you have to do and get it over with," he ground out.

Brave words and nothing less than she'd expect from a man who refused to admit to any sort of weakness, but as she probed at the raw edges of his wound with surgical tweezers, then irrigated the area with warm water, the tendons on his neck stood out like cords.

Finally, with a clean dressing in place, she said, "That's about it for now."

"Good. Hand me my jacket and I'll be on my way."

He struggled to sit up, turned gray in the face and toppled back against the pillows.

Her patience snapped at that. "Try not to be a bigger fool than you already are, Niko Leonidas! The only place you're going is to bed, and you won't need your jacket for that."

He eyed her malevolently. "*Ade apo tho re,* Emily. You're beginning to annoy me."

"Not half as much as you're annoying me. Giorgios, grab his good arm and help me get him upstairs. We'll put him in the room adjoining mine—and I suggest," she added sweetly, addressing Niko again, "that you don't fight me on this. You've suffered enough pain for one night."

Although his glower was black as thunder, he offered no further resistance except to mutter, "Your bedside manner could use improvement, woman. Escaping rebel forces was a walk in the park compared to this."

But by the time they got him upstairs and into the bed Damaris had rushed to prepare, he had no fight left in him. "Clean sheets," he murmured on a ragged sigh. "Never thought they'd feel so good."

A moment later, he was asleep.

Emily left the connecting door between their rooms open and checked on him frequently during the remainder of the night, concerned as much about his rising temperature as the injury causing it. At one point, he opened his eyes and stared at her in the dim light as if he didn't know who she was. Another time, she heard him muttering her name deliriously and, placing the back of her hand against his cheek, realized he was burning up. Without knowing the extent of any vessel damage, she daren't give him aspirin and had to settle for sponging him down with tepid water. It helped temporarily, but never managed to subdue the fever completely.

From the outset, she'd known that what she could do for him would be, at best, a stopgap measure, and had hoped the new day would make him more amenable to accepting the kind of treatment only a physician could provide. But when, despite her efforts, his temperature spiked dangerously just before dawn, she knew she couldn't afford to wait for his permission, and phoned Pavlos's family physician.

She and the doctor had developed a strong mutual respect in the months since she'd come to Greece, and he brushed aside her apologies for disturbing him at such an ungodly hour. "I'll come at once," he said, after listening without interruption as she related the situation.

He arrived just as the sun was rising, subjected Niko

to a thorough examination, treated the infected gunshot wound and wrote out a prescription for topical and oral antibiotics. "Be glad you have a first-class nurse in residence, young man," he told Niko, when he was done. "You'd be hospitalized otherwise, whether or not you like it."

Then turning to Emily before he left, he added quietly, "Change his dressing regularly, and make sure he takes in plenty of fluids to replace what he's lost. If you're at all concerned that he's not getting enough, don't hesitate to call and we'll rehydrate him intravenously. Other than that, bed rest and medication should do the trick. Unless I hear from you sooner, I'll stop by again in the morning."

For two days, Emily was unconditionally happy. She had her man safe, close by and on the road to recovery. Although he slept a good part of the time, he always sensed when she was near. "Hey, angel," he'd murmur drowsily, fumbling for her hand, and her heart would swell with love.

The reprieve was short-lived. By the Thursday, he was chafing at being confined to bed and insisted that moving around was the best way to regain his strength. On Friday, he made it downstairs for breakfast, which was all it took for hostilities to resume between him and his father. And as usual, she found herself caught in the middle.

"What are you doing down here?" Pavlos demanded testily when he saw him.

"I have better things to do than lie around in bed all day, old man."

"Such as what?" Emily put in, horribly afraid she knew the answer.

"Unfinished business," he replied cryptically.

"If by that you mean going back to Africa and getting shot again, forget it."

"Don't tell me what to do, Emily. You're not my keeper."

"No, I'm the woman who loves you."

"More fool you," Pavlos chipped in, "because you have a jealous rival, my dear, and it's called death. He flirts with it constantly and has done for years."

"*Pre sto diavolo*—go to the devil, old man!" Niko retorted irascibly. "You know nothing about what motivates me, and even less about my relationship with Emily."

"I know she deserves a man willing to give her more than you ever will."

"Someone like you, I suppose?"

"At least she wouldn't be pacing the floor wondering where I am half the time."

"Because you can barely make it as far as the front door under your own steam."

They were like two lions fighting over the day's kill, the older one battling for dominance over a younger, more powerful adversary, and it sickened her.

"I could strangle the pair of you!" she exploded. "You're both so full of Greek pride, you can't see past it to what you're doing to one another. Or maybe you can, and you don't care."

"Stay out of it, Emily," Niko warned her. "This is between him and me."

"I won't!" she said, so angry she almost stamped her foot. "Pavlos is your father, for pity's sake, and you're his only child. You're all the family either of you has left and it's past time you put this senseless feud aside and made peace with one another. I know I would, were I in your place."

"But you're not," Niko said, so coldly that she shivered, "so can we agree to disagree and leave it at that? What you and I do in the bedroom is one thing, but you don't hear me interfering in your life the rest of the time. I'd appreciate it if you'd afford me the same sort of courtesy."

If he'd slapped her, she couldn't have been more shocked. "I thought we were about more than what happened in the bedroom."

He looked almost as shattered as she felt. "We are," he muttered, raking a furious hand through his hair. "I love you, you know that."

She'd once believed those three words were all it took for a man and a woman to make their relationship work, but she'd been wrong. They meant nothing if they came wrapped in resentment and soured what was once beautiful.

"Maybe you do," she said dully, "but not nearly enough."

CHAPTER ELEVEN

BEFORE he could respond to her accusation, let alone refute it, she was gone from the room. Seconds later, the front door slammed, drowning out the sound of her racing footsteps.

"That went well." Pavlos sneered. "Have anything planned for an encore?"

"Butt out," he growled, and turned to go after her.

"Do her a favor." The old man's voice followed him down the hall. "Let her alone. She's better off without you."

Maybe she was, but it wasn't in Niko's nature to give up without a fight. He'd be dead by now, if it were. And they'd invested too much of themselves in each other for it to end like this, over careless words spoken in the heat of the moment.

Wrenching open the door with his good hand, he stood on the step and shaded his eyes against the late morning sun. She'd already cleared the circular parking area and was swerving past an outraged peacock, which happened to be obstructing her path as she fled across the south lawn.

Intent on stopping her, Niko gave chase. Another dumb

move, he soon realized. Every bone in his body crunched as he hit the ground running. He covered no more than about forty meters before he was gasping for breath, and his shoulder was throbbing almost as badly as it had when he'd first been shot. He hadn't a hope of catching anything that moved, let alone a woman bent on putting as much distance between him and her as she was. And if that wasn't indignity enough, his father was now standing in the open doorway, watching the whole debacle.

"Emily!" The effort of raising his voice almost brought Niko to his knees.

She swung back to face him. *"What?"*

He couldn't answer. His lungs were bursting and black dots danced before his eyes. Humiliated by his weakness, not to mention his audience, he bent over, his chest heaving.

Seeing the shape he was in, she made her slow way back to him. "I already know how cruel you can be," she said, "but I had no idea you were stupid, too. You've probably made your wound bleed again and undone all the progress you made. Keep it up and you'll wind up in hospital, whether or not it's where you want to be."

"I want to be with you," he wheezed.

"Whatever for? We have nothing in common outside the bedroom, remember?"

"We both know that's not true."

"Then why did you say it?"

"Because I was—*am* frustrated as hell. I can no more tolerate not being in charge of my life than I can abide being on the receiving end of my father's grudging hospitality. The sooner I move back to the penthouse, the better for everyone."

"You're in no condition to go back to the penthouse," she informed him flatly.

"Too bad. I'm going anyway. Pavlos and I bring out the worst in each other. We always have." He grabbed at her hand. "Come with me, angel. It's Friday and we have the whole weekend ahead. Let's spend it together, making up for lost time."

"I don't know about that. Given your recent history, I doubt you're going to be feeling very…energetic."

"My upper torso might not be quite up to par, but below the waist everything's working just fine," he assured her. "Fully recovered or not, I want you so badly it hurts. More than that, I need you."

"You're only saying that to get your own way."

Annoyed, he snapped, "I thought you knew me better than that, Emily, but since you apparently don't, let me make one thing clear. I've yet to resort to lying in order to get a woman to sleep with me, and if you think that's what I'm doing now, then perhaps you should just keep running in the other direction and not look back." He released her hand and took a step away. "There, you're free. Off you go."

She bit her lip. A lone tear drizzled down her cheek. "I can't. I love you."

"Then why are we standing here arguing?"

"I don't know," she said and, closing the distance between them, buried her face against his neck.

"Go with him," Pavlos said, when she told him Niko was set on returning to the penthouse after lunch, then surprised her by adding, "and don't worry about being back here on Monday. Stay a week, or however long it takes to get him back on his feet. Judging from what I just saw, he's not quite the iron man he'd like to think he is."

"But you hired me to look after you," she protested, although they both knew he hadn't needed a resident nurse in days.

"Right now, he needs you a lot more than I do."

"I'm afraid you're right."

"Then pack a bag and be on your way. How are you getting into the city?"

"By taxi."

"No need. Giorgios will take you in the Mercedes. It'll be more comfortable for superhero."

She dropped a kiss on his cheek. "Thank you, Pavlos. You're an old softie under all that grump."

He swatted her away with rough affection. "Watch your mouth, girl, and don't be so quick with the gratitude. My son's about as cussed an individual as you could ask to meet, and I don't expect you'll have an easy time with him."

But she didn't care if she didn't have easy, as long as she had time.

They'd no sooner arrived at the penthouse than it started to pour with rain. Huge drops danced wildly on the terrace. Veils of cloud swirled outside the floor-to-ceiling windows, bringing an early dusk to the afternoon and obscuring the outside world. They didn't care. Wrapped in splendid isolation and with days of being together stretching before them, they didn't need sunshine. All they needed was each other.

That night, they sent out for dinner, ate it by candlelight and retired early. Knowing the day had wearied him, Emily didn't anticipate they'd make love, nor did she mind. She was happy simply to lie beside Niko in his big bed and feel the steady beat of his heart beneath her hand because, a week ago, she'd been afraid she'd never do so again. But he was alive, they were together, and that was all that mattered.

Proximity, though, was a powerful aphrodisiac and desire stole over them in quiet waves, with none of the tempestuous urgency they were used to. He turned on his side and his leg brushed hers, hair-roughened skin against smooth, warm thigh. His hand whispered over her hips to the hem of her short nightie and drew it up past her bottom. His mouth searched out hers and he uttered her name in muted invitation when she reached down and found him already hard.

All silken, pulsing heat, he positioned himself between her legs and slid inside her. They moved together in a slow, sweet symphony, adoring one another with soft murmurs of love. They climaxed in unison, the passion unspooling between them, lazy as waves rolling ashore. They fell asleep locked in each other's arms, sated with pleasure, and awoke to a morning washed clean and sparkling with sunshine.

So began a week she knew she would remember for the rest of her life. Sometimes they slept late. Other times, they went grocery shopping, arriving early at the markets to choose from a bewildering selection of food, and coming home loaded with goodies. Succulent lamb for souvlaki, or ground beef for moussaka. Fresh prawns and squid, cheese and olives for mezedes.

Ignoring Niko, who laughed and reminded her they were buying for two, not an army, she lingered at the fruit and vegetable stands, choosing jewel-toned egg-plant, vivid green peppers and bright red tomatoes, as well as lemons, tangerines and melons. She went to the bakery for bread still warm from the oven, and a quaint little shop at the entrance to the Plaka that sold honey, coffee, yogurt and nuts.

She learned to make tzaziki and saganaki. Even tried her hand at baklava. Although he had a housekeeper who usually came in every couple of days when he was in residence, Emily sent her away, preferring to change the bed linens and take care of the laundry herself, while Niko caught up by phone with what was happening at the airfield.

They took walks around the city. Visited museums and ancient churches. Explored art galleries and antique shops. Sometimes they'd go out for a meal. Mostly they stayed home, preferring to be alone.

They made love whenever and wherever the mood took them. Suddenly, urgently, in the late afternoon, on the rug in front of the fire in the living room, with the scent of burning apple wood filling the air. Sleepily, in the middle of the night, spurred by heaven only knew what dreams might have woken them. Wildly, hilariously, on the desk in his study, while he tried to conduct a serious phone conversation with Dinos at the office.

They lazed on the big overstuffed couch in the living room and read or listened to music, taking unhurried pleasure in simply being in the same room together.

It was like being married, except marriage was one subject they never discussed. To do so would have meant talking about the future which, in turn, would have brought that other world into focus. The one that took him away from her. Better to live in a fool's paradise.

But that dreaded other world intruded anyway, evidenced by a restlessness in him that increased as he regained his strength. Phone calls to the office weren't enough to satisfy him. He started spending time at the airfield again, an hour or two at first until, by the middle of the second week, he was back at work pretty much full-time. Domesticity had palled, even if his desire for her hadn't. He was raring for something more challenging than building fires or checking the firmness of tomatoes in the marketplace.

"I'm the boss," he said when she remonstrated with him. "Bosses are supposed to lead, not sit at home and let others do the job for them."

Matters came to a head on the third Sunday. All day, he'd been on edge. Finally, with evening closing in and Christmas carols playing on the stereo, he poured them each a glass of wine and came to sit next to her on the couch. "I have something to tell you, *karthula*," he began.

She knew what it was, without his having to elaborate. "You're leaving again."

"Yes."

"When?"

"Tomorrow."

"With so little advance notice?"

"Not exactly. I've known for a couple of days now that I'd be going."

"Where to this time?"

He looked at the fire, at the red roses she'd arranged in a vase on a side table, at the book lying facedown on the arm of the couch. He looked anywhere but at her, and her stomach turned over in a sickening lurch of prescience. "Oh, no," she whispered on a trembling breath. "Please tell me you're not going back to that horrendous place."

"I must," he said.

"Why? To get shot again, fatally this time?"

"People there are in terrible straits and they need help. And I need you to understand that I can't turn my back on them."

Anger welled up in her and she struck out at him, slamming her fist against his right arm. "What about what *I* need, Niko, or doesn't that matter to you?"

"I have given you all of myself."

"No. You give me what's left over after you take care of other people."

"Not so. You're what keeps me sane when the world around me erupts into madness. Before we met, I didn't care if I never came home. Now, I live for the time that we can be together again."

"Sure you do," she said, tears clogging her voice. "I'm the warm body that makes you forget the horrors you left behind, but it doesn't change the fact that you care more about strangers than you'll ever care about me."

"I don't deserve that, Emily."

"I don't deserve to be left waiting and wondering if you'll come back to me in one piece or a body bag."

"No, you don't," he said, setting down his wine and going to stand at the glass doors leading to the terrace, "which is why I never promised you forever. I've always known I couldn't give it to you."

So there it was, the end of the affair, delivered with the

uncompromising honesty that was his trademark. They'd finally run out of borrowed time and the tomorrow she'd tried so hard to postpone stood on the doorstep.

Hollow with pain, she said, "We were never a good fit, were we?"

"Never," he admitted, after a horrible, tension-filled pause.

"Always a ships-passing-in-the-night sort of thing."

"That about covers it."

But his voice was all rusty, as if he'd choked on a peanut. And she…she was perilously close to sobbing. She had followed in her parents' footsteps and gambled everything for the pleasure of living in the moment. And in doing so had lost everything. Their biggest mistake had become hers, too.

"So…o…o." She drew out the word on a long, quivering sigh. "I guess this is goodbye."

"I guess it is."

"It's for the best."

"Probably."

She dug her fingernails into her palms; bit the inside of her lip until she tasted blood. "I'll collect my stuff and get out of here. You must have a lot to do and don't need me underfoot."

He didn't argue, just straightened his shoulders and turned back to confront her, his face unreadable. "Fine. I'll drive you back to the villa."

And subject them both to more suffering? "No," she said. "There's a taxi stand right outside your building. I'll take a cab."

She left her untouched wineglass next to his and went upstairs to the bedroom to throw clothes, shoes and toiletries haphazardly into her suitcases. She had to get away quickly, before she fell down on her knees and begged him not to leave her.

At last she was ready. All that remained to be done was walking away from him. If there'd been a back entrance to the penthouse, she'd have taken it and spared them both the agony of a last goodbye, but he remained in the living room which opened off the long hall leading to the foyer.

"I think I've got everything," she said, staring straight ahead because, if she looked into his jade-green eyes one more time, she'd lose it completely.

"Anything you've forgotten, I'll send to the villa."

"Thanks." She swallowed painfully. "Take care of yourself."

"You, too."

She tried to open the door. Fumbled with a latch, which refused to budge. Was dimly aware of movement in the room behind her and renewed her efforts, not wanting him to come and help.

She could not look at him, or speak to him, or let him come near her again. She could not.

Eyes streaming, she made one last effort. The blasted latch clicked, but still the door refused to budge because, she realized, staring blurrily through her tears, he was holding it shut. Over the tormented thud of her heart she heard his voice so close behind her that his breath wafted warm and damp over her nape. "Emily, don't go," he begged. "It doesn't have to end like this."

She wilted, empty of pride and so full of hurt that she had no fight left in her. Dropping her luggage, she turned in his arms and clung to him, accepting that she was as helpless to refuse him as she was to change the course he'd set himself long before he met her. "I'm so afraid for you," she sobbed.

"I know, sweetheart," he said, kissing her eyes, her tears. "I know."

Hounded by the remorseless hunger, which had held them in thrall from the first, they sought the only comfort left to them and went at each other like mad things, giving the lie to any notion that being apart was better than being together. She clawed at him, desperate in her need, raking her hands down his shirt-front to tear open the buttons. He pinned her against the door, yanked up her skirt and ripped off her panties. Freeing himself from his jeans, he hoisted her off her feet, pulled her legs around his waist, and drove into her as if she was all that stood between him and damnation.

After that, there was no question of her leaving. Instead they tried to do what they'd done so successfully for over two weeks. They tried to play house.

He sorted the clothes he'd take with him in the morning. She folded them, the way a good wife would, and put them neatly in the canvas carryall that held enough to see him through as many days as he'd be gone. Too many, she noticed, counting three pairs of jeans, eight shirts and as many changes of undershorts and socks.

They tried to talk about anything except where he'd be tomorrow night at that time, but the conversation stalled at every turn and they'd subside into stricken silence before making another valiant attempt at normality.

They sat down to dinner, but abandoned the table when neither of them could eat. Their gazes met and held, and broke apart again when the emotion in their depths threatened to overwhelm them.

"Let's stop this," he finally said. "Come to bed, *khriso mou*. Let me hold you in my arms and love you one last time before I go."

She tried, fusing her body with his in a desperate, hopeless attempt to stop time. Amassing his every word, his every touch, and hoarding them against an empty future. She wished she could shut down her mind and simply listen to her body. But the specter of his flying off into the teeth of danger, of death, haunted her. It left her drained, deprived of everything that gave her life meaning. "Please don't go," she finally beseeched him. "If you love me at all, please stay and keep me with you."

"I can't," he said.

And she couldn't, either. He was an adventurer, at heart as much a rebel as those he fought against, albeit for different reasons. Risking life and limb gave him a rush she'd never understand. She needed stability—a real home, a husband, children—and she couldn't live suspended indefinitely on the fine edge of sanity, wanting what he couldn't give her.

Light from the en suite bathroom filtered into the room, crowding the corners with shadows but providing enough illumination for her to watch him sleeping. With the hours racing by much too fast, she committed to memory the curve of his mouth, the clean line of his jaw and cheekbones, his lashes, so long and thick he could sweep a street with them.

Beyond the windows, the sky grew imperceptibly lighter, precursor of a new and hellish dawn shouting that today was their last day. She did not want to hear or see it, and closing her eyes, she pressed her body close to his, inhaling through every pore the very essence of all that he was.

6:30 a.m.

Time to make a move.

Deactivating the alarm clock before it disturbed the silence, Niko took a moment to savor the warmth of her body next to his. Feigning sleep himself, he'd listened to her crying softly throughout the night. It had taken every last milligram of self-control for him not to reach for her and tell her what he knew she wanted to hear.

I'll send someone else in my place, and stay with you. We'll get married, make a home together, raise a family.

Exhaustion had claimed her before temptation got the better of him. Now she slept, with strands of her pale blond hair spread over his shoulder as if to bind him to her. She looked young, beautiful. Defenseless as a child, and unutterably sad.

He had done that to her. What had started out to be no more than a harmless flirtation designed to show Pavlos that his trust in her was misplaced, had blossomed out of control. Niko had seen it coming, but had done nothing to put an end to it. She had captivated him like no other woman he'd ever met, and he'd made the fatal mistake of falling in love with her.

Worse, selfish bastard that he was, he'd let her fall in love with him. And now he had to leave her because he knew that happy-ever-after wasn't in the cards. Of his fifteen employees, ten were pilots. The youngest was single and still living at home. Five of the remaining nine were divorced, victims of a career that demanded too much of the women who'd once loved them enough to take their names and bear their children.

He did not want that for her, for them. He'd rather lose her now, with the good memories still intact, than wait until all the joy and passion had turned bitter with resentment.

6:31 a.m.

Stealthily he eased himself off the bed, collected his clothes and, as he'd done before, went downstairs to shower and dress in the guest suite. As a rule, he stood under the jets an indecently long time because there was no telling when he'd next have access to hot water or clean towels. But that morning he made quick work of preparing for the day ahead.

6:49 a.m.

Ready to go. A better man than he'd ever be would have picked up his bag and left. He couldn't go without a last farewell, and went to the library to find pen and paper.

I love you enough to set you free to live the kind of life you're looking for, he wrote. *The man who can give it to you will be lucky indeed. Be happy, Emily.*

Then stopping by the living room, he plucked a rose from the bouquet she'd arranged, and stole back upstairs.

She lay exactly as he'd left her. He ached to kiss her. To whisper her name. To taste her mouth one more time.

For once, he did the right thing. He placed the note and the rose on his pillow and left her.

CHAPTER TWELVE

"He's gone again," Pavlos said, his wise old eyes absorbing everything in a single glance. "He's left you."

Too awash in misery to put a brave face on things, Emily collapsed into the chair next to his. "Yes."

"So what now?"

"I think I must go, too, Pavlos. There's nothing more for me here." Except a rose already wilting, a note that put a final end to hope and a heart in shreds.

"There's me."

She shook her head sadly. "I've taken advantage of your generosity too long already."

"Rubbish! You nursed me back to health, put up with my bad temper and—"

"And now you're well again." Or as well as he'd ever be. His hip had healed to a degree, but his eighty-six-year-old body was worn-out, and there wasn't a thing she or anyone else could do about it.

"You gave me a reason to get out of the bed in the morning," he insisted. "I've grown fond of you. You're like a daughter to me and will always have a place in my home."

For a moment, she was tempted. To be needed,

wanted; to be part of a family, however small…hadn't she longed for just such peace of mind and heart ever since she was nine? But common sense told her she'd find neither in this house. She'd never hear the doorbell without hoping it was Niko come to tell her he'd changed his mind, that he wanted forever after all, and he wanted it with her.

If Pavlos had been truly alone, it might have been different, but he had the devoted Giorgios and Damaris to take care of his daily needs, and a family doctor who visited three times a week. She'd be leaving him in good hands.

"I'm fond of you, too, and I'll never forget your kindness," she told him gently, "but my life is in Vancouver. I have a house there. Friends, a career, financial and professional obligations to honor."

"And I'm not enough to make you turn your back on them." He sighed and nodded acceptance. "Will you keep in touch?"

"Of course."

"I don't suppose I have to tell you that my son is a fool."

"No more than I was, Pavlos."

"I tried to warn you, girl."

"I know you did."

The trouble was, his warning had come too late. It had been too late from the moment she and Niko had set eyes on each other. The attraction between them had blazed out of control, instantaneous combustion bent on destroying anything that stood in its path. The fear that she might live to regret giving in to it had dissolved in the lilting excitement, the sheer *aliveness* of being in love. Nothing compared to it.

What she hadn't known was that when it ended, it

took more than it had ever bestowed. Without Niko she was empty, incomplete. She had known him less than three months and in that time he had turned her life upside down, stolen everything she had to give, and left her with nothing.

Or so she believed when she said goodbye to Pavlos. And perhaps, if she'd chosen a different career, she might have ascribed the mood swings and exhaustion she brought home with her to the unavoidable emotional fall-out of a love affair gone wrong. But nursing school had taught her well. She was attuned to her body and as the old year came to an end, she hardly needed a home pregnancy test to confirm the cause of the fatigue and faint but undeniable nausea that hounded her every waking hour.

The future Niko had insisted no one could predict was staring her in the face with a certainty that eliminated any possibility that she might one day come to forget him. He would be with her always in the shape of his child.

The realization shattered the blessed numbness, which had cushioned her since the day he'd left. She was a twenty-seven-year-old, highly trained medical professional, for pity's sake! Of all people, she should have known how to protect herself from an unplanned pregnancy. How could she have been so careless?

Except she hadn't been, nor had Niko. Even at their most spontaneous they'd taken precautions, to the point that he'd joked about buying condoms in bulk, to cut down on the number of trips to the drugstore! But there'd been a few times during their last two weeks together that they'd almost left it too late to be safe. Idiot that she was to have exposed herself to such risks, she must have conceived then.

Her doctor, whom she went to see in late January, soon put paid to that theory. "You're well into your second trimester, Emily. About sixteen weeks along, I'd say."

"I can't be." Unless…had they cut things too fine on the boat? Been too carried away by the newness of their affair to be as responsible as they should have been?

"Are you sure you last menstruated at the end of October?"

"Pretty sure," she said, vaguely recalling her period had been lighter than usual. Nothing more than spotting, but she hadn't paid much attention at the time. She'd been too busy falling in love.

"What about the father?"

"What about him?"

"Are you going to tell him?"

"No."

"Why not?"

"Because we're not together anymore. He's not into parenthood, at least with me."

That night, she lay in bed, surrounded by all the comforting things that spelled home. The blue and white toile de jouy wallpaper she'd hung herself. The handmade wedding ring quilt she'd bought at auction, three years ago. Her reproduction four-poster bed and matching rosewood bombe chest of drawers. The silver-framed photograph of her parents and two small oil paintings she'd found at an estate sale, the summer she'd graduated from nursing school.

They were proof she didn't need a man around, she

told herself. Closer to her due date she'd put a rocking chair in the alcove near the window, where she'd nurse her baby, and a white bassinet next to her bed. When he grew too big for that, she'd turn the second bedroom into a nursery. Paint clouds on the ceiling. Stencil unicorns and pixies on the walls—oh, and a guardian angel, because every child had to have a guardian angel, even if he couldn't have a father.

A father...Niko...

Memories of him rushed to the forefront of her mind. Of his warm breath tickling her neck when he leaned over to kiss her good morning. His mouth against hers, his voice in her ear.

Of his long, strong body and olive skin. The planes of his chest, the swell of muscle over his shoulder, the lean, taut curve of his buttocks.

Of his beautiful face, and his mesmerizing eyes and the way they turned dark when the passion he tried so hard to contain rode roughshod over him.

Of his laughter, his wicked sense of humor... *You've left me with an erection that would do a stallion proud, Emily....*

Oh, to hear him laugh again! To see him, to hold him!

As winter turned to spring, she struggled to put the past behind her, but it wasn't easy with his baby growing inside her. Wouldn't have been even if she wasn't pregnant.

Any mention of humanitarian aid brought him vividly alive in her mind. A melody they'd listened to together, the scent of aftershave on another man, a stranger, when it belonged only to him, were enough to turn a good day bad. He was in her heart, in her soul.

But in every other respect, she was alone. Alone and

pregnant, because although he'd paid lip service to loving her, when put to the test, the father of her unborn child chose to risk life and limb in some benighted corner of the world, rather than risk his heart to her.

Well, let him, she'd tell herself, furious at her own weakness. She'd had her fill of reluctant charity, growing up as she had in her aunt's house where she'd never been welcome. If Niko couldn't commit to her without reservation, she didn't want him at all.

Anger was so much easier to bear than grief, even if they did both boil down to the same thing in the end.

"Will you be able to manage financially?" her friends asked when they heard she was about to become a single parent.

"Yes," she said, the irony not escaping her that her baby's grandfather was responsible for the substantial savings she'd amassed. "I have it all planned out. I can work for another five months, then after the birth, take a year's maternity leave, and when that ends, hire a live-in nanny to look after the baby."

But her calculations misfired. On the twelfth of May when she was only thirty-three weeks into her pregnancy, and contrary to anything she or her doctors had reason to expect, she gave birth to a three pound, eleven ounce daughter.

As a nurse, she knew that a mildly preterm baby's chances of surviving without lasting complications were excellent. As a mother, she wore herself to a shadow fretting over the tiny, delicate creature who had taken her heart by storm from the second she entered the world.

She named her Helen and brought her home when

she weighed five pounds. "At least she looks all there," the well-meaning woman next door remarked, stopping by the next day to inspect the new arrival. "For a preemie, that is."

Emily's friends were somewhat more encouraging. "She's adorable, so petite and feminine," they agreed, flocking around the bassinet.

To Emily, she was the most beautiful baby ever born. She brought light to a life which, since the day Niko left, had been too often filled with darkness. Sitting in the rocking chair, with her baby at her breast and the dogwood trees blooming outside the window, Emily found a measure of peace that had eluded her for much too long.

Spring melded into summer. If it wasn't too hot, Emily would tuck Helen into her stroller and take her for walks in the park or along the seawall. She'd nurse her in the shade of a sun umbrella on the patio.

She'd kept her promise to stay in touch with Pavlos, and at first they'd exchanged frequent e-mails but, as the months came and went, they'd written to each other less often. He never mentioned Niko, had little to say about anything really, and she decided against telling him about her pregnancy. What was the point in upsetting him?

After Helen was born, she wasn't so sure she'd made the right decision. Would learning he was a grandfather bring a little joy into Pavlos's life, or merely create an even deeper rift between father and son? More to the point, could he keep it a secret from Niko?

She had no doubt that, should he find out she'd had his baby, Niko would feel obligated to do the honorable thing and marry her. And that, she knew, would merely invite long-term misery for everyone. He would never

settle happily for domesticity, and she wouldn't—
couldn't live with his career choice. No child needed a
daredevil for a father. Better to have no father at all than
one who, as Pavlos had once pointed out, flirted with
death every time he went to work.

As summer advanced, Helen continued to thrive.
Although still small for her age, she gained weight
steadily, clocking in at over six and a half pounds when
she was three months old.

One morning, Emily had put her down for her
morning nap and was folding laundry at the kitchen
counter when she received a distraught phone call from
Giorgios. Pavlos had taken a turn for the worse and was
not expected to recover. He had refused to be admitted
to hospital and was asking for her.

"What about his son?" she said. "Has he been contacted?"

"We have tried, but he is far away."

Typical! she thought. Why stick close to home and
your ailing father, when you could be somewhere else
giving your all to strangers?

"Will you come, Emily?"

How could she refuse? Pavlos needed her. "Yes, but
it'll take me a little time to make the arrangements."

"I am afraid he does not have much time left."
Giorgios's voice broke. "He is tired of fighting to live,
Emily. Many times, he asks me, 'What for do I wake up
each morning to an empty house?'"

"You tell him he has to hold on," she said fiercely.
"Don't you dare let him die before I get there."

* * *

She and Helen arrived at the villa by taxi two days later. Obtaining a passport for her baby at such short notice had taken some doing, but Emily had appealed to a sympathetic government official who, when he'd heard her situation, had cut through the bureaucratic red tape in record time.

As the cab rounded the last curve in the driveway and the villa came into view, nothing seemed to have changed. The palm trees rose tall against the deep blue sky. The flower beds blazed with color under the sun. Proud as ever, the peacocks strutted over the immaculate lawns.

Inside, the house told a different story. The atmosphere was somber, oppressive, although her showing up with a baby caused something of a stir.

"Yes, she's mine," Emily said to a stunned Damaris. Then, to Giorgios, "Am I in time?"

"*Neh.* When he heard you were coming, he found new strength. He is awake and just a few minutes ago asked how soon you would be here."

Lifting Helen from her infant seat, she said, "Then let's not keep him waiting any longer."

She had witnessed death in all its guises many times in her career, but even though she thought herself prepared, she was shocked when she saw Pavlos. He lay against his pillows, so frail and shrunken that a stiff breeze could have blown him away. His face was the color of parchment, his eyes closed, and had it not been for the shallow rise and fall of his chest, he might have already been dead.

"Hold her for me for a second, will you?" she whispered, passing Helen to Damaris, and approached his bed. "Hello, darling," she said softly.

He opened his eyes. "You came," he said, his voice a pale imitation of what it once had been.

"Of course."

"You're a good girl."

Stifling a rush of grief, she took Helen from Damaris and laid her in his arms. "I've brought someone with me," she said. "Say hello to your granddaughter, Pavlos."

He gazed at Helen who stared up at him from big blue eyes. Almost inaudibly, he whispered, "She is Niko's child?"

"Yes."

Tears trickled down his face. "I never thought to see the day. *Yiasu, kali egoni.* Hello, my little one."

"Her name's Helen."

"A good Greek name." The breath rattled in his beleaguered lungs. "A beautiful name for a beautiful child."

"I thought you'd approve."

He tore his eyes away from Helen. "How could I not? She is of my blood and has you for her mother. Tell me all about her."

"Tomorrow," she said, seeing that he was tiring fast. "For now, Pavlos, try to get some sleep."

He groped for her hand. "Sleep will come soon enough, girl, and we both know it is not one from which I will awake. Talk to me while there is still time. I want to know everything."

"Stay with him," Damaris murmured, scooping Helen into her arms again. "I will look after the little one."

"Take Giorgios with you when you go," Pavlos

wheezed. "His mournful face and death bed vigil weary me."

"Poor man," Emily said, when they were alone. "He loves you so much, Pavlos, and all this…" She indicated the oxygen tank and other hospital paraphernalia in the room. "It probably scares him."

"I know, and it hurts me that he is so overwrought. I would spare him seeing me like this, if I could. He has been more of a son to me than Niko ever was."

"Niko loves you, too."

"Save me the platitudes, girl! I am dying. If he cares about me at all, why is he the only one not here now?"

Footsteps crossing the adjoining sitting room came to a halt in the open doorway. "But I *am* here," Niko said. "I came as soon as I heard."

CHAPTER THIRTEEN

HORRIFIED, Emily froze, battered by panic and such a welter of conflicting emotions that her instinct was to run as far and as fast as she could to escape him. Anything to suppress the surge of longing aroused by the sound of his voice, the craving to touch him again. Anything to prevent his finding out about Helen. But what if he'd already seen her and recognized her as his? And even if he hadn't, how could she justify leaving Pavlos when he was clutching her hand so desperately?

Reining in her emotions, she drew on the control which had served her so well as a critical care nurse. With deceptive calm, she swiveled in the chair and in one sweeping glace took in everything about him from the top of his head to his dusty flight boots.

He looked like hell. Fatigue smudged his eyes, he hadn't shaved in days and he needed a haircut. Judging by their appearance, he must have slept in his jeans and shirt longer than was good for them or him, and the crystal was cracked on his flight computer watch. But more than all else, he looked unutterably sad.

"I'll leave the pair of you alone together," she muttered, rising to her feet.

"No," Pavlos wheezed, his eyes beseeching her.

Niko crossed the room and pressed her down on the chair again. "Please stay, angel," he said. "What I have to say is as much for you as for my father."

"Don't you dare upset him."

"I won't."

He pulled a chair close on the far side of the bed and took his father's other hand. The contrast between them, the one so big and strong and deeply tanned, the other so weak, with every vein showing through the paper-thin skin, was painfully moving to behold.

"If you're here to dance on my grave," Pavlos said, the faintest spark of the old hostility charging his words, "you needn't have rushed. I'm not dead yet."

"And I thank God for that, *Patera*, because I want to tell you I'm sorry I've made such a poor job of being your son."

"An *epiphaneia* at this late date?" Pavlos let out a croak of feeble laughter. "What brought that on?"

"I have just come back from a hell where political corruption and genocide rule the day. I've witnessed mothers ripped away from their newborn infants, fathers murdered before their children's eyes and been powerless to prevent either. I've met thousands of orphans infected by diseases, which will kill them before they grow to be adults. I have buried a dead baby and wept over his grave because there was no one else to mourn him."

Momentarily overcome, he cleared his throat and rubbed his thumb lightly over the back of his father's hand. "In the end, the devastation and ruin defeated me. What was I doing, trying to mend broken families in a foreign country when my own was falling apart at home? By what right had I held you at a distance, *Patera*, when your greatest sin was wanting to give me a better life than you had when you were young?"

"You're my son," Pavlos said. "Stubborn and proud and hell set on making your own way in the world, just as I was at your age. And you wanted to make that world a better place."

"Yes, I did. But I neglected you in the process. Have I left it too late to ask your forgiveness?"

With great effort, Pavlos lifted his other hand and laid it alongside Niko's stubble-covered jaw. "Ah, my foolish boy," he said hoarsely. "Don't you know it's never too late for a father to welcome his son home again?"

Niko started to cry then, harsh, horrible, rasping sobs that tore through his body. Emily couldn't bear it. Springing up from her chair, she stumbled to the French doors in the sitting room and ran out to the terrace.

At the far end, a path led away from the villa and wound through the gardens to a marble bench set in a shady arbor screened from the house by a grove of lemon trees. Reaching it, she sank down on the seat's cool, hard surface and wrestled with the demons plaguing her.

She had fought so hard to get over Niko. To shut herself off from dreams of him vivid enough that she awoke with the scent of his skin, the silken touch of his intimate flesh, taunting her. She'd struggled to find a foothold in a world without him. To build a safe, secure, contented life around her baby.

And for what? To fall for him all over again in less time than it took to blink, swayed by tears she'd never thought to see him shed, and words she'd never believed she'd hear him utter? Casting aside his indomitable pride, he'd revealed his innermost heart and in so doing, had walked right back into hers.

She could not allow it. Could not risk being dragged back into the morass of misery where loving him had landed her before. She had a child to protect now. Helen needed a mother who was whole, not half a woman pining for what she couldn't have. If she acted quickly and discreetly, she could leave the villa without anyone being the wiser. It was the best thing, the only thing to do.

Mind made up, she went around the side of the house to let herself in the front door, and came face-to-face with a harassed Georgios. "I've been looking for you, Emily. Your little one is screaming with hunger and Damaris cannot comfort her."

Right on cue, Emily's breasts started to leak and a quick glance at the clock on the wall showed her it had been over two hours since she'd last nursed her baby. Leaving would have to be postponed a little longer. "Please ask Damaris to bring her to me in the drawing room. It's cooler in there."

"If you'd rather be upstairs, everything's ready in your suite."

"Thanks, Giorgios," she said, "but now that Niko's arrived, I won't be staying here after all."

"Pavlos will be disappointed."

"I don't think so. We had our time together. Now it's his son's turn."

Niko sat with his father until he drifted off to sleep, then quietly left the bedroom and went in search of Emily. He and Pavlos had made peace at last. Now it was time to mend things with her. He'd hurt her badly. Hurt them both, for reasons which, in retrospect, struck him as unforgivably egotistical on his part. Well, no more. Things would be different from now on.

The house was silent as a tomb. An unfortunate comparison, he thought with a pang. Already the scent of death, indefinable but all too familiar, pervaded the atmosphere. But as he drew level with the pillared entrance to the formal day salon, a place so seldom used that he couldn't remember the last time he'd set foot in it, a soft, dovelike murmur caught his attention.

Thinking a bird might have flown in from the garden, he stepped quietly into the room and instead discovered Emily sitting by the open window, a lightweight shawl of some sort draped over her shoulder, her head bent attentively over the infant at her partially exposed breast.

The shock almost felled him. Yes, he'd urged her to find a man who could give her what he'd thought he never could, but not once in all the months they'd been apart had it occurred to him that she'd take his advice to heart so quickly or so thoroughly.

As though sensing she was being observed, she looked up and caught him staring. Her eyes widened and quickly, almost defiantly, she drew the shawl over the baby—a newborn, from what he'd been able to observe, probably no more than a few weeks old.

"Well," he said, affecting amusement when what he most wanted to do was howl with disappointed outrage, "I hardly expected this."

She tilted one shoulder in a dismissive little shrug. "What can I say? The day's been full of surprises."

He angled a glance at the baby, although all he could

see were its tiny legs and the little red soles of its feet poking out beneath the shawl. "Boy or girl?"

"Girl."

"Does she look like you?"

"Some people think so."

"Lucky her. And you're happy?"

"Deliriously. I have everything I ever wanted."

"Really?" He'd never have guessed. She was fidgety, tense, the picture of uneasiness. Rearranging the shawl needlessly. Looking anywhere but at him.

There was something else not right about the picture of contentment she was trying to present, and watching the nervous fluttering of her fingers, he all at once realized what it was. "In that case," he said, "why aren't you wearing a wedding ring?"

Of all the questions she'd feared he might ask, this one had never crossed her mind, and she briefly considered trying to come up with an inspired lie to throw him off the scent. Since she'd done such a good job of fooling him into thinking she'd found some other man to take his place, why not continue with the charade? But suddenly she'd had enough of the deceit and the subterfuge. She'd tell him the truth, or at least an edited version of it, and if he persisted in leaping to all the wrong conclusions, that was hardly her problem. "Because I'm not married," she said.

"Why not?"

"I rushed into a relationship with the wrong man, we went our separate ways and I'm bringing up my baby alone. Don't look so disapproving. It was my choice, and hardly unique in today's world. Hundreds of women make the same decision every day."

"You're not one of those women, Emily," he said. "You should have held out for the husband you always wanted."

"Well, I didn't. I had a baby instead."

His unforgettable green eyes scoured her face, undermining her resolve to remain coolly disinterested. "It's not too late for you to have both."

"I'm afraid it is. There aren't too many men out there willing to take on another man's child."

"There's me," he said. "If you'll have me, I'll marry you."

She was so unprepared for his answer that she almost dropped Helen. "Don't be ridiculous! The Niko Leonidas I know doesn't invest in marriage."

"That man doesn't exist anymore. He grew up and learned what was important in life."

"He used to believe helping those in need was important."

"He still does."

Bristling, she said, "I'm not in need, Niko. I can manage very well on my own."

"You misunderstand. What I'm saying is that I haven't abandoned the causes I've supported all these years. I still believe in doing my part and I always will. I just don't need to keep proving it by playing Russian roulette with my own life. There are other, more effective ways to make a difference."

"Marrying me isn't one of them," she said. But oh, how she wished it were!

He crossed the room in swift strides and came to where she sat. "Listen to me," he implored. "I love you. Give me a chance to show you how much. Let me make a home for you and your baby. Let me be a father to her. I don't care who else's blood runs in her veins. That she's yours is reason enough for me to love her as if she were my own."

"Oh…!" She pressed her trembling lips together and fought to hold back the tears. "This is so not what I expected when I woke up this morning."

"Me, neither. If you need time to think about it—"

"We both do, Niko. Right now your father needs you more than I do, and you're too emotionally fragile to be making any other major decisions."

"Not to the point that I don't know my own mind. In deference to my father, I won't pressure you to accept my proposal now, but I won't be put off indefinitely."

"There's more at issue here than just you and me, Niko. My situation…well, it's not exactly what you think."

"Do you love me?"

"Yes."

"Are you married?"

"I've already told that I'm not."

"Then there are no issues that can't be worked out."

He ran his hands down his crumpled shirt and dusty jeans. "Look, I'm a mess, inside and out. I'm going home to get cleaned up and pull myself together, but in the event that you're worried my proposal is some spur-of-the-moment impulse on my part—"

"Is it? You are a man who likes to rush to the rescue, after all."

"The person I'm rescuing this time is myself, Emily. It's taken me a long time, but I've finally set my priorities straight. Only a fool discards the treasures that bless his life. I was on my way home to tell my father that even before I heard he was dying. To my lasting regret, I've left it too late to make it up to him for all the wasted years. I won't make the same mistake with you."

He left her then, but not as he had before. Not empty of everything but despair. She'd once read that when it rains in the desert, all the cacti burst into glorious flower. For such a long time her spirit had been arid as a desert, but his words made hope bloom in every corner of her heart and fill it to overflowing.

While he was gone, Giorgios came to tell her Pavlos was awake again. She went to him immediately.

His tired eyes brightened when he saw she'd brought Helen with her and he tried to reach out to hold her, but the effort was too much for him and he sank back against the pillows. His pulse was weak and erratic, his breathing labored as his poor old heart struggled to keep working, and he soon drifted asleep again.

Niko joined her not long after and took up his post on the other side of the bed.

Sensing his presence, Pavlos muttered haltingly, "You here, son?"

"I'm here, *Babas*."

"You'll be a rich man when I go."

"Not as rich as I'd be if you stayed."

"Not enough time left for that, boy. It's up to you and Emily now."

"I know."

"You take good care of her."

"I will."

"And my granddaughter. Be a better father to her than I ever was to you."

Startled, Niko shot Emily a quick glance, but he said only, "I won't let you down, *Babas*."

"Never have, boy," Pavlos said, his voice barely above a whisper. "Always made me proud...should have told you before now."

He never spoke. He subsided into sleep again, deeper this time, his respirations so shallow they barely moved the sheet covering him. Emily busied herself checking the IV solution and oxygen, hoping to avoid the inevitable question about his father's comment, but Niko's attention remained fixed on Pavlos.

An hour passed, and then another. Helen squirmed and scrunched up her face, the prelude, Emily knew, to a very vocal demand for food. "I'll nurse her in the other room so she doesn't disturb him," she told Niko.

"Don't take too long," he said.

Afternoon slipped toward dusk. Giorgios brought tea and sandwiches. Damaris took Helen and put her to bed in a drawer she'd taken from a dresser, which was lined with soft blankets. The doctor paid a call, met Emily's gaze, shook his head regretfully and said he'd be by again in the morning.

Throughout the night, Emily and Niko kept vigil. Lost in their own thoughts of the man who'd made such an indelible impression on them both, they spoke little. At six o'clock the next morning, Pavlos died.

"He's gone, Niko," she said. "It's over."

He nodded, bent his head and gathered his father's frail body in his arms.

Leaving him to make his private farewell, she slipped from the room and went out to the terrace. In the half-light of dawn, the flower beds shone like pale clumps of stars. It was going to be another beautiful late August day. The first of many without Pavlos.

She didn't hear Niko join her until he spoke. "He was rambling, wasn't he, when he said the baby's mine?"

"No," she said, too sad and exhausted to prevaricate. The truth had to come out sooner or later, it might as well be now. "You're her biological father."

"That's impossible. We always used protection."

"We couldn't have been as careful as we thought,"she said.

"How old is she? She looks practically newborn."

"She's three months old."

"How much does she weigh?"

"Nearly seven pounds now, but she was less than four at birth. She looks small because she was born seven weeks early."

He almost staggered. "Why didn't you tell me?"

"I tried to when you found me with her yesterday. You wouldn't let me."

"I'm not talking about yesterday afternoon, Emily. I'm talking about the last nine or ten months. I would have married you at once, if I'd known."

"I know you would. I didn't want you on those terms. I still don't."

"I was afraid that might be the reason," he said. "I seem to have a real talent for screwing up the relationship that means the most to me."

And he walked back into the house, a man so bowed down with sorrow that she couldn't bear to watch him.

CHAPTER FOURTEEN

SHE saw little of him in the week that followed. Arranging the funeral and the myriad tasks associated with it kept him occupied. Pavlos had many business associates and the stream of callers coming to the villa to pay their respects was endless.

Emily helped poor Damaris, who was run off her feet providing refreshments, and spent many quiet hours in the gardens with Helen, wondering what the future held. Although he'd made time to get to know his daughter, Niko treated Emily more like a sister than a lover. Had she ruined their chances by keeping their baby a secret? she wondered.

She received her answer when he sought her out as she sat in the shade of an olive tree, on the lawn overlooking the Saronic Gulf. For the last two days, they'd had the villa to themselves again, but it was too lovely an afternoon to spend indoors.

"We've pretty much laid the past to rest, Emily," he announced, dropping down beside her on the blanket she'd spread on the grass. "Now we have to take care of the future. I said I wouldn't rush you for an answer to my proposal, and I've tried to keep my distance, but I'm afraid I've run out of patience."

Her mouth dropped open. "Are you saying you still want to marry me?"

"More than I've ever wanted anything in my life. The question is, do you trust me enough to want to marry me?"

"Why wouldn't I trust you?"

"Well, let's see. I showed myself to be devious and unscrupulous by trying to expose you as a fraud. I seduced you, then agreed that we weren't a good match and might as well end our relationship. I left you, and you had a baby you didn't dare tell me about because you quite rightly thought I'd make a lousy father. Shall I go on?"

"No. We've laid the past to rest, remember, so let's do as you suggest and talk about the future."

"Okay. Here's what I've decided. Although I'll continue to support the causes I hold dear, I'm retiring as a pilot and sharing management of the company with Dinos. I intend to take an active role in overseeing my father's investments as he always wished me to do. Giorgios and Damaris have been very loyal to my family, so if you and I get married and you're agreeable, I'd like to live here and keep them and the rest of staff on. How am I doing so far?"

"Very well. I couldn't ask for better."

"Is that a yes to my proposal?"

"I'm not sure," she said coyly. "You moved into the villa a week ago and have been sleeping in a room down the hall from mine and your daughter's ever since. Do you plan to keep on doing that?"

"Not if you'll let me sleep in yours."

"Then it's a yes."

He closed his eyes and let out a long, slow breath. "Thank you for that, angel," he said. "I've been a very sad and lonely man since my father died, disappointed in myself on many levels and so afraid I'd blown any chance I might have had with you."

"I've been sad, too, Niko," she said, "but it hasn't changed the way I feel about you. I love you. I always will."

"I love you, too, so much more than you'll ever know. I love our daughter and will protect you both for the rest of my life."

That night, they lay together in bed with Helen between them. After fussing all evening, she'd finally fallen asleep.

"How beautiful she is," Niko whispered, his gaze tracking her face feature by feature. "Her ears are like little shells and look how tiny her nose is."

"She has your dark hair," Emily told him.

"She has your mouth.'

She smiled. "She is *our* baby."

"Yes," he said. "And I think you should put her in the drawer so that we can practice making another just like her, *mana mou*."

They made love, taking slow delight in rediscovering each other. He traced his tongue over the pale blue veins in her swollen breasts. She kissed the scar on his shoulder where he'd been shot. With hands and mouths and whispered words of love, they found the magic they once thought they'd lost and made it new and wonderful again. And when, at last, he entered her, they clung together and let the passion roll over them in sweet, endless waves and carry them to the far shores of ecstasy.

Afterward, Emily curled up in his arms and, hearing Helen whimper in her sleep, murmured drowsily, "We really must buy her a proper crib, don't you think?"

"Tomorrow, my darling," he said, bringing his mouth to hers in a lingering good-night kiss.

He tasted of lemons and sunshine and all things Greek. Of the fabulous turquoise sea, the dazzling mango-tinted sunsets, the ethereal dawns.

He tasted of forever.

CONSTANTINE'S DEFIANT MISTRESS

SHARON KENDRICK

CHAPTER ONE

IT WAS hearing his name on the radio which made her senses scream. Laura never had time for newspapers—even if her dyslexia hadn't made reading so difficult—she relied on the morning news programme to keep her up to date. Usually she only listened with half an ear, and usually she wasn't remotely interested in anything to do with international *finance*.

But Karantinos was an unusual name. And it was Greek. And didn't anything to do with that beautiful and ancient land put her senses on painful alert for very obvious reasons?

She had been busy making bread—sprinkling a handful of seeds into the dough before she popped the last batch into the oven. But with shaking hands she stopped dead-still and listened—like a small animal who had found itself caught alone and frightened in the middle of a hostile terrain.

'Greek billionaire Constantine Karantinos has announced record profits for his family shipping line,' intoned the dry voice of the news-reader. 'Playboy Karantinos is currently in London to host a party at the Granchester Hotel, where it is rumoured he will announce his engagement to Swedish supermodel Ingrid Johansson.'

Laura swayed, gripping the work surface to support herself, her ears scarcely able to bear what she had just heard, her heart pounding with a surprisingly forceful pain. Because she had preserved Constantine in her heart, remembering him just as he'd been when she'd known him—as if time had stood still. A bittersweet memory of a man who still made her ache when she thought of him. But time never stood still—she knew that more than anyone.

And what had she expected? That a man like Constantine would stay single for ever? As if that lazy charm and piercing intellect—that powerhouse body and face of a fallen angel—would remain unattached. She was just surprised that it hadn't happened sooner.

She could hear the sounds of movement from above as she took off her apron. But her heart was racing as she mechanically went through her morning routine of tidying up the kitchen before going upstairs to wake her son. She often told herself how lucky she was to live 'over the shop', and although helping run a small baker's store hadn't been her life's ambition, at least it gave her a modest income which she supplemented with occasional waitressing work. But most of all it provided a roof over their heads—which was security for Alex—and that was worth more than anything in Laura's eyes.

Her sister Sarah was already up, yawning as she emerged from one of the three poky bedrooms, running her fingers through the thick dark curtain of her hair, which so contrasted with her sister's finer, fairer mane.

'Mornin', Laura,' Sarah mumbled, and then blinked as she saw her older sister's face 'What the hell's happened? Don't tell me the oven's gone on the blink again?'

Mutely, Laura shook her head, then jerked it in the direction of her son's bedroom. 'Is he up yet?' she mouthed.

Sarah shook her head. 'Not yet.'

Laura glanced at the clock on the wall, which dominated her busy life, and saw that she had ten minutes before she had to get Alex up for school. Pulling Sarah into the small sitting room which overlooked the high street, she shut the door behind them and turned to her sister, her whole body trembling.

'Constantine Karantinos is in London,' she began, the whispered words falling out of her mouth like jagged little fragments of glass.

Her sister scowled. 'And?'

Laura willed her hands to stop shaking. 'He's throwing a party.' She swallowed. 'And they say he's getting engaged. To a Swedish supermodel.'

Sarah shrugged. 'What do you want me to say? That it's a surprise?'

'No... But I...'

'But what, Laura?' demanded Sarah impatiently. 'You can't seem to accept that the no-good bastard you slept with hasn't an ounce of conscience. That he *never gave you another thought.*'

'He—'

'He what? Refused to see you? Why, you couldn't even get a single meeting with the great man, could you, Laura? No matter how many times you tried. He's never even taken your phone calls! You were good enough to share his bed—but not good enough to be recognised as the mother of his child!'

Laura shot an agonised look at the closed door, straining her ears as she wondered if Alex had done the unheard-of and managed to get himself out of bed without his mother or his auntie gently shaking him awake. But then, seven-year-old boys were notoriously bad at getting up in the morning, weren't they? And they became increasingly curious as they got older…kept asking questions she wasn't sure how to answer…

'Shh. I don't want Alex to hear!'

'Why not? Why shouldn't he know that his father happens to be one of the richest men on the planet—while his mother is working her fingers to the bone in a bread shop, trying to support him?'

'I don't want to…' But her words tailed off. Didn't want to *what* exactly? Laura wondered. Didn't want to hurt her beloved son because it was the duty of every mother to protect her child? Yet she had been finding it increasingly difficult to do that. Just last month Alex had come home with a nasty-looking bruise on his cheek, and when she had asked him what had happened he had mumbled and become very defensive. It had only been later that she'd discovered he'd been involved in some kind of minor skirmish in the playground. And later still that she had discovered the cause, when she'd gone tearing into the school, white-faced and trembling, to seek a meeting with the headmistress.

It transpired that Alex was being bullied because he looked 'different'. Because his olive skin, black eyes and towering height made him look older and tougher than the other boys in his class. And because the little girls in the class—even at the tender ages of six and seven—had been following the dark-eyed Alex around like eager little puppies. Like father, like son, she had thought with a pang.

Laura had felt a mixture of troubled emotions as she'd gone home that day. She'd wanted to ask her son why he hadn't hit back—but that would have gone against everything she had taught him. She had brought him up to be gentle. To reason rather than to lash out. For two pins she would have withdrawn her son from the school and sent him somewhere else—but she didn't have the luxury of choice. The next nearest state school was in the neighbouring town, and not only did Laura not have a car but the bus service was extremely unreliable.

Lately her son had been asking her more and more frequently about *why* he looked different. He was an intelligent little boy, and sooner or later he wouldn't allowed her to fob him off with vague and woolly pieces of information about a father he had never seen. If only Constantine would just *talk* to her. Acknowledge his son. Spend a little time with him—that was all she wanted. For her beloved boy to know a little of his heritage.

She was distracted while she gave Alex his breakfast, and even more distracted during the short walk to his school. Although it was almost the summer holidays, the weather had been awful lately—nothing but rain, rain, rain—and this morning the persistent drizzle seemed to penetrate every inch of her body. She shivered a little, and tried to chatter brightly, but she felt as if she had a heavy lead weight sitting in the pit of her stomach.

Alex looked up at her with his dark olive eyes and frowned. 'Is something wrong, Mum?' he questioned.

Your father is about to marry another woman and will probably have a family with her. Telling herself that the blistering shaft of jealous pain was unreasonable under the circumstances, she hugged her son to her fiercely as she said goodbye.

'Wrong? No, nothing's wrong, darling.' She smiled brightly, and watched as he ran into the playground, praying that the head teacher's recent lecture on bullying might have had some effect on the little savages who had picked on him.

She was lost in thought as she walked back to the shop. Hanging up her damp coat in the little cloakroom at the back, she grimaced at the pale face which stared back at her from the tiny mirror hung on the back of the door. Her grey eyes looked troubled, and her baby-fine hair clung to her head like a particularly unattractive-looking skull-cap. Carefully, she brushed it and shook it, then crumpled it into a damp pleat on top of her head.

Pulling on her overall, she was still preoccupied as she walked into the shop, where her sister was just putting on the lights. Five minutes until they opened and the first rush of the day would begin—with villagers keen to buy their freshly baked bread and buns. Laura knew how lucky she was to have the life she had—lucky that her sister loved Alex as much as she did.

The two girls had been orphaned when Sarah was still at school, after their widowed mother had died suddenly and quietly in the middle of the night. A stricken Laura had put her own plans of travelling the world on hold, unsure what path to take to ensure that Sarah could continue with her studies. But fate had stepped in with cruel and ironic timing, because Laura had discovered soon after that she was carrying Alex.

Money had been tight, but they had been left with the

scruffy little baker's shop and the flat upstairs, where they had spent most of their childhood years. They had always helped their mother in the shop, so Laura had suggested modernising it and carrying on with the modest little family business, and Sarah had insisted on studying part-time so that she could help with Alex.

Up until now the scheme had worked perfectly well. And if the shop wasn't exactly making a huge profit, at least they were keeping their heads above water and enjoying village life.

But recently Sarah had started talking longingly of going to art school in London, and Laura was horribly aware that she was holding her back. She couldn't keep using her little sister as a part-time child-minder, no matter how much Sarah loved her nephew—she needed to get out there and live her own life. But then how on earth would Laura cope with running a business and being as much of a hands-on mum as she could to Alex? To Alex who was becoming increasingly curious about his background.

Sarah was giving the counter a final wipe, and looked up as Laura walked into the shop. 'You still look fed up,' she observed.

Laura stared down at the ragged pile of rock-cakes and boxes of home-made fudge under the glass counter. 'Not fed up,' she said slowly. 'Just realising that I can't go on hiding my head in the sand any longer.'

Sarah blinked. 'What are you talking about?'

Laura swallowed. Say it, she thought. Go on—*say* it. Speak the words out loud—that way it will become real and you'll *have* to do it. Stop being fobbed off by the gatekeepers who surround the father of your son. Get out there and *fight* for Alex. 'Just that I've got to get to Constantine and tell him he has a son.'

Sarah's eyes narrowed. 'Why the new fervour, Laura?' she asked drily. 'Is it because Constantine is finally settling down? You think that he's going to take one look at you and decide to dump the Swedish supermodel and run off into the sunset with you?'

Laura flushed, knowing that Sarah spoke with the kind of harsh candour which only a sister could get away with— but her words were true. She had to rid herself of any romantic notions where the Greek billionaire was concerned. As if Constantine would even *look* at her now! He certainly wouldn't fancy her any more—for hadn't hard work and a lack of time to devote to herself meant that her youthful bloom had faded faster than most? At twenty-six she sometimes felt—and looked—a whole decade older than her years. And even if the fire in her heart still burned fiercely for the father of her son she had to douse the flames completely.

'Of course I don't,' she said bitterly. 'But I owe it to Alex. Constantine has *got* to know that he has a son.'

'I agree. But aren't you forgetting something?' questioned Sarah patiently. 'Last time you tried to contact him you got precisely nowhere—so what's changed now?'

What *had* changed? Laura walked slowly towards the door of the shop. She wasn't sure—only that perhaps she'd realised time was running out, that maybe this was her last chance. And that she was no longer prepared to humbly accept being knocked back by the tight circle which surrounded the formidable Greek. She was fired up by something so powerful that it felt as if it had invaded her soul. She was a mother, and she owed it to her son.

'What's changed?' Slowly, Laura repeated Sarah's words back to her. 'I guess *I* have. And this time I'm going to get to him. I'm going to look him in the eye and tell him about his son.'

'Oh, Laura, exactly the same thing will happen!' exclaimed Sarah. 'You'll be knocked back and won't get within a mile of him!'

There was a pause. Laura could hear the ticking of her wristwatch echoing the beating of her heart. 'Only if I go the conventional route,' she said slowly.

Sarah's eyes narrowed. 'What are you talking about?'

Laura hadn't really known herself up until then, but it was one of those defining moments where the answer seemed so blindingly simple that she couldn't believe she hadn't thought of it before. Like when she'd decided that they ought to start making their own loaves on the premises rather than having them delivered from the large bakery in the nearby town—thereby enticing their customers in with the delicious smell of baking bread.

'The radio said he's giving some big party in London,' she said, piecing her whirling thoughts into some kind of order. 'In a hotel.'

'And?'

Laura swallowed. 'And what industry has the fastest turn-over of staff in the world? The catering industry! Think about it, Sarah. They'll…they'll need loads of extra staff for the night, won't they? Casual staff.'

'Just a minute…' Sarah's eyes widened. 'Don't tell me you're planning—'

Laura nodded, her heart beating faster now. 'I've done waitressing jobs at the local hotel for years. I can easily get a reference.'

'Okay, so what if you do manage to get on the payroll?' Sarah demanded. 'Then what? You're going to march over to Constantine in your uniform, in the middle of his fancy party, and announce to him in front of the world, not to mention his soon-to-be wife that he has a seven-year-old son?'

Laura shook her head, trying not to feel daunted by the audacity of her own idea but her fervour refused to be dampened. 'I'll try to be a bit more subtle about it than that,' she said. 'But I'm not going to leave until he's in full possession of the facts.'

She reached up and turned over the sign on the shop door from 'Closed' to 'Open'. Already there was a small cluster of shoppers waiting, shaking off the raindrops from their umbrellas as they filed into the shop.

Laura pinned a bright smile to her lips as she stood behind the counter and took her first order, but the irony of her plan didn't escape her. After all, she had been waitressing when she'd first met Constantine Karantinos, and had tumbled into his arms with embarrassing ease.

Afterwards she had looked back and wondered how she could have behaved in a way which had been so completely out of character. And yet it had been such a golden summer in those carefree months before her mother had died, and she'd felt as if she had the world at her feet as she saved up to go travelling.

She had been an innocent in every sense of the word—but a few months of waitressing in a busy little harbour town had trained her well in how to deal with the well-heeled customers who regularly sailed in on their yachts.

Constantine had been one of them, and yet unlike any of them—for he'd seemed to break all the rules. He'd towered over all the other men like a colossus—making everyone else fade into insignificance. The day she had first set eyes on him would be imprinted on her mind for ever; he had looked like a Greek god—his powerful body silhouetted against the dying sun, his dark and golden beauty suggesting both vigour and danger.

She remembered how broad his shoulders had been, and how silky the olive skin which had sheathed the powerful muscle beneath. And she remembered his eyes, too—as black as ebony yet glittering like the early-morning sunlight on the sea. How could she have resisted a man who had seemed like all her youthful fantasies come to life—a man who had made her feel like a woman for the first and only time in her life?

She remembered waking up in his arms the next morning to find him watching her, and she had gazed up at him, searching his face eagerly for some little clue about how he might feel. About her. About them. About the future.

But in the depths of those eyes there had been…nothing.

Laura swallowed.

Nothing at all.

CHAPTER TWO

'YES, Vlassis,' Constantine bit out impatiently, as he glanced up at one of his aides, who was hovering around the door in the manner he usually adopted when he was about to impart news which his boss would not like. 'What is it?'

'It's about the party, *kyrios*,' said Vlassis.

Constantine's mouth flattened. Why had he ever agreed to have this wretched party in the first place? he found himself wondering. Though in his heart he knew damned well. Because there had been too many mutterings for much too long about people in London wanting to enjoy some of the legendary Karantinos wealth. People always wanted to get close to him, and they thought that this might give them the opportunity. And it was always interesting to see your friends and your enemies in the same room— united by those twin emotions of love and hate, whose boundaries were so often blurred.

'What about it?' he snapped. 'And please don't bother me with trivia, Vlassis—that's what I pay other people to deal with.'

Vlassis looked pained, as if the very suggestion that he should burden his illustrious employer with trivia was highly offensive to him. 'I realise that, *kyrios*. But I've just received a message from Miss Johansson.'

At the mention of Ingrid, Constantine leaned back in his chair and clasped his fingers together in reflective pose. He knew what the press were saying. What they always said if he was pictured with a woman more than once. That he was on the verge of marrying, as most of his contemporaries had now done. His mouth flattened again.

Perhaps one of the greatest arguments in favour of marriage would be having a wife who could deal with the tiresome social side of his life. Who could fend off the ambitious hostesses and screen his invitations, leaving him to get on with running the family business.

'And?' he questioned. 'What did Miss Johansson say?'

'She asked me to tell you that she won't be arriving until late.'

'Did she say why?'

'Something about her photo-shoot overrunning.'

'Oh, did she?' said Constantine softly, his black eyes narrowing in an expression instinctively which made Vlassis look wary.

Unlocking his fingers, Constantine raised his powerful arms above his head and stretched, the rolled-up sleeves of his silk shirt sliding a little further up over the bunched muscle. Slowly he brought his hands down again, lying them flat on the surface of the large desk. The faint drumming of two fingers on the smooth surface was the only outward sign that he was irritated.

Ingrid's coolness was one of the very qualities which had first attracted him to her—that and her white-blonde Swedish beauty, of course. She had a degree in politics, spoke five languages with effortless fluency—and, standing at just over six feet in her stockinged feet, she was one of the few women he had ever met who was able to look him in the eye. Constantine's mouth curved into an odd kind of smile. As well as being one of the few *natural* blondes he'd known…

When they'd met, her unwillingness to be pinned down, her elusiveness when it came to arranging dates, had contrived to intrigue him—probably because it had never happened before. Most women pursued him with the ardour of a hunter with prized quarry in their sights.

But over the months Constantine had realised that Ingrid's evasiveness was part of a game—a master-plan. Beautiful enough to be pursued by legions of men herself, she had recognised the long-term benefits of playing hard-to-get with a man like him. She must have realised that Constantine never had to try very hard, so she had made him try very hard indeed. And for a while it had worked. She had sparked his interest—rare in a man whose natural attributes and huge wealth meant that his appetite had become jaded at an early age.

She had been playing the long game, and Constantine had allowed himself to join in; Ingrid knew what she wanted—to marry an exceptionally wealthy man—and deep down he knew it was high time he took himself a wife. And surely the best kind of wife for a man like him was one who made few emotional demands?

He didn't want some clingy, needy female who thought that the world revolved around him. No, Ingrid came close to fitting almost all his exacting criteria. Every hoop he had presented her with she had jumped through with flying colours. Why, even his father approved of her. And, although the two men had never been close, Constantine had found himself listening for once.

'Why the hell don't you marry her?' he had croaked at his son, where once—before age and ill-health—he would have roared. 'And provide me with a grandson?'

Good question—if you discounted his father's own foolish views on love. Didn't there come a time when every man needed to settle down and produce a family of his own? A boy to inherit the Karantinos fortune? Constantine frowned. Circumstances seemed to have been urging him on like a rudderless boat—and yet something about the sensible option of marrying Ingrid had made him hold back, and he couldn't quite work out what it was.

How long since they had seen one another? Constantine allowed his mind to flick back over the fraught and hectic recent weeks, largely filled with his most recent business acquisition. It had been ages since Ingrid had been in his bed, he realised. Their paths had been criss-crossing over the Atlantic while their careers continued their upward trajectory. Constantine gave a hard smile.

'What time is she arriving?' he questioned.

'She hopes before midnight,' said Vlassis.

'Let's hope so,' commented Constantine, as a faint feeling of irritation stirred within him once more. But he turned to a pile of papers—to the delicate complexity of an offshore deal he was handling. And, as usual, work provided a refuge from the far more messy matter of relationships. For Constantine had learned his lesson earlier than most—that they brought with them nothing but pain and complications.

He left the office around six and headed for the Granchester, whose largest penthouse suite he always rented whenever he was in town. He loved its glorious setting, overlooking lush green parkland, its quiet luxury and the discretion of its staff. And he liked London—just as he liked New York—even if they were too far from the sea for him to ever let complete relaxation steal over him....

To the sound of opera playing loudly on the sound system, he took a long, cold shower before dressing in the rather formal attire which the black-tie dinner warranted. His eyes glittered back at him as he cast a cursory glance at himself in the mirror.

Slipping on a pair of heavy gold cufflinks, he made his way downstairs, his eyes automatically flicking over to his people, who were discreetly peppering the foyer. He knew that his head of security would be unable to prevent the paparazzi from milling around by the entrance outside, but there was no way any of them would be getting into the building to gawp at the rich and the powerful.

Ignoring the gazes of the women who followed his progress with hungry eyes, he walked into the ballroom and looked around. The Granchester had always been a byword for luxury—but tonight the hotel had really surpassed itself. The ballroom was filled with scented blooms, and chandeliers dripped their diamond lights...

A soft voice cut into his thoughts.

'Could…could I get you a drink, sir?'

For a brief moment the voice stirred a distant memory—as faint as a breath on a still summer's day. But then it was gone, and slowly Constantine turned to find a waitress standing staring up at him—chewing at her lip as if she hadn't had eaten a meal in quite a while. His eyes flicked over her. With her small, pinched face and tiny frame she looked as if she probably *hadn't* eaten a meal in ages. Something in her body language made him pause. Something untoward. He frowned.

'Yes. Get me a glass of water, would you?'

'Certainly, sir.' Miraculously, Laura kept her voice steady, even though inside she felt the deep, shafting pain of rejection at the way those black eyes had flicked over her so dismissively. She had tried to hold his look for as long as was decently possible under the circumstances—willing him to look at her with a slowly dawning look of incredulity. But instead, what logic told her would happen had happened. *The father of her son hadn't even recognised her!*

Yet had she really bought into the fantasy that he might? That he would stare into her eyes and tell her that they looked like the storm clouds which gathered over his Greek island? He had said that when he had been charming her into his bed, and doubtless he would have something suitable in his repertoire for any woman. Something to make every single woman feel special, unique and amazing. Something which would make a woman willingly want to give him her virginity as if it were of no consequence at all.

It had been her moment to tell him that he had a beautiful little son—while there was no sign of the supermodel girlfriend all the papers had been going on about—and she had blown it. The shock of seeing him again, coupled with the pain of realising that she didn't even qualify as a memory, had made her fail to seize the opportunity. But surely you couldn't just walk up to a man who was essentially a total stranger and come out with a bombshell like that?

Laura hid her trembling fingers in her white apron as she quickly turned away—but the emotional impact of seeing Constantine again made her stomach churn and her heart thump so hard that for a moment she really thought she might be sick.

But she couldn't afford to be sick. She had to stay alert—to choose a moment to tell him what for him would be momentous news. And it wasn't going to be easy. Getting an agency placement to waitress at the Karantinos party had been the easy bit—the hard stuff was yet to come.

'What the hell do you think you're doing?' demanded a severely dressed middle-aged woman as Laura walked up to the bar to place her order.

Laura smiled nervously at the catering manager, who had summoned all the agency staff into a cramped and stuffy little room half an hour earlier to tell them about the high expectations of service which every Granchester customer had a right to expect. 'I just offered the gentleman a drink—'

'Gentleman? *Gentleman*? Do you know who that *is*?' the woman hissed. 'He's the man who's *giving* this party which is paying your wages! He's a bloody world-famous Greek shipping tycoon—and if anyone is going to be offering him drinks then it's going to be me. Do you understand? I'll take over from now on. What did he ask for?'

'Just…just water.'

'Still or sparkling?'

'He…he didn't say.'

The manager's eyes bored into her. 'You mean you didn't ask?'

'I…I… No, I'm sorry, I'm afraid I didn't.' Inwardly,

Laura squirmed beneath the look of rage on her supervisor's face, and as the woman opened her mouth to speak she suspected that she was about to be fired on the spot. But at that moment there was some sort of hubbub from the other end of the ballroom, as the harpist arrived and began making noisy demands, and the manager gave Laura one last glare.

'Just do what you're supposed to do. Offer him both still and sparkling, and then fade into the background—you shouldn't find *that* too difficult!' she snapped, before hurrying away towards the musician.

Laura tried to ignore the woman's waspish words as she carried her tray towards Constantine. But inside she was trembling—mainly with disbelief that she had managed to get so close to him. And thrown into the complex mix of her emotions at seeing him again was also her body's unmistakable reaction to seeing the biological father of her son. It was something she stupidly hadn't taken into account—the powerful sense of recognition at seeing him. The sense of familiarity, even though this man was little more than a stranger to her.

Because here was Alex in adulthood, she realised shakily—or rather, here was a version of what Alex *could* become. Strong, powerful, prosperous. And wasn't that what every mother wanted for her son? A lion of a man, as opposed to a sheep.

Whereas the Alex she had left back at home being looked after by a frankly cynical Sarah—well, that Alex was headed in a completely different direction. Bullied at school and living a life where every penny mattered and was counted—how could he possibly achieve his true potential like that? What kind of a future was she offering him?

And any last, lingering doubt that she must be crazy to even contemplate a scheme like this withered away in that instant. Because she owed Alex this.

It didn't matter if her pride was hurt or the last of her stupid, romantic memories of her time with Constantine was crushed into smithereens—she owed her son this.

But as Laura approached him again, it was difficult not to react to him on so many different levels. His had always been an imposing presence, but the passing of the years seemed to have magnified his potent charisma. There had been no softening of the hard, muscular body—nor dimming of the golden luminance of his skin. And, while there might be a lick of silver at his temples, his wavy dark hair was as thick as ever. But with age had come a certain cool distance which had not been there before. He carried about him the unmistakable aura of the magnate—a man with power radiating from every atom of his expensively clad frame.

Laura felt the erratic fluttering of her heart. Yet none of that mattered. His eyes were still the blackest she had ever seen, and his lips remained a study in sensuality. She still sensed that here was a man in the truest sense of the word—all elemental passion and hunger beneath the sophisticated exterior.

'Your water, sir,' she said, trying to curve her mouth into a friendly smile and silently praying that he would return it.

Hadn't he once told her that her smile was like the sun coming out? Wouldn't that stir some distant memory in his mind? And didn't they say something about the voice always striking a note of recognition—that people changed but their voices never did?

She spoke the longest sentence possible under the circumstances. 'I...I wasn't sure if you wanted still or sparkling, sir—so I've brought both. They both come from...from the Cotswolds!' she added wildly, noticing the label. A fact from a recent early-morning farming programme on the radio came flooding back to her. 'It's...um...filtered through the oolitic limestone of the Cotswold Hills, and you won't find a purer water anywhere!'

'How fascinating,' murmured Constantine sardonically, taking one of the glasses from the tray and wondering why she sounded as if she was advertising the brand. She didn't *look* like the kind of out-of-work actress who would moonlight as a waitress, but you could never be sure. 'Thanks.'

He gave a curt nod and, turning his back on her, walked away without another word and Laura was left staring at him, her heart pounding with fear and frustration. But what had she expected? That he would engage her in some small-talk which would provide the perfect opportunity for her to tell him he had a son? Start remarking that the slice of lemon which was bobbing around in his glass of fizzy water was vastly inferior to the lemons he grew on his very own Greek island?

No. The smile hadn't worked and neither had the voice. Those black eyes had not widened in growing comprehension, and he had not shaken his coal-dark head to say, in a tone of disbelief and admiration, *Why, you're the young English virgin I had the most amazing sex with all those years ago! Do you know that not a day goes by when I don't think about you?*

Laura chewed on her lip. Fantasies never worked out the way you planned them, did they? And fantasies were dangerous. She mustn't allow herself to indulge in them just because she had never really got over their one night together. She was just going to have to choose her moment carefully—because she wasn't leaving this building without Constantine Karantinos being in full possession of all the facts.

The evening passed in a blur of activity—but at least being busy stopped her from getting too anxious about the prospect which lay ahead.

There had been a lavish sit-down dinner for three hundred people, though the space beside Constantine had remained glaringly empty. It must be for his girlfriend, thought Laura painfully. So where was she? Why wasn't she sticking like glue to the side of the handsome Greek who was talking so carelessly to the women in a tiara on the other side of him. *It was a royal princess!* Laura realised. Hadn't she recently come out of a high-profile divorce and walked away with a record-breaking settlement?

Laura had managed to pass right by him with a dish of chocolates, just in time to hear the Princess inviting him to stay on her yacht later that summer—but Constantine had merely shrugged his broad shoulders and murmured something about his diary being full.

The candlelight caught the jewels which were strung around the neck of every woman present—so that the whole room seemed to be glittering. In the background, the harpist had calmed down, and was now working his way through a serene medley of tunes.

It was not just a different world, Laura realised as she carried out yet another tray of barely touched food back to the kitchens, it was like a completely alien *universe*. She thought of the savings she had to make so that Alex would have a nice Christmas, and shuddered to think how much this whole affair must be costing—why, the wine budget alone would have been more than the amount she lived on in a single year. And Constantine was paying for it all. For him it would be no more than a drop in the ocean.

The guests had now all moved into the ballroom, where the harpist had been replaced by a band, and people had started dancing. But the minutes were melting by without Laura getting anywhere near Constantine, let alone close enough to be able to talk to him. People were clustering around him like flies, and it was getting on for midnight. Soon the party would end and she'd be sent home—and then what?

There was a momentary lull before a conversational buzz began to hum around the ballroom, and then the dancing crowd stilled and parted as a woman began to slowly sashay through them, with all the panache of someone whose job it was to be gazed at by other people. Her flaxen fall of hair guaranteed instant attention, as did the ice-blue eyes and willowy limbs which seemed to sum up her cool and unattainable beauty.

She wore a dazzling white fur stole draped over a silver dress, and at over six feet tall she dominated the room like the tallest of bright poppies. And there was really only one person in the room who was man enough not to be dwarfed by her impressive height—the man she was headed for as unerringly as a comet crashing towards earth.

'It's Ingrid Johansson,' Laura heard someone say, and then, 'Isn't she *gorgeous*?'

Convulsively, she felt her fingers clutching at her apron as she watched the blonde goddess slink up to Constantine and place a proprietorial hand on his forearm before leaning forward to kiss him on each cheek.

Constantine was aware of everyone watching them as Ingrid leaned forward to kiss him. 'That was quite an entrance,' he murmured, but inside he felt the first faint flicker of disdain.

'Was it?' Ingrid looked into his eyes with an expression of mock-innocence. 'Must we stay here, *alskling*? I'm so tired.'

'No,' Constantine said evenly. 'We don't have to stay here at all—we can go upstairs to my suite.'

To Laura's horror she saw the couple begin to move towards the door, and she felt her forehead break out into a cold sweat.

Now what?

She saw some of the bulkier security men begin to follow them, and the slightly disappointed murmur from the rest of the guests as they began to realise that the star attractions were leaving. Soon Constantine would be swallowed up by the same kind of protection which had shielded him so effectively from her all those years ago…

And then a terrible thought occurred to her—a dark thought which came from nowhere and which had never even blipped on her radar before. Or maybe she had simply never allowed it to. What if it *hadn't* been his security people who had kept her away from him all those years ago? What if he'd *known* that she was trying to make contact? And what if he'd actually *read* the letter she'd sent, telling him about Alex, and had decided to ignore it?

What if he had simply *chosen not to have anything to do with his own son*?

A cold, sick feeling of dread made her skin suddenly clammy, but Laura knew it was a chance she had to take. If that had been the case, then maybe she would find out about it now. And if he chose to reject his son again...well, then she wanted to see his face while he did it.

She went over to the bar and ordered a bottle of the most expensive champagne and two glasses.

'Put it on Mr Karantinos's account,' she said recklessly, and took the tray away before the barman could query why the order hadn't gone through room service.

Her flat, sensible shoes made no sound as they squished across the marble foyer, but within the mirror-lined walls of the lift she was confronted with the reality of her appearance and she shuddered. Hair scraped back into a tight bun, on top of which was perched a ridiculous little frilly cap. A plain black dress hung unflatteringly over her knees and was topped with a white-frilled apron.

She looked like a throwback to another age, when people in the service industry really *were* servants. Laura was used to wearing a uniform in the bread shop—what she was not used to was looking like some kind of haunted and out-of-place ghost of a woman. A woman who must now go and face one of the world's most noted beauties, who happened to be sharing a bed with a man whose child Laura had borne.

The lift glided upwards and stopped with smooth silence at the penthouse suite, its doors sliding open to reveal

Laura's worst fears. Two dark and burly-looking men were standing guard outside the door. So now what? Fixing on a confident smile, which contradicted the awful nerves which were twisting her stomach like writhing snakes, Laura walked towards the door.

One of the guards raised his eyebrows. 'Where do you think you're going?'

His accent was thickly Greek, and somehow it only added tension to her already jangled nerves. Laura's smile widened, though a bead of sweat was trickling its way slowly down her back. 'Champagne for Mr Karantinos.'

'He told us he didn't want to be disturbed.'

Because of what was at stake, Laura found herself digging deep inside herself, finding courage where she had expected to find fear. Her smile became conspiratorial; she even managed a wink. 'I think he's about to announce his engagement,' she whispered.

The other guard shrugged and jerked his head in the direction of the door. 'Go on, then.'

Rapping loudly on the door, Laura heard a muffled exclamation—but she knew she couldn't turn back now. She had to get this over with—because if she left it much longer she might find them…find them…

Blocking out the unbearable thought of Constantine and the supermodel beginning to make love, Laura pushed open the door, and the scene before her stamped itself on her gaze like a bizarre tableau.

There was Constantine, staring hard at the supermodel. And there was Ingrid staring back at him, her expression disbelieving. She had removed her fur wrap, and her dress

was nothing but a sliver of silver which clung to her body
and revealed the points of her nipples.

They both looked round as she walked in.

'What the hell do you think you are doing?' demanded
Constantine, and then frowned as he saw the tray she was
carrying. 'You don't just walk into my suite like this—and
I didn't order champagne.'

Not even he was cold-hearted enough to celebrate the
fact that he'd just finished with his girlfriend—even though
Ingrid was still standing there staring at him as if she didn't
quite believe it.

Putting the tray down on a table before she dropped it,
Laura looked up at him, her voice low and trembling. 'I
need to talk to you.' She glanced over at the model, who
was glaring at her. 'Alone, if that's all right.'

'Who the hell is this?' snapped Ingrid.

He had absolutely no idea, and for one moment
Constantine wondered if the insipid little waitress was
some kind of set-up. Were her male accomplices about to
burst in with cameras? Or did her uniform conceal some
kind of weapon? Hadn't kidnap attempts been suspected
enough times in the past?

But he remembered her from the ballroom—her
pinched, pale face and her inappropriate babbling on about
some type of water. She didn't look like the kind of woman
capable of any kind of elaborate subterfuge. And her expression was peculiar; he had never seen a woman look quite
like that before—and it made him study her more closely.

Her cheeks were pale but her grey eyes were huge, and
she looked as if she was fighting to control her breathing.
Her breasts—surprisingly pert breasts for such a tiny

frame, he thought inconsequentially—were heaving like someone who had just dragged themselves out of the water after nearly drowning.

'Who are you?' he demanded hotly. 'And what do you want?'

'I told you,' answered Laura quietly. 'I need to talk to you. Alone, if I may.'

Constantine's eyes narrowed as some primeval instinct urged him to listen to what this woman was saying. And something in her strange urgency told him to ensure that they had no audience. He turned to the supermodel, praying that she wouldn't make the kind of scene which some women revelled in when a man had just ended a relationship.

'I think you'd better leave now, don't you, Ingrid?' he questioned quietly. 'I have a car which will take you wherever you want to go.'

For a moment Laura felt eaten up with guilt and shame as she saw the supermodel's stricken face, and her heart went out to her. Because what woman wouldn't be able to identify with the terrible battle taking place within the gorgeous blonde? Anyone could see she wanted to stay— but it was also easy to see from the obdurate and cold expression on Constantine's face that he wanted the supermodel out of there.

Oh, this was just terrible—and it was all her fault. Awkwardly, she shifted from one foot to the other. 'Look, perhaps I can…come back.'

'*You* are not going anywhere,' snapped Constantine as he flicked her a hard glance. 'Ingrid was just leaving.'

At this, Ingrid's mouth thinned into a scarlet line. 'You

bastard,' she hissed, and marched out of the suite without another word.

For a moment there was silence, and Laura's heart was pounding with fear and disbelief as she lifted up her hands in a gesture of apology. 'I'm sorry—'

'Shut up,' he snapped, two fists clenching by the shafts of his powerful thighs as a quiet fury continued to spiral up inside him. 'And don't give me any misplaced sentiments. Do you think you can hysterically burst in here making veiled threats and then act like a concerned and responsible citizen who cares about the havoc she's wreaked along the way? Do you?'

Nervously, Laura sank her teeth into her bottom lip. She supposed she deserved that—just as she supposed she had no choice other than to stand there and take it. Maybe if she let him vent his anger then he would calm down, and they could sit down afterwards and talk calmly.

His black eyes bored into her like fierce black lasers. 'So who *are* you?' he continued furiously. 'And why are you really here?'

Brushing aside her hurt that he *still* didn't recognise her, Laura tried again. 'I. . .' It sounded so bizarre to say it now that the moment had arrived. To say these words of such import to a man who was staring at her so forbiddingly. But then Alex's face swam into the forefront of her mind, and suddenly it was easy.

She drew a deep breath. 'I'm sorry it has to be this way, but I've come to tell you that seven years ago I had a baby. Your baby.' Her voice shaking with emotion, she got the final words out in a rush. 'You have a son, Constantine, and I am the mother of that son.'

CHAPTER THREE

CONSTANTINE stared at the trembling waitress who stood before him, and who had just made such a preposterous claim. That *she* was the mother of *his* son. Why, it would almost be laughable were it not so outrageous.

'That is a bizarre and untrue statement to make,' he snapped. 'Especially since I don't even know you.'

Laura felt as if he had plunged a stiletto into her heart, but she prayed it didn't show on her face. 'Then why didn't you have the guards take me away?'

'Because I'm curious.'

'Or because you know that deep down I could be telling the truth?'

'Not in this case.' His lips curved into a cruel smile. 'You see, I don't screw around with waitresses.'

It hurt. Oh, how it hurt—but presumably that had been his intention. Laura forced herself not to hit back at the slur, nor to let herself wither under his blistering gaze. 'Maybe you don't now—but I can assure you that wasn't always the case.'

Something in her calm certainty—in the way she stood there, facing up to him, despite her cheap clothes and lowly demeanour—all those things combined to make Constantine consider the bizarre possibility of her words. That they might be *true*. He looked deep into her eyes, as if searching for some hint of what this was all about, but all he saw was the stormy distress lurking in their pewter depths, and suddenly he felt his heart lurch. Eyes like storm clouds.

Storm clouds.

Another memory stirred deep in the recesses of his mind. 'Take down your hair,' he ordered softly.

'But—'

'I said, take down your hair.'

Compelled by the silken urgency of his voice, and weakened by the derision in his eyes, Laura reached up her hand. First, off came the frilly little cap, which she let fall to the floor—she certainly wouldn't be needing *that* again. Then, with trembling fingers, she began to remove the pins and finally the elastic band.

It was a relief to be free of the tight restraints and she shook her hair completely loose, only vaguely aware of Constantine's sudden inrush of breath.

He watched as lock after lock fell free—one silken fall of moon-pale hair after another. Fine hair, but masses of it. Hair which had looked like a dull, mediocre cap now took on the gleaming lustre of honey and sand as it tumbled over her slight shoulders. Her face was still pale—and the dark grey eyes looked huge.

Storm clouds, he thought again, as more memories began to filter through, like a picture slowly coming into focus.

A small English harbour. A summer spent unencumbered by the pressures of the family business. And a need to escape from Greece around the time of the anniversary of his mother's death—a time when his father became unbearably maudlin, even though it had been many years since she had died.

His father had promised him far more responsibility in the Karantinos shipping business, and that summer Constantine had recognised that soon he would no longer be able to go off on the annual month-long sailing holiday he loved so much. That this might be the last chance he would get for a true taste of freedom. And he'd been right. Later that summer he'd gone back to Greece and been given access to the company's accounts for the first time— only to discover with rising disbelief just how dire the state of the family finances was. And just how much his father had neglected the business in his obsessive grief for his late wife.

It had been the last trip where he was truly young. Shrugging off routine, and shrugging on his oldest jeans, Constantine had sailed around the Mediterranean as the mood took him, lapping up the sun and feeling all the tension gradually leave his body. He hadn't wanted women—there were always women if he wanted them—he had wanted peace. So he'd read books. Slept. Swum. Fished.

As the days had gone by his olive skin had become darker. His black hair had grown longer, the waves curling around the nape of his neck so that he had looked like some kind of ancient buccaneer. He'd sailed around England to explore the place properly—something he'd always meant to do ever since an English teacher had read him stories about her country. He'd wanted to see the improbable world of castles and green fields come alive.

And eventually he'd anchored at the little harbour of Milmouth and found a cute hotel which looked as if it had been lifted straight out of the set of a period drama. Little old ladies had been sitting eating cream cakes on a wonderful emerald lawn as he strolled across it, wearing a faded pair of jeans and a T-shirt. Several of the old ladies had gawped as he'd pulled out a chair at one of the empty tables and then spread his long legs out in front of him. Cream cakes which had been heading for mouths had never quite reached their destination and had been discarded—but then he often had that effect on women, no matter what their age.

And then a waitress had come walking across the grass towards him and Constantine's eyes had narrowed. There hadn't been anything particularly *special* about her—and yet there had been something about her clear, pale skin and the youthful vigour of her step which had caught his attention and his desire. Something familiar and yet unknown had stirred deep within him. The crumpled petals of her lips had demanded to be kissed. And she'd had beautiful eyes, so deep and grey—a pewter colour he'd only ever seen before in angry seas or storm clouds. It had been—what? Weeks since he had had a woman? And suddenly he'd wanted her. Badly.

'I'm afraid you can't sit there,' she said softly, as her shadow fell over him.

'Can't?' Even her mild officiousness was turning him on—as was the pure, clean tone of her accent. He looked up, narrowing his eyes against the sun. 'Why not?'

'Because…because I'm afraid the management have a rule about no jeans being allowed.'

'But I'm hungry,' he murmured. 'Very hungry.' He gave her a slow smile as he looked her up and down. 'So what do you suggest?'

As a recipient of that careless smile, the girl was like putty in his hands. She suggested serving him tea at an unseen side of the hotel, by a beautiful little copse of trees. Giggling, she smuggled out sandwiches, and scones with jam and something he'd never eaten before nor since, called clotted cream. And when she finished work she agreed to have dinner with him. Her name was Laura and it made him think of laurels and the fresh green garlands which ancient Greeks wore on their heads to protect them. She was sweet—very sweet—and it was a long time since he'd held a woman in his arms.

The outcome of the night was predictable—but her reaction wasn't. Unlike the wealthy sophisticates he usually associated with, she played no games with him. She had a vulnerability about her which she wasn't afraid of showing. But Constantine always ran a million miles from vulnerability—even though her pink and white body and her grey eyes lured him into her arms like a siren.

In the morning she didn't want to let him go—but of course he had to leave. He was Constantine Karantinos—heir to one of the mightiest shipping dynasties in the whole of Greece—and his destiny was not to stay in the arms of a small-town waitress.

How strange the memory could be, thought Constantine—as the images faded and he found himself emerging into real-time, standing in a luxury London penthouse with that same waitress standing trembling-lipped in front of him and telling him she had conceived a child that night. And how random fate could be, he thought bitterly, to bring such a woman back into his life—and with such earth-shattering news.

He walked over to the drinks cabinet and poured himself a tumbler of water—more as a delaying tactic than anything else. 'Do you want anything?' he questioned, still with his back to her.

Laura thought that a drink might choke her. 'No.'

He drank the water and then turned round. Her face looked chalk-white, and something nagged at him to tell her to sit down—but his anger and his indignation were stronger than his desire to care for a woman who had just burst into his life making such claims as these.

A son....

'I wore protection that night,' he stated coldly.

Laura flinched. How clinical he sounded. But there was no use in her having pointless yearnings about how different his reaction might have been. She knew that fantasies didn't come true. Try to imagine yourself in his shoes, she urged herself. A woman he barely knew, coming back into his life with the most momentous and presumably unwelcome news of all.

'Obviously it failed to do what it was supposed to do,' she said, her voice as matter-of-fact as she could make it.

'And this child is you say…how old?'

'He's seven.'

He felt the slam of his heart and an unwelcome twist of his gut. Constantine turned and stared out of the vast windows which overlooked the darkened park before the unwanted emotions could show on his face. A son! Above the shadowed shapes of the trees he could see the faint glimmer of stars and for a moment he thought about the stars, back home, which burned as brightly as lanterns. Then just as suddenly he turned back again, his now composed gaze raking over her white face, searching for truth in the smoky splendour of her eyes.

'So why didn't you tell me this before?' he demanded. 'Why wait seven long years? Why now?'

Laura opened her mouth to explain that she'd tried, but before she had a chance to answer him she saw his black eyes narrow with cynical understanding.

'Ah, yes, but of course,' he said softly. 'Of course. It was the perfect moment, wasn't it?'

Laura frowned. 'I don't know what you're—'

But her thoughts on the matter were obviously superfluous, for ruthlessly he cut through her words as if he were wielding a guillotine. 'You wait long enough to ensure that I can have no influence—even if the child *is* mine. How is it that the old saying goes? *Give me a child until he is seven and I shall give you the man.*' He took a step towards her, his posture as menacing as the silken threat in his voice. 'So what happened? Did you read the papers and hear that that Karantinos stock has soared, and then decide that this was the optimum time to strike? Did you think that coming out with this piece of information now would put you in a strong bargaining position?'

'*B-bargaining* position?' echoed Laura in disbelief. He might have been talking about a plot of land…when this was their *son* they were discussing.

His voice was as steely cold as his eyes. 'I don't know why you're affecting outrage,' he clipped out. 'I presume you want money?'

Automatically, Laura reached her hand out and steadied herself on a giant sofa—afraid that her trembling knees might give way but determined not to sit down. Because that would surely put her in an even weaker position—if she had to sit looking up at him like a child who had been put on the naughty chair. But even her protest sounded deflated. 'How dare you say that?' she whispered.

'Well, why else are you here if you haven't come looking for a hand-out?'

'I don't have to stay here and listen to your insults.'

'Oh, but I am afraid that you do. You aren't going anywhere,' he said with silky menace as he glittered her a brittle look. 'Until we get this thing sorted out.'

This thing happened to be their son, thought Laura—until she realised with a pang that maybe the Greek's angry words had the ring of truth to them. Because Alex was *her* son, not his. Constantine had never been a part of his life. *And maybe he never would be.* For a moment she felt a wave of guilt as Constantine's black gaze pierced through her like a sabre.

'Just by telling me you have involved me—like it or not,' he continued remorselessly as his gaze burned into her. 'Didn't you realise that every action has consequences?'

'You think I don't know that better than anyone?' she retorted, stung.

Something in her response renewed the slam of his heart against his ribcage, and Constantine narrowed his eyes, searching for every possible flaw in her argument the way he had learnt to do at work—an ability that had made him a formidable legend within the world of international shipping. 'So why didn't you tell me about this before—like seven years ago?'

She still wanted to turn and run, but she doubted that her feet would obey her brain's command to walk, let alone run. 'I tried…' She saw the scorn on his face. 'Yes, I tried! I tried tracking you down—but you weren't especially easy to trace.'

'Because I hadn't meant it to be anything more than a one-night stand!' he roared, steeling himself against the distressed crumpling of her lips.

'Then don't you talk to *me* about consequences,' she whispered.

There was a pause as he watched her struggling to control her breathing, her grey eyes almost black with distress. 'So what happened?' he persisted.

Laura sucked in a low, shuddering breath. 'I managed to find out the address and phone number of your head-quarters in Athens.' She had been completely gobsmacked to discover that her scruffy jeans-wearing, slightly maverick Greek lover turned out to be someone very important in some huge shipping company. 'I tried ringing, but no one would put me through—and I sent you a letter, but it obviously never reached you. And I've tried several times since then.'

Usually around the time of her son's birthday, when Alex would start asking questions, making her long to be able to introduce the little boy to his father.

'The result has always been the same,' she finished bitterly. 'It doesn't matter how I've broached it or what approach I've made—every time I've failed to even get a phone call with you.'

Constantine was silent for a moment as he considered her words, for now he could imagine exactly what must have happened. An unknown English girl ringing and asking to be put through to Kyrios Constantine—why, she would have been swatted away as if she were a trouble-some fly buzzing over a plate of food. Likewise any letters. They would have been opened and scrutinised. Who would have made the decision not to show him? he wondered, and then sighed, for this was something he *could* believe.

The ancient Greek troop formation of a tightly-knit and protective group known as the phalanx still existed in modern Greece, Constantine thought wryly. It was not the right of his workers to shield him, but he could see exactly why they had done it. Women had always shamelessly pursued him—how were his staff to have known that this woman might actually have had a case. *Might*, he reminded himself. Only *might*.

There was a pause. 'Do you have a photo?' he demanded. 'Of the child?'

Laura nodded, swallowing down her relief. At last! And surely asking to see a picture of Alex was a good sign? Wouldn't he set eyes on his gorgeous black-eyed son and know in an instant that there could only be one possible father? 'It's…it's in my handbag—downstairs in the staff cloakroom. Shall I go and get it?'

He was strangely reluctant to let her out of his sight. As if she might disappear off into the night and he would never see her again. *But wouldn't that be the ideal scenario?* The question came out of nowhere, but Constantine pushed it away. He stared down into those deep grey eyes and inex-plicably his mouth dried. 'I'll come with you.'

'But I'll…'

Black brows were raised. 'You'll what?'

She had been about to say that she would be sacked if she were seen strolling through the hotel with one of the guests—but, come to think of it, it wasn't as if she was planning to work here again. 'People will talk,' she said. 'If you're seen accompanying one of the waitresses to the staff cloakroom.'

'So let them talk,' he snapped. 'I think it is a little late in the day for you to act concerned after your dramatic entrance into my suite!' And he pulled open the door and stalked out, leaving Laura to follow while he spoke in rapid Greek to the two guards.

They rode down in the penthouse lift, which seemed to have shrunk in dimension since the last time she had been in it. Laura was acutely aware of his proximity and the way his powerful frame seemed to dominate the small space. She was close enough to see the silken gleam of his skin and to breathe in that heady masculine tang which was all his. Close enough to touch…

And Constantine knew that she was aware of him; he could sense it in the sudden shallowness of her breathing— the way a pulse began fluttering wildly beneath the fine skin at her temple. Did she desire him now, as women always did, and was anger responsible for the answering call in his own body? The sudden thick heat at his groin? The furious desire to open her legs and bring her right up against him, so that he could thrust deep into her body and spill out some of his rage? What was it about this plain little thing which should suddenly have him in such a torrent of longing?

He swallowed down the sudden unbearable dryness in his throat as the lift came to a halt and the door slid open on some subterranean level of the hotel he hadn't known existed. Laura began to lead the way through a maze of corridors until she reached the women's cloakroom.

'Wait here,' she said breathlessly.

But he reached out and levered her chin upwards with the tips of his fingers, feeling her tremble as he captured her troubled gaze with the implacable spotlight of his own.

'Don't run away, will you?' he murmured, with silky menace.

Laura stilled. In the light of all the vicious accusations he had hurled at her, his touch should have repelled her—but it did no such thing. To her horror, it reminded her of what it was like to be touched by a man, and the hard, seeking certainty of this man's particular touch.

With an effort she jerked her head away. 'I wasn't pl-planning to.'

'Hurry up,' he ordered, as the heat at his groin intensified—for he had seen the sudden darkening of her eyes and sensed her body's instinctive desire for him. That in itself was nothing new—women always desired him—what perplexed him was the answering hunger which stirred in his blood.

Laura nodded. 'I…I can't stay in this uniform. I'd better change while I'm in there—so I may be a couple of minutes.'

'I'll wait,' he ground out, but her words triggered an unwanted series of explicit and strangely powerful memories as the door closed behind her. Of the young woman who had shed her clothes with such unashamed pleasure—taking him into her pink and white body and gasping out her pleasure. Had that same woman conceived his child that night? he found himself asking, the question spinning round and round in his brain as he stared at the dingy wall of the staff corridor.

Laura took off her uniform and, leaving it neatly folded

beside one of the laundry baskets, she pulled on her jeans, T-shirt and thin jumper—she'd experienced too many cold winters not to have learnt the benefits of layering. Then she picked up her handbag and waterproof jacket and walked outside, to where Constantine stood in exactly the same spot, like a daunting dark statue.

Beneath the harsh glare of the overhead light, she began delving around in her handbag until she pulled out the picture of Alex taken at school, just a few months ago—she handed it to him.

Constantine stared down at it in silence for a long moment. The child had black eyes and a faint olive tint to his skin, and the dark curls of his hair looked as if an attempt had been made to tame them especially for the photo—but already they were beginning to escape. He remembered his own hair being just as stubborn at such an age.

Narrowing his eyes, he studied the image more carefully. The child was smiling, yes—but there was an unmistakable wariness about that smile, and Constantine felt a sudden wild leap of protectiveness, mixed in with an innate sense of denial. As if the logical side of his mind refused to accept that he could start the evening by hosting a glittering party and then the evening would end with a paternity claim foisted on him out of the blue. That he should suddenly be a father. He shook his head.

'He looks just like you!' Laura blurted out, wanting him to say something—anything—to break this tense and awful silence.

An icy feeling chilled his skin. He had never felt quite so out of control as he now found himself—not since his mother had died and he had watched his father fall to pieces before his eyes, and had decided there and then that love did dangerous things to a man. 'Does he?'

'Oh, yes.'

'That proves nothing,' he snarled as he thrust the photograph back into her hand. 'For all I know this might just be a very clever scam.'

Laura swayed, unable to believe that he would think her so cold and calculating. So *manipulative*. So sexually free and easy. But why shouldn't he think that? He didn't know her—just as she didn't know him. Though the more of himself he revealed, the more she was beginning to dislike him. Had he forgotten that she had gone into his arms an innocent, unable to resist the powerful sexual pull he had exerted?

'B-but you knew that I was a virgin that night,' she reminded him painfully.

He shrugged, as if her words meant nothing—but the concept of a woman's purity was both potent and important to a man as traditional as Constantine. He forced himself to remember his incredulity that a young woman should so casually give her virginity to a man she knew she would never see again. Or had *he* been naïve? With her he had played the man he had never allowed himself to be— the itinerant traveller without a care in the world. What if her sweet and supposed ignorance of his wealth and his status had all been an act? Suppose she'd seen his yacht and started asking questions in between serving him tea and having dinner with him? Wouldn't that make her eagerness to lose her innocence to a man who was little more than a stranger more understandable?

Constantine had spent his whole life being surrounded

by people who wanted something from him—maybe this woman was no different.

'You *told* me you were a virgin, but those could have simply been words. And, yes, I know that you gasped as I entered you,' he said brutally, before pausing to add a final, painful boast. 'But women always do—maybe it is something to do with my size, or my technique.' He shrugged as her fingertips flew to her lips, hardening his heart against her obvious distress. 'Maybe you thought that affecting purity would guarantee you some sort of future with the kind of man you were unlikely to meet again. That if I thought you were a virgin I would think more highly of you—rather than just as a woman who had casual sex with a man she'd just met.'

Laura felt ill. It was as if he had taken her memories of the past and ground them to dust beneath his heel. 'Well, if you think that,' she said, putting the photo back in her wallet with trembling fingers, 'then there's nothing more to be said, is there?'

But Constantine moved closer, so close that she could feel his body heat, and she hated the thought that flashed through her mind without warning. This was the man who had planted a seed in her body…whose child had grown within her. The image was so overwhelming that it made her instinctively shudder. And wasn't nature famously canny, if cruel—conditioning women to desire the biological father of their child, even if that man was utterly heartless? Laura swallowed, because now he was lowering his head towards her so that she was caught in the intense ebony blaze of his eyes. Surely he wasn't going to…?

But he was.

He caught her against him, crushing her tiny frame against his and enfolding her within his powerful arms. She could feel the fierce hard heat of his body where it touched hers, and knew that she should cry out her protest—but she could no sooner stop this than she could have stopped the earth spinning around the sun.

His mouth came down to capture hers, and even though Laura was desperately inexperienced when it came to men she could sense the simmering anger which lay behind his kiss. This was a kiss which had more to do with anger than desire. But that didn't stop her responding to it—didn't stop her body flaring up with desire as if he had just ignited it with some hidden fuse. *He despises me*, was her last sane thought as the expert touch of his mouth made her lips part willingly beneath his.

His hands were tight around her waist and her own were splayed over the hard chest, where she could feel the rapid thundering of his heart. And through the kiss Laura made a little sound of disbelief—wondering how she could respond with such melting pleasure to a man who clearly viewed her with utter contempt.

The sound seemed to startle him, for just as suddenly as he had taken her in his arms he let her go, so that she had to steady herself against the wall as she stared up at him.

'Wh-what was that all about?' she breathed.

What, indeed? With an effort, Constantine controlled his ragged breathing and stared at her, shaking his head as if to deny the intensity of that kiss. It had been all about desire, he told himself fiercely—a powerful desire which was no respecter of circumstance or status. And how ex-traordinary that he should feel such overwhelming lust for this washed-out little waitress. Inappropriate, too—when to do so would surely weaken his case against her preposterous claim.

He looked down at her, his heart pounding so powerfully in his chest and his groin so hard with need that for a moment he couldn't think straight. 'You will need to get a DNA test done as quickly as possible,' he grated.

Laura's eyes widened in distress. 'But… But…'

'But what?' he cut in scornfully, and gave a short laugh as the aftermath of the kiss faded and reality flashed in like a sharp knife. 'Did you really think that I was going to acknowledge the boy as a Karantinos heir—giving him access to one of the world's greatest fortunes—simply because you say so and because the boy bears a passing resemblance to me?'

'But you—'

'Yes, he looks Greek,' he finished witheringly. 'But for all I know you might be one of those women who turn on for Greek men.' He gave a blistering smile as his gaze raked over her kiss-swollen lips. 'I think you've just demonstrated that to both our satisfaction.'

Laura slumped back against the wall and stared up at him. Was that why he had kissed her—to make her look morally loose? And then to follow it up with a cold-blooded demand that she prove Alex was his child? 'Why, you…you *bastard*!' she gasped.

Constantine reflected that women were remarkably unimaginative when it came to insults. And didn't they realise that *they* were the ones who put themselves into situations which gave men ammunition to criticise them?

But inside he was hurting for reasons he wasn't even

close to understanding—a state of being so rare for him that it made him want to hurt back, and badly.

'I should be careful about my choice of words, if I were you, Laura,' he informed her coldly. 'It isn't *my* parentage which is in doubt. If tests prove that the boy is mine, then I will take responsibility—but first you're going to have to prove it.'

CHAPTER FOUR

'WHAT do you mean, he wants a DNA test?'

Laura stared at her sister, trying to snap out of the terrible sense of weariness which seemed to have settled over her like a dank cloud. After leaving the Granchester last night she had spent a few restless hours in a cheap London hotel before catching the first train back to Milmouth—her mind still spinning with all the hurtful things Constantine had said to her. On the plus side, she had arrived back in time to take Alex to school, but now she was back in the shop, Sarah having coped with the morning rush of customers. This quiet spell meant that Laura was now forced to face Sarah's furious interrogation.

She shrugged her shoulders listlessly—she had gone through every emotion from anger and indignation through to sheer humiliation and had worn herself out with them. 'It's fairly self-explanatory, isn't it? He wants a DNA test done. He wants proof that Alex is his son.'

'Did you show him the photo?'

'Of course I did.'

'And?'

There was a pause while Laura thought about how best

to put it, strangely reluctant to repeat Constantine's wounding words. Was it her own hurt pride which stopped her from telling her sister how much he clearly despised her and all she stood for? 'He said that although Alex looked Greek he couldn't possibly risk acknowledging an heir to such a vast fortune as his without proof.'

'The bastard!'

And even though she'd hurled exactly the same word at him last night, Laura now found herself in the bizarre position of putting forward a contrary point of view. One that she had been thinking about during her early morning train journey. 'I can see his point,' she said carefully. 'I mean, he doesn't know that he's the only possible contender who could be Alex's father, does he?'

'Didn't you tell him?'

'No.' His anger had been too palpable; the mood between them too volatile. Why, he'd even accused her of using her virginity as a bargaining tool. 'And even if I had he might not have believed me. Why should he?'

Sarah frowned. 'Laura—I don't believe this! You're not *defending* him, are you?'

'Of course I'm not,' replied Laura stiffly.

But the truth was far more complex. She *could* see Constantine's point—even though it hurt her to the core that he should think her capable of having lots of partners and just wanting to foist paternity on the richest candidate. The way she had acted the day she'd met him had been uncharacteristic behaviour she'd never repeated—but Constantine wasn't to know that, was he?

'For all he knows, there might have been a long line of Greek lovers in my life,' she told her sister fiercely, blinking furiously to stop the rogue tears from pricking at her eyes.

'What? All of them sailing their yachts into Milmouth?' questioned Sarah sarcastically. 'I didn't realise our town was twinned with Athens!'

'Very funny,' said Laura as she pulled on her apron.

But at least Sarah's acerbic comments had helped focus her mind, and she went on the internet at lunchtime— cursing the dyslexia which made her progress slow as she laboriously pored over websites which offered information about DNA-testing. Sitting in the cramped little corner of the sitting room where they kept the computer, she studied it until she was certain she knew all the facts—and she was startled by the sudden sound of her cellphone ringing. She used it mainly for emergencies—only a few people had the number—and this was one she didn't recognise.

But the voice she did. Instantly.

'Laura?'

Briefly, she closed her eyes. Away from the cruel spotlight of his eyes, it was all too easy to let the honeyed gravel of Constantine's faintly accented voice wash over her. It tugged at her senses, whispering over her suddenly goosebumpy skin, reminding her of just how good a man's kiss could make a woman's starved senses feel.

Appalled at the inappropriate path of her thoughts—especially when he was forcing Alex to go through the indignity of a DNA test—Laura sat up straight and glared at the computer screen. Get real, she told herself furiously.

'Hello, Constantine.'

'Ah, you recognised my voice,' he observed softly.

'Funny that, isn't it? Yet, strange as it may seem, there

aren't scores of Greek men growling down the telephone at me.'

Detecting a distinctively spiky note in her voice, Constantine frowned. Was she daring to be sarcastic—to *him*? And under such circumstances, too? 'You know why I'm calling?'

'Yes.'

'You will agree to the DNA test?'

Laura gripped the phone tightly. What choice did she have? 'I suppose so.'

'Good.' Leaning back in the sumptuous leather of his chair, Constantine surveyed the broad spectrum of the glittering London skyline. 'I've been making some enquiries and I can either arrange for you to have it done at my lawyer's office here in London—or he tells me that he can arrange for you to use somewhere closer to you, if that's more convenient.'

She heard an unexpected note of silky persuasion in his voice, and suddenly Laura was glad that she had done her research, glad that she wasn't just going to accept what the powerful and autocratic Greek was telling her. *What it was in his best interests to tell her.*

'I'm not using a lawyer's office,' she said quietly.

There was a disbelieving pause. 'Why not?'

'Because I believe that doing so carries all kinds of legal implications,' she said. 'This test is being done to establish paternity to your satisfaction; it is not a custody claim. So I'm doing the test at home on a purely need-to-know basis.'

Another pause, longer this time. Constantine had not been expecting her to query his wishes—to be honest, he had expected her simply to accept his agenda. Because people always did; they bowed to the dominance of his will. So just who did this mousy little waitress think she was to dare to oppose his wishes? He lowered his voice. 'And if I object?'

'You aren't in any position to object!' she declared, refusing to let that silky tone intimidate her. 'You're the one who wants this damned test—who is going to force me to take a swab from my seven-year-old son's mouth. Have you thought what I'm going to tell him? How I'm going to explain *that* to a seven-year-old boy?'

'And didn't you think through any of this before you came to me?' he flared back.

The terrible truth was that she *hadn't* thought through all the repercussions—instead she had been swept along by feelings which had been too primitive to allow any room for reason. She had felt an overpowering sense of injustice—because Constantine might be about to marry another woman and have a family with *her* without realising that he had another son who might know nothing but penury and spend his life living in the shadows. And she had thought he would recognise her—remember the night they had spent together with surely a *bit* of fondness. And then, in true fairy-tale fashion, she had imagined him acknowledging his son with a certain amount of Greek pride.

And it was about you, too, wasn't it? prompted the uncomfortable voice of her conscience. *Aren't you forgetting to put that into the equation? You were unreasonably jealous of the woman you thought was going to share his life—even though you had no right to be. And your actions helped contribute to the fact that the supermodel stormed out of the hotel suite, didn't they?*

'Or did you think I was just going to roll over like a pussycat and sign you a big, fat cheque?' he persisted.

She had been about to admit her hastiness and lack of forethought, but his hateful remark made her bite it back. What an unremittingly cruel man he could be. Perhaps she had opened a whole can of worms, and Alex might be about to discover what kind of man his father really was. 'I—I'll organise the test,' she said shakily.

Constantine heard the faint tremble in her voice, and unwillingly he frowned. He remembered the photo of the little boy with the stubborn curls and the wariness which had peeped out from his black eyes. Could he really put the child through the worry of a test? Had she not proved herself by now? Because surely if she had been bluffing then she would not have dared sustain such a fiction for so long. And the fact that he had been trying to block from his mind now came slamming into focus—that little boy was *his* little boy.

'Forget the test,' he said suddenly.

Staring out at Milmouth high street, where the hazy sunshine spilling onto the cobbled streets seemed to mock at her dark mood, Laura froze. 'F-forget it?' she questioned incredulously. 'Why?'

'I've changed my mind,' he said slowly.

Laura's lips parted—she was scarcely able to believe what she'd just heard. Constantine magnanimously telling her that the test was unnecessary when he was the one who had insisted on it in the first place—like a teacher at school deciding to let her off a hastily handed-out detention. He has all the power, she realised bitterly. And she still wasn't clear what the motives were for his sudden about-face.

'But you said you wanted proof.'

'I no longer need it. I believe you,' he said unexpectedly.

'You believe that he's your son?'

'Yes.' There was a long silence as Constantine acknowledged the power of the single word of admission which would now change his whole life—whether he liked it or not. 'Yes, I believe he's my son,' he said heavily, as if the full statement would reinforce that fact to both of them. He had known it the moment he had stared at the photo and seen those disobedient curls—and on some subliminal level he had accepted it even before that. Because some instinct had told him to—an instinct he had not understood at the time and probably never would.

'But...why?' Her confused words cut into the turmoil of his thoughts. 'Why now, after all you said? All you accused me of?'

Constantine curled his hand into a tight fist and stared at it. All he had said had been rooted in denial; he hadn't *wanted* to believe her. He had been reluctant to accept the enormity of the possible consequences if what she said *had* been true. But suddenly he allowed himself to see that this news could have all kinds of benefits—and perhaps it had dropped into his life at just the right time. A solution had begun to form in his mind—as perfect a solution as such circumstances would allow. All he needed was to convince her to go along with it.

The determination which had driven him to rebuild one of the most powerful companies in his native Greece now emerged in a different form. A form which could be used to tackle a private life which had suddenly become complicated. Constantine's mouth hardened, and so did his groin as he remembered the way she had let him kiss her in that scruffy little hotel corridor last night. Of *course* she would go along with his wishes! She wasn't exactly the kind of woman who was going to turn down a golden opportunity if it fell into her lap, now, was she?

For a moment he was tempted to put his proposition to her there and then—until he was reminded that she had shown signs of stubbornness. Better to have her as a captive audience and to tell her face to face. Better to allow his lips and his body to persuade her if his words couldn't.

'Your co-operation has convinced me that you are telling the truth,' he said silkily. 'A woman like you would be unlikely to pit herself against an adversary like me if she was lying.'

The unexpected reprieve made Laura blink her eyes rapidly. 'Th-thank you,' she said, after taking a moment to compose herself—though when she thought about it afterwards she realised that she had completely missed the sting behind his words.

Constantine was aware that this was the moment to choose—when she was both vulnerable and grateful. 'We'll need to discuss some kind of way forward,' he said smoothly. 'Obviously, if I am the child's father, then there are a great many possibilities available to us all in the future.'

Laura felt a conflicting mixture of fear and hope. She didn't like to ask what he meant in case she came over as greedy, or grasping—but her senses had been put on alert. His sudden mood-switch from anger and accusation to honeyed reasonableness was unsettling—she felt like a starving dog, about to leap on a tasty-looking piece of meat, only to discover that it was a mangy old stick. What did he want?

'Such as?' she questioned cautiously.

'I don't really think it's the kind of discussion we should be conducting on the phone do you, *mikros minera*?' His voice deepened. 'So why don't we meet somewhere and talk it over like two sensible adults?'

It didn't seem to matter how many times she swallowed—Laura just couldn't lose the parchment-dryness which seemed to be constricting her throat. Why did she feel as if she was being lured into some trap—as if Constantine Karantinos was taking her down some path to an unknown and not particularly welcome destination? She snatched a glance at her watch. She was already ten minutes over her lunch break, and Sarah would go mad if she was much longer.

'Okay,' she said cautiously. 'I'll meet you. Where and when?'

'As soon as possible,' he clipped out. 'Let's say tomorrow night. I can come there—'

'No!' The word came out in a burst before she steadied her voice. 'Not here. Not yet. People will talk.'

'Why will they talk?' he bit back, more used to his presence at a woman's side being flaunted.

Laura stared out of the window to where she could see the distant glimmer of the sea. Did he have no idea about a small town like this and the ongoing mystery of Alex's paternity? Her night with the handsome Greek had been clandestine enough, and no one had known about it. Previously innocent and still relatively naïve, her pregnancy had come as a complete shock. If Laura's mother had still been alive, it might all have been different—she would have been there to support her and help her face the rest of the world.

As it was, Laura had felt completely on her own—not wanting to burden her young sister with any of her fears about the future. She had been proud and defiant from the moment she'd started to show right up to the moment she'd brought her baby home from the hospital.

Alex had been so very cute, and Laura so tight-lipped about his parentage, that people had given up asking who his father was—even if they still sometimes wondered.

But imagine if a man as commanding and as striking as Constantine should suddenly show up in Milmouth! His black hair and golden-olive skin were exactly the same physical characteristics which marked her son out at school. Why, she might as well take out a front-page advertisement in the *Milmouth Gazette*! People would talk and word might reach Alex—and whatever Alex was going to be told it needed to be carefully thought out beforehand. Oh, *what* was she going to tell her beloved son?

'Because people always talk,' she said flatly. 'And I don't want my son hearing speculative gossip.'

Constantine frowned. 'Where, then? London?'

'London's not easy for me to get to.'

'I can send a car for you.'

How easily practical problems could be solved when you had money, thought Laura. But a Greek billionaire's limousine was just as striking as its owner. 'No, honestly—there's no need for that. I'll meet you in Colinwood—it's our nearest big town.'

Constantine waved away the secretary who had appeared at the door of his vast office, carrying a bundle of papers. 'And is there a good restaurant there?'

She thought about what Colinwood had to offer. 'There's a hotel called the Grapevine, which is supposed to have a good restaurant, but I won't be eating because I like to have tea with my…my son,' she said. And besides, if the evening turned out to be really uncomfortable then she'd be trapped, wouldn't she? Forced to sit enduring food she didn't really want to eat and growing silent every time the waiter appeared. 'I'll meet you in the bar at nine.'

'Very well,' he said softly, and put the phone down— feeling slightly perplexed that she had not instantly fallen in with his wishes as he had expected her to do. *As women always did.*

Laura sat in silence for a moment after the connection was broken, and then ran back down to the empty shop, blurting out her news before her sister had a chance to berate her for being late.

'I'm meeting him for a drink tomorrow night. He's changed his mind about the DNA test.'

Sarah paused in the middle of brushing some icing sugar off the counter. '*Why?*'

Laura shook her head, and a terrible combination of fear and excitement shivered over her skin. 'I *don't know*,' she whispered. 'I just don't know.'

CHAPTER FIVE

DURING the build-up to her meeting with Constantine, Laura tried to carry on as usual—but inside she was still a seething cauldron of nerves, fear, and a terrible sense of *excitement,* too. And how she hated that heart-pounding awareness that she was going to see him again…that she *wanted* to see him again.

Even her choice of clothes for the outing proved a headache—she wasn't used to going out on dates and so had no idea what to wear. And this *wasn't* a date, she reminded herself—in fact, it was anything but. She knew it was wrong to go looking all dressed-up—it might look as if she was *expecting* something, mightn't it? But he had only ever seen her dressed as a waitress—or naked—and she had her pride. She didn't want him to look at her and wonder what the hell he had ever seen in her.

So, the following evening, she tucked Alex into bed and went to shower and change. It was a hot, sticky evening, and a light, flowery dress was about the only thing she had which was suitable—but it worked with bare legs and strappy wedge sandals. She added some seed pearls which had belonged to her mother, and went into the sitting room to face her sister's assessment.

'No make-up?' questioned Sarah critically as she looked her up and down.

'I am wearing a *bit*.'

'Hardly going to knock his socks off looking like that, are you?'

'That was never my intention,' said Laura as she picked up her handbag. 'Anyway, I'll see you later.' She wobbled her sister a smile as nerves came back to assail her. 'And thanks for babysitting.'

'Any time. Ring me if you want rescuing.'

'And how are you going to rescue me?' asked Laura, her mouth curving into a wry smile. 'By sending in the cavalry?'

She caught the bus to Colinwood—a pretty journey, which took in part of the dramatic coastline before tunnelling into lanes lush and thick with summer greenery. Normally she might have enjoyed just sitting back and taking in the scenery, but her heart was full of fear and the sky was heavy with the yellow-grey clouds which preceded a storm. As Laura alighted in the market square in the still and heavy air, she could already feel the oppressive beads of sweat which were prickling at her forehead.

The Grapevine was already quite full—mainly with young professionals, as well as couples out together for the evening. Laura found herself watching them the most—their close body contact proclaiming to the world that they were in love.

She knew that envy was an unappealing trait, but sometimes she just couldn't help herself. She wondered what it must be like to do things the 'right' way round. To fall in love and get engaged and then married. To have a man sit and hold your hand and look as if he had found heaven on earth. She tried to imagine the shared joy of a first baby—the breathless wonder of news being broken to friends and relatives. Not like her—with her unplanned pregnancy and her young son who had never laid eyes on his father...

She saw Constantine immediately—somehow he had bagged the best table in a quiet corner which commanded an enviable view of the stunning gardens outside. A waitress was buzzing around him, smiling for an extra beat as she placed a small dish of olives in front of him, smoothing her manicured hand down over a slender hip as if she wanted to draw his attention to it.

Please give me the strength to stand up to him, Laura said to herself silently as she picked her way through the room towards him, trying to fix her face into a neutral expression. But what kind of expression did she wear in circumstances like these?

Constantine watched her, observing her with a clinical detachment made easier by the fact that she was not wearing a uniform tonight. Tonight her long, fine hair was fizzing down over her shoulders—he could see its brightness as she approached. And she wore a thin little summer dress which made the most of her firm, young body and slender frame. The shoes she wore were high and drew attention to her legs. Amazing legs, he thought suddenly, as if remembering why she had captivated him all those years ago—and then instantly regretted it as she walked up to his table.

'H-hello, Constantine.'

He should have risen to greet her, but his trousers were stretched so tightly across his groin that he did not dare move. It wasn't textbook behaviour—but then he reminded himself that this wasn't exactly a textbook situation. They weren't out on some kind of cute, getting-to-know-you evening; they were here to discuss a small child. And once again the shimmering of some unknown emotion whispered at his heart.

'Sit down,' he drawled.

'Thanks.' She perched on the edge of the plush leather banquette, her skin clammy and her heart thumping loudly with nerves. It was so hot in here! When he handed her a glass of wine, she automatically took it with boneless fingers, even though she'd decided on the way over that alcohol was a bad idea. She took a sip. 'Have…have you been waiting long?'

There was silence for a moment, and Constantine leaned back, taking his time as he studied her, noting the way her knees were pushed tightly together and the stiff set of her slender shoulders. Her body language screamed out her tension—and he knew then that this was not going to be a walk-over. 'No, I've only just arrived,' he said, and in the fading light his eyes glittered. 'So…that's the niceties out of the way. Have you told the boy anything yet?'

Laura shook her head. She wished he would stop looking at her like that. As if he was stripping her completely bare with his black eyes. 'No.'

Fractionally, he leaned towards her. 'Do you realize,' he said softly, 'that I don't even know his name?'

It sounded like an accusation, and maybe it was— though it was actually the first time he'd asked. She sucked in a breath, disorientated by his proximity. *What if he hates the name I've chosen?* she thought—*in that inexplicable*

*way that people often did take against names because they
reminded them of someone or something from their past.*

'It's Alex,' she said quietly. 'Short for Alexander.'

There was a moment of silence before Constantine let
out a long, low breath. It was a name which meant warrior.
A proud name which carried with it all the weight and
honour of his heritage. 'A Greek name,' he observed.

'Yes. It seemed somehow *appropriate*.'

He felt a wave of something approaching helplessness
wash over him. 'In a situation which was entirely *inappropriate*?' he countered—because didn't giving the child a
name make him seem real in a way that a photo never
could? A person was beginning to emerge from the scraps
of information he was being fed. A person about whom he
knew absolutely *nothing*. 'What else did you decide was
appropriate?' he snapped.

Laura recoiled from the anger which was emanating in
heated waves from his powerful frame, and she put her
wine glass down on the table before it slid from her fingers.
'We can't keep apportioning blame!' she said in a low
voice. 'What happened *happened*. We can't change it—we
just have to deal with the situation as it is.'

'And the situation is what?' he retorted. 'A woman who
is clearly living from hand to mouth having sole charge of
my son and heir? Don't you think it's time I had a little
input into his life as well, Laura?'

'Of…of course I do. That's why I'm here.' She stared
at him, twisting her fingers nervously in her lap. 'We could
arrange a first meeting, if you like.'

He gave a short laugh. 'Slot me into the diary like an
appointment at the dentist, you mean? You want me turning

up on a Saturday afternoon to take a reluctant child for a hamburger while he counts away the minutes he has to spend with this stranger?'

Laura bit her lip. 'I didn't mean like that.'

'No? Then just what *did* you mean?' His black eyes blazed into her. 'What kind of future had you anticipated when you made contact with me again?'

His dominance was formidable, and Laura felt herself swamped by its dark power. *'I don't know,'* she admitted desperately.

Constantine's mouth hardened. 'Well, I *do*. I have given it a lot of thought and weighed up all the possibilities.' He had spoken to his lawyers, too—but maybe now was not the best time to tell her *that*. He lowered his voice, the way he did in the world of business when he was about to close a deal. 'And there is a future which makes perfect sense for all parties. Which is why I want you to accompany me to my island home in Greece, Laura, occupying the only position which is appropriate.' He paused, and his eyes gleamed like cold, black stones as he looked at her. 'As my wife.'

CHAPTER SIX

LAURA stared at Constantine, her heart beating wildly, scarcely able to believe her ears. 'Your *wife*?' she repeated incredulously. 'Why on earth would I want to marry *you*?'

'*Want* has nothing to do with it,' he iced back, outraged at her shocked and unflattering response. '*Need* is a far more fitting word. For a start, you need money.'

'I never said—'

'You're a *waitress* who also works in a damned shop!' he shot out.

The beating of her heart increased. 'How did you know that?'

His lips twisted. How naïve she was! 'It wasn't difficult. I got someone to find out for me.'

Laura swallowed. 'You mean you've been *spying* on me?'

Dismissively, he batted the question away, with an arrogant flick of his hand. If only it were as easy to bat away the memory of the photos his private detective had dropped in front of him: Laura taking the boy to school in clothes which were clearly too small for him. Not to mention the pictorial evidence of his son growing up in some scruffy apartment over a seedy little shop.

But it was more than that. There had been the dawning realisation that perhaps this trembling little waitress might actually make ideal marriage material. Poor and desperate—wouldn't she be so swept away by his power and his riches that she would be completely malleable, so that he could mould her to the image of his perfect wife? And of course added to all this was the inexplicable fact that he hadn't been able to stop thinking about that stolen kiss in the dark basement of the hotel… Why, even now the memory of it made him want to do it all over again. It was crazy. It was inexplicable. And it was as potent as hell…

He scowled, forcing his mind back to her ridiculous claim that she'd been spying on him. 'Don't be hysterical, Laura,' he snapped. 'When a woman comes to a man in my position, making claims of enormous significance, it is inevitable her background will be investigated. For all I knew you might have had some male partner at home, his eyes fixed greedily on the main chance—seeing your ex-lover as a meal ticket.'

'You…you…*cynic*…' she breathed.

'Or simply a realist?' he countered. 'Oh, come on—you can lose the outrage, *agape mou*. You see, I *know* the corrupting power of money. And I've seen what people will do in its pursuit.'

Laura stared at him. His *wife*? Had he really just asked her to be his wife? 'But I thought you were marrying that other woman—'

'What other woman?'

She saw his eyes narrow dangerously and wished she hadn't started this. 'The Swedish supermodel,' she said reluctantly.

'Who told you that?'

'I heard it on the radio,' she admitted, and from the look of slowly dawning comprehension which crossed his face she wished she'd kept quiet. Because now she sounded like some kind of stalker.

'You shouldn't believe a word the media tells you,' he snapped. 'But at least that explains why you suddenly appeared out of nowhere the other night.' His eyes fixed her with icy challenge. 'Actually, the press have been trying to marry me off for years—but *I* will chose whom and when to marry, not the media!'

She stared up at him, full of bewilderment. 'I still don't understand…after everything you've said—why you want to marry *me*.'

'Don't you? Think about it. Marriage has always been on a list as something that perhaps I ought to do when I get around to it—but there's been no real sense of urgency. Until now.' His black eyes glittered. 'You see, I possess a vast fortune, Laura,' he elaborated softly, 'and my father is old and frail. His greatest wish is to see me provide him with an heir. This could be a surprisingly easy way of accomplishing both objectives.'

Laura shook her head. 'But that's so…*cold-blooded*!'

'Is it?' He gave a cynical laugh. 'Unlike you, I have not grown up on a diet of believing in romance and happy-ever-after.' In fact, he knew better than anyone that reality never matched up to dreams, and that emotion robbed men of sense and of reason. He lowered his voice. 'Why not look at it practically rather than emotionally? Marriage will serve a purpose—it will legitimise my son and it will give you all the financial security you could ever need.'

But deep down Laura's suspicions were alerted. It would also give Constantine power, she recognised. And once he had that power wouldn't he be tempted to use it against her? Pushing her to the sidelines until he dominated Alex's life as she suspected that he could all too easily? Everything that she'd fought and worked for could be threatened by this man's undeniable wealth and charisma.

'No! No and no and no!' she flared back, as the emotion and the humid atmosphere of the bar began to tighten her throat. Suddenly she needed to get away from Constantine's heady proximity and the danger he represented.

Grabbing her handbag, she stood up—and without another word walked straight out of the bar, uncaring of the sudden lull in conversation from the couples around them, or the curious eyes watching her as she tried not to stumble in her high wedges.

Outside in the fast-fading light the atmosphere was just as sticky, and the heady scent of roses was almost overpowering. Laura dimly wondered if she should take off her shoes and run to the bus stop in an effort to escape from him, when she felt a hand gripping her arm. Constantine spun her round to face him, his black eyes blazing.

He stared at her, a nerve working furiously in his cheek. Because no woman had ever said no to him before. And no woman ever turned her back on him, either.

'Don't you ever walk out on me like that again!' he bit out.

'I'm a free agent and I can do exactly as I please!'

'You think so?' His mouth hardened with lust. 'Well, in that case, so can I!'

Without warning he pulled her right up against him— so close that she could feel every hard sinew. And she wanted to resist him—just as she was resisting his demand that she marry him. But it seemed that her body had other ideas. To her horror she found herself wanting to sink against him. Into him.

Did he sense that? Was that why he gathered her closer still—with a small moan of what sounded like his own surrender?

In the pale light, he tilted her face up. 'Now, this *is* a time when the word *want* is appropriate. And you want me, Laura—just as I want you. Don't ask me why, but I do,' he ground out, and he drove his mouth down onto hers.

She had meant to gasp out her protest, but instead her lips opened beneath his like a sea-anemone, and suddenly her feelings ran away with her. Was it anger or frustration which fuelled her desire, causing her fingers to clutch at his shoulders—finding the butter-soft silk of his shirt and the hard sheath of the muscular flesh beneath? Or was it something infinitely more dangerous—the fierce clamour of her heart for a man who would never grant her access to his?

'*Oh,*' she breathed, as she felt his free hand move down to splay with intimate freedom over the globe of one buttock, and a shudder rocked through her as her body melted into his.

'*Theos mou!*' he ground back in response. Through waves of hunger, which came with a strength he had not been anticipating, Constantine pulled her into a darkened recess at the side of the building and continued to plunder her mouth with kiss upon kiss. The fingers which had been on her bottom now slipped underneath the little sundress, and he slid his hand round until it lay over the cotton-covered warmth of her mound. He felt her gasp out a little cry. Her passion had not abated over the years, he thought grimly. Nor had her eagerness dulled or softened around the edges. He felt himself grow so hard that he thought he would explode.

Should he do it to her here? Unzip his trousers and thrust himself in her sweet, wild wetness? He moved his hand over what felt like a pair of functional cotton panties.

'If only you weren't wearing any…then how easy it would be,' he commented unevenly.

His graphic words broke into the darkly erotic spell which had captivated her, and Laura opened her eyes to see the face of Constantine—taut and tight with sexual hunger. Reality washed over her like a cold shower. *What the hell was she doing? Standing there while he put his hand between her legs and incited her to…to…*

'Stop…stop it,' she whispered.

'Stop what?'

'T-touching me.'

'But you like it. You know you do.' He moved a finger against her and heard her breathing quicken. 'Don't you?'

'*Oh.*'

His fingertips continued to tease her moist heat—and even in the dim light he could see the sudden dilation of her eyes before the lids came down to obscure them. She relaxed against him once more and he felt her imminent surrender. Should he carry on? Bring her to an orgasm she would be unable and unwilling to prevent? Kiss away the gasping little sounds as those sweet spasms pulsed through her? It would be a turn-on to watch her, and perhaps she would be more amenable to his plans if he had her glowing and basking in his arms afterwards.

But at that moment he heard the sound of a car approaching, and saw the powerful beam of its headlights snaking up the drive. He realised just what he was doing. He, Constantine Karantinos, was standing by the side of a hotel, making out with a woman, in an aroused state such as he had not been in since his teenage youth!

'Let's go upstairs,' he murmured, his lips soft as they whispered over the long pale line of her neck.

Through the mists of sweet, sensual hunger warning bells sounded like fire alarms in her head, and Laura opened her eyes in confusion. 'Up-upstairs?' she echoed blankly.

'Mmm. Much more comfortable there. Enormous bed. Enormous pleasure.' He kissed her neck and guided her fingers to where he was hard and aching for her. 'Enormous everywhere,' he whispered, on an arrogant boast.

But Laura shrank back, snatching her hand away from his tantalising heat as she looked up at him, aghast. 'You have a *room* here?'

'A suite, actually. Not the best I've seen—but not bad.'

'Let me get this straight.' Her heart was pounding. 'You thought…you thought that I'd just meekly go to bed with you?'

He smiled. 'Meekly is not the word I was hoping for, *agape mou*—since your response so far tells me that you are a very passionate woman. But then as I recall you always were,' he added softly.

And it was those last words of his which were almost her undoing—because they gave the situation a *faux* intimacy, almost as if they had some kind of tender, shared past between them. But they didn't, she reminded herself painfully. What they had shared had been nothing but a powerful sexual chemistry which had flared out of control. And just because that sexual chemistry was as explosive as ever, it didn't mean she had to give in to it. To behave in a way which would afterwards have him insulting her as if she were no better than a cheap little tramp.

'I'm not going upstairs with you,' she said sharply, pulling herself out of his arms and tugging her dress down defiantly as she moved away from the alcove.

To Constantine's astonishment, he could see that she meant it. Had he thought that she would capitulate as easily as she had done all those years ago? The way women always did? For a moment frustrated longing pulsed around his veins as he searched her face for a sign that she might be on the verge of changing her mind, but there was none.

With the steely self-control for which he was renowned he forced his own desire to evaporate, like droplets of water sizzling onto a hot Greek street. There would be plenty of time for sex once she had agreed to his other demands—and, banishing the tantalising memory of her heated response to him, Constantine switched to the real reason he was here.

'Hasn't that little interlude convinced you that we could make a creditable stab at matrimony?' he questioned softly as he followed her, his feet crunching over the soft gravel.

'How delightfully you put it—but the answer is still no.' Her knees still weak, Laura sank down onto a wooden bench in full view of the main entrance into the hotel, where cars were coming and going. Let him *dare* try to start touching her here!

Constantine sat down next to her. Was this like a boardroom battle? he wondered. With her supposedly stubborn resistance being used as a lever to increase her demands? He gave a small smile. She would soon learn that *he* called all the shots. 'I'd like to know what your main objection to my proposal is?' he questioned silkily.

'Why—Alex, of course,' she shot back. 'Do you really think I can just announce to him that I'm marrying his father—whom he's never even met—and that we're all going off to Greece to live happily ever after?'

'Why not?'

'Why *not*? Don't you know *anything* about children?'

'Actually, no, I don't,' he snapped. 'Since I've been denied that opportunity up until now!'

Laura swallowed as she stared into the shadowed flint of his features. Be reasonable, she told herself as she worked out what to say. Because if she expected him to come round to her way of thinking then she was going to have to be convincing. And convincing a man like this about anything wasn't going to be easy. She had to show him how it would look from a little boy's point of view.

Her voice softened. 'Alex's life is here in England—it's all he's ever known. Don't you think that suddenly landing all this in his lap would be overloading him with too much, too soon? Tearing him away from his home and his school? A new father who turns up out of the blue and a new life he has no say in? What if Greece doesn't work out?'

'We will make it work out,' he vowed grimly.

And in a way that stubborn insistence only reinforced her determination. Laura suddenly got an ominous vision of the finality of being trapped in a loveless marriage with a man like Constantine, and a shiver ran down her spine. 'You can't *make* things happen like that,' she said. 'Human beings aren't puppets that you can play with and control. I don't think you realise the impact of taking a child who's never even been abroad and plonking him in a foreign land.'

His body tensed as if she had hit him, and he clenched his fists. 'Don't ever…*ever*…refer to Greece as a "foreign land" in front of me or in front of my son,' he hissed. 'It is the land of his forebears with a rich and glorious heritage. And one which I intend that he will learn about.'

The fingers which had tightened into two fists now slowly unfurled, and Laura found herself watching them with a horrible kind of fascination.

'I want contact with Alex,' he continued inexorably. 'And I want him to meet his grandfather. Those two things are non-negotiable—so how do you intend to let me go about doing it, Laura?'

And Laura knew then that she didn't have to be stuck on an island to be trapped. Entrapment could be emotional as well as geographical, she realised—and in a way her fate had been sealed from the moment she had made contact with him again. She could see the determination etched on his face, and she realised that there was no way she was going to be able to escape his demands. Which meant that she had to fashion them to best suit her and Alex's purpose. And no one could deny that it was in a child's best interests to learn about his father—no matter what *she* thought about him.

She laced her fingers together. 'I think it's best for Alex to get to know you…gradually.'

'And how do you suggest I do that?' he demanded. 'Start coming into that bread shop you run and buying some damned bun every morning?'

If the circumstances hadn't been so fraught then Laura might almost have laughed, because the image of this powerful Greek going into her little village shop was both bizarre and amusing. But there was no place for humour here; this was deadly serious. Yet neither was there was any need for him to be so scathing about her method of earning a living. Working in a shop wasn't up there with being a supermodel, but it was honest and it was decent—even if it didn't reap the huge kind of rewards which *he* obviously considered essential.

'Of course I don't,' she said stiffly.

'*My* life and *my* work are in Greece,' he clipped out.

'I realise that.' Just as hers and Alex's was here—a cultural and geographical world away. Laura's mind starting spinning as she searched desperately for some sort of solution to their dilemma, when suddenly a thought occurred to her. Unseen in the folds of her cheap summer dress, her fingers tightened as an idea of breathtaking simplicity came to her. 'But the long summer holidays are coming up,' she said slowly.

Constantine stilled. 'And what has that got to do with anything?'

'I could come to Greece,' she said carefully. 'But not as your wife. A complete lifestyle change would unsettle Alex—but he could cope with the kind of situation he's used to.'

'You aren't making any sense,' he snapped.

'Well, I…I presume that your father employs staff at his home in Greece?'

'Of course he does.'

'How many?'

'I am not in the habit of keeping an inventory,' he drawled. But her eyes continued to regard him steadily and he gave an impatient kind of sigh. 'There is a permanent house-keeper who lives within the complex, and several people who come in from the village to help out.'

'And do…do any of them have children?'

'Not young children, no—but there are plenty of those in the village.' He frowned. 'What the hell does that have to do with anything?'

Laura let out a long breath. 'I know exactly what we can do,' she breathed. 'You take me on for the summer as a temporary member of staff. I can work in your father's house—'

'Work in my father's house?' he roared in disbelief, staring at her as if she had taken complete leave of her senses. 'Doing *what*?'

Laura lifted her chin up, determined not to be intimidated by the fierce blaze from his eyes. 'The skills of which you've already been so very critical—I can clean and make beds. I can serve food. I can even cook—though not to any cordon bleu standard.'

Constantine stared into her face. 'Such lowly and subservient pursuits!' he bit out. 'What kind of a woman would want this?'

A woman with pride, thought Laura ardently. And a woman with dignity—or rather one who was trying to claw back some of the poise which always seemed to fly out of the window whenever Constantine was around.

'Meanwhile, Alex gets a few weeks in the sun,' she carried on, her enthusiasm growing now. 'If he plays with other children he can learn a little Greek, and they can learn English. It'll do him good to have a holiday—and in that relaxed environment he can get to know you.'

There was an ominous kind of silence while Constantine mulled over her words—there was no doubt that he was surprised by the humbleness of her request. She wanted to come to his house as a *servant*! And yet maybe it would work out better this way—for wouldn't it place strain on his father's heart to suddenly produce a seven-year-old grandson out of nowhere? And wouldn't she be more expendable as a servant than as a wife? Easier to dispose of afterwards, if her presence began to grate on him, without having to go through all the publicity and disruption of a divorce?

He stared at her, aware that her impudent idea was distracting him from the most important question of all. 'And when do you propose telling Alex that I'm his father?' he asked softly.

The eyes she turned to him were huge. 'Can we...can we wait until the moment is right?'

He hardened his heart against the tremulous appeal in her voice. 'I will not wait for ever, Laura,' he warned.

'No. No, I can understand that. We will tell him as soon as it's appropriate. I promise. Oh, thank you. Thank you, Constantine.' She flashed him a grateful smile, but the look he gave in response was like ice.

'This is not a situation I am happy with,' he bit out.

How hard the years had made him, she thought fleetingly. He was a completely different person from the rufflehaired man who had sailed in and out of her life all those summers ago.

And what about her? Had *she* changed that much? Laura bit her lip. Quite honestly, that brief period of freedom and sexual awakening had been so unlike anything she had known since that she had almost completely forgotten it.

Or maybe she had just blocked it from her mind. Maybe it was too painful to remember being carefree and unencumbered by worry.

She forced her mind back to practicalities. 'The only problem I can think of is that I'm going to need a replacement to help my sister in the shop while I'm away—but I assume you'd be able to help me sort that out?'

The *only* problem? he thought. Was she crazy? He could see a few more than that.

'I can fix that,' said Constantine heavily—because for the first time in his life he had not got what he wanted. Despite her reduced circumstances and tiny stature, he could see that here was a woman who had her mind set on something, and nothing he could do or say was going to change her mind. Was this a unique version of mother-love? he wondered bitterly. A mother fighting tooth and nail for what was best for her child?

Briefly, Constantine found himself wondering what it must be like to have a mother who felt like that about you. A mother who cared about your welfare more than she cared about her own—but he vetoed the thought instantly. He never wasted time thinking about things which were beyond his own comprehension.

It was one of the reasons behind his success.

CHAPTER SEVEN

LAURA was aware of a surprisingly green oval rising up to meet them as the helicopter landed with the agility of a large moth. Ringed with silver-white sand, from the sky the island had looked like a jewel in the middle of a sea so intensely blue that she'd felt quite shaken with the beauty of it all.

And shaken by her first ever trip in a helicopter, of course.

She stole a glance at Alex, who also seemed complctely rapt by the splendour unfolding before him, and wondered what kind of effect this trip was going to have on him. Because although she'd insisted on travelling out to Greece on a regular airline, since 'servants don't arrive in private jets,' as she had told Constantine firmly, there had been a helicopter waiting at Athens airport to whisk them off to the island of Livinos.

It had all proved a little distracting—and Laura found herself wondering if experiencing these enormous riches from such an early age had been instrumental in fashioning Constantine's character? She stared out at the gradually slowing helicopter blades. Of course it had! Your early experiences always shaped your development like nothing else. If he'd been used to snapping his fingers from an early age and getting whatever it was he wanted then no wonder he was so autocratic and demanding.

She held Alex's hand tightly as she helped him down from the helicopter, with his beloved blue bear clutched tightly to his chest. He'd been worried that the scruffy old toy was too babyish to bring with him—but Laura had insisted the bear come too. Heaven only knew he wouldn't go to sleep without him.

Thinking she heard someone call her name, she looked up, her eyes narrowed against the blinding heat of the hot sun, and there, standing beside a four-wheel drive, was the man who had been dominating her thoughts all week.

Constantine! Here! Her mouth dried and her heart began to race erratically as he fixed his piercing gaze on them. So much hung on what happened next, and for Alex's sake she prayed that this first meeting would be a success as they made their way across the scorching tarmac towards the Greek billionaire.

Constantine felt a sudden lurching of his heart as he watched them approach, unprepared for the powerful feelings which came surging over him as he stared at the boy. The photos he had seen had made him take seriously her claim that the child was his—even though he had done his best to deny it at the time. But seeing him now, in the living and breathing flesh—well, that was something entirely different. Put a hundred—no, a thousand seven-year-old boys in front of him and Constantine would have instantly picked out this particular boy as having sprung from Karantinos loins.

He sucked in a ragged breath as they grew closer, his heart now pounding with a terrible combination of recognition and regret—that they were strangers to one another, and yet he knew that they were linked in the most primeval way of all.

With an effort he tore his gaze away from Alex and let it travel instead to Laura, whose eyes were fixed on him with a certain amount of trepidation. As well they might be. Constantine's lips curved with contempt. Another cheap little dress and a pair of sandals which had seen better days—and her fine hair all mussed up in a cloud around her head. Had she deliberately come here today emphasising her lowly status, after stubbornly insisting that she be employed in the house as a member of staff? Was she perhaps hoping that he might make some kind of generous settlement on her if she insisted on highlighting the differences between them?

Yet despite the anger he felt towards her there was a fair amount of it directed at himself, for the inexplicable lust he still felt for her. That his groin should instantly ache with an unquenchable desire to make love to her—this pale and insipid little shop-worker who had turned down his offer of marriage!

But he composed his face into a smile of welcome as they grew closer—because he was clever enough to know that he could never win the boy if he was seen to be openly critical of his mother.

'C-Constantine,' stumbled Laura. 'I...well, I certainly wasn't expecting to find you here to meet us.'

'What an unexpected pleasure it must be,' he murmured sardonically, but his eyes were fixed on the child and he was aware of a strange beating of his heart. 'Hello, Alex.'

Alex turned a confused face up towards Laura 'Who's this, Mum?'

Constantine crouched down so that he was on a level with the boy, wondering if there would be some kind of instant recognition on the part of his son—but of course there was none. Had he perhaps been secretly hoping that Laura might already have told him—that there would be some kind of touching scene outside the airport? But things like that only happened in movies, he told himself grimly. This was real life.

Usually he did not care what kind of impression he made—people could either take him or leave him. His careless attitude stemmed from the fact that other men were always anxious to be his friend, while women were eager to be his lover. But now he realised that unexpectedly his heart was beating fast with something approaching concern. I want him to like me, he thought fiercely. I *need* him to like me.

'My name is Constantine Karantinos,' he said softly. 'And you are going to be staying in my father's house.'

Alex nodded, as if this were nothing untoward, and Laura supposed that after the excitement of the day itself he would have calmly accepted being told he was taking a trip to the moon. 'Is it a nice house?'

'Oh, it's a very nice house,' answered Constantine, with a smile of rare indulgence. 'With a big swimming pool.'

Alex blinked. 'You mean, just for us?'

'Just for us,' replied Constantine gravely.

Alex bit his lip in the way he always did when he was worried, and Laura's heart turned over as she watched him. 'But I'm not very good at swimming,' he said.

Constantine wondered why. 'Then we shall have to teach you—would you like that?'

Alex nodded, his dark eyes wide. 'Yes, please!'

'Let's get in the car, then.' And Constantine helped the child into the back seat and strapped him in, before stepping back to allow Laura to pass.

His eyes narrowed as she moved close enough for him to be able to get the drift of some light scent, and despite its cheapness he swallowed with another unexpected wave of lust.

'You look...' He allowed his gaze to drift over her pale skin and pinched expression and saw her bite her lip in response to his critical scrutiny. 'Pretty tired,' he conceded.

'Yes,' said Laura, thinking that tired didn't even come close—she felt physically and mentally exhausted. Truth to tell, she hadn't had a full night's sleep since she'd met Constantine at the Grapevine that night—plus she'd been working some of Sarah's shifts, to make up for the time she was going to take off. 'It's been a long week,' she said wearily.

For a moment—just for a moment—he felt the faintest tug of sympathy. For the first time he noticed that the grey eyes were shadowed, and that her pale skin was almost translucent with fatigue.

'Then for heaven's sake get in the car and relax,' he said roughly, climbing into the driver's seat himself and starting up the engine, while the helicopter pilot put their small and rather battered suitcases in the boot.

'Wow! Get in, Mum!' Alex enthused. 'It's huge.'

Uncomfortably conscious of trying to keep as much of her pale, bare legs hidden as possible, Laura got in next to her son. She caught sight of a pair of black eyes mocking her as they glanced at her from the rearview mirror, and her reaction to that unmistakably sensual look was instinctive, though completely unwelcome. She felt the weak, thready patter of her heart and the icing of her skin, but she stared straight ahead at his broad shoulders and prayed that he would just let her get on with her work while he got down to the important business of getting to know Alex. Did he realise that she was determined to fight her desire for him—since no good could come out of their renewing a sexual relationship?

'Do you live near the sea?' piped up Alex.

'No place on the island is far from it,' answered Constantine. 'And if you're very lucky you might see one of the Karantinos ships sailing by.'

Alex failed to keep the sense of wonder from his voice. 'You mean *real* ships?'

Constantine laughed. 'Yes. Very real. And very big.'

'I'd love that,' said Alex wistfully, and then bit his lip in the way he'd unconsciously picked up from his mother. 'But Mum will be working, won't she? And she says I'm not to get in anyone's way.'

There was an awful silence, and if there had been a dark corner nearby then Laura would have gone away and crawled into it. She had never felt sorry for herself—ever. She had always embraced hard work and considered it a part and parcel of bringing up a child out of wedlock. But Alex's words prompted a deep dislike of her predicament—and of what it was doing to her son.

His words had set them apart. Making him sound like some servant's child from a different century—almost as if he was going to be sent up the chimney and asked to sweep it! And Constantine clearly felt it, too—because once more he caught her gaze in the driving mirror, but this time the look was not remotely sensual, it was spitting with a slow, burning anger. As if it was an insult to *his* honour to hear his son speaking in such a way.

'You must not worry about your mother's working hours,' he said abruptly. 'Since I know that she will be happy for you to enjoy yourself.'

'I just don't want her to feel left out,' said Alex loyally, and Laura could have wept. It was supposed to be *her* protecting him, and not the other way round.

'Of course you must let Constantine show you all his ships,' said Laura, as if she discussed the ownership of ships every day of her life.

'I used to live here when I was about your age,' said Constantine conversationally.

'Oh, *wow*!' Alex sighed. 'Lucky you.'

Something in the boy's wistfulness made a rush of unwilling memories come flooding back—and for once Constantine could not block them out. In many ways it had been a textbook and idyllic upbringing—with none of the stresses surrounding life spent in the city. The beauty of Livinos, and the ability to swim and to fish and to climb trees without fear—those were gifts which every other child on the island had experienced. He hadn't needed to be the son of a wealthy man to enjoy the carefree freedoms of childhood in this part of Greece.

But, essentially, it had been a lonely time for Constantine. Materially rich but emotionally neglected by a mother who had never been there—even when she had been physically present. His beautiful, fragile mother, who had captivated his father like a moth to a flame—who had consumed all those around her but given little back. Who had not known—nor been able to learn—how to love the strong-minded baby she had given birth to.

'Look out of the window, Alex,' said Constantine gently. 'As well as some of the most wonderful beaches you will ever see, we have mountains, and forests of cedar, oak and pine. And mines of silver and gold.'

'*Gold*?' spluttered Alex. 'Not really?'

'Yes, really. It was first discovered by the Parians, who came from the island of Paros.'

This time Laura sent Constantine a silent message. *Stop it,* her eyes appealed. *Stop painting for him the kind of pictures he has only ever seen in films or books before. Please don't make his life in England fade into pale and boring insignificance.*

And Constantine read the appeal perfectly, deliberately choosing to ignore it. Did she really expect him to play his heritage down, when it was his son's heritage, too? His expression didn't alter.

'We have white marble, too,' he continued. 'Which is exported all over the world. And there are all the other components which are an essential part of Greek life—fruit and honey and olives. Now, look closely as we drive up this road, Alex, and you will see my father's house.'

House, he had said, noted Laura suddenly, her quibble forgotten as she gazed curiously out of the window. Not home. Did that have any significance? But then she peered out through the window and her breath caught in her throat as the most beautiful place she had ever seen suddenly came into view.

Surrounded by orange and lemon trees, the villa was large and imposing, dominating the landscape while somehow managing to blend into it. It stood almost at the top of the mountain, and the views around it were panoramic. Dark sapphire brush-strokes of a sea threw off a brilliant light, and as Laura opened the car door she could smell the scent of pine and citrus and hear the unfamiliar sound of beautiful birdsong.

'We're here,' said Constantine, as he held his hand out to help Alex down. The boy took it as naturally as breathing.

How easily Alex is learning to trust him, thought Laura—knowing that she should be glad for her son's sake, and yet unable to prevent the strange spike of envy which tugged at her stomach.

The huge front door opened and a middle-aged woman wearing a floral pinafore dress came out immediately to meet them—as if she had been standing waiting for their arrival.

'I'll introduce you to Demetra,' Constantine said, an odd glint in his eyes. 'She's in charge of the staff here—so you'll be directly answerable to her. Oh, and don't worry—she speaks excellent English, so you won't have any problems understanding her instructions, Laura.'

Instructions. Answerable. His words brought Laura tumbling back down to earth with a crash. And with a shock she realised that all the privileges she had been enjoying up until that moment were now about to evaporate. She was to become one of the domestic staff. *But that's what you wanted*, she reminded herself painfully. *That's what you insisted on.*

At least she had spent the last few evenings poring over a phrasebook—but her usual slowness with reading coupled with the difficulty of the complex Greek language meant that she had retained only a few words. Still, now was the time to start using them.

'*Kalimera*,' she said, with a nervous smile at the older woman.

Demetra's eyes swept over Laura in rapid assessment, and she said something in Greek to Constantine, to which he made a drawled reply. It seemed to satisfy her, for she nodded and returned the smile.

'*Kalimera*, Laura. You are very welcome at Villa Thavmassios.' Her eyes crinkled fondly as she stared at Alex's dark curls. 'And this your boy?'

'Yes, this is Alex.' Laura gave a Alex a little push, and to her relief he stepped forward and shook the Greek woman's hand, just the way she'd taught him to. Demetra gave a delighted exclamation before enfolding him in a bear-hug, and Laura bit back a smile as she saw Alex send her a horrified look of appeal.

'We bring children from the village to play with you, Alex,' said Demetra. 'And my own son is home from university—he is a very fine sports student. He teach you to swim and to fish. You would like that?'

'Yes, please,' said Alex shyly, as Demetra finally let him go. She said something else to Constantine, but he shook his head.

'*Ochi*,' he said in negation, and then smiled. 'Shall I show you to your room now, Alex?' Then he turned to Laura, almost as if it was an afterthought. 'And I might as well show you yours,' he added softly.

Laura tried to tell herself not to react to the unmistakable provocation in those dark eyes—telling herself that nothing was going to happen because she didn't want anything to happen. But even as she made the silent vow she had to fight to suppress the glimmer of longing which had begun to whisper its way over her skin.

Liar. You know that you want him. That you would give a king's ransom for his lips to rove all over your naked body.

Laura's cheeks flushed, and she could feel their colour intensify simply because Constantine was looking at her with that hateful half-smile playing around his lips— as if he knew exactly what she was thinking. As if he knew that her breasts were prickling and her heart racing like a piston. Her fist clenched around the strap of her handbag and she dug her nails into it—as if she were digging them into his rich, silken flesh.

What on earth was going on? Why was she suddenly reacting to him as if she was the kind of woman who was prey to carnal desires, when nothing could be further from the truth?

Nothing.

Why, there hadn't been a single man in her life since Constantine had sailed away all those years ago— because the truth was that she had never wanted another man in the way she'd wanted him, even if single motherhood didn't exactly encourage romantic entanglements. But suddenly Laura's lack of another lover seemed more like a failure rather than anything to be proud of. As if she was one of those pathetic women who had been carrying a flame for a man who'd never even given her a second thought. Who hadn't even remembered that they'd been lovers!

His voice cut across her thoughts. 'Ready?' he questioned.

Forcing a smile, she took Alex's hand. 'Let's go and see your room, darling.'

The villa was cool and huge—it made her Milmouth apartment look like a shoebox—and Laura found herself wondering how long it would take to get her bearings.

Alex's suitcase had already been brought into a bright room which had been transformed into a small boy's dream. There was a bookcase filled with any number of books, and a table on which sat a drawing block and a rainbow collection of colouring pens. A giant castle reposed in one corner—with small figures of knights and horses—and a beautiful wooden train-set sat curved and just itching to be put in motion.

Seeing the castle, Alex turned to Constantine with a look of breathless excitement on his face.

'Did Mum tell you I liked horses?' he demanded excitedly.

'I thought that all little boys liked horses,' answered Constantine solemnly.

'Can I play with it? Now?'

'That is what it is there for. You play with it while I show your mama her room—which is just along the corridor— then we will go downstairs and eat something, and later on you can swim. Would you like that?'

Alex's eyes were like dark, delighted saucers. 'Oh, *yes!*' And he ran over to the castle.

Laura looked up at Constantine, fighting to keep her emotions in check—but, whichever way you looked at it, the Greek tycoon had gone out of his way to make the small boy feel welcome, and she found that she was having to blink back sudden tears. She wanted to say thank you, but the look which had darkened his features into a steely mask was not one which readily invited gratitude.

'Let's go,' said Constantine softly, and Laura's heart was pounding heavily as they walked along the cool, marbled corridor. She felt like a prisoner whose fate had been sealed, yet she was filled with a terrible kind of excitement when Constantine halted before a door. As he threw it open, all she could see was a bed.

'What did Demetra say to you outside?' she questioned quickly, wanting something—anything—to distract her attention from that bed.

'That you looked too small and too slight for any kind of physical work.'

'And what did you tell her?'

Constantine paused as he stared down into the stormy beauty of her grey eyes, registering the dormant strength which lay within her petite frame. 'I told her that you were no stranger to hard work,' he said unexpectedly.

'Oh.' The words caught her off-guard, and Laura found herself feeling ridiculously warmed by the nearest thing to a compliment he'd paid her. She looked up at him, heart racing. 'Why, thank you—' But she got no further, because Constantine's gaze was raking over her face. He took her hand, pulling her inside the bedroom, shutting the door on the rest of the world.

'Be very clear about this, Laura. I don't want your thanks,' he said softly. 'I want you. *This...*' And suddenly he was kissing her with a fervour which sapped the last of her resistance. Her knees sagged and she fell against him as with a low moan he tightened his arms around her, his lips prising hers open with effortless mastery.

It was a frantic, seeking kiss, and for a few seconds Laura gave herself up to it completely. She felt the lick of his tongue exploring hers, the sweet pressure of his mouth as it seemed to plunder deeper and deeper within her mouth—until she felt as if he had stripped her bare with his kiss. Suddenly she was vulnerable. Too vulnerable.

She could feel her breasts begin to prickle as they pushed against the hard wall of his chest, and an unbearable aching clamoured at the fork of her thighs. She wanted him to lift her skirt up. She wanted him to touch her. She wanted...

Had she silently transmitted those wishes to Constantine? Because suddenly he was making them all come true. His hand was impatiently rucking up the cotton of her sundress and splaying with indolent possession over the cool silk of her inner thigh.

'Constantine,' she moaned into his mouth, and the sound seemed to incite him.

'Ah, *ne, ne,*' he breathed, as he deepened the kiss, moving his fingertips upwards so that they scorched their way over the moist fabric of her panties and he felt her buck beneath him. Would there be time? he wondered distractedly as his hand moved down to his belt.

Through the hot heat of a fierce sexual hunger which seemed ready to consume her Laura felt the sudden tension in his body, and became graphically aware of his growing hardness. And with a certainty born of instinct rather than experience she saw just where all this was leading. Was that the rasping of a zip she could hear? With a stifled cry of horror and recrimination she tore her lips away and pushed helplessly at the solid wall of his chest, but her head dipped against it for support.

'We…we mustn't,' she breathed against his racing heart. 'You know we mustn't.'

Constantine caught his breath before disengaging himself, propelling her away from him as if she had suddenly become poison in his arms. He turned away to adjust his trousers even as hot, sexual hunger coursed round his veins, and it was a moment or two until he had composed himself enough to face her.

And in a way he knew she was right to stop things before they went too far, but—damn her—he didn't *want* her to be right! Especially when she was so turned on and struggling to control her breath. *He* was the one who always controlled the situation, and women the ones who clung to him like limpets as they waited for his command. The whole encounter had lasted only a couple of minutes but fierce frustration made him turn on her.

'Do you always conduct yourself in such a way?' he accused hotly. 'Using your eyes to beg silently for a man to *take you* when your son is just along the corridor? How many times has he witnessed his mother in an intimate embrace with a man, Laura—tell me that? How many?'

Laura's mouth opened in an 'oh' of protest. 'Never,' she breathed fiercely, shaking her head so that her hair flew round it like a cloud. 'Never, ever.'

'A woman who turns on as quickly as you do? I don't believe you,' he said with soft scorn.

'Don't you? Well, that's your problem, not mine, Constantine—you can believe what you damned well like!' Injustice bubbled up in her blood to replace the aching fires of frustration. Why should he apportion blame solely to *her*? Smoothing her hands down over her heated cheeks, she stared at him. 'You had nothing to do with what just happened, of course—you were just standing there like an innocent while I threw myself at you.'

'I wouldn't advise that you go down the accusation path,' he drawled arrogantly. 'Because when a woman has sent out the unmistakable message that she wants a man to make love to her then I'm afraid that nature has programmed that man to follow through.'

Laura stilled as she stared at him in horror. *Had* she? Her heart began to pound anxiously. Maybe she had—though certainly not consciously—and yet wasn't his reaction to it about as insulting as it was possible to get? As if kissing her had been nothing more than a conditioned response for him, while for her it had been…

What? Her betraying body shivered with sweet memory. What had it been? Like being transported straight to paradise without stopping? Or—even worse—a reactivation of that passionate longing he had awoken in her the very first time she'd looked into his eyes all those years ago? When she'd believed in love at first sight and had cried for months after he'd gone.

But such emotion was completely wasted. *He doesn't like you*, she reminded herself bitterly—*and he certainly doesn't respect you*. For him you're just another willing body in a long line of willing bodies who have been welcoming him into their arms all his life.

Once she had been blinded by youth and inexperience and his sheer charisma, and she had willingly fallen into bed with him. But now things were different. She had too much to lose to risk throwing it all away on some feel-good sex which would leave her physically satisfied but emotionally bereft. Sex which he might use against her to paint a black picture of her morals. Or which might prejudice her attempts to have a reasonable relationship with him for the sake of his son.

'Shall we just put it down to experience and make sure it doesn't happen again?' she questioned unsteadily.

Black eyes mocked her. 'You think it's that easy? That desire is like a tap you can just turn on and off at will?'

'I think you can try.'

'But I don't want to try,' he said softly. 'And what is more I don't intend to.'

Their eyes met in a silent battle of wills, and Laura felt her mouth dry, hating the fact that his thinly veiled threat thrilled her instead of shocking her. 'I think that…that you'd better leave now while I freshen up and then help get Alex properly unpacked,' she said. But she couldn't help noticing the pulse which beat so frantically at his throat as his gaze continued to rake over her in a look of unashamed sexual hunger.

Laura swallowed as she turned away and walked over to the window, blind to the beauty of the sapphire sea and cerulean sky outside, suddenly realising how difficult this whole situation was going to be. But you're here as his *employee*, she reminded herself. So why not remind him of that? Put some space and some barriers between the two of you. Remind yourself that you are most certainly not equals.

She turned round and fixed the kind of smile to her lips which she gave to the Milmouth office workers when they came into the shop for their lunchtime sandwich. 'So…what happens next in terms of me starting work?'

Constantine gave a slow smile. He knew exactly what she

was doing—but he recognised that it was a kind of game she was playing. So let her be confronted by the reality of waiting on him and see how she liked *that!* 'Tonight you and Alex will eat with Demetra, and she will familiarise you with our customs. She will tell you what she expects from you and answer any questions you might have,'

'You mean…you…won't be there?' questioned Laura tentatively.

'No, *agape mou*,' he said softly. 'I'm going out.'

'Out?' she echoed, aware that she sounded crestfallen. And *possessive*?

'Indeed I am.' His black eyes glittered. 'As your new husband I should not, of course, have dreamt of abandoning you on your first evening. But this was the choice you made, Laura—and you must live with the consequences even if they are not to your liking.'

'At least I can live with my conscience,' she said tightly.

'Well, bravo for you!' he mocked, as he finished tucking in his silk shirt. 'And tomorrow Alex will join me and my father for lunch. The child will meet his grandfather for the first time.'

'That's good.' Laura stared at him, suddenly aware of just how little she really knew about him. 'And…your mother?'

There was an infinitesimal pause before he spoke. 'My mother died many years ago,' he said.

'Oh, I'm sorry,' said Laura, interpreting his flat tone as grief, knowing from her own experience that the dead must always be acknowledged, even if the subject sometimes made you feel miserable. 'What happened?' she questioned gently.

'She died of pneumonia a long time ago,' he said, his face stony. 'But my family history need not concern you, Laura.'

'It's Alex's family history, too,' she reminded him, taken aback by the sudden venom in his tone.

'Then I will discuss such matters with Alex,' he said. 'And it's pointless looking at me with those wounded grey eyes—because as my wife you could have legitimately shared such discussions. As it is there are plenty of other things to occupy you. So why don't you run along and speak to Demetra.'

He paused deliberately, enjoying seeing the flush of colour to her cheeks, wanting to rub in the subservience she had insisted on. Wanting to wound her as she had somehow wounded him, though he couldn't for the life of him work out how. 'And then prepare to wait on my table,' he finished cuttingly.

CHAPTER EIGHT

LAURA awoke to that confusing sensation of being in a strange room and not realising quite where she was—until she saw the stripes of bright sunlight shafting in through the bottom of the shutters and felt unaccustomed warm air wafting her body. She was in Greece—on the Karantinos island—and all night long she'd dreamt of Constantine, remembering the coldness in his voice when she'd tried to ask him about his mother, his dismissing her and her questions with a crisp arrogance clearly intended to drive home her reduced status in his household.

Some time during the night she must have kicked off the crisp cotton sheet, and now she was lying sprawled and exposed in a little nightdress which had ridden up over her hips during her very restless sleep. Which was surprising, given how tired she'd been following a delicious supper eaten with Demetra and her son in the cosy informality of the large kitchen.

Afterwards she and Alex had gone for a walk around the vast estate, with Demetra's son, Stavros, acting as their guide. The young Greek student had pointed out all the bright constellations in the night sky and Alex had had the time of his life as a brand-new world of astronomy had opened up for him.

And then Laura sat bolt upright in bed. Alex! She hadn't heard a peep out of him all night—when she'd tucked him and Blue Bear up in bed he'd barely been able to murmur goodnight before he was out for the count. What if he'd had nightmares? Got up and gone looking for her? Or wanted a drink and found himself lost in this vast and unknown house?

Grabbing her matching wrap, she hurried from her room and burst into Alex's room—to find it completely empty. 'Alex!' she gasped.

'He's outside,' came a voice from behind her, and she whirled around to find Constantine standing in the doorway of the room—an unfathomable look on his face as he studied her.

Aware that her hair was unbrushed and her eyes still full of sleep, Laura blinked. 'Outside where?'

'By the pool—with Demetra's son.'

'You mean you left my son—'

'*Our* son,' he corrected.

'With someone who's virtually a stranger—by a swimming pool when he *can't even swim that well*!'

'Oh, for heaven's sake—do you really think I would have placed him in any danger? I've known Stavros all his life, and he swims like an eel!' he snapped. 'I've been with them all morning, and apparently you all had dinner together last night. They've been getting along famously. If you hadn't overslept you could have seen that for yourself.' His expression darkened. 'What I want to know is why he can't damned well swim in the first place?'

'Because...'

'Because *what*, Laura?' he queried archly.

'Because—' Oh, what was the point in hiding anything from him? 'Well, the lessons were expensive...' Her voice tailed away as she realised he was looking at her in disbelief.

'Expensive?' he repeated incredulously.

She thought he sounded as if he were trying out a new and unknown word. But how *could* he understand what it was like to have to make every penny count when he had spent a life with an abundance of wealth?

'He has football coaching at the weekends instead,' she justified. 'And I couldn't afford everything.'

'So here we have my son, the pauper,' he said bitterly. 'A Karantinos heir living on the breadline!'

Laura swallowed, suddenly realising how exhausted he looked—as if he hadn't had a wink of sleep all night. His black eyes were hooded and tired, and the dark shadow at his jaw suggested that he might not yet have shaved. The expensively dressed Greek billionaire was a world away from this barefoot and elemental-looking man in faded jeans and T-shirt who stood in front of her.

It seemed all too disturbingly intimate and familiar—a glimpse of the old Constantine—and Laura shrank back, suddenly and dangerously aware of his proximity and the fact that while he was fully dressed she was wearing very little. Nothing but a very short wrap over an equally short night-dress that barely came to the middle of her bare thigh. And from the sudden tightening of his features the realisation had begun to dawn on him at precisely the same moment.

Without another word, Laura turned and walked out of the room and back along the corridor to her own—but to her horror and shameful excitement, she realised that Constantine was right behind her.

'No,' she whispered ineffectively, as he shut the door behind him and she felt his warm breath on her neck.

'Oh, yes,' he said grimly, turning her round as if she were a mannequin in a store window. 'You should not walk around the house half-naked if you don't want this particular outcome—nor make big eyes at me and allow your body to tremble with such obvious hunger whenever you come near me.'

Afterwards, she'd try to tell herself that she had done everything to resist him—but that would be a complete lie. She did nothing. Nothing but stare up at him, her parched lips parting with unashamed yearning, a tiny little whimper of desire escaping from them as he moved closer still. And then it was too late. His kiss was like dynamite, his touch the fire which made it combust—and Laura went up in flames.

'*Oh*,' she moaned, clawing at his shoulders as he caught her by the waist and brought her up hard against the aroused cradle of his desire, so that she could feel the shockingly unfamiliar hard ridge of him pressing up against her through his jeans.

With an uncharacteristic disregard for foreplay, he slid up her nightdress and this time found her bare and ready for him, giving a little groan of delight as he tangled his fingers in her hair and then greedily delved inside her honeyed moistness as she gasped out her fevered response. He closed his eyes helplessly as she swayed against him, her hips moving with sudden instinct against his fingers.

Laura clung to him, her love-starved body hungry for his kiss and for everything else she knew he could give her.

His fingers were moving purposefully between her legs now, and he was driving his mouth down on hers in a kiss which quite literally took her breath away—a kiss she never wanted to end.

And then she felt a change taking place in her body; the rhythm of his fingers was changing pace—quickening against her blossoming heat. She felt the wild beat of her heart—the momentary lull before she tumbled over—her body spasming helplessly against his hand, his kiss silencing her little gasps of fulfilment as she slumped weakly against him until the last of her orgasm died away.

'Constantine,' she breathed eventually, her cheeks flushed and her heart beating fast. 'Oh, Constantine.'

'I want you,' he whispered fiercely into her ear. He guided her hand to lie over the achingly hard ridge in his jeans. 'Feel how much I want you.'

And she wanted him, too. But it was broad daylight in the middle of the morning, and she had responsibilities which were far more urgent that the siren call of her body. 'N-Not now…' The words stumbled out of her mouth. 'A-And not here. We can't. You know we can't.'

Through the dark, erotic mists of his desire came her unsteady voice of reason. At first he tried to ignore it—but something at its very heart made Constantine still and pull his lips away from hers, to stare down into the flushed confusion of her face, the tumbled gold of her unbrushed hair.

His heart was thundering so powerfully he could barely think, let alone speak. 'You think that it is right to deny me pleasure now that you have taken your own? Is that right?'

Dumbly, she shook her head.

Fuelled by a savage wave of frustration, he felt the slow

flare of anger begin to burn. 'You think you can keep tantalising me and that I will be like a tame puppy who will just keep trotting behind you and taking whatever it is that you dish out to me? Letting you turn me down, time and time again—so that I can't sleep at night for thinking about your pale, curved body? Taking me so far with your sweet, soft promise and then acting outraged? Is that what men usually let you do, Laura?'

She was too busy catching her breath to rise to the taunt.

'Have you become a *tease*, Laura?' he persisted.

Her lips were trembling, 'No. *No*.'

'Just a woman who promises so much, who lets a man touch her so intimately and then freezes up? If that isn't your definition of a tease, then I'd like to know what is.'

Frustratedly, she shook her head—knowing that he spoke nothing but the truth. She was acting like a naïve little virgin around him, when they both knew she was anything but. The kind of woman who would let a man only go so far... Was that because she thought that her continued resistance to full-on sex might make him respect her? When just one look at the contemptuous mask of his features proved that respect was the very last thing he was feeling?

And what of her *own* desires? Hadn't she been living like a nun for the past eight years? Though it had not felt like denial because no one had moved her to passion. But Constantine had. Constantine still did. It was all there for the taking if only she could accept that it would just be no-strings sex.

'I'm not saying I don't want you—how could I when I've just proved the very opposite?' she whispered. 'Just not now and not here—when Alex might come back from the pool and start looking for me.'

His unyielding expression did not alter. 'So, when?'

Laura could have wept. How matter-of-fact he sounded. It had taken a lot for her to say that, and yet it was as if the significance of her declaration was irrelevant and all he wanted was to pin her down to a time and a place. Her breath came out in a shuddering sigh, but she knew that she couldn't back out of it now, even if she wanted to.

'Come to me tonight,' she whispered. 'Late. When the house is quiet and when I know for sure that Alex is asleep.'

He felt the urgent leap of anticipation at his groin and he stared deep into the storm clouds of her eyes. Taking her slender waist between his hands, he bent his head to graze his lips over hers, feeling her tremble as he did so. Had she learnt somewhere along the way that a woman's most effective weapon was resistance? Was that why she had applied it so effectively, making him desire her with a power which set his blood on fire for her?

And yet with Laura it did not feel like a game she was playing with him in an attempt to ensnare him. This felt real—as if she was fighting herself as well as fighting him.

'I shall spend the whole day thinking about it, *agape mou*,' he murmured. 'Imagining you naked in my arms. Pinned beneath my body as I drive into you over and over again. Yes, I will come to you tonight.' He smiled as he brushed an indolent finger over her trembling lips. 'Now, hurry up and get dressed before I change my mind about waiting.'

With a mounting feeling of disbelief, Laura watched as he left the room, hugging her flimsy little wrap closer to her still flushed and trembling body.

She felt calmer after she'd showered and dressed and pulled on the floral pinafore Demetra had given her to wear. Not the most flattering garment in the world—but that wasn't supposed to be its function, was it?

She stared at her rather drab image in the mirror. It was stupid to feel ashamed of waitressing when it was a job she had done with pride and efficiency during many periods of her adult life. But this felt different, and maybe that was because it *was*. She was going to have to wait on the father of her child and pretend that he meant nothing to her.

Shutting the door quietly behind her, Laura went outside to find Alex splashing around with Stavros in the shallow end of an enormous swimming pool.

'Mum!' he yelled. 'Look! Stavros is teaching me breaststroke!'

Laura smiled as the seal-dark wet head of the student emerged from the water. 'Thank you, Stavros.'

The student grinned as he gestured for Alex to come forward. 'I like to teach, and he shows promise. Young children learn quickly. Come, Alex, show your mama what you can do.'

Alex doggy-paddled over to the edge of the pool and stared up at her, and Laura's heart turned over as she saw the look of pure joy on his little face. 'Don't get tired, will you, darling?' she said.

'*Mum*!'

'Did you have breakfast?'

'Yes, I had it with Constantine.' Alex grinned. 'We had yoghurt—with *honey*! And Constantine and me went and picked oranges from the tree and then we squeezed them!'

She gazed down at him, thinking how easily her son

had slotted into life here—already. *And* how easily he seemed to be slotting into a relationship with Constantine, too. Why, he must have felt as if he had landed in heaven with all the space and beauty which surrounded him

The dark flicker of fear invaded her heart once more. Fear that Alex might just fall in love with Greece and the powerful man who had fathered him—and might not want to return with her to their grey and penny-pinching life back in England…

'Lovely, darling,' she managed to say. 'Well, I'm supposed to be working, so I'd better go and see what Demetra wants me to do.'

Laura made her way to the kitchen to find Demetra, who seemed to have assumed the role of mother hen. First she insisted that Laura sit outside and eat some bread and honey, and drink some of the thick, strong coffee.

'You are too thin,' Demetra commented as she pushed a bowl of bread towards her. 'A woman needs her strength.'

Tell me about it, thought Laura wryly, as she sliced a peach into gleaming rose-tinged slices. But mental strength was surely just as important as the physical kind—and you couldn't build *that* up with bread and honey! But she felt oddly moved by the older woman's kindness—because it had been so long since someone had fussed over her like this.

And at least working was therapeutic—it was hard to stay troubled when your fingers were busy chopping salads and stuffing vine leaves. Demetra showed her how to make a sweet pastry dish which was soaked in lemon syrup after baking—as well as a pudding studded with nuts and raisins and flavoured with cinnamon and cloves.

Laura leaned back against the range. 'Where did you learn how to cook like this, Demetra?'

'Oh, I have cooked all my life,' answered Demetra simply. 'First for my husband and then for my living. You see, I was widowed when Stavros was just a baby, and so I came here to work for the Karantinos family. They have been good to me. And Kyrios Constantine is a good man,' she added fiercely. 'He used to fish with my husband—and when he died he put Stavros through school and university and made sure the boy wanted for nothing.'

The housekeeper's words of praise for Constantine pre-occupied Laura as she began to lay the table on the terrace, beneath a canopy of leaves. But the last thing she needed was to hear praise lavished on him. She wanted to put him out of her mind—at least until tonight.

'Do you know, I could stay here all day watching you do that?' murmured a deep voice from the shadows, and Laura whirled round to find Constantine at the other end of the terrace, his black eyes fixed on her. Clearly fresh from the shower, with tiny droplets of water bejewelling the black hair, he had changed from jeans and T-shirt into dark trousers and a thin silk shirt, and he had shaved, too.

'How long have you been standing there?' she accused, her heart beginning to race with a ridiculous excitement.

He began walking towards her, his progress made slow by an exquisitely painful arousal. 'Long enough to see that delightfully old-fashioned pinafore dress stretched tight over the delectable curve of your bottom,' he murmured. 'Making me want to touch it again, quite urgently.'

Laura sent an agonised glance in the direction of the kitchen, even though the rattle of china told her that

Demetra was not within earshot. 'Constantine, don't. Please. Somebody might hear.'

His black eyes mocked her. 'Ah, Laura! You see how already we are colluding like lovers—even though we are not yet lovers? For that pleasure I must wait—and I am not a man who is used to waiting.'

'No, I can believe that,' she said quietly, holding the tray in front of her as if it were a shield.

He lowered his voice until it was nothing but a silken caress which whispered over her skin. 'Do you know that I feel as a man in prison must feel, ticking off the seconds and the minutes and the hours?'

Laura swallowed. 'Constantine—'

'So that the whole day seems stretched out in front of me like a piece of elastic,' he continued inexorably. 'Which is tightening unbearably—tighter and tighter— until the time when it snaps and I can once more feel your lips on mine and your honeyed heat as it welcomes me into your body.'

'Stop it,' she whispered as the siren song of desire began a slow pulsing through her veins 'Please, stop it. Or how will I compose myself in front of the others?'

'You didn't think through the potential problems of making such an erotic date with destiny, did you?' he taunted.

She hadn't counted on being on such an erotic knife-edge, no. 'Do you think your father's going to ask me anything?'

'If he does, then just answer his questions truthfully,' he said, his whole mood suddenly sobering. 'If you think you can manage that.'

'You're…making it sound as if you think I'm a liar,' said Laura unsteadily, trying to read his expression—but it would have been easier to have sought some sort of meaning from a statue.

Constantine shook his head. 'I haven't quite decided what you are,' he said softly. 'Or just what your agenda is.'

Her heart slammed against her ribcage. 'Who says I have an agenda?'

'Women always do—it's in their genetic make-up.'

'You're a cynic, Constantine.'

'No, *agape mou*,' he contradicted softly. 'I am simply a very rich man who has seen female ambition in its every form. And you—of all women—have the opportunity to try to take me for everything you can get your hands on.'

'You think that I'd do that?' she demanded breathlessly.

'I told you—I haven't made up my mind yet,' he returned.

And yet Laura had confounded every one of his expectations of her. Her refusal to marry him and her stubborn insistence on coming here to work instead had left him feeling unsettled. After a lifetime spent dodging matrimonial commitment to some of the world's most eligible women, he had assumed that this humble waitress would leap at the chance of being a rich man's wife—yet she had done the very opposite. So was she simply being devious, or principled?

'Now—if you'll excuse me—I have some business calls I need to make before lunch.' His eyes glittered with erotic intent. 'And roll on midnight, my stormy-eyed little temptress, so that we can at last finish off what we've started.'

For a moment after he'd gone Laura stood rooted to the spot—unable to believe how a man could switch so quickly from desire to distrust and then back to desire again. She finished laying the table for lunch, and then went to help Alex get ready.

'Is Constantine's daddy very old?' he wanted to know, as he wriggled into a brand-new T-shirt.

'I believe so, darling—and he hasn't been too well recently, so you must be well-behaved.' Surprisingly, Alex let her attempt to tame his dark waves into shape and, stepping back, her eyes shone with maternal pride as she looked at him. 'But I know you will.'

The lunch table looked beautiful—with little pots of purple and white flowers dotted everywhere—and Stavros and Alex sat at their places, waiting until Constantine appeared with his father. Laura watched as they made slow progress across the terrace, the old man leaning heavily on a stick.

He's so *old*, realised Laura suddenly. Why, he must be in his mid-eighties. Which meant that he... She frowned as she worked out what age he'd have been when Constantine was born. Fifty, at least. Had his wife also been elderly? she wondered. Was that why she'd succumbed to a bout of pneumonia?

Kyrios Karantinos was, as Constantine had said, very frail—but it was easy to see how handsome he must once have been. He had the most amazing bone structure, and Laura found herself wondering with a pang whether Alex would look a little like this when he was an old man. Whether Constantine would.

And whether she would still be around to see it.

The faded eyes looked her up and down as he waved Constantine away and looked at Laura. Was it wrong to play the part of being some kind of waitress in this elderly man's house? she wondered, as a sudden pang of guilt washed over her. But it *wasn't* a part, was it? She *was* a waitress. This was far more honest than turning up here as

Constantine's new bride, married to a man who seemed to alternate between despising and desiring her—now, that really *would* have been a living lie. And one that any father would surely veto.

Nervously, Laura smoothed down the front of her pinafore dress. 'I'm very pleased to meet you, Kyrios Karantinos,' she said.

'My son tells me that you met in England?'

'Yes, sir.'

'And that you persuaded him to let you come and work here for the summer?'

'That's right. It seemed a great opportunity to give my son a holiday.'

There was a momentary pause before he gestured towards the curly-haired little boy in his new shorts and T-shirt. 'And this is your little boy?'

'Yes, this is Alex.'

The faded eyes were now turned in the direction of the child, and for a moment Laura thought that she saw them narrow. But the moment passed, and slowly he sat down and began asking Alex about his morning. To Laura's delight and pride her son began to chatter away. He began to tell the old man about his swimming lesson, and she longed to stay and listen, but Constantine was raising his hand to get her attention.

Her cheeks burned as she met the mocking look in his black eyes and registered the arrogant tone in his voice as he clipped out an order for wine. He's enjoying this, she thought to herself suddenly as she hurried out towards the kitchen. He's enjoying rubbing in my subservient status.

She tried to tell herself not to be affected by Constantine's sardonic scorn, but that was easier said than done. When he gestured arrogantly for the bread basket she found herself wanting to hurl its contents at his hateful head. Or to tip the cool yoghurt and cucumber dish of *tzatziki* all over his lap.

In fact, she was so busy keeping everyone's glasses filled and bringing out dish after dish that Laura had no real opportunity to take in what was going on—much as she longed to listen to what Alex was saying to his grandfather, or to see whether the old man showed any sign of guessing who the little boy really was. And it felt peculiar to be serving her own son his lunch in the guise of a waitress.

Never had she felt more of an outsider than she did during that seemingly endless meal—it was as if she was an observer, watching a play unfold before her. As if she had no real place anywhere.

And wasn't there a rather frozen lack of communication between Constantine and his own father? As if the two men tolerated each other rather than loving one another? Is that the kind of role model Constantine is planning to provide for Alex? she wondered, feeling suddenly fearful. That of emotional containment?

But at least Alex himself seemed to have come into his own, blossoming in a way she had never seen him doing before. He was lapping up all the attention, she realised. From Constantine, from his father, and from young Stavros, too. *Because he wasn't used to the company of men.* For the first time she could see how limiting his life must be, living with two women in a cramped apartment above a village shop.

And all the time she was aware of Constantine watching the scene too, his shuttered black eyes hidden behind the dark lashes, his gaze drifting to the animated features of the little boy. Had he sat at that very table and chattered away like that when he was Alex's age? she wondered.

She watched as he began to peel an orange for his son, her gaze drawn inexorably to the strong fingers as they pulled away petal-shaped segments of the peel. Shadows fell from the high-angled slash of his cheekbones and the sensual curve of his lips had relaxed into a half-smile. And then he suddenly looked up, and the ebony spotlight of his gaze swept over her, and she found herself flushing as he raised his glass in her direction.

'Can you fetch me some more ice for my water?' he questioned carelessly, and Laura's colour heightened as she nodded and went off to the kitchen in search of some.

He watched her go. Watched the high, tempting curves of her buttocks thrusting against the dowdy clothes, and once again he felt his heart-rate soar. What was it this plain little creature had which made his body ache like this? he asked himself bitterly. Was it because she was the mother of his child? Or because she was the only virgin he had ever bedded? Perhaps his desire for her was stronger than anything he had ever known simply because she had refused him time and time again. More importantly, would this terrible hunger cease once he had possessed her? His lips curved. Of course it would. As if someone like her could hold his attention for more than one night!

Laura returned, carrying the ice, and bent to put some in his glass, temptingly aware of the tantalising warmth of his body and the faint trace of his musky scent. Was he silently laughing at the image she presented as she served him—and when those black eyes swept over her in insolent assessment what did they see? A too-slight woman serving drinks in an unflattering floral pinafore dress? A mother who had willingly put herself in the role of outcast by waiting at her lover's table?

Laura wondered if that was all they saw. Perhaps his gaze was perceptive enough to delve beneath the surface and guess at her feelings of apprehension and vulnerability. Was he feeling quietly triumphant as he anticipated the assignation she had so willingly agreed to tonight—and might he use it against her? *To do what?*

She thought of all the empty promises she had made to herself—that she would not succumb to the overwhelming chemistry which still sizzled between them. That she would protect her heart from pain by not getting close to him in any way.

And then she thought of their midnight assignation, closing her eyes as her body registered an automatic thrill of anticipation—despite the damning quality of the words he had whispered. What had they been? *Ah, yes. To finish off what they'd started.*

Laura bit her lip as she carried out a dish of almonds to the table. Was there any scenario more potentially heartbreaking than the one which lay ahead of her?

CHAPTER NINE

A CRACK of light slanted across the floor as the door opened, and Laura held her breath as she saw the dark and formidable shape of Constantine standing silhouetted there. If he thought she was sleeping, would he creep away again? she wondered. Would he remember that she had been working and perhaps might need her rest? Spare her this sensual ordeal which she suspected might open the door to a terrible kind of heartache? And yet her heart was pounding so hard that she was certain he must be able to hear its frantic beat.

A low laugh beside the bed put paid to her half-hearted hopes. 'Surely you don't expect me to believe you are asleep do you, *ghlikos mou*?' he questioned softly.

She heard the rasp of a zip, and then the soft thump of something slithering to the ground—presumably his jeans—before a rush of air to her skin as he peeled the sheet away from her body and climbed into bed. Laura trembled as she felt that first contact with his warm, muscular flesh.

'You're...*naked*,' she breathed.

'What did you expect?' With comfortable assurance he hooked his arms around her and drew her close, the glitter of his eyes discernible in the moonlight, his breath warm on her face. 'Ah…perhaps you wanted to watch me strip?'

'I….' His easy provocation left her feeling cheated and out of her depth. *He does this kind of thing all the time,* she reminded herself—*and he has no idea that it's been eight long years since you slept with a man. This man.* Had she mistakenly hoped that there might be some kind of wooing, and that he might be gentle with her? Perhaps taking her tenderly in his arms and tossing her a few compliments, before beginning a slow lovemaking? Was she *crazy*?

'Meanwhile, you…are most definitely *not* naked,' he murmured, as he skated his hand down over one cotton-covered hip, and she heard the faint deprecation in his voice. 'Shame on you, Laura—I cannot believe you always wear something this unflattering in bed when you make an assignation with your lover.'

She guessed that now was not the time to tell him that this was her first such assignation. But she realised that Constantine hadn't been expecting a reply—his question had merely been the precursor to skimming the nightie up and over her head, and tossing it over the side of the bed like a flag of surrender. She shivered as her nakedness was revealed.

'Cold?' he murmured, as his lips found the line of her jaw and began to whisper along its curve.

'N-no.'

'Surely not scared?'

Scared? She was *terrified*—because didn't sex play havoc with a woman's emotions? And weren't hers already see-sawing their way towards chaos and a terrible feeling of vulnerability? But she shook her head, unwilling to admit to fear or doubt or anything else which might put her at even more of a disadvantage in his arms.

'Good.' He lifted his hand to smooth some of the fine mass of pale hair away from her face. 'You see, you have made me wait too long for this, Laura. Much too long…longer than any other woman would have dared or been able to. You have driven me half mad with temptation—do you realise that?' His voice was unsteady as he drove his mouth down on hers with a hunger so fierce that it made his body shudder, and her hands reached up to cling to him so that even his taunting words about other women were forgotten beneath the power of his kiss.

Constantine groaned as her lips opened eagerly to welcome him and he felt the softness of her breasts. His fingers skimmed her body, reacquainting themselves with all its curves and secret places, luxuriating in the soft, silken feel of her skin—and he groaned again.

He had found the delay before getting into her bed almost unendurable—their snatched and teasing foreplay something he had not experienced since he was a teenager—and it had been compounded by the fact that she was the mother of his child. For once his feelings were less than straightforward—she had captured his imagination as well as his desire. But in the sweetness of the moment all that was forgotten, and now she was so compliant beneath his embrace that Constantine knew this was all going to happen very quickly. Too quickly.

And perhaps Laura sensed it too, because she suddenly pulled away from him, her eyes huge in her face.

'Contraception?' she whispered.

'You?'

'I don't…have anything.'

Swearing softly in Greek, he reached blindly for the jeans he'd left on the floor until he found a condom. Gingerly he slid it on, and then pulled her soft body back into his arms. 'Let's hope it's a little more reliable than last time,' he drawled.

Laura stiffened as the impact of his words hit home, and half tried to pull away from him. 'That's a hateful thing to say.'

'You want to hide from the truth? Is that it?'

'I think there's a time and a place for everything—and that remark was wrong on just about every level.'

He gave a brief half-smile. 'You dare to scold me, *ghlikos mou*?' Before she could answer, he tipped her chin upwards and stared down at her with erotic intent. 'But then you dare to do many things which surprise me, Laura. Now, where was I? Was it here?' He lowered his head until his mouth found the lobe of her ear and whispered over its plump little oval. 'Or here?' His lips moved to hers, felt them tremble, and that involuntary little shudder moved him more than it should have done.

He kissed silent her little cries, his greedy fingers exploring her body with a thoroughness which left her gasping—finding her most vulnerable places and tantalising her until he felt her squirm with impatient longing. And her fervour filled him with a strange kind of disquiet, even while it set his senses on fire. 'Are you always this eager?' he murmured.

'Are you?' she parried.

No, he thought suddenly. No, he was not—but then this was the only woman who had had his child grow within her body. 'That doesn't answer my question,' he said unevenly.

No, it didn't—and while Laura knew that there was no earthly reason why she should respond, instinct told her that her answer would please him. And why not please him when he was in her arms and in her bed and soon to be in her body?

'I am only this eager with you,' she said, her voice dipping a little with sexual shyness. 'For you are the only lover I have ever known.'

There was a moment of disbelief while he sucked in a ragged breath, and suddenly the power of that thought made him feel momentarily weak—or as weak as Constantine was ever capable of being. 'The *only* one?' he demanded.

'Yes. And now will you please shut up about it? Or you'll give me a complex.'

He groaned as she kissed him back, boldly tracing her soft and seeking lips over every inch of his body, and then he gave a low laugh as he took her soft breast in his hand and stroked it.

He held back until he could hold back no longer, and then he touched her once again between the sweet haven of her thighs and felt her quiver with pleasure. Tearing his lips away from hers, he stared down into her face for an infinitesimal moment before—with one long, delicious stroke—he filled her and let out a long moan of pleasure.

The feel of him inside her again after so long was a sweet shock—but Laura barely had time to accommodate him, or to savour the sensation of Constantine moving within her, thrusting deep into her body and deep into her heart. Because all too quickly she was spiralling once more towards that dizzy destination he'd led her to that very afternoon, when he had brought her to orgasm with his fingers. But this was something else. This was the real thing. *He* was the real thing. Her heart gave a sudden lurch in time with her limbs.

'Oh, *Constantine*,' she cried, and she felt tears spilling from beneath her eyelids. '*Constantine!*'

Smothering her little gasps with his lips, he felt her bucking uncontrollably beneath him, and the spasming of her body sent his own pleasure hurtling right off the radar. He waited until he could wait no longer—until his orgasm took him under completely, instead of his more usual controlled riding it out, like a wave. And the unexpectedness of that surrender momentarily took his breath away.

Afterwards, he felt as though she had taken something from him, but he wasn't quite sure what. Abruptly he rolled away from her, and lay beside her on the rumpled sheets, staring at the moon-dappled ceiling, waiting for her words—the words that women always said at moments like these, when they were at their weakest. Praise, adoration and undying love—Constantine had heard them all in his time. Words which were his due and yet words he often scorned because of their transparent predictability. Yet Laura said nothing.

He turned his head to look at her—she was lying perfectly still, with her eyes closed and her pale hair spread out like a fine cloud across the pillow. She was so still she might almost have been sleeping—the fading gleam of tears drying on her heated cheeks the only clue as to what had just taken place. She must have sensed that his gaze was on her, yet still she did not open her eyes and look at him.

Which made the next step easy, didn't it? An early exit

from her bed—which was what he had planned on making all along. Besides, he preferred sleeping on his own once his passion had been spent, and the cloying emotions of waking up with a woman always left him cold. So why the hell was he lying here in a state of indolent bliss, heavy-limbed and unwilling to stir?

For a moment Laura didn't move, couldn't think—her equilibrium thrown off kilter by what had just happened between them. She found herself biting back inappropriate words—telling him that sex with him was one of the most glorious things which had ever happened to her, and so was he. Telling him that she had been a rash and stupid fool to have turned down his offer of marriage and please could she reconsider? But as her shattered senses returned to something approaching normality she knew she had to put some distance between them in order to protect herself.

Because sex could make you feel too close to a man—it could make you start concocting all kinds of emotional fantasies about that man. And hadn't she just been doing exactly that? Imagining herself half way in love with him? She should never forget that the man in question had a heart of stone—why, he'd moved as far away from her as possible as soon as their bodies had stilled. And hadn't he made this 'assignation' of theirs sound completely unemotional—mechanical, even? Well, then, pride should make her do the same.

'I think…I think that perhaps you'd better go now,' she suggested huskily.

Constantine, who had been mentally preparing himself to do exactly that, stilled. '*Go*?' he echoed in soft disbelief.

She risked opening her eyes then, and wished she

hadn't—for in the bright moonlight Constantine lay on the bed like a beautiful dark statue, with the rumpled sheet which lay carelessly over one narrow hip only just covering his manhood.

Laura swallowed. 'Well, yes. I mean…Alex might come in early and I don't… Well, I don't want him to find us in bed together.'

'How very admirable of you, Laura,' he murmured, but inside his feelings were at war. He felt anger that she—*she*—should be the one to eject Constantine Karantinos from her bed—and yet this went hand in hand with an undeniable and fierce approval that she should demonstrate such sound morality around his impressionable young son.

He pushed the sheet back from his inconveniently hardening body and watched the way that her nipples were peaking in response. He saw the movement of her throat as she swallowed down her desire, and the way her eyes were now drawn irresistibly to his groin. 'Though if you continue to lie there looking at me like that, then I might just change my mind,' he said thickly.

The statement—or was it a question?—hung on the air as she saw the sudden tension return to his body, and Laura's tongue snaked around her lips, her thighs parting by a fraction as she shifted uncomfortably on the bed.

Constantine rolled over. Kissed her nipple. Heard her gasp as he stroked between her legs and then slicked on a condom. Suddenly she was urging him inside her, and it seemed like only seconds before she felt her spasming helplessly around him and he followed her almost immediately, his mouth pressed against her shoulder as he bit out his fulfilment. But he withdrew from her as soon as the last sweet wave shuddered away, moving from the bed with an elegant grace as he began to pull on his clothes.

'Constantine—'

Zipping up his jeans, he looked down at the flushed and startled expression on her face. 'Mmm?'

'Maybe...' Her voice was tentative. 'Maybe I might change my mind this time. About you staying. As long as you leave early.'

Although he was now on the much more familiar ground of a woman trying to inveigle him back into her bed, Constantine narrowed his eyes with a slowly smouldering anger. Did she really think he was the kind of man who would pander to her whims—the kind of man to be played with as a kitten played with a mouse? Wasn't she in danger of over-estimating her appeal to him?

His mouth twisted. 'I don't think so, *agape mou*. Alex is asleep down the hall—and until he knows that I am his father, then I don't think it's a good idea if he finds me in your bed, do you? Sweet dreams,' he said softly, and turned and left the room without another word.

For a moment Laura just lay there, watching the door close behind him, her body still glowing with the aftermath of pleasure but her heart aching with a terrible kind of pain. Had she mistakenly thought that sex might bring about some sort of closure? Maybe give her some guidance about how she was going to extricate herself and Alex from this situation while causing the least amount of hurt all round?

If so, then she had been hugely mistaken. Because behind all the passion she had felt Constantine's bitterness, and the knowledge that it could take her to a dark, dark place.

She must have drifted off to sleep, because when she opened her eyes she was surprised to find it was six o'clock. The house was still silent and for a moment she lay there, reliving the night before and its horribly unsatisfactory ending. She showered and dressed, and spent ten minutes tugging the rumpled bed back into some sort of order before going to the other end of the corridor and poking her head around Alex's door.

He was fast asleep, his dark lashes feathering down into two sooty arcs, the faint colour to his skin an indication that he had been playing in the sunshine. He looked really contented, she thought with a sudden glow—and her heart felt a little lighter as she went down to the empty kitchen and made herself a coffee.

Taking the cup outside, she went to stand at the top of the stone steps at the end of the garden and stood looking out to sea, where the giant crimson globe of the sun was rising up over the milky horizon. It was such a beautiful place, she thought wistfully—and yet it seemed to have its own shadows and secrets. Though maybe every place on earth did.

Later, she was busy constructing a giant plate of fruit for breakfast, while Demetra pounded away at some dough and bemoaned the fact that the village no longer had a bakery, when Laura heard a rapid clicking sound and looked up.

'What's that?' she questioned.

Demetra paused. 'Oh, the helicopter.' She shrugged. 'It will be Kyrios Constantine, going to Athens.'

'To…to *Athens*?' questioned Laura shakily, her heart crashing uncomfortably against her ribcage. She told herself that it was unreasonable of her to expect him to inform her of his movements. But didn't last night's love-making entitle her to the common courtesy of him at least coming to say goodbye? She could see Demetra looking at her curiously, and found herself struggling to say something suitably conventional. What would a casual servant say at such a time? 'Er…the pilot lives on the island, does he?'

'Oh, he needs no pilot,' answered Demetra. 'Kyrios Constantine flies the helicopter himself!'

'And is he…working in Athens?' questioned Laura

'Work, yes—and probably women, too.' Demetra's eyes crinkled conspiratorially. 'Always the women—they flock to Kyrios Constantine like ants around the honeypot.'

The housekeeper's words made her hand jerk, and the fruit knife she was holding inadvertently nicked her thumb. Laura quickly put it down as a small spot of crimson blood welled up and began to drip onto the wooden table.

CHAPTER TEN

'YOU'VE cut your thumb,' observed Constantine softly.

'Oh, it's nothing.'

'Nothing?' he murmured. 'Come here—let me see.'

Laura squirmed as he took the injured digit in his hand and even that innocent contact sent her senses spiralling. Earlier that day he had flown back, after spending three nights in Athens, and while she was ridiculously pleased to see him she couldn't dispel her terrible aching insecurity and jealousy at the thought of what he might have been doing there.

They were sitting by the edge of the sea, on a beach more beautiful than any beach she could ever have imagined—just her, Alex and Constantine, who had insisted that she and her son both needed to see more of the island, especially as today was officially her day off.

Alex had spent the morning playing with a magnificent sandcastle which his father had constructed while demonstrating a sweet kind of patience which had made Laura's heart turn over with an aching wistfulness. Because it was like glimpsing the sun appearing from behind a thick, dark cloud. This was the Constantine who usually lay hidden behind that formidable exterior—the one he rarely allowed people to see. The side he had shown her all those years ago...the side which had made him all to easy to love—and still did.

They had just eaten salads and cheese for lunch, and now their son was lying in the cool shade of a rock, fast asleep—a cute cotton hat shielding his little face from the occasional sand-fly. It felt strange to be out like a normal family—without her floral pinafore dress and the subtle sense of subservience which she adopted whenever she put it on. And strange too to be in the company of the man she had not seen since he had left her room after that passionate night of lovemaking.

When he had left without a word about why or where he was going, she reminded herself.

'How did you do it?' questioned Constantine as he continued with his mock-examination of her thumb, which was raising her heart-rate significantly.

'I...I cut it on a fruit knife.'

'Clumsy of you, Laura.'

'Yes.' She wanted to tell him not to touch her like that—yet she knew that such words would sound like hysterical nonsense, because to the outside world it would look like nothing more than an innocent assessment of her thumb. But to Laura it felt as if he were trailing sizzling fire where he made contact. As if her nerve-endings became instantly raw and clamouring wherever his fingertips brushed against them.

And yet conversely she wanted him to touch her in a far more inappropriate way altogether. To have him pull her into his arms—to at least give *some* indication that they'd actually been lovers. But of course he did not touch her, and Laura tried to tell herself it was because Alex was nearby.

'So…what were you doing in Athens?' she questioned suddenly, even though she had vowed she would not.

For a moment Constantine didn't answer as he let her hand go, an odd, mocking kind of smile curving the corners of his lips. 'I don't think that's any of your business, do you?'

It was the response of her worst nightmares, and it made all her uncertainties bubble to the surface. Heart pounding with fear, she glanced quickly over at Alex, but he was fast asleep, worn out by the morning and oblivious to the low, urgent tones of his parents. 'Did you go straight from my bed to another's?'

His black eyes sent her a mocking challenge. 'Why? Is that the kind of behaviour you normally indulge in yourself?'

She clenched her hands into tiny fists. 'You know very well that you're the only person I've ever slept with!'

On hearing this for a second time, Constantine felt his heart accelerate into a thundering kind of triumphant beat. He was Greek, and he was pure alpha-male, and he would have been lying if her declaration hadn't thrilled him to every fibre of his being—but he was damned if he would let it show.

'Ah, if only I could say the same, *agape mou*,' he sighed regretfully.

Tears stung her eyes. 'Why do you delight in hurting me?' she demanded, realising too late how vulnerable that made her sound. But Constantine didn't seem to have noticed.

'Don't you think that hurt is an inevitable part of a relationship?' he returned with a shrug. 'Of *all* relationships?'

She disregarded his careless use of the word 'relationship,' because the clue was in the emphasised word and Laura seized on it. 'Is that what happened with you, Constantine? You got hurt?'

'I've seen how women can hurt and manipulate, yes.'

'Girlfriends, you mean?'

'No, not *girlfriends*,' he answered scornfully.

'You mean…your mother?' she guessed, as she remembered the odd, strained look on his face when he'd mentioned her.

He shrugged in affirmation but didn't bother to reply. Hopefully she might take the hint and quit interrogating him.

'What happened?'

Did she never learn when to leave well enough alone— that her probing questions were unwelcome? 'What happened happened a long time ago,' he snapped. 'So forget it.'

Laura leaned a little closer. 'But I don't want to forget it. This is Alex's grandmother we're talking about, and one day he may want to know. Won't you tell me, Constantine? Please?'

What was it about her softly spoken question that sparked a need to reply—*to confide about things he had never told another?* he wondered, raking his dark hair back from his brow in frustration. He was a man who never confided, who was strong for everyone. The buck stopped with Constantine and it had done for many years, but now words came spilling from his lips like a stream of dark poison.

'She was years younger than my father—decades, in fact. A beautiful, fragile beauty who bewitched him—and because he was almost fifty when they married her youth and her beauty hit him like a hurricane. When a man has never known passion until late in life it can take him over like a fever.' He shrugged. 'He neglected everything in pursuit of a love she was ill-equipped to return—but then she was incapable of loving anyone but herself.'

'Even you?' said Laura slowly.

Her question broke into the tumult of his thoughts, but Constantine was in too far to stop now. 'Even me,' he answered, and the admission was like a hammer blow—for was there not something almost shameful about admitting that the most fundamental bond of all, between mother and child, had simply not existed in their case? But the precise side of Constantine's nature meant that he needed to attempt to define it.

'She was one of those people who did not seem to be of this earth—she was too fey and too delicate, and she did not look after herself,' he continued. 'She partied and drank wine instead of eating—smoked cigarettes instead of breathing in the pure Greek air. And when she died her enchantment still did not end—for my father went to pieces. He became one of those men who are obsessed by a ghost and who live in a past which only really exists in their own imagination. It was only when I took over the business properly that I was able to see just how badly he had let things go.'

Laura stared at his hard and beautiful features, transformed now into a mask hardened by pain and memory. So even his father had not been there for him—which explained the lack of closeness between the two men. 'I'm so sorry,' she said simply.

He turned, angry with her, but far angrier with himself for having unleashed some of the dark secrets of his soul. 'I do not want your sympathy,' he snapped.

'But I think that—'

'And neither do I want your advice—no matter how well intentioned! You are a woman from humble circumstances who knows nothing of this life of privilege which you have entered solely because you are the mother of my son! And you would do well to remember your place here!'

Laura reached for her sunglasses and rammed them down over her eyes before he could see the tears which were brimming up behind her lids. *Remember your place here.* How cheap did that make her feel? His words were barely any different from her own thoughts about them occupying different worlds—but, oh, how it hurt to hear them flung at her with such venom. He didn't like women, she realised—and, while it was easy to see why, it wasn't going to change, was it? Nothing *she* said would ever change it.

She saw Alex begin to stir—had their low but angry words wakened him? she wondered guiltily. But her primary feeling was of relief that she would no longer have to endure any more hurt provoked by Constantine's cruel comments. And she would protect herself from further heartache by staying as far away from him as possible.

'I think in view of what's just been said that we should try to avoid each other as much as possible while I'm still here,' she whispered.

Constantine's eyes narrowed. 'Are you *crazy*?' he questioned silkily, and without warning he splayed his hand over the sun-warmed expanse of her thigh, watching with triumph as her lips parted involuntarily in a soundless little gasp of pleasure. He lowered his voice. 'We may as well enjoy the one good, satisfactory thing which men and women *do* give each other. And—just for the record—I've done nothing but work in Athens; there have been no other women.' His black eyes gleamed with predatory anticipation. 'To be perfectly frank, your passion has left me unable to think of any other woman but you, *agape mou*.'

'And should I be flattered by that?' she questioned bitterly.

'I think perhaps you should,' he murmured.

But Laura was already scrambling to her feet and packing up the picnic basket.

'Oh, and Laura?' he said softly.

She looked up, some new steely quality in his voice warning her that what he was about to say would be more than another remark about their sexual chemistry. 'What?'

'I think it's about time we told Alex who I really am, don't you?'

Laura bit her lip. She had known this would happen, and it was happening sooner than she had hoped. But what was the point in delaying any more? Wouldn't that look as if they were hiding something shameful rather than giving them the opportunity to bond? Just because change was disrupting—and just because Laura was afraid of how telling Alex might affect their lives—it didn't mean that she could keep putting it off because it suited *her*.

'And your father?' she said softly. 'He'll need to know, too. Alex shouldn't be expected to keep the news to himself.'

In the end, the moment for telling Alex came quite naturally later that afternoon, when the three of them were sitting in the main town square of Livinos. Alex was eating ice-cream—an elaborate concoction of lemon and chocolate curls—and it seemed that every island resident stopped to ruffle his dark curls as they passed by.

'Why does everyone keep patting my head?' he questioned, not unhappily. 'And what do they keep saying to you?'

'By and large, the Greek people love having children around,' said Constantine, and Laura felt her heart lurch as she thought about his own mother. *But he's told you quite emphatically that he doesn't want your sympathy*, she reminded herself.

'Some of the older ones say that you look very much as I did at the same age,' added Constantine carefully.

'Do I?'

There was a pause. 'Very much so,' said Constantine gruffly, and then he looked across the table at Laura. She nodded. 'Do you have any idea why that might be?'

To Laura's surprise, Alex didn't answer straight away—just glanced from Constantine, to her, and then back to Constantine again. His dark eyes fixed on his father's face, a look of hope and longing tightening his boyish little features.

'Are you my daddy?' he asked.

Had it been the spoonful of ice-cream Alex had insisted on giving him which had caused this damned lump in his throat, making him momentarily incapable of words? Constantine swallowed. 'Yes, I am,' he said eventually.

There was no Hollywood movie scene of the son flinging himself onto his father's lap—that would have been too much in the circumstances. As they began to walk back towards the villa, Laura noticed Alex's fingers creep up towards the hand of the man by his side. And that Constantine took his son's little hand and was clasping it firmly, while looking fixedly ahead and blinking furiously, as if some piece of grit had just flown into his eye.

That evening, Constantine—with Laura standing nervously by his side—told his father that the Karantinos family did indeed have an heir, and that he had a grandson.

The old man stared at his son for a long moment and then gave a short laugh. 'You think I haven't already guessed that?' he questioned quietly. 'That you could bring a young child into this house out of the blue, with some flimsy excuse about him and his mother needing a holiday, a child who is the mirror-image of you at the same age, and that I would not realise that he was yours?'

Laura tried not to stare as she felt emotion build up like a gathering storm. She saw the old man take one tentative step forward, and silently willed the two men to embrace—to try to wipe out some of the heartache and bitterness which had built up between them. But Constantine took a corresponding step backwards—a step so subtle that many people would not have noticed. But Laura noticed. *Damn you, Constantine*, she thought furiously. *Damn you and your hard and unforgiving soul*. And his father noticed, too—for the lined face momentarily crumpled before he turned to look at her and nodded.

'You have a fine child in Alex, my dear. A happy and contented son for you to be proud of.'

'Th-thank you,' said Laura tremulously. 'It may seem odd to you that we kept it secret, but—'

Kyrios Karantinos shook his head. 'I can understand that circumstances may have been difficult,' he said gently. 'For I am not a complete ogre.' This was accompanied by a mocking glance at the silent figure of Constantine. 'Far better to approach things cautiously than to dive in. And Alex—he is happy to learn of the news?'

'He's ecstatic,' said Laura truthfully. As far as Alex was concerned it was *Constantine this* and *Constantine that*. Constantine had quickly become the centre of the impressionable young boy's universe. She'd watched the relationship developing between them and seen how badly her boy wanted a father—a man as a role-model. And Constantine never showed his fierce side with Alex, realised Laura.

'We must have a party to celebrate!' announced Kyrios Karantinos suddenly. 'We could invite some people over from the mainland. It's a long time since we've thrown a big party.'

And, to Laura's surprise, Constantine nodded.

'Why not?' he questioned, with a shrug of his broad shoulders.

Laura turned away before either of them noticed the conflict of emotions she suspected were criss-crossing over her face, knowing that it was wrong to feel scared—but she did.

Despite their differences, the two proud men were gearing themselves up to announce to the world that the Karantinos family now had an heir—and the importance of such an heir to such a family could not be over-estimated. But aside from the bloodline issue there was something else which was just as important…and deep-down Laura hoped that Constantine and his father might be making the first steps towards a true reconciliation.

But where did that leave her? And Alex? She wanted him to forge a close relationship with both his father and his grandfather—of course she did. It was just the future which worried her now. Because how on earth were they going to handle it when she took Alex back to England at the end of the holidays? When he left sunshine and luxury behind him and returned to an old life which was looking greyer by the minute?

CHAPTER ELEVEN

'WHAT the hell are you doing?' demanded Constantine as he walked into the kitchen.

'What does it look like?' questioned Laura steadily, finding herself in the awkward situation of having to pretend to be normal and pleasant to Constantine in a situation which defied definition—made doubly difficult by the fact that she had been writhing passionately underneath the man in question in the early hours of that very morning. Pushing the erotic memory from her mind, she positioned another olive on one of the little feta tartlets, wanting to look at something—anything—other than the mocking distraction of his black eyes.

'Laura, put the damned dish down and look at me!'

Laura complied—knowing that if she didn't want to create discord then she didn't really have a lot of choice. 'What is it?'

'Why…?' He drew a deep breath. 'Why are you helping out in the kitchen?'

'Because we both agreed that would be my role here.'

'No, Laura,' he said heavily. '*You* insisted on it and *I* was railroaded into agreeing.'

'That must have been a first,' she said gravely.

Unwillingly, his mouth twitched. 'Very probably,' he agreed, before the sight of her beautiful body in that hideous-looking floral pinafore made the smile die instantly. 'I don't want you doing any more of this kind of work in the house and neither does my father. It is no longer appropriate. You are Alex's mother—and at the party tonight you will be introduced to the people of Livinos as such, not serving damned pastries to the guests!'

'But won't...?' She could feel her heart racing with nerves. How would the Karantinos family's friends and neighbours accept her—a pale little English waitress—as the mother of the Karantinos heir?

'Won't what?'

'Won't people think it strange? I mean, it's a small island. Everyone's going to want to know why I've been working here and now suddenly I've been revealed as the mystery mother. Why, even Demetra's been dying to ask, but she's so loyal to you and your father that she wouldn't dare.'

'I do not *care* what other people think,' he iced back. 'It is what *I* think that matters.'

'If you knew just how arrogant that sounded—'

His black eyes glittered. 'You didn't seem to be complaining about my arrogance when I ordered you to strip for me last night, *agape mou*. In fact, you told me that you had never been so turned on in your life.'

Laura flushed. Well, no—but characteristics which worked well within the bedroom did not always work in everyday life. 'Oh, very well,' she said quickly, in an effort to change the subject. 'I'll come to the party—if you insist.'

Fleetingly, it struck him as ironic that she—of all

people—should sound as if she were conferring upon him a favour, when just about every other female of his acquaintance would have bitten his hand off for an invitation to what would be an undeniably glittering event.

'You will, of course, need something to wear.'

Laura felt her body stiffen with tension. 'What's the matter with the clothes I brought with me?' she questioned defensively. 'Too small-town and humble for the Karantinos family? Is that it?'

'Frankly, yes,' he drawled, his eyes mocking her as she took an angry step towards him. '*Ne*, just try it,' he murmured. 'Go on, Laura. Jab an angry finger at my chest and we both know what will happen. Except that it won't, because we can't—since Alex is having a chess lesson with my father just along the hall and Demetra is getting half the women in the village to bake bread for her. That is why I'm not able to ravish you here in the kitchen, or by the pool—or anywhere else for that matter.' He paused and he gave the flicker of a smile. 'So maybe you'll lose that indignation when I tell you about the dresses I've bought for you.'

Laura stared at him. 'You've…bought me *dresses*?'

He nodded as he met her uncomprehending look with one of his own. *Didn't* all *women like to be bought beautiful dresses?* he wondered. In his experience, the more money you lavished on a female, the more she adored you for it. 'When I was in Athens I took the opportunity to pick some up. You see, I knew that this kind of situation was bound to arise at some time, and that you'd need to look the part of a Karantinos woman.'

Her heart raced with anger and shame and hurt. Look

the *part*? Because she was playing a role instead of being the real thing? Of course she was—or that would be how Constantine saw it.

The arrogant swine! He had bought her finery with his millions so that she would blend in, had he? Well, for once in her life—she would make sure she did the exact opposite and stand out at his wretched party!

'How very kind of you,' she said, mock-demurely, and saw him frown. 'I'll go and look at them.'

'No. Not now,' he said softly, and caught her wrist, bringing it up to his lips and whispering them against the fine tracery of veins which clothed the thready hammering of her pulse.

Just that brief touch weakened her, and Laura swayed and closed her eyes. 'Don't,' she whispered. 'You've just said yourself that the house is full of people.'

'Which is why we're going for a drive.'

Laura swallowed. 'Alex—'

'Is fine with my father. I've checked. Now, take off that damned pinafore and let's get going.'

Minutes later they were zipping their way along an isolated coastal road in a little silver sports car she hadn't seen before. 'Where exactly,' she questioned, 'are we going?'

'You'll see.'

The wind whipped through her hair and Laura felt ridiculously light-hearted. 'Suddenly you're an international man of mystery?'

'If that's what you'd like me to be,' he declared evenly, but her bright mood had affected him too, and he smiled.

Their destination turned out to be a beautiful stone house set back from the beach—but its simple beauty went unnoticed because they were barely inside the door before Constantine started kissing her and tugging at the zip of her dress.

'Aren't you going to…show me around?' she gasped.

'Aren't you?' he countered, and then closed his eyes as his fingers found her soft breasts. 'Come on, Laura. Show me around your body, *oreos mou*, show me deep inside your body—for that is the only place I want to go right now.'

His erotic words only spurred on Laura's own frantic desire. Half-clothed, they sank onto the marble floor—its cool surface contrasting perfectly with his hot flesh as it covered hers, their gasps morphing into ecstatic shuddered cries which split the silence.

Afterwards, they lay there—both with a fine dew of sweat drying on their skin—and Constantine stroked the mass of blonde hair which clouded her shoulders.

'Hot?'

'Boiling.'

'Fancy a swim?' he questioned idly.

Lazily, she stirred against his body, and yawned. 'I didn't bring a costume.'

Regarding her discarded panties, he splayed his hand possessively over one bare, warm globe of her bottom. 'Who says you'll need one? You can swim naked, my beauty.'

'Providing fodder for any passing voyeurs?' she said primly, even though she shivered beneath his touch and at the blatantly untrue compliment which had sprung from his lips.

Constantine laughed. 'It's utterly private and we won't be observed by a soul,' he said softly. 'That's why I brought us here. To see your body by daylight—for I am tired of having to be furtive. Of having to sneak into your room at night as if we are committing some sort of crime. I want the freedom to cry out when I come, and to watch while you do, too. To watch you walk around unfettered. I want to have sex with you in the sea, Laura,' he said thickly. '*Oreos mou*, I want to have sex with you all day long—until our bodies are exhausted and our appetites sated.'

It wasn't the most romantic declaration she had ever heard, but it echoed Laura's own haunting desire for him. With her body she could show him her passion, even if her heart and her lips were prevented from giving voice to it. You could love a man with your lips in a different way than using them to tell him, she thought. And Constantine was right—the freedom to behave without constraint was completely intoxicating…

The afternoon sun was still bright when they drove back. Laura tried to tell herself that they were too exhausted for much conversation, but it was more than that. Her head was full of spinning thoughts.

Constantine had remained true to his vow that he was going to make love to her until they were both exhausted—she had never known that it was possible for desire to be ignited over and over again. He had made love to her on the beach, and then carried her down to the sea to wash the grains of sand from her skin. But the act of washing had awoken their sensual hunger once more—he had made her gasp and giggle until at last he had pulled her wet body against his and let the sea foam surge deliciously over their nakedness. Slippery and salty, she had let him part her legs beneath the water and felt their warm flesh join once more beneath the waves. And Constantine had been right—the freedom to make love without worrying about being overheard or seen was utterly intoxicating.

She thought about the party which lay ahead, and which until fairly recently would have terrified the life out of her. But that had been before this journey here to Livinos—a journey which had taught her as much about herself as about Greek life.

It had taught her that she loved the man who sat beside her, despite his cold heart which had been so damaged in his own childhood that it seemed to have no hope of healing. She loved him because he was Alex's father—but she suspected that she had loved him all those years ago, when she had given him her virginity so joyfully on that warm summer night. For wasn't love at first sight both the great dream and yet the admittedly rare reality of human relationships? Even if it hadn't been reciprocated it didn't mean it had necessarily gone away—and since she had become his lover that feeling had been growing as inexorably as a new shoot towards the spring sunshine. Hadn't the afternoon they'd just spent added to the magic?

She glanced at his hard and rugged profile as he stared at the coastal road ahead. The wind whipped through the black, tousled curls and the dark glasses shaded his eyes against the light—preventing her from reading anything of his own thoughts.

But who was she kidding? Those ebony eyes never gave anything away. And neither did he. He could buy her new dresses so that she wouldn't disgrace him at his fancy party— but he couldn't give her any of his heart or his soul even if he wanted to. He had locked those away a long time ago.

Back at the villa, they parted without a kiss or embrace— only the briefest of glittering looks from Constantine reminding her of how they'd spent the afternoon.

'I'll see you later,' he said softly, and resolutely turned his back on her before he was tempted to kiss her again.

Laura watched him go. Maybe for him it had just been an afternoon of amazing sex, she thought. He probably wasn't—like her—stupidly reliving every glorious second of it and pretending that it had anything to do with emotion.

It was with heightened colour that she went off to find Alex, who was now playing tennis with Stavros.

He waved his arm at her in greeting, and then adopted a fierce expression on his little face, wanting desperately to show his mother how good he'd become at the game.

How he'd grown to love sport, she thought tenderly. She stood by the side of the tennis court and watched as her son batted the ball over the net with what looked like incredible natural skill to her proud, motherly eye. Alex had been on a journey too, she recognised—he had realised some of his own dormant talents as well as getting to know his Greek family. And deep down she knew that nobody would ever dare bully him again. Laura watched as they changed ends, wondering once again how on earth he would ever be able to bear to leave this paradise of a place to go back to the very different life he knew in England.

She went to her room and showered off the sand, slipping into jeans and a T-shirt before surveying the garments Constantine had bought her, which someone had hung up in her wardrobe while she'd been out at the beach house. And although she'd told herself that she wasn't going to swoon over a few expensive articles of clothing she found herself doing just that.

Finest silk, cashmere and organza were here—represented in gowns which unbelievably fitted her like a glove.

She twirled in front of the mirror in a vivid emerald silk. Though maybe it wasn't unbelievable at all—for wasn't Constantine one of those men who seemed to instinctively know more about a woman's body than she did?

But Laura didn't have a clue about dressing up. She'd never had the time, the money or the opportunity before—and suddenly she found herself longing for advice. Surely she could phone Sarah? She hadn't spoken to her sister for ages, and she missed her. With her artistic streak, Sarah had a brilliant eye and knowledge of clothes—she'd know which of these dresses would be most suitable.

She walked through the house, looking for Constantine, but he was nowhere to be found—only Kyrios Karantinos was in his study, sitting hunched over a book. He looked up as she tapped on the door.

'Looking forward to the party?' he questioned with a smile.

Laura wondered what he'd say if he had any idea of the confused emotions which were swirling around inside her. 'I'm not quite sure what to wear,' she admitted. 'And I wondered if it would be okay to use the telephone to ring my sister in England?' She hesitated, but then thought of the Karantinos billions and her own modest income. 'I've...I've got a cellphone, but it's...'

The old man gave a small smile as he gestured towards the telephone on the desk and began to get up. 'Please— say no more and come in. You must feel free to use the phone whenever you like, my dear.' His smile became a little wider. 'It is quite clear to me that Constantine has not ended up with a materialistic woman!'

She wanted to tell him that Constantine had not 'ended

up' with this woman at all. 'Thank you—but I can go somewhere else to make the call. I don't want to push you out of your own study.'

'I was leaving shortly anyway.' He looked at her. 'I've been wondering what your future plans are?' he questioned, his faded eyes narrowing. 'Or maybe I shouldn't ask?'

Laura hesitated, knowing that she should not confide in Constantine's father—for mightn't Constantine see that as some kind of betrayal? 'No arrangements have been made yet,' she said uncertainly.

'You're good for him,' the old man said suddenly.

'No—'

'*Yes*. Better than anyone else has ever been for him.' A ragged sigh left his lips, as if it had been waiting for a long time to escape, and the old man looked at her with pain in his faded eyes. 'Better than I or his mother ever were, that's for sure.'

'I don't think—'

'I was a *bad* father—a very bad father,' interrupted Kyrios Karantinos fervently. 'I know that. I worshipped his mother—I was one of those foolish men who become obsessed by a woman. She dazzled me with her beauty and her youth so that I couldn't see anything but her.' There was a pause. 'And that kind of love is dangerous. It is blind. It meant that I could not tell the difference between fantasy and reality—and somewhere along the way was a very small and confused boy, cut adrift by the very two people who should have been looking out for him.' He gave a shuddering sigh. 'We both neglected him.'

How her heart ached for that little boy. 'Have you...have you tried to explain all this to Constantine?' she ventured cautiously. 'Tried to tell him how it was? I mean, how…how *sorry* you are now?'

'Oh, maybe a million times,' he admitted. 'But my proud and successful son will only hear what he wants to hear, and he finds the past too painful to revisit. Forgive me, Laura—for I do not mean to speak ill of him. You see…I love him.' His voice trembled. 'And I am an old man.'

She stared at him, suddenly understanding the subtext which lay behind his words. Soon he might die. And then the painful past might never be resolved—instead spreading its poisonous tentacles far into the future.

Briefly, he squeezed her arm and then left the study, and Laura stared out of the window at the beautiful Greek day, her heart almost breaking as she thought about the terrible distance between the two men which might never be bridged.

But she was here with a purpose. And—even if her worries about what to wear seemed rather flippant in comparison to what Kyrios Karantinos had just told her—she gathered together her troubled thoughts before dialling England.

It was strange speaking to her sister—it felt as if a lifetime had passed since they had last spoken—and Sarah was sounding very bubbly. 'The girl Constantine hired to work in the shop is *lovely*!' she enthused, and her voice dipped mischievously. 'And she has this *cousin*…he's called Matthius and he's just *gorgeous*!'

Aware of the rapidly spiralling cost of the call, Laura butted in. 'Sarah, I need your advice about clothes…'

Once Sarah had been given a brief run-down on all the dresses in the picture, she was emphatic. Laura must wear her hair up—'because sometimes when you wash it it goes into a cloud, and you end up looking like Alice in

Wonderland.' And she should opt for the most fitted dress—'because what's the point of having a great figure if you can't show it off?'

That evening, Laura's hands were trembling as she swept an extra layer of mascara onto her lashes. She couldn't ever remember feeling this nervous before a party before—but maybe that wasn't so surprising. She'd overseen Alex getting dressed—Constantine had ensured that his son would be suitably kitted-out, too—and her heart had swelled with pride when she saw her little boy in a pair of long, dark trousers and a white shirt and little bow-tie. He looked so *Greek*, she thought.

But he is Greek. Or at least half-Greek.

Suddenly filled with fear, she stood in front of the mirror, but her head was so buzzing with disquiet that for a moment she did not see the image which reflected back at her. *Alex isn't going to want to leave this place*, she realised with a sinking heart. And could she really blame him?

Her eyes focussed on the mirror at last, and Laura blinked because for a moment it felt as if she was looking at a complete stranger. A sleek and sophisticated stranger with a costly dress and big, dark eyes?

There was a tap at the door and she turned round to see it opening. Constantine was standing there—his dark expression completely unreadable as he looked her up and down.

Nervously, Laura swallowed. 'Do you…do you like it?'

'I'm not sure,' he drawled.

'But you bought it! You're the one who wanted me to wear something grand.'

'*Ne.* I know I did,' he said slowly. He just had not been expecting such a complete…*transformation*. On the model in the showroom—who had flirted with him quite outrageously until his stony indifference had caused her to stop—the dress had looked completely different. But the blue satin moulded Laura's curves so closely that it looked as though she had been dipped in a summer sky. Above the low-cut bodice her skin glowed softly golden, and the curve of her breasts was a perfect swell. Her fine blonde hair was piled high on her head, with just a couple of recalcitrant locks tumbling down by the side of her face like liquid gold.

And her face! She rarely wore much make-up—sometimes nothing and she always looked as sexy as hell—but tonight the unaccustomed darkening of her eyes and the slick of gloss to her lips made her look like a siren. Every man would look at her and want her, thought Constantine—and a nerve flickered furiously at his temple.

'Do you like it?' repeated Laura, half tempted to tear the damned thing off and put on the little floral dress she'd brought with her from England.

'You look very *beautiful*,' said Constantine carefully. Putting his hand in his pocket, he withdrew a slim leather case. 'You'd better have these.'

'What are they?'

He flipped the lid open to reveal a bright scattering of ice-white jewels, and it took Laura's disbelieving eyes a couple of seconds to realise that she was in fact looking at a diamond necklace and a pair of long, glittering earrings.

'I can't wear these,' she breathed.

'Why not?'

'What if I lose one?'

'Don't worry—they're insured,' he said carelessly as he

clipped the exquisite necklace around her neck. 'Put on the earrings, Laura.'

With trembling fingers she complied, and the piled up hairstyle complemented the waterfall earrings brilliantly as she stood before him for his assessment.

'Perfect,' he said softly. 'Now you look like a Karantinos woman.'

But as they walked out together towards the strings of lights which were already twinkling against the darkening sky Laura felt like a prize pony in a show, decked out with unfamiliar ribbons and with its mane plaited.

She was an impostor, she thought. A fraud. Externally she carried all the displays of wealth which would be expected of the mother of Constantine's son. But inside? Inside she felt like a cork from a bottle which was lost on a vast and tossing ocean.

The party had all the elements for a successful evening, and the guests were determined to enjoy the fabled Karantinos hospitality. The weather was perfect, the finest wines flowed, and the village women had outdone themselves with the food. But part of Laura wished that she could hide behind the anonymity of her waitress's uniform instead of being subjected to the curious looks of the women of Livinos and—even more intimidating—of the society beauties who had flown in from Athens. They seemed to have no qualms about failing to hide their surprise when they were introduced to Laura. And neither did they abstain from flirting with Constantine.

Maybe she couldn't blame them, for he drew the eye irresistibly; no other man came even close to him. His hair looked ebony-black when contrasted against the snowy whiteness of his dinner jacket, which emphasised his powerful physique. And Alex stayed close by his side as Laura heard him being introduced over and over again as 'my son'.

My son, too she thought bitterly, ashamed of the great flood of primitive jealousy and fear which washed over her.

Because one look around at all the good and the great gathered here tonight was enough to ram home the extent of Constantine's power and influence. And not just here in his native Greece. Why, a world-famous architect had flown in from New York especially for this party!

But Laura knew how to behave. She knew that people couldn't tell how you were feeling if you disguised your nerves and concerns behind a bright party smile. It must be working too, because several of the men went out of their way to be charming to her.

The toast—to health and happiness and the continuation of the Karantinos bloodline—was taken early, so that Kyrios Karantinos could retire. He looked exhausted, thought Laura—and she accompanied him back to the house, keen to see he got there safely as well as enjoying a break from the sensation of being watched by the other guests.

She managed to get an excited Alex into bed before midnight, and by the time she had pulled the sheet over Blue Bear he was fast asleep. It was late, she reasoned. Too late to go back—and she was exhausted, too. All that endless smiling and trying not to sound like some gauche little woman who had shoe-horned her way into the life of the Greek billionaire by getting pregnant had completely wiped her out.

She showered and slipped into bed—half hoping that Constantine would not come to her tonight and half praying that he would. Couldn't she lose this terrible sense of insecurity in the warm haven of his arms? Forget life and all its problems in the dreamy pleasure of his lovemaking? Even if those feelings came crowding back in the moment he left.

The door opened and Constantine stood there unmoving—still in his dinner suit—just staring at the bed in silence before walking into the room and quietly shutting the door behind him.

'H-hello,' she said, sitting up and feeling rather stupid—why hadn't he come over to pull her hungrily into his arms?

'Can you get up and put some kind of robe on?' he asked, in a strained and distant kind of voice.

'Sure.' She looked up at him for some kind of hint as to what this was all about—but then she wished she hadn't. Because it was like a cruel flashback to all those years ago when she had looked into his eyes and seen nothing.

Nothing at all.

CHAPTER TWELVE

'Is…is something wrong?' asked Laura tentatively.

Constantine turned round. The silky gown came to mid-thigh, and covered her in all the right places—but it did nothing to disguise the luscious curves and he did not want to be distracted by her body. Not yet.

'Nothing is wrong,' he said coolly. 'Why don't you sit down?'

He indicated the long window seat, which was scattered with squashy embroidered cushions, and Laura sank down onto it, wondering why he was talking to her in that strange tone. And why he hadn't kissed her. 'Why are you acting like this?' she asked, bewildered.

'I'm not *acting* like anything,' he ground out. 'I'm just wondering why you ran back to your room without saying goodnight to any of our guests?'

'Because they weren't *my* guests, they were *yours*!' she returned. 'They weren't here to see me, but you—and your father—and your son. I only had curiosity value as the woman who had given birth to him. Once they had seen me, I was superfluous to requirements.'

'Not to some of the male guests, you weren't!' he snarled. 'They could hardly stop undressing you with their eyes!'

'Well, you have only yourself to blame for that, Constantine,' she hissed back. 'Since you're the one who bought me the dress!'

'And I don't know why I did!'

'Oh, yes, you do,' she contradicted hotly. 'Because I just wasn't good enough, looking the way I normally look. You were afraid that I'd show you up!'

'I didn't want you to feel awkward.'

'You don't think I felt *awkward* with half a million pounds worth of diamonds strung around my neck?' She glanced over at the leather box. 'And can you please take them away with you? Just having them in the room makes me nervous.'

'Laura, why are you being like this?' he exploded.

Why, indeed? Because he made her feel cheap? As if the real Laura could only be tolerated if she was dressed up to look like someone else? *Because he would never love her as she wanted to be loved?* She raked her loose hair away from her face and looked at him in the bright moonlight which flooded in from the unshuttered windows.

'Being like *what*? *You're* the one who's burst in here with a face like ice!' she returned. 'So have you come here for something specific? Because I'm tired and I'd like to get to sleep.'

His eyes narrowed—it was the first time she had not melted automatically into his arms, eager for the closeness of his body.

'Yes, I came here for something specific,' he said, and his mouth hardened as he bit the words out. 'To ask you once again to marry me.'

It was ironic, thought Laura fleetingly, how something which you had only ever pictured in your wildest dreams should dissolve when it happened in real life. This was different from the last time he'd asked her—when they'd barely known each other. Because now they did. Now they were lovers who had shared time with one another—so that him asking her to marry him could be given proper consideration.

A proposal of marriage from the man she loved—supposedly the one thing her aching heart longed for. And yet it had been delivered with all the warmth of a giant chunk of ice floating in an Arctic sea.

She drew in a deep breath. 'Presumably to legitimise your son?'

He looked at her. Hadn't they been through too much for him to dress up the truth with niceties? He shrugged. 'Of course.'

Laura could have wept—or hurled the nearest object at his hard-hearted head. But since that happened to be the diamond set she didn't dare risk it.

He sensed her displeasure. 'Of course there would be more to our marriage than that.'

'There would?' she questioned hopefully.

He nodded. 'We have shown that we can live compatibly, *ne*?' His voice softened into a tone of pure silk. 'And in bed—or out of it—we are pure dynamite together, *agape mou*. You know that.'

Yes, she knew that—but wasn't that the most frightening thing of all? To have physical chemistry up there as one of the main reasons for being together. Because didn't everyone say that it faded in time? And then what would they be left with? A cold shell of a marriage. Already she could imagine the reality of such a marriage, and an icy chill made her begin to shiver, despite the heavy warmth of the night.

'No,' she said.

'No?' His voice was incredulous, and he took a step forward. 'How can you say no when you know that it is what Alex would want,' he said, his voice dangerously soft. 'What Alex *wants*.'

Her fingers flew to her throat and she stared at him in fear. 'Have you asked him? Gone behind my back to get him to side with you?' she demanded hoarsely.

His mouth twisted. 'You think me capable of such an act, Laura? No, I have not—but you know that what I say is true. The boy loves it here—you have only to look at him to see how much he has blossomed since he arrived.'

Guilt shafted through her heart. Hadn't she thought the very same herself—and had he guessed that? 'But that's…*blackmail*,' she whispered.

No. It was fighting for what was truly his—something which he had discovered meant more to him than all his properties and ships and the international acclaim he enjoyed. His son meant far more to him than the continuation of a bloodline…young Alex had crept into his heart and found a permanent home there. Was Laura prepared to ride rough-shod over their son's wishes purely for her own ends?

'Ask him,' he taunted. 'Go on—ask him!'

But Constantine's cruel words focussed Laura's mind on what really mattered, and now she got up and faced him, staring mulishly up at him. It was true that he towered over her, and made her feel ridiculously small, but she didn't care. She might be small but she certainly wasn't insignificant. And he *would* hear her out!

'No, I *won't* ask him—because I wouldn't marry you if you were the last man on earth!' she hissed. 'A man so cruel and so cold that he can't bear to forgive his own father. Even though that father has asked him time and time again to forgive him for all the wrongs he admits he did!'

'Have you been speaking with my father?' he demanded furiously.

'And what if I have? Is that such a heinous crime?' she retorted. 'Am I supposed to ask your permission if I want to speak to somebody?'

'You dare to accuse me of going behind *your* back, and now I discover that you have done exactly the same!' he thundered.

'Oh, please don't try and get out of it by using logic!' she flared, showing a complete lack of it herself. 'Your father made mistakes, yes—and so did your mother. Though it sounds to me as if she couldn't help her own behaviour, and some people are like that. Weak. Unable to give love—even to their own children. And *they can't help it*, Constantine—they were born that way!'

He clenched his fists in fury. How dared she? How *dared* she? 'Have you quite finished?'

That intimidating tone would have silenced many people, but Laura was too passionate to stop. This meant far too much for her to be able to stop. 'No, I have *not* finished! I can't believe you even made the suggestion that I marry you. You're still angry about the coldness of your own childhood and yet you want to subject Alex to more of the same!'

'What the hell are you talking about, Laura?'

This was painful; maybe too painful—and Laura was not prepared to go as far as admitting that if they married then the balance of love would be as one-sided as in his parents' own marriage. Because he didn't realise she loved him, did he? And wouldn't it give him power over her if he did?

'I'm talking about bringing a child up within a loveless marriage—it's just not fair. Things would only get worse between us—never better—and as Alex grew he would have to tiptoe around our feelings and our animosities. What kind of example is that to set him?' she said, her voice beginning to tremble as she thought of her darling son. 'What hope is there for him to be happy in his own life if he looks around and sees discord all around him? How can he believe in love and happiness for himself if he never sees an example of it at home, Constantine?'

Her breath had deserted her and her words died away. She had nothing left to say—but she did not think she needed to. For Constantine's face had suddenly become shuttered. And his eyes—always enigmatic—now looked like strange, cold stones. As if a light had gone out behind them.

'This is what you think?' he demanded.

'Yes,' she whispered, although it broke her heart to admit it. 'Because it's the truth.'

For a moment there was silence—a heavy and uncomfortable kind of silence—and then Constantine's mouth hardened.

'Very well, Laura,' he said, in a voice of pure steel. 'I can see the sense behind your words, since they are—as you say—the truth. And at least if you go then I will no longer have to endure your intolerable interference in things which do not concern you.'

She prayed her lips would not crumple, nor her eyes give her pain away. 'Constantine—'

But he silenced her with his next statement. 'We will need to make plans. And we must do it so that everyone benefits as far as possible. You will require financial assistance. *No!*' He held his hand up peremptorily, anticipating her objections. A harsh note of bitterness entered his voice. 'This is not the time for pretty displays of unnecessary pride,' he spat out. 'You are the mother of my son and I insist that you have an adequate income to support him in a manner which I hope we can both agree on. I want him to go to a school where he isn't bullied—'

'Who told you that?'

'He did, of course,' he said impatiently. 'Not in so many words—but it was clear to me that he is not as happy as he could be. He needs a school where there is plenty of sport, and you need enough money to take that haunted look out of your eyes, never to have to supplement your income with damned waitressing jobs again. And I...' He drew a deep breath as pain like he had never known rushed in to invade the heart he had tried to protect for so long. 'I want to see as much of Alex as possible—we'll need to come to some agreement on that.'

She wanted to reach out to him. To tell him that he could see as much of Alex as he wanted—to reassure him and to comfort him that they would do the best they possibly could. But there was something so icy and forbidding about his words and demeanour that she did not dare. Suddenly he had become a stranger to her. 'Of course,' she said stiffly.

'I will arrange for you to return to England as soon as possible. I think that best, in the circumstances. My lawyers will be in touch on your return. But I want some time alone with Alex tomorrow morning.' He drew a deep breath as reality hit him, seeming to turn his whole body into stone. He forced the next words out. 'To say goodbye to my son.'

CHAPTER THIRTEEN

'But Mum, *why* do we have to go home?'

Laura's smile didn't slip, even though her face felt as if it had been carved out of marble—but during the sleepless night which had followed her furious row with Constantine she had decided the best way to handle questions like this. And the best way was to present her and Alex leaving Livinos as something perfectly normal. *Which it was.*

'Well, we only ever planned to come out for a few weeks,' she reminded him. 'Remember?'

'It's been less than that,' said Alex sulkily. 'And I like it here.'

She knew that—and it broke her heart to have to drag him away—but what choice did she have? He'd been happy in England before and he would be happy again—especially if there was no more bullying and if he changed schools, as Constantine himself had suggested. And didn't all the books on child-rearing say that the worst thing you could do was to subject your children to a hostile atmosphere and infighting between parents? She could do worse than remind herself of the bitter words she and Constantine had exchanged last night if she needed any more convincing that the two of them were basically incompatible.

'Anyway,' said Laura, with a brightly cheerful smile, even though the thought of the future terrified her, 'you'll be coming back to Livinos lots…to see your daddy. And he'll be coming to England to take you out. You'll…well, you'll have the best of both worlds, really, Alex!'

Alex bit his lip, as if he couldn't bring himself to agree with this. 'Can I go swimming with Stavros, please?'

Laura felt her heart threaten to break as she saw his pinched little face. 'Of course you can,' she whispered. 'But you've only got a couple of hours. The helicopter will be leaving straight after lunch, and we mustn't be late.'

He didn't say another word as she took him outside to find the affable Greek student, and Laura stood there, watching the two of them heading towards the pool area, her eyes full of rogue tears which she fiercely blinked back.

Returning to her room, she finished packing—folding her cheap clothes into neat piles and then stuffing them into the equally cheap suitcase. For a brief moment her fingers strayed towards the costly gowns Constantine had bought her, and then strayed back again. Because what was the point of taking them back to England? They had been purchased with the sole purpose of making her look like a Karantinos woman—and she wasn't one and never would be. She had no right to wear the exquisite garments and they had no place in her life—where on earth could she possibly wear them in Milmouth?

Packing up Alex's stuff was harder—because here she really was tempted to take some of the wonderful toys and books Constantine had provided for him. But even if they took a whole load back—where on earth would they find room to accommodate them in their tiny apartment? And besides, they would always be here for him when he visited.

Laura swallowed the sudden acrid taste of fear. Because wasn't that an additional cause of her fretting heart? The fact that Alex would have his wonderful little world kept intact here—a world of toys and swimming pools, boats and planes, and the growing knowledge that he was heir to the fabulous Karantinos fortune…not simply the son of a struggling single mother. Would the day come when he chose to live out the Greek side of his heritage—rejecting her and the country of his birth?

Alex wouldn't *do* that, she told herself desperately—but still the fear ate away at her.

Their packing completed, Laura stole a glance at her watch. She had already said a brief and upsetting farewell to Constantine's father, and to Demetra, too. Goodbyes were awful at the best of times, but these felt a million times worse—loaded down with the terrible and aching significance of all that she was leaving behind. And most upsetting of all was the thought of leaving Constantine.

Was she being crazy? Wouldn't it make more sense if she gritted her teeth and accepted the fact that, while he didn't love her, Constantine would provide a secure childhood for Alex?

But not a *loving* childhood, she reminded herself. And she knew that this was about far more than her ego being bruised because Constantine didn't love *her*. Why, he couldn't even forgive his father. How could she let Alex exist in an emotionally cold world like that?

Laura glanced at her watch. The time was ticking away,

and her stomach was churning with the kind of slow dread she got before an exam. What the hell was she going to do between now and the arrival of the helicopter, which would whisk them to Athens to catch the private jet which this time she had been unable to refuse? Maybe she would take one last lingering tour of the beautiful grounds which surrounded the Karantinos property.

Slipping out of the villa into the dappled sunlight, Laura thought how strange the atmosphere around the place seemed today. Was it because Constantine was nowhere to be seen? Or maybe it was just her.

She could hear the distant splash of Alex and Stavros larking around in the pool, and she could see a sleek white yacht down on the sapphire waters of the sea—but none of it seemed real. She felt as if she was insubstantial; a ghost of a woman who walked through the fruit orchards and tried to focus on the scent of the pine trees rather than the tearing ache in her heart.

Walking further across the property than she had ever ventured before, she came across a small bougainvillaea-tumbled grove. It was a scented, secret sort of place, reached through a dusty tract of olive trees and shaded from the glaring heat of the sun by tumbling blooms, and she sank down on a stone bench, wishing that she'd drunk some water before leaving the house.

For a while she sat there, trying to decide about what she would do when she got back to Milmouth. Maybe she'd think about selling more local produce in the shop—asking villagers if they wanted to shift any leftover crops from large gluts of home-grown vegetables. That would benefit everyone in the community, wouldn't it? But the question seemed to have no real relevance in her life. *Please help me to feel part of that community again,* she prayed. *And not like some sad woman who's left her heart and her soul behind in this paradise.*

'Hiding away, are you, Laura?'

A deep and familiar voice shattered the silence, and Laura's heart leapt as Constantine stepped into the grove—his hard face shuttered, the dappled light casting shadows over the high slash of his cheekbones. She looked up into his eyes, but met nothing but cool curiosity in their ebony depths.

'Why would I be hiding?' she questioned, her voice sounding light in contrast to the hard thundering of her heart.

He shrugged as he sat down beside her. 'This isn't a place you usually frequent.'

'Then how did you know I was here?'

There was a pause. 'I followed you.'

Another pause. Longer this time. And now her heart was beating so hard and so fast that Laura could barely stumble the words out. 'Wh-why would you do that?'

His eyes rested on the lightly tanned length of her slender thighs, their shape clearly outlined by the thin cotton dress she wore. Why, indeed? Because she continued to mesmerise him—even though he had vowed not to let her? Constantine's mouth twisted as he felt the slow throb of blood to his pulse points. How many times had he told himself that she exerted an allure simply because she had refused him—because she had done the inexplicable and turned down his offer of marriage for a second time?

He met the wide grey eyes which were observing him so guardedly, and noted the fall of fine blonde hair which was hanging around her narrow shoulders like a pale cloud.

Had she read one of those books which advised holding out in order to increase her worth as a woman? He felt the stab of desire jerking insistently at his groin. Well, she would learn soon enough that he would not be played with—not any more. She had had her chance and that chance would not return. But in the meantime he would have her one last time!

'Why, Constantine?' she persisted. 'Why did you follow me?'

He picked up her unresisting hand and studied it. 'Oh, I don't know.' Running the pad of this thumb questingly over the centre of her palm, he felt her shiver. 'Any ideas?'

Laura felt her already dry throat grow completely parched. His touch. His proximity. The sudden glint from his eyes. All those things were making her feel weak and helpless.

She told herself to pull her hand away. To move. To distract him.

So why did she stay exactly where she was? Letting Constantine stroke enchanting little circles over her skin and feeling herself tremble in response?

'Mmm, Laura?' he questioned, as he shifted his body a little closer on the bench. 'Any ideas?'

'N-no.'

'Really? How remarkably unimaginative of you, *agape mou*. Why, I'm quite disappointed that someone whom I have coached so tirelessly in the art of love shouldn't immediately take advantage of a sweet and final opportunity presenting itself like this.'

His words were in a muddle in her head. Dangerous words—of which *final* seemed to be the most dangerous of all. *You both know it's over*, she told herself desperately—

so why are you letting him pull you onto his lap? And why aren't you stopping him from sliding your panties right down, from putting his fingers between your legs and...

'Constantine!' she gasped.

He kissed her to shut her up—but also because he wanted to kiss her. *Needed* to kiss her. To punish her and to make her hurt as he was hurting. But the kiss didn't stay that way—infuriatingly, it transformed itself into a terrible aching hunger which could be eased in only one way. He tore his mouth away and shuddered out a harsh entreaty.

'Undo my jeans.'

Laura didn't even hesitate before she tremblingly obeyed—indeed, she thought that she might have been scrabbling at his belt even before that terse instruction had been whispered in her ear.

She gasped again as she freed him—marvelling at the sheer power of him. He looked and felt so big and so erect in her tiny hand as she stroked on the condom he gave her. And then he began impatiently to tug at the jeans, until they had slithered down to his ankles. He didn't even bother to kick them off. Instead, he just lifted her up, as if she were made of cotton wool, bringing her down deep onto his aching shaft and kissing her again with a fierce hunger—sensing that her shuddering little cries of fulfilment were only minutes away. As were his. A few ecstatic movements of her hips and he was groaning into her mouth as he felt himself spasming against her own honeyed contractions.

Afterwards, she collapsed against him, burying her head on his shoulder, willing the tears not to come, and wondering why everything felt so confused. Why had he done this—and why had she let him? Registering that sex had a dark power which managed to distort what had seemed such a straightforward decision, she found herself wondering if she had been wrong to tell him she was leaving.

If he asks me again to stay, then I might just say yes, she thought weakly—but the next thing she knew was Constantine firmly lifting her off him.

'Straighten your clothes,' he said abruptly as he began to pull up the zip of his jeans. He hated his weakness around her—the way he couldn't seem to resist her when every logical pore in his formidable body told him that it should be easy. Would she see this as another little triumph? he wondered bitterly. Another perfect demonstration of how she had the powerful Constantine Karantinos eating out of her hand?

'I'll leave you to find your own way back,' he finished, raking angry fingers back through the tousled waves of his black hair.

And then he was gone, and Laura could hardly believe what had just taken place. How she could have let him arrive and just…*do* that to her? But she *had* let him. More than let him—had squirmed with pleasure and enjoyed every erotic second of it—so if Constantine had now lost all respect for her as a woman then she had only herself to blame.

But in a way her orgasm had emptied her of all feeling and all emotion—and at least that made the last preparations for her departure bearable. So that she was able to chat excitedly to Alex about the conkers which would be on the autumn trees in England—ignoring the morose set of his little face in response. Only once did her composure threaten to buckle, and that was when Constantine clasped his son in a hug which went on and on.

Then he ruffled the little boy's dark curls and smiled. 'I'll come and see you soon in England,' he said.

Alex's crumpled face was turned upwards, as if he had just seen the first light in a dark sky. 'When?'

'How does next month sound?'

'Oh, it sounds wonderful, Papa.'

The helicopter blades whirred round and round, and Laura glanced out of the window to see Constantine staring up intently at his son. She felt a real pang of remorse. Was she doing a wrong and selfish thing by taking Alex back to England? Yet how many women would willingly trap themselves on an island this size with a man who didn't love them?

The island retreated as the craft took off, but Constantine stood there long after the black speck had grown smaller and smaller and then finally disappeared, his shoulders bowed with the weight of something too painful to analyse.

Something which made all the Karantinos billions fade into pale insignificance.

CHAPTER FOURTEEN

As THE last of Alex's footsteps died away, Laura closed the front door and let out a long sigh of something which felt like relief. *Please let him have a nice day with my sister,* she prayed silently. *Please remove some of the inevitable disappointment which has clouded my son's face since returning home from Greece last week.* A week which had felt more like a year.

It was strange to be back in England, and even stranger to be back in their small flat which no longer seemed to feel like home. *And why was that?* she wondered guiltily. Because it was small and poky after the vast Karantinos villa? Or because the powerful presence of Constantine was absent—making the place seem soulless?

'I miss my papa,' Alex had told her on more than one occasion—in a way which tore at Laura's conscience.

And, so do I, she thought. *So do I.* A decision she had made for all the best reasons was now proving to be unbearable—and it seemed that she had no one in the world to turn to or confide in.

Because even Sarah seemed to have moved on. Her sister

had been hurtling up to London at every opportunity to see Matthius—the cousin of the Greek student Constantine had roped in to help while Laura had been away. It seemed that like Demetra, Mattius was also a member of the Constantine Karantinos fan-club, having convinced Sarah that the billionaire was only arrogant and cold to the many people who wanted something from him—but that to friends and family he was loyalty personified.

For Laura, who was trying desperately hard to put the Greek tycoon from her mind, this was the last thing she wanted or needed to hear. Was it her stricken face which had made Sarah offer to take Alex out for the day? Or the fact that she couldn't seem to settle to anything and was driving everyone mad?

Whatever the reason, it was very kind of her sister, and Laura knew it was good for Alex to have something to occupy his thoughts other than the life he had left behind on Livinos. But the free day yawned emptily ahead of her, and Laura found herself wondering how she was going to fill the aching hours ahead when she heard a loud banging on the door. She ran back into the hall to throw it open with more than a little relief.

'Now what have you forgotten—?' she began to say, but the words died on her lips when she saw who was standing there. Not Alex. Nor Sarah. But…

Constantine?

Laura swallowed, shaking her head a little, blinking back the stupid sting of disbelieving tears as she stared up at him. She'd been thinking about him non-stop. Dreaming about him constantly. Her thoughts about him had driven her half mad and her heart had been unable to stop aching—so that for a moment it just felt like an extension of all her desires that he would somehow magically appear. As if the man who stood in front of her wasn't real. As if he couldn't be real.

But he was. Laura stared at the formidable physique of Constantine Karantinos—standing on her doorstep, with his dark hair all windswept and a look on his face she had never seen before. Had she forgotten just how gorgeous he was? How strong and how vital? How he could dominate a space simply by existing in it?

'Constantine,' she breathed, and her heart began to pound with frantic yearning. She wanted to touch him. To throw her arms around him. To whisper her fingertips wonderingly along the hard, proud line of his jaw—as if only touch alone would convince her that he was really here. 'Wh-what are you doing here?' she questioned.

It was then that she realised. Of course! He had come to see his son. Their heartbreaking farewell on the airstrip must have made him vow to come and see Alex earlier than he had intended. And even though she would have liked some warning that he was about to appear, so that she wouldn't have answered the door in a scruffy old pair of jeans and a T-shirt which had seen better days, she managed a brisk kind of smile.

Think of Alex, she told herself—he's the one who matters.

So she was able to look up at him with genuine regret. 'Oh, what a pity. Alex has just gone out.'

'I know he has.'

She looked at him blankly. 'You do?'

'Yes. I rang Sarah this morning and asked her if she would take him out for the day.'

'You rang Sarah?' she repeated. 'And she...*agreed*?'

'Yes, she did.'

Laura blinked at him in confusion. It was true that her sister no longer seemed to think that he was the devil incarnate—but agreeing to Constantine's request behind her back sounded awfully like *collusion*, and...and... Well, it threw up all kinds of questions. 'But *why*?' she whispered.

He raised his dark brows in sardonic query. 'Do you want me to tell you when I'm standing on the doorstep?'

Registering the faintly reprimanding tone of his question, she pulled the door open wider. 'No. No, of course not. Come in.' But as he passed her she had to clutch the door handle to balance herself—his very proximity was producing a terrible wave of weakness and longing which threatened to destabilise her.

He was standing in their cramped little hallway—making it look even smaller, if that were possible—and Laura shook her head uncomprehendingly. Because if he wasn't here to see Alex, then...then...

'Please tell me why you're here,' she said, her voice a whisper as thready as her erratic heartbeat.

His black gaze was calculating. 'No ideas at all, Laura?'

Numbly, she shook her head, and it was then that Constantine realised that there was no easy way to do this—or she wasn't going to make it easy for him—and maybe that was the way it should be. Maybe he too needed to experience doubt and uncertainty, as well as the fear that she might reject him again.

But words describing feelings didn't come easy when you'd spent a lifetime avoiding them—and for a moment he felt like a man who had found himself on a raft in the middle of the ocean, unsure of which direction to take. He sucked air into lungs which suddenly felt empty.

'I have thought about everything you said that last night. About love and about the past.' He saw the way she was staring at him, her pale face fierce, chewing on her bottom lip the way she always did when she was concentrating hard. 'And the impact of both those things on the present and the future.' There was a pause. 'They were things I didn't want to hear,' he whispered. 'Things I tried to block my ears to. But somehow—I couldn't do it. And when my anger had died away, I realised that you were right. That I needed to forgive my father—and in a way I needed to forgive my mother, too.'

'Constantine—'

'So that's what I've come to tell you. That I have. I have had a long talk with my father and told him…'

Momentarily his voice tailed away, and Laura lifted up her hand. 'You don't…have to tell me if you don't want to,' she whispered, seeing the pain of memory etched on his hard features and finding that it was hurting her, too.

'Oh, but that's where you're wrong. You see, I do, Laura. I need to tell you plenty of things—just as I did my father.' He sucked in another breath—because although Constantine was a brave man, opening up his heart to her like this took courage of a different kind. 'I told him that it was now time for us to be a true father and son to each other—and for him to be a grandfather to Alex.'

Laura nodded as his sudden appearance at last began to make sense. She guessed what was coming. He was going to ask her to take Alex back to Greece, to help facilitate his relationship with his father—a man too old and infirm to travel great distances. And, although it wasn't ideal, Laura knew she was going to say yes. It didn't matter if he wasn't offering her the dream ticket of love *with* marriage—she'd settle for whatever she could get. For everyone's sake. Because she'd had a chance to live the alternative—a life without Constantine—and that life was bleak. Like a vase which was permanently empty of flowers. And didn't she have more than enough love to go round—for all of them? Couldn't she perhaps show him *how* to love—with the hope that one day he might be able to give a little love back to her? Was it pathetic of her to be prepared to settle for that?

'That sounds perfect,' she agreed.

Constantine's eyes narrowed. 'Does it?' he questioned, and suddenly his voice sounded harsh. 'Not to me, it doesn't.'

And now a very real fear lanced through her. Perhaps he *wasn't* asking her to marry him at all—hadn't he already asked her twice and she'd turned him down? Would a proud man like this really ask her a third time? Why, she was probably being completely arrogant in not accepting that deep down he'd been delighted to see the back of her. 'Why not?' she breathed painfully.

He stared at her. The bare feet. The shapeless jeans—and a T-shirt which Demetra would probably have used to polish the tiles with. It was inconceivable that such a woman as Laura had captured his heart, but captured it she had—and so tightly that at this moment it was threatening to burst right out of his chest. Her physical ensnarement of him had never been in any doubt—but her purity and loyalty to him as a lover thrilled him to the very core of his being. As did her fierce determination to protect her son, and her admirable refusal to accept his offer of marriage, showing him that she was not a woman who could be bought by his colossal wealth.

'Because I have been a fool,' he declared hotly. 'I have failed to see what was right beneath my very nose—that you, Laura, are the woman who makes me laugh, who challenges me. The woman who is not afraid to tell me the truth. Who kisses more sweetly than I ever thought it possible to kiss. Who makes diamonds look dull and starlight seem mediocre.'

He drew a ragged breath, knowing that he had still not gone far enough—but admitting love for the first time in his life was hard for a man who had only ever seen warped examples of that emotion.

He stared at her, his heart pounding in his chest, aware as he looked at her that if he said it he had to mean it. *Really* mean it. And suddenly it was easy.

'You are the woman I love,' he said softly. 'I love you, Laura. I love you so much.'

'Oh, Constantine…' she breathed, scarcely able to believe what he was saying to her. But just one look at the incredible tension on his beautiful face told her that every word was true.

'But the question is do you love *me*?' he demanded.

Was he *crazy*? 'Yes—*yes*!'

'As fiercely as I do you?'

'Oh, yes!'

'Then for the third time of asking—and because I am finally running out of patience—will you please marry me, Laura?'

Her smile broke out, so wide it felt as if it would split her face in two. 'Yes! Oh, God, yes. I love you. I *love* you,

Constantine! I've loved you for so long that I don't know any other way—but, oh, I can't tell you how wonderful it is to actually be able to say it out loud!'

'Promise me you'll never stop saying it,' he declared, amazed at his own need to hear it.

'Oh, I won't—my sweet, darling Constantine.'

He pulled her into his arms, and this time he really *did* destabilise her, for her knees gave way—but Constantine was holding onto her as tightly as could be as he began to kiss her. And this kiss was different from any other they had ever shared. It was tender and healing as well as passionate, and it sealed their love properly—ending all twists and turns along the way which had brought them here to this point.

And if it was a kiss which was mingled with their tears—then didn't that somehow make it sweeter and more precious still?

EPILOGUE

THE wedding took place in Greece—with Sarah as bridesmaid and Alex carrying two platinum rings on a little cushion. Knowing the sensibilities of young boys, Laura had told him that he didn't *have* to be involved in the ceremony, but Alex had insisted. He was so happy, Laura realised—blissfully contented that his mother and his father were going to be married at last.

It was a small ceremony, with a big party afterwards, and because it was held on the island it meant that the press could be kept largely in check. Unexpectedly, the message of congratulations which brought most satisfaction to bride and groom was sent by the supermodel formerly known as Ingrid Johansson, who was now Mrs Ingrid Rockefeller, and living in luxury in the centre of Manhattan. It read:

You did me a favour, *alskling*—I have now a man who adores me, and we were married last month.

Laura had long ago realised that Constantine had already finished with the supermodel when she had burst into his life again, but it gladdened her heart to know that the Swedish beauty was happy.

Sarah had landed herself a place at art school in London, and was planning a new life for herself there. So they'd sold their bakery shop and the flat for a very respectable sum which had gone towards buying her an apartment near her college. And Sarah—after a little persuasion—had allowed Laura and Constantine to pay off the balance of her new home.

'You've helped me for years,' Laura had told her fiercely. 'So please let me pay back something for all your time and kindness.'

It was decided that Alex would go to the school on Livinos until he was old enough to continue his studies on the mainland—just as his father had done. And, as well as taking an intensive course in Greek, Laura was planning to open a bakery on the island. Demetra had moaned about the lack of a bread shop often enough, and Laura recognised that she had a real gift for making a small business work. Two local women had been employed to help her, and if other babies came along—well, then Laura knew there were heaps of people she could call on.

But for now the shop gave her a role and a purpose on Livinos—it meant that she was more than just Constantine's new wife, and that was important to her. And, she suspected, to him. One of the reasons he had fallen in love with her—so he told her on their wedding night—was because she was so proud and independent. She was the only woman he'd ever known who hadn't coveted diamonds.

In fact, this lack of enthusiasm for fine jewels had

proved to be the only problem in the blissfully problem-free time leading up to their wedding.

'It is traditional for the groom to give his beautiful bride a gift,' he murmured, pulling her into his arms and drifting his lips against hers. 'But—since diamonds don't impress you—what on earth can I give you as a wedding present that is equally precious, *agape mou*?'

And Laura smiled, because the question was superfluous. She already had the thing she most wanted—the most precious thing on this earth. The love of a man she adored.

Constantine's love.

THE GREEK TYCOON'S ACHILLES HEEL

LUCY GORDON

PROLOGUE

THE lights of the Las Vegas Strip gleamed and glittered up into the night sky. Down below, the hotels and casinos rioted with life and money but the Palace Athena outshone them all.

In the six months since its opening it had gained a reputation for being more lavish than its competitors, and today it had put the seal on its success by hosting the wedding of the beautiful, glamorous film star, Estelle Radnor.

The owner of the Palace, no fool, had gained the prestige of staging her wedding by offering everything for free, and the gorgeous Estelle, also no fool where money was concerned, whatever might be said of her taste in men, had seized the offer.

The wedding party finished up in the casino, where the bride was photographed throwing dice, embracing her groom, throwing more dice, slipping an arm around the shoulders of a thin, nondescript young girl, then throwing more dice. The owner watched it all with satisfaction, before turning to a young man who stood regarding the performance sardonically.

'Achilles, my friend—'

'I've told you before, don't call me that.'

'But your name has brought me such good luck. Your excellent advice on how to make this place convincingly Greek—'

'None of which you've taken.'

'Well, my customers *believe* it's Greek and that's what matters.'

'Of course, appearance is everything and what else counts?' the young man murmured.

'You're gloomy tonight. Is it the wedding? Do you envy them?'

'Achilles' turned on him with swift ferocity. 'Don't talk nonsense!' he snapped. 'All I feel is boredom and disgust.'

'Have things gone badly for you?'

A shrug. 'I've lost a million. Before the night's out I'll probably lose another. So what?'

'Come and join the party.'

'I haven't been invited.'

'You think they're going to turn away the son of the wealthiest man in Greece?'

'They're not going to get the chance. Leave me and get back to your guests.'

He strolled away, a lean, isolated figure, followed by two pairs of eyes, one belonging to the man he'd just left, the other to the awkward-looking teenager the bride had earlier embraced. Keeping close to the wall, so as not to be noticed, she slipped away and took the elevator to the fifty-second floor, where she could observe the Strip.

Here, both the walls and the roof were thick glass, allowing visitors to look out in safety. Outside ran a ledge which she guessed was there for workmen and window cleaners, but inaccessible to customers unless they knew the code to tap into the lock.

She was staring down, transfixed, when a slight noise made her turn and see the young man from downstairs. Moving quietly into the shadows, she watched, unnoticed, as he came to stand nearby, gazing down a thousand feet at the dazzling, distant world beneath.

Up here there were only a few lamps, so that customers could look out through the glass. She had a curious view of his face, lit from below by a glow that shifted and changed colour. His features were lean and clean-cut, their slight sharpness emphasised by the angle. It was the face of a very young man, little more than a boy, yet it held a weariness—even a despair—that suggested a crushing burden.

Then he did something that terrified her, reaching out to the code box and tapping in a number, making a pane of glass slide back so that there was nothing but air between him and a thousand foot drop. Petra's sharp gasp made him turn his head.

'What are you doing there?' he snapped. 'Are you spying on me?'

'Of course not. Come back in, please,' she begged. 'Don't do it.'

He stepped back into comparative safety, but remained near the gap.

'What the hell do you mean, "don't do it"?' he snapped. 'I wasn't going to *do* anything. I wanted some air.'

'But it's dangerous. You could fall by accident.'

'I know what I'm doing. Go away and let me be.'

'No,' she said defiantly. 'I have as much right to take the air as you. Is it nice out there?'

'What?'

Moving so fast that she took him by surprise, she slipped past him and out onto the ledge. At once the wind attacked her so that she had to reach out and found him grasping her.

'You stupid woman!' he shouted. 'I'm not the only one who can have an accident. Do you want to die?'

'Do you?'

'Come inside.'

He yanked her back in, stopping short in surprise when he saw her face.

'Didn't I see you downstairs?'

'Yes, I was in the Zeus Room,' she said, naming the casino. 'I like watching people. That place is very cleverly named.'

'You know what Zeus means, then?' he asked, drawing her away to where they could sit down.

'He was the King of the Greek gods,' she said, 'looking down on the world from his home on the top of Mount Olympus, master of all he surveyed. That must be how the gamblers feel when they start playing, but the poor idiots soon learn differently. Did you lose much?'

He shrugged. 'A million. I stopped counting after a while. What are you doing in a casino, anyway? You can't be more than fifteen.'

'I'm seventeen and I'm…one of the bridal party.'

'That's right,' he said, seeming not to notice the way she'd checked herself at the last moment. 'I saw her embracing you for the camera. Are you a bridesmaid?'

She regarded him cynically. 'Do I look like a bridesmaid?' she demanded, indicating her attire, which was clearly expensive but not glamorous.

'Well—'

'I don't really belong in front of the cameras, not with that lot.'

She spoke with a wry lack of self-pity that was attractive. Looking at her more closely, he saw that she wore no makeup, her hair was cut efficiently short, and she'd made no attempt to enhance her appearance.

'And your name is—?' he queried.

'Petra. And you're Achilles. No?' The last word was a response to his scowl.

'My name is Lysandros Demetriou. My mother wanted to call me Achilles, but my father thought she was being sentimental. In the end they compromised, and Achilles became my second name.'

'But that man downstairs called you by it.'

'It's important to him that I'm Greek because this place is built on the idea of Greekness.'

To his delight she gave a cheeky giggle. 'They're all potty.'

They took stock of each other. He was as handsome as she'd first sensed, with clean cut features, deep set eyes and an air of pride that came with a lifetime of having his own way. But there was also a darkness and a brooding intensity that seemed strange in this background. Young men in Las Vegas hunted in packs, savouring every experience. This one hid away, treasuring his solitude as though the world was an enemy. And something had driven him to take the air in a place full of danger.

'Demetriou Shipbuilding?' she asked.

'That's the one.'

'The most powerful firm in Greece.' She said it as though reciting a lesson. 'What they don't want isn't worth having. What they don't acquire today they'll acquire tomorrow. If anyone dares to refuse them, they wait in the shadows until the right moment to pounce.'

He grunted. 'Something like that.'

'Or maybe you'll just turn the Furies onto them?'

She meant the three Greek goddesses of wrath and vengeance, with hair made of snakes and eyes that dripped blood, who hounded their victims without mercy.

'Do you have to be melodramatic?' he demanded.

'In this "pretend" Greek place I can't help it. Anyway, why aren't you in Athens grinding your enemies to dust?'

'I've done with all that,' he said harshly. 'They can get on without me.'

'Ah, this is the bit where you sulk.'

'*What?*'

'During the Trojan war Achilles was in love with this girl. She actually came from the other side, and was his prisoner, but they made him give her back, so he withdrew from the battle and sulked in his tent. But in the end he came out and started fighting again. Only he ended up dead. As you could have done on that ledge.'

'I told you I wasn't planning to die, although frankly it doesn't seem important one way or the other. I'll take what comes.'

'Did she do something very cruel?' Petra asked gently.

In the dim light she could barely see the look he turned on her, but she sensed that it was terrible. His eyes were harsh and cold in the gloom, warning her that she'd trespassed on sacred ground.

'Stop now!' howled the Furies. 'Run for your life before he strikes you dead.'

But that wasn't her way.

'She?' he asked in a voice that warned her.

She laid a gentle hand on his arm, whispering, 'I'm sorry. Shouldn't I have said that?'

He rose sharply and strode back to the gap in the glass wall and stood gazing out into the night. She followed cautiously.

'She made me trust her,' he whispered.

'But sometimes it's right to trust.'

'No,' he insisted. 'Nobody is ever as good as you think they are, and sooner or later the truth is always there. The more you trust someone, the worse it is when they betray you. Better to have no illusions, and be strong.'

'But that would be terrible, never to believe in anything, never to love or hope, never be really happy—'

'Never to be wretched,' he said harshly.

'Never to be alive,' she said with gentle urgency. 'It would be a living death, can't you see that? You'd escape suffering, but you'd also lose everything that makes life worth living.'

'Not everything. There's power. You'd gain that if you did without the other things. They're only weaknesses.'

'No,' she said, almost violently. 'You mustn't give in to that way of thinking or you'll ruin your life.'

'And what do you know about it?' he demanded, angry now. 'You're a child. Has anyone ever made you want to smash things and keep on smashing until nothing is left alive—including yourself?'

'But what do you gain by destroying yourself inside?' she demanded.

'I'll tell you what you gain. You don't become—like this.' He jabbed a finger at his heart.

She didn't have to ask what he meant. Young as he was, he lived on the edge of disaster, and it would take very little to push him over. That was why he dared to stand here, defying the fates to do their worst.

Pity and terror almost overwhelmed her. Part of her wanted to run for her life, get far, far away from this creature who might become a monster if something didn't intervene. But the other part wanted to stay and be the one to rescue him.

Suddenly, without warning, he did the thing that decided her, something terrible and wonderful in the same moment. Lowering his head, he let it fall against her shoulder, raised it, dropped it again, and again and again. It was like watching a man bang his head against a brick wall, hopelessly, robotically.

Appalled, she threw her arms around him and clutched a restraining hand over his head, forcing him to be still. His despair seemed to reach out to her, imploring her comfort, saying that only she could give it to him. To be needed so desperately was a new experience for her and, even in the midst of her dismay, she knew a kind of delight.

Over his shoulder she could see the drop, with nothing to protect him from it. Nothing but herself. She gripped him tight, silently offering him all she could. He didn't resist, but now his head rested on her shoulder as though the strength had drained out of him.

When she drew back to see his face the bitter anguish had gone, leaving it sad and resigned, as though he'd found a kind of peace, albeit a bleak and despairing peace.

At last Lysandros gave her a faint smile, feeling deep within him a desire to protect her as she had tried to protect him. There was still good in the world. It was here in this girl, too innocent to understand the danger she ran just by being here with him. In the end she would be sullied and spoiled like the rest.

But not tonight. He wouldn't allow it.

He tapped a number into the code pad and the glass panel closed.

'Let's go,' he said, leading her away from the roof and down into the hotel.

Outside her door he said, 'Go inside, go to bed, don't open this door to anyone.'

'What are you going to do?'

'I'm going to lose a lot more money. After that—I'm going to do some thinking.'

He hadn't meant to say the last words.

'Goodnight, Achilles.'

'Goodnight.'

He hadn't intended what he did next either, but on impulse he leaned down and kissed her mouth gently.

'Go in,' he said. 'And lock your door.'

She nodded and slipped inside. After a moment he heard the key turn.

He returned to the tables, resigned to further losses, but mysteriously his luck turned. In an hour he'd recovered every penny. In another hour he'd doubled it.

So that was who she was, a good luck charm, sent to cast her spell and change his fortunes. He only hoped he'd also done something for her, but he would probably never know. They would never meet again.

He was wrong. They did meet again.

But not for fifteen years.

CHAPTER ONE

THE Villa Demetriou stood on the outskirts of Athens on raised ground, from which the family had always been able to survey the domain they considered theirs. Until now the only thing that could rival them had been the Parthenon, the great classical temple built more than two thousand years before, high on the Acropolis, far away across the city and just visible.

Recently a new rival had sprung up, a fake Parthenon, created by Homer Lukas, the one man in Greece who would have ventured to challenge either the Demetriou family or the ancient gods who protected the true temple. But Homer was in love, and naturally wished to impress his bride on their wedding day.

On that spring morning Lysandros Demetriou stood in the doorway of his villa, looking out across Athens, irritated by having to waste his time at a wedding when he had so many really important things to deal with.

A sound behind him made him turn to see the entrance of Stavros, an old friend of his late father, who lived just outside the city. He was white-haired and far too thin, the result of a lifetime of self-indulgence.

'I'm on my way to the wedding,' he said. 'I called in to see if you fancied a lift.'

'Thank you, that would be useful,' Lysandros said coolly. 'If I arrive early it won't give too much offence if I leave early.'

Stavros gave a crack of laughter. 'You're not sentimental about weddings.'

'It's not a wedding, it's an exhibition,' he said sardonically. 'Homer Lukas has acquired a film star wife and is flaunting her to the world. The world will offer him good wishes and call him names behind his back. My own wish for him is that Estelle Radnor will make a fool of him. With any luck, she will.

'Why did she have to come to Athens to get married, anyway? Why not make do with a false Greek setting, like that other time?'

'Because the name of Homer Lukas is synonymous with Greek shipbuilding,' Stavros said, adding quickly, 'after yourself, of course.'

For years the companies of Demetriou and Lukas had stood head and shoulders above all others in Greece, or even in the world, some reverently claimed.

They were opponents, foes, even outright enemies, but enemies who presented a civilised veneer to outsiders because it was profitable to do so.

'I suppose it might be a real love-match,' Stavros observed cynically.

Lysandros raised his eyebrows. 'A real—? How many times has she been married? Six, seven?'

'You should know. Weren't you a guest at one of the previous weddings, years ago?'

'Not a guest. I just happened to be in the Las Vegas hotel where it was held and watched some of the shenanigans from a safe distance. And I returned to Greece the next day.'

'Yes, I remember that. Your father was very puzzled—pleased, but puzzled. Apparently you'd told him you wanted nothing more to do with the business now or ever again. You vanished for two years, but suddenly, out of the blue, you just walked in the door and said you were ready to go to work. He was even afraid you wouldn't be up to it after…well…'

He fell silent, alarmed by the grim look that had come over Lysandros's face.

'Quite,' he said in a quiet voice that was more frightening than a shout. 'Well, it's a long time ago. The past is over.'

'Yes, and your father said that all his fears were groundless because when you returned you were different, a tiger who terrified everyone. He was so proud.'

'Well, let's hope I terrify Homer Lukas. Otherwise I'm losing my touch.'

'Perhaps you should be scared,' Stavros said. 'Such threats he's been uttering since you recently bilked him and his son of billions. *Stole* billions, according to him.'

'I didn't steal anything, I merely offered the client a better deal,' Lysandros said indifferently.

'But it was at the last minute,' Stavros recalled. 'Apparently they were all assembled to sign the contracts, and the client had actually lifted the pen when his phone rang and it was you, giving him some information that you could only have acquired "by disgraceful means".'

'Not as disgraceful as all that,' Lysandros observed with a shrug. 'I've done worse, I'm glad to say.'

'And that was that,' Stavros resumed. 'The man put the pen down, cancelled the deal and walked out straight into your car, waiting outside. Rumour says Homer promised the gods on Olympus splendid offerings if only they would punish you.'

'But I've remained unpunished, so perhaps the gods weren't listening. They say he even uttered a curse over my wedding invitation. I hope he did.'

'You're really not taking anyone with you?'

Lysandros made a non-committal reply. He attended many weddings as a duty, sometimes with companions but never with one woman. It would interest the press too much, and send out misleading signals to the lady herself, which could cause him serious inconvenience.

'Right, let's get going,' Stavros said.

'I'm afraid I'll have to catch you up later,' Lysandros excused himself.

'But you just said you'd go with me—'

'Yes, but I've suddenly remembered something I must do first. Goodbye.'

There was a finality in the last word that Stavros dared not challenge.

His car was waiting downstairs. In the back sat his wife, who'd refused to come in with him on the grounds that she hated the desolate house that seemed to suit Lysandros so perfectly.

'How can he bear to live in that vast, silent place with no family and only servants for company?' she'd demanded more than once. 'It makes me shiver. And that's not the only thing about Lysandros that makes me shiver.'

In that, she knew she was not alone. Most of Athens would have agreed. Now, when Stavros had described the conversation, she said, 'Why did he change his mind about coming with us?'

'My fault. I stupidly mentioned the past, and he froze. It's almost eerie the way he's blotted that time out as though it never happened, yet it drives everything he does. Look at what happened just now. One minute he was fine, the next he couldn't get rid of me fast enough.'

'I wonder why he's really going to leave early.'

'He'll probably pass the time with a floozy.'

'If you mean—' she said a name, 'she's hardly a floozy. Her husband's one of the most influential men on the—'

'Which makes her a high class floozy, and she's keeping

her distance now because her husband has put his foot down. Rumours reached him.'

'He probably knew all the time,' his wife said cynically. 'There are men in this city who don't mind their women sleeping with Lysandros.'

Stavros nodded. 'Yes, but I gather she became too "emotional", started expecting too much, so he dropped the husband a hint to rein her in if he knew what was good for him.'

'Surely even Lysandros wouldn't be so cruel, so cold-blooded—'

'That's exactly what he is, and in our hearts we all know it,' Stavros said flatly.

'I wonder about *his* heart,' she mused.

'He doesn't have one, which is why he keeps people at a distance.'

As the car turned out of the gate Stavros couldn't resist looking back to the house. Lysandros stood there at the window, watching the world with a brooding air, as though it was his personal property and he had yet to decide how to manage it.

He remained there until the car had vanished through the gates, then turned back into the room, trying to clear his mind. The conversation had disturbed him and that must be quickly remedied. Luckily an urgent call came through from his manager at the port of Piraeus, to say that they were threatened with union trouble. Lysandros gave him a series of curt orders and promised to be there the next day.

Today he would attend Homer Lukas's wedding as an honoured guest. He would shake his rival's hand, show honour to the bride, and the watching crowds would sigh with disappointment not to see them at each other's throats, personally as well as professionally.

Now, more than ever, his father's advice rang in his head. *'Never, never let them know what you're thinking.'*

He'd learned that lesson well and, with its aid, he would spend today with a smile on his face, concealing the hatred that consumed him.

At last it was time for his chauffeur to take him to the Lukas estate. Soon he could see Homer's 'Parthenon', in which the wedding was to take place, and it loomed up high, proclaiming the residence of a wealthy and influential man.

A fake, he thought grimly. No more authentic than the other 'Greek setting' in Las Vegas.

His thoughts went back to a time that felt like another world and through his mind danced the girl on the roof, skinny, ordinary, yet with an outspoken innocence that had both exasperated and charmed him. And at the last moment, when she'd opened her arms to him, offering a comfort he'd found nowhere else in the world and he'd almost—

He slammed his mind shut. It was the only way to deal with weakness.

He wondered how she'd come to be one of the wedding party; probably the daughter of one of Estelle Radnor's numerous secretaries.

She might be here today, but it was probably better not to meet again after so long. Time was never kind. The years would have turned her into a dull wife with several children and a faithless husband. Where once she had sparkled, now she would probably seethe.

Nor had he himself been improved by time, he knew. A heaviness had settled over him, different from the raging grief that had possessed him in those days. That had been a matter of the heart and he'd dealt with it suitably, setting it aside, focusing on his head, where all sensible action took place.

He'd done what was right and wise, yet he had an uneasy feeling that if he met her now she would look right through him—and disapprove.

At last they arrived. As he got out of his car and looked around he had to admit that Homer had spent money to great effect. The great temple to the goddess Athena had been re-created much as the original must have looked when it was new. The building was about seventy metres by thirty, the roof held aloft by elegant columns. Marvellous statues abounded, but the greatest of all was the forty-foot statue of Athena, which had mysteriously developed the face of Estelle Radnor.

He grimaced, wondering how long it would be before he could decently depart.

But, before he could start his social duties, his cellphone shrilled. It was a text message.

I'm sorry about what I said. I was upset. You seemed to be pulling away when we'd been growing so close. Please call me.

It was signed only with an initial. He immediately texted back.

No need to be sorry. You were right to break it off. Forgive me for upsetting you.

Hopefully that would be an end to it, but after a moment another text came through.

I don't want to break off. I really didn't mean all those things. Will I see you at the wedding? We could talk there.

This time it was signed with her name. He responded.

We always knew it couldn't last. We can't talk. I don't wish to subject you to gossip.

The answer came in seconds.

I don't care about gossip. I love you.

Madness seemed to have come over her, for now she'd stepped up the intensity, signing *your own forever*, followed by her name. His response was brief.

Please accept my good wishes for the future. Make sure you delete texts from your phone. Goodbye.

After that he switched off. In every way. To silence a

machine was easy. It was the switching off of the heart and mind that took skill, but it was one he'd acquired with practice, sharpening it to perfection until he would have guaranteed it against every female in the world.

Except perhaps one.

But he would never meet her again.

Unless he was very unlucky.

Or very lucky.

'You look *gorgeous*!'

Petra Radnor laughed aside the fervent compliment from Nikator Lukas.

'Thank you, brother dear,' she said.

'Don't call me that. I'm not your brother.'

'You will be in a couple of hours, when your father has married my mother.'

'Stepbrother at most. We won't be related by blood and I can yearn after you if I want to.'

'No, I think you'll be the brother I've always wanted. My *kid* brother.'

'Kid, nothing! I'm older than you.'

It was true. He was thirty-seven to her thirty-two, but there was something about him that suggested a kid; not just the boyish lines of his face but a lingering immaturity that would probably be there all his life.

Petra liked him well enough, except for his black moods that seemed to come from nowhere, although they also vanished quickly.

He admired her extravagantly, and she justified his admiration. The gaunt figure of her teen years had blossomed, although she would always be naturally slender.

She was attractive but not beautiful, certainly not as the word was understood among her mother's film-land friends.

She had a vivid personality that gleamed from her eyes and a humour that was never long suppressed. But the true effect was often discovered only after she'd departed, when she lingered in the mind.

To divert Nikator's attention, she turned the conversation to Debra, the starlet who would be his official companion.

'You two look wonderful together,' she said. 'Everyone will say what a lucky man you are.'

'I'd rather go with you,' he sighed.

'Oh, stop it! After all the trouble Estelle took to fix you up with her, you should be grateful.'

'Debra's gorgeous,' he conceded. 'At least Demetriou won't have anything to match her.'

'Demetriou? Do you mean Lysandros Demetriou?' Petra asked, suddenly concentrating on a button. '*The* Lysandros Demetriou?'

'There's no need to say it like that, as though he was important,' Nikator said at once.

'He certainly seems to be. Didn't he—?'

'Never mind that. He probably won't have a woman on his arm.'

'I've heard he has quite a reputation with women.'

'True. But he never takes them out in public. Too much hassle, I guess. To him they're disposable. I'll tell you this, half the women who come here today will have been in his bed.'

'You really hate him, don't you?' she asked curiously.

'Years ago he was involved with a girl from this family, but he ill-treated her.'

'How?'

'I don't know the details. Nobody does.'

'Then maybe she ill-treated him,' Petra suggested. 'And he reacted badly because he was disillusioned.'

He glared at her. 'Why would you think that?'

'I don't know,' she said, suddenly confused. A voice had whispered mysteriously in her mind, but she couldn't quite make out the words. It came from long ago, and haunted her across the years. If only—

She tried to listen but now there was only silence.

'She fled, and later we heard that she was dead,' Nikator continued. 'It was years ago, but he knew how to put the knife in, even then. Be warned. When he knows you're connected with this family he'll try to seduce you, just to show us that he can do it.'

'Seduce?' she echoed with hilarity. 'What do you think I am—some helpless maiden? After all this time around the film industry I've learned to be safely cynical, I promise you. I've even been known to do a bit of "seducing" myself.'

His eyes gleamed and he reached out hopeful hands. 'Ah, in that case—'

'Be off,' she told him firmly. 'It's time you left to collect Debra.'

He dashed away, much to her relief. There were aspects of Nikki that were worrying, but that must wait. This was supposed to be a happy day.

She checked her camera. There would be an army of professional photographers here today, but Estelle, as she always called her mother, had asked her to take some intimate family pictures.

She took one last look in the mirror, then frowned at what she saw. As Nikator had said, she looked gorgeous, but what might be right for other women wasn't right for Estelle Radnor's daughter. This was the bride's big day, and she alone must occupy the spotlight.

'Something a little more restrained, I think,' Petra murmured.

She found a darker dress, plainer, more puritanical. Then she swept her luxuriant hair back into a bun and studied herself again.

'That's better. Nobody will look at me now.'

She'd grown up making these adjustments to her mother's ego. It was no longer a big deal. She was fond of Estelle, but the centre of her life was elsewhere.

The bride had already moved into the great mansion, and now occupied the suite belonging to the mistress of the house. Petra hurried along to say a last encouraging word before it was time to start.

That was when things went wrong.

Estelle screamed when she saw her daughter.

'Darling, what are you thinking of to dress like that? You look like a Victorian governess.'

Petra, who was used to her mother's way of putting things, didn't take offence. She knew by now that it was pointless.

'I thought I'd keep it plain,' she said. 'You're the one they'll be looking at. And you look absolutely wonderful. You'll be the most beautiful bride ever.'

'But people know you're *my* daughter,' Estella moaned. 'If you go out there looking middle-aged, what will they say about *me*?'

'Perhaps you could pretend I'm not your daughter,' Petra said with wry good humour.

'It's too late for that. They already know. You've got to look young and innocent or they'll wonder how old *I* am. Really, darling, you might try to do *me* credit.'

'I'm sorry. Shall I go and change?'

'Yes, do it quickly. And take your hair down.'

'All right, I'll change. Have a wonderful day.'

She kissed her mother and felt herself embraced as warmly as though there'd never been an argument. Which, in a sense, was true. Having got her own way, Estelle had forgotten it had ever happened.

As she left the room Petra was smiling, thinking it lucky

that she had a sense of humour. Thirty-two years as Estelle Radnor's daughter had had certain advantages, but they had also demanded reserves of patience.

Back in her room, she reversed the changes, donning the elegantly simple blue silk dress she'd worn before and brushing her hair free so that it fell gloriously about her shoulders. Then she went out into the grounds where the crowds were gathering and plunged into introductions. She smiled and said the right things, but part of her attention was elsewhere, scanning the men to see if Lysandros Demetriou had arrived.

The hour they had spent together, long ago, now felt like a dream, but he'd always held her interest. She'd followed his career as far as she could, gathering the sparse details of his life that seeped out. He was unmarried and, since his father's death had made him the boss of Demetriou Shipbuilding, he lived alone. That was all the world was allowed to know.

Occasionally she saw a photograph that she could just identify as the man she'd met in Las Vegas. These days his face looked fearsome, but now another face came into her mind, a naïve, disillusioned young lover, tortured out of his mind, crying, 'She made me trust her,' as though that was the worst crime in the world.

The recent pictures showed a man on whom harshness had settled early. It was hard to realise that he was the same person who'd clung to her on that high roof, seeking refuge, not from the physical danger he'd freely courted, but from the demons that howled in his head.

What had become of that need and despair? Had he yielded to the desire to destroy everything, including his own heart?

What would he say to her if they met now?

Petra was no green girl. Nor was she a prude. In the years since then she'd been married, divorced, and enjoyed male company to the full. But that encounter, short but searingly intense, lived in her mind, her heart and her senses. The awareness of an overwhelming presence was with her still, and so was the disappointment she'd felt when he'd parted from her with only the lightest touch of the lips.

Now the thought of meeting Lysandros Demetriou again gave her a frisson of pleasurable curiosity and excitement. But strangely there was also a touch of nervousness. He'd loomed so large in her imagination that she feared lest the reality disappoint her.

Then she saw him.

She was standing on the slope, watching the advancing crowd, and even among so many it was easy to discern him. It wasn't just that he was taller than most men; it was the same intense quality that had struck her so forcefully the first time, and which now seemed to sing over the distance.

The pictures hadn't done him justice, she realised. The boy had grown into a handsome man whose stern features, full of pride and aloofness, would have drawn eyes anywhere. In Las Vegas she'd seen him mostly in poor light. Now she could make out that his eyes were dark and deep-set, as though even there he was holding part of himself back.

Nikator had said no woman would be with him, and that was true. Lysandros Demetriou walked alone. Even in that milling crowd he gave the impression that nobody could get anywhere near him. Occasionally someone tried to claim his attention. He replied briefly and passed on.

The photographer in Petra smiled. Here was a man whose picture would be worth taking, and if that displeased him at first he would surely forgive her, for the sake of their old acquaintance.

She took a picture, then another. Smiling, she began to walk down until she was only a few feet in front of him. He glanced up, noticed the camera and scowled.

'Put that away,' he said.

'But—'

'And get out of my sight.'

Before she could speak again he'd passed on. Petra was left alone, her smile fading as she realised that he'd looked right through her without a hint of recognition.

There was nothing to do but move on with the crowd and take her place in the temple. She tried to shrug and reason with herself. So he hadn't recognised her! So what? It had been years ago and she'd changed a lot.

But, she thought wryly, she could dismiss any fantasies about memories reaching over time. Instead, it might be the chance to have a little fun.

Yes, fun would be good. Fun would punish him!

The music started as the bride made her entrance, magnificently attired in fawn satin, looking nowhere near fifty, her true age.

Petra joined the other photographers, and forgot everything except what she was meant to be doing. It was an ability that had carried her through some difficult times in her life.

Lysandros was seated in the front row. He frowned at her as if trying to work something out, then turned his attention to the ceremony.

The vows were spoken in Greek. The bride had learned her part well, but there was just one moment when she hesitated. Quickly, Petra moved beside her, murmured something in Greek and stepped back. Lysandros, watching, frowned again.

Then the bride and groom were moving slowly away, smiling at the crowd, two wealthy, powerful people, revelling in having acquired each other. Everyone began to leave the temple.

'Lysandros, my friend, how good to see you.'

He turned and saw Nikator advancing on him, arms outstretched as though welcoming a long-lost friend. Assuming a smile, he returned the greeting. With a flourish Nikator introduced his companion, Debra Farley. Lysandros acted suitably impressed. This continued until everyone felt that enough time had elapsed, and then the couple moved on.

Lysandros took a long breath of relief at having got that out of the way.

A slight choke made him turn and see the young woman with the luscious fair hair. She was laughing as though he'd just performed for her entertainment, and he was suddenly gripped by a rising tension, neither pleasure nor pain but a mysterious combination of both, as though the world had shifted on its axis and nothing would ever be the same again.

CHAPTER TWO

'YOU did that very convincingly,' Petra said. 'You should get an Oscar.'

She'd spoken in Greek and he replied in the same language.

'I wasn't as convincing as all that if you saw through me.'

'Oh, I automatically disbelieve everyone,' she said in a teasing voice. 'It saves a lot of time.'

He gave a polite smile. 'How wise. You're used to this kind of event, then? Do you work for Homer?' He indicated her camera.

'No, I've only recently met him.'

'What do you think of him?'

'I've never seen a man so in love.' She shook her head, as if suggesting that this passed all understanding.

'Yes, it's a pity,' he said.

'What do you mean?'

'You don't think the bride's in love with him, surely? To her, he's a decoration to flaunt in her buttonhole, in addition to the diamonds he's showered on her. The best of her career is over so she scoops him up to put on her mantel-piece. It almost makes me feel sorry for him, and I never thought I'd say that.'

'But that means someone has brought him low at last,' she

pointed out. 'You should be grateful to her. Think how much easier you'll find it to defeat him in future.'

She was regarding him with her head on one side and an air of detached amusement, as though he was an interesting specimen laid out for her entertainment. A sudden frisson went through him. He didn't understand why, and yet—

'I think I can manage that without help,' he observed.

'Now, there's a thought,' she said, apparently much struck. 'Have you noticed how weddings bring out the worst in people? I'm sure you aren't usually as cynical and grumpy as now.'

This was sheer impertinence, but instead of brushing her aside he felt an unusual inclination to spar with her.

'Certainly not,' he said. 'I'm usually worse.'

'Impossible.'

'Anyone who knows me will tell you that this is my "sweetness and light" mood.'

'I don't believe it. Instinct tells me that you're a softie at heart. People cry on your shoulder, children flock to you, those in trouble turn to you first.'

'I've done nothing to deserve that,' he assured her fervently.

The crowd was swirling around them, forcing them to move aside. As they left the temple, Lysandros observed, 'I'm surprised Homer settled for an imitation Parthenon.'

'Oh, he wanted the original,' she agreed, 'but between you and me—' she lowered her voice dramatically '—it didn't quite measure up to his standards, and he felt he could do better. So he built this to show them how it ought to have been done.'

Before he could stop himself he gave a crack of laughter and several people stared at the sight of this famously dour man actually enjoying a joke. A society journalist passing by stared, then made a hasty note.

She responded to his laughter with more of her own. He led her to where the drinks were being served and presented her with a glass of champagne, feeling that, just for once, it was good to be light-hearted. She had the power of making tension vanish, even if only briefly.

The tables for the wedding feast were outside in the sun. The guests were taking their places, preparing for the moment when the newly married couple would appear.

'I'll be back in a moment,' she said.

'Just a minute. You haven't told me who you are.'

She glanced back, regarding him with a curious smile. 'No, I haven't, have I? Perhaps I thought there would be no need. I'll see you later.'

Briefly she raised her champagne glass to him before hurrying away.

'You're a sly devil,' said a deep voice behind him.

A large bearded man stood there and with pleasure Lysandros recognised an old ally.

'Georgios,' he exclaimed. 'I might have known you'd be where there was the best food.'

'The best food, the best wine, the best women. Well, you've found that for yourself.' He indicated the young woman's retreating figure.

'She's charming,' Lysandros said with a slight reserve. He didn't choose to discuss her.

'Oh, don't worry, I'll back off. I don't aspire to Estelle Radnor's daughter.'

Lysandros tensed. 'What are you talking about?'

'I don't blame you for wanting to keep her to yourself. She's a peach.'

'You said Estelle Radnor's daughter.'

'Didn't she tell you who she was?'

'No,' Lysandros said, tight-lipped. 'She didn't.'

He moved away in Petra's direction, appalled at the trap into which he'd fallen so easily. His comments about her mother had left him at a disadvantage, something not to be tolerated. She could have warned him and she hadn't, which meant she was laughing at him.

And most men would have been beguiled by her merriment, her way of looking askance, as though that was how she saw the whole world, slightly lopsided, and all the more fun for that.

Fun. He barely knew the word, but something told him she knew it, loved it, even judged by it. And she was doubtless judging him now. His face hardened.

It was too late to catch her; she'd reached the top table where the bride and groom would sit. Now there would be no chance for a while.

A steward showed him to his place, also at the top table but just around the corner at right angles to her—close enough to see her perfectly, but not talk.

She was absorbed in chatting to her companion. Suddenly she laughed, throwing back her head and letting her amusement soar up into the blue sky. It was as though sunshine had burst out all over the world. Unwillingly he conceded that she would be enchanting, if—*if* he'd been in a mood to be enchanted. Fortunately, he was more in control than that.

Then she looked up and caught his eye. Clearly she knew that her little trick had been rumbled, for her teasing gaze said, *Fooled you!*

He sent back a silent message of his own. *Wait, that's all. Just wait!*

She looked forward to it. Her smile told him that, causing a stirring deep within him that he had to conceal by fiercely blanking his face. People sitting close by drew back a little, wondering who had offended him.

There was a distant cheer and applause broke out as Mr and Mrs Homer Lukas made their grand entrance.

He was in his sixties, grey-haired and heavily built with an air of natural command. But as he and his bride swept into place it suited him to bend his head over her hand, kissing it devotedly. She seemed about to faint with joy at his tribute, or perhaps at the five million dollar diamond on her finger.

The young woman who'd dared to tease Lysandros joined in the applause, and kissed her mother as Estelle sat down. The crowd settled to the meal.

Of course he should never have mistaken her for an employee. Her air of being at home in this company ought to have warned him. And when she moved in to take close-up photographs both bride and groom posed at her command.

Then she posed with the happy couple while a professional photographer took the shots. At this point Nikator butted in.

'We must have some of us together,' Lysandros could just hear him cry. 'Brother and sister.'

Having claimed a brother's privilege, he snaked an arm about her waist and drew her close. She played up, but Lysandros spotted a fleeting look of exasperation on her face, and she freed herself as soon as possible, handing him back to Debra Farley like a nurse ridding herself of a pesky child.

Not that he could blame Nikator for his preference. In that glamorous company this creature stood out, with her effortless simplicity and an air of naturalness that the others had lost long ago. Her dress was light blue silk, sleeveless, figure-hugging, without ornament. It was practically a proclamation, as though she were saying, *I need no decoration. I, myself, am enough.*

No doubt about that.

As the party began to break up he made his way over to her. She was waiting for him with an air of teasing expectancy.

'I suppose that'll teach me to be more careful next time,' he said wryly.

'You were a little incautious, weren't you?'

'You thought it was a big joke not to tell me who you were while I said those things about your mother.'

'I didn't force you to say them. What's the matter with you? Can't you take a joke?'

'No,' he said flatly. 'I don't find it funny at all.'

She frowned a little, as though confronting an alien species. 'Do you find anything funny—ever?'

'No. It's safer that way.'

Her humour vanished. 'You poor soul.'

She sounded as though she meant it, and the hint of sympathy took him aback. It was so long since anyone had dared to pity him, or at least dared to show it. Not since another time—another world—long ago...

An incredible suspicion briefly troubled his mind. He ordered it gone and it obeyed, but reluctantly.

'If you feel I insulted your mother, I apologise,' he said stiffly.

'Actually, it's me you insulted.'

'I don't see how.'

She looked into his face with a mixture of incredulity, indignation, but mostly amusement.

'You really don't, do you?' she asked. 'All this time and you still haven't—you *really* haven't—? Well, let me tell you, when you meet a lady for the second time, it's considered polite to remember the first time.'

'For the second—? Have we ever—have we—?'

And then the suspicion wouldn't be banished any longer. He *knew*.

'It was you,' he said slowly. 'On the roof—in Las Vegas—'

'Boy, I really lived in your memory, didn't I?'

'But—you're different—not the same person.'

'I should hope not, after all this time. I'm the same in some ways, not others. You're different too, but you're easier to spot.

I was longing for you to recognise me, but you didn't.' She sighed theatrically. 'Hey ho! What a disappointment!'

'You didn't care if I recognised you or not,' he said flatly.

'Well, maybe just a little.'

An orchestra was getting into place and the dancing area was being cleared, so that they had to move to the side.

He was possessed by a strange feeling, of having wandered into an alien world where nothing was quite as it looked. She had sprung out of the past, landing in his path, challenging him with memories and fears.

'Even now I can't believe that it's you,' he said. 'Your hair's different—it was cut very short—'

'Functional,' she said at once. 'I was surrounded by film people making the best of themselves, so I made the least of myself as an act of adolescent defiance.'

'Was that all you could think of?'

'Consider my problem,' she said with an expansive gesture. 'The average teenager goes wild, indulges herself with wine, late nights, lovers—but everyone around me was doing that. I'd never have been noticed. So I cut my hair as badly as possible, bought cheap clothes, studied my school books and had early nights. Heavens, was I virtuous! Boring but virtuous.'

'And what happened?' he asked, fascinated.

She chuckled. 'My mother started to get very worried about my "strange behaviour". It took her a while to accept the fact that I was heading for the academic life.'

'Doing what?'

'I've made my career out of ancient Greece. I write books, I give lectures. I pretend to know a lot more than I actually do—'

'Like most of them,' he couldn't resist saying.

'Like most of them,' she agreed at once.

'Is your mother reconciled?'

'Oh, yes, she's terribly impressed now. She came to one of my lectures and afterwards she said, "Darling that was wonderful! *I didn't understand a word.*" That's her yardstick, bless her. And in the end it was me who introduced her to Homer.' She looked around. 'So you could say I'm to blame for all this.'

It was time for the dancing. Homer and Estelle took the floor, gliding about in each other's arms until the photographers had all had their fill.

'Aren't you taking any pictures?' he asked.

'No, mine's just the personal family stuff. What they're doing now is for the public.'

Nikator waved as he danced past with Debra in his arms. Petra sighed.

'He may be in his late thirties but he's just a silly kid at heart. What it'll be like when he takes over the firm I can't—' She broke off guiltily, her hand over her mouth. 'I didn't say that.'

'Don't worry. You didn't say anything the whole world doesn't already know. It's interesting that you're learning already.'

There was a sardonic edge to his voice, and she didn't have to ask what he meant. The two great families of Greek shipbuilding survived by getting the edge on each other, and inevitably that included spying. The kind of casual comment that others could risk might be dangerous.

The dance ended and another one began. Debra vanished in the arms of a powerful producer, and Nikator made his way in Petra's direction.

'Oh, heavens, dance with me!' she breathed, seizing Lysandros and drawing him onto the floor.

'What are you—?' Somehow he found his arms around her.

'Yes, I know, in polite society I'm supposed to wait for you to ask me,' she muttered, 'but this isn't polite society, it's a goldfish bowl.'

He felt she couldn't have put it better.

'But your fears may be misplaced,' he pointed out. 'With you being so boring and virtuous he probably wasn't going to ask you at all.'

'He has peculiar tastes.' She added hurriedly, 'And I didn't say that, either.'

She was like quicksilver in his arms, twisting and turning against him, leading him on so that he moved in perfect time with her and had to fight an impulse to tighten his grip, draw her against his body and let things happen as they would. Not here. Not now. Not yet.

Petra read him fairly accurately, and something thrilled in her blood.

'Don't you like dancing?' she asked after a while.

'This isn't dancing. It's swimming around that goldfish bowl.'

'True. But we annoyed Nikator, which is something gained.'

She was right. Nikator's expression was that of a child whose toys had been snatched away. Then Lysandros forgot everything except Petra. Her face was close to his and the smile in her eyes reached him directly.

'What will you do after this?' he asked.

'Stay here for a few days, or weeks. It's a chance for me to do some research. Homer has great contacts. There's a museum vault that's never opened for anyone, but he's fixing it for me.'

He glanced down at the slender, sensual body moving in his arms, at the charming face that seemed to smile more naturally than any other expression, and the blue eyes with their mysterious, tantalising depths, and he knew a sense of outrage. What was this woman doing in museums, investigating the dead, when everything in her spoke of life? She belonged not in tombs but in sunlight, not turning dusty pages but caressing a man's face and pressing her naked body against his.

The mere thought of her nakedness made him draw a sharp breath. The dress fitted her closely enough to give him a good idea of her contours, but it only tempted him to want more. He controlled his thoughts by force.

'Is visiting museums really your idea of being lucky?' he asked slowly.

'I'm going to see things that other scholars have been struggling to see for years. I'll be ahead of the game.'

'But isn't there anything else you want to do?' he asked.

'You mean, what's a woman doing worrying her little head about such things? Women are made for pleasure; serious matters should be left to men.'

Since this came dangerously near to his actual thoughts he was left floundering for a moment. He wished she hadn't used the word 'pleasure'. It was a distraction he could do without.

'I didn't mean it like that,' he managed to say at last, 'but when life offers you so many more avenues—'

'Like Nikator? Yes, I could throw myself into his arms, or anything else he wanted me to throw myself into—careful!'

'Sorry,' he said hastily, loosing his fingers, which he'd tightened against her instinctively.

'Where was I? Ah, yes, exploring avenues.'

'Forget Nikator,' he snapped. 'He's not an avenue, he's a dead end.'

'Yes, I'd managed to work that out for myself. I'm not seventeen any more. I'm thirty-two, in my dotage.'

In her dotage, he thought ironically, with skin like soft peach, hair like silk and eyes that teased, inviting him just so far and warning him against going any further. But she was right about one thing. She was no child. She'd been around long enough to discover a good deal about men, and he had an uneasy feeling that she could read more about him than he wanted her—or anyone—to know.

'If you're fishing for compliments you picked the wrong man,' he said.

'Oh, sure, I'd never come to you for sweet nothings, or for anything except—yes, that would be something—' She hesitated, as though trying to phrase it carefully. 'Something you could give me better than any other man,' she whispered at last.

He struggled not to say the words, but they came out anyway. 'And what's that?'

'Good financial advice,' she declared. 'Aha! There, I did it.'

'Did what?'

'I made you laugh.'

'I'm not laughing,' he said through twitching lips.

'You would be if you weren't trying so hard not to. I bet myself I could make you laugh. Be nice. Give me my little victory.'

'I'm never nice. But I'll let you have it this once.'

'Only this once?' she asked, raising her eyebrows.

'I prefer to claim victory for myself.'

'I could take that as a challenge.'

Then there was silence as their bodies moved in perfect time, and she thought that yes, he was a challenge, and what a challenge he would be; so different from the easy-going men with whom she'd mostly spent her life. There was a darkness about him that he made little attempt to hide, and which tempted her, although she knew she was probably crazy.

'Do your challenges usually work out as you plan?' he asked.

'Oh, yes,' she assured him. 'I won't settle for anything less than my own way.'

'I'm exactly the same. What a terrible battle looms ahead.'

'True,' she said. 'I'm trembling in fear of you.'

He didn't speak, but a slow smile overtook his face—the smile of a man who didn't believe her and was planning a clever move.

Petra had a strange feeling that the other women on the dance floor were staring at her. Most of them had slept with Lysandros, she'd been warned, and suddenly she knew it was true. Their eyes were feverish, full of memories, hot, sweet and glorious, followed by anguish. Mentally they raked her, undressed her, trying to imagine whether she would please him.

And that was really unnerving because she was trying to decide the same thing.

They spoke to her, those nameless women, telling her that he was a lover of phenomenal energy, who could last all night, untiring, driving her on to heights she'd never reached before, heights she wanted to discover.

There was one woman in particular whose greedy gaze caught her attention. Something about the extravagantly dressed, petulant creature made Petra wonder if this was the most recent of Lysandros's conquests—and his rejections. Her eyes were like the others, but a thousand times more bitter, more murderous.

Then Lysandros turned her in the dance, faster and faster, taking her to a distant place where there was only the whirling movement that shut out the rest of the world. She gave herself up to it completely, wanting nothing else.

Would she too lie in his arms in a fever of passion? And would she end up like the others, yearning wretchedly from a distance?

But something told her that their path together wouldn't be as simple as that.

Suddenly they were interrupted by a shout from a few yards off. Everyone stopped dancing and backed away, revealing the bride and groom locked in a passionate embrace. As befitted a glamorous couple, the kiss went on and on as the crowd cheered and applauded. Then some of the others began to embrace. More and more followed suit until it seemed as though the whole place was filled with lingering kisses.

Lysandros stood motionless, his arm still around her waist, the other hand holding hers. The space between them remained barely a centimetre. It would take only the slightest movement for him to cover that last tiny distance and lay his lips on hers. She looked up at him, her heart beating.

'What a performance!' he exclaimed, looking around and speaking in disapproving tones. 'I won't insult you by subjecting you to it.'

He released her, stepping back and giving her no choice but to do the same.

'Thank you,' she said formally. 'It's delightful to meet a man with a sense of propriety.'

She could have hit him.

'I'm afraid I must be going,' he said. 'I've neglected my affairs for too long. It's been a pleasure meeting you again.'

'And you,' she said crisply.

He inclined his head courteously, and in a moment he was gone.

Thunderstruck, she watched him, barely believing what had happened, and so suddenly. He was as deep in desire as herself. All her instincts told her that beyond a shadow of doubt. Yet he'd denied that desire, fought it, overcome it, *because that was what he had decided to do.*

This was a man of steely will, which he would impose no matter what the cost to himself or anyone else. He'd left her without even a glance back. It was like a blow in the stomach.

'Don't worry. Just be patient.'

Petra looked up to see the woman who'd caught her attention while they'd danced. Now she recalled seeing her arrive at the wedding with one of the city's most wealthy and powerful men. She was regarding Petra with a mixture of contempt and pity.

'I couldn't help watching you—and Lysandros,' she said,

moving nearer. 'It's his way, you see. He'll come just so close, and then withdraw to consider the matter. When he's decided that he can fit you in with his other commitments he'll return and take his pleasure at his own time and his own convenience.'

'If I agree,' Petra managed to say.

The woman gave a cold, tinkly laugh.

'Don't be absurd, of course you'll agree. It's written all over you. He could walk back right this minute and you'd agree.'

'I guess you know what you're talking about,' Petra said softly.

'Oh, yes, I know. I've been there. I know what's going through your head because it went through mine. "Who does he think he is to imagine he can just walk back and I'll yield to him on command?" But then he looks at you as if you're the only woman in the world, and you do yield on his command. And it'll be wonderful—for a while. In his arms, in his bed, you'll discover a universe you never knew existed.

'But one day you'll wake up and find yourself back on earth. It will be cold because he's gone. He's done with you. You no longer exist. You'll weep and refuse to believe it, but he won't answer the phone, so after a while you'll have to believe it.'

She began to turn away, but paused long enough to say over her shoulder, 'You think you'll be different, but with him no woman is ever different. Goodbye.'

CHAPTER THREE

THE party went on into the evening. Lights came on throughout the false Parthenon, music wafted up into the sky, assignations were made, profitable deals were settled. Petra accompanied Estelle into the house to help her change into her travelling clothes.

The honeymoon was to be spent on board the *Silver Lady*, Homer's yacht, refurbished for the occasion and currently moored in the port of Piraeus, about five miles away. Two cars bearing luggage and personal servants had already gone on ahead. There remained only the limousine to convey the bride and groom.

'Are you all right?' Estelle asked, glancing at her daughter's face.

'Of course,' Petra said brightly.

'You look as if you were brooding about something.'

In fact she'd been brooding about the stranger's words.

'When he's decided that he can fit you in with his other commitments he'll return and take his pleasure at his own time and his own convenience.'

That was not going to happen, she resolved. If he returned tonight he would find her missing.

'Do you mind if I come to the port to see you off?' she asked suddenly.

'Darling, that would be lovely. But I thought you'd be planning a wild night out.'

'Not me. I don't have your energy.'

In the car on the way to the port they drank champagne. Once on board, Homer showed her around the stately edifice with vast pride, finishing in the great bedroom with the bed big enough for six, covered with gold satin embroidered cushions.

'Now we must find a husband for you,' he declared expansively.

'No, thank you,' Petra hurried to say. 'My one experience of marriage didn't leave me with any desire to try again.'

Before he could reply, her cellphone rang and she answered.

'I'm afraid my manners left something to be desired,' said a man's voice. 'Perhaps I can make amends by taking you to dinner?'

For a moment she floundered. She had her speech of rejection ready prepared but no words would come.

'I'm not sure—'

'My car's just outside the house.'

'But I'm not there. I'm in Piraeus.'

'It won't take you long to return. I'll be waiting.'

He hung up.

'Cheek!' she exploded. 'He just takes it for granted I'll do what he wants.' Seeing them frowning, she added, 'Lysandros Demetriou. He wants to take me to dinner, and I wasn't given much chance to say no.'

'That sounds like him,' Homer said approvingly. 'When he wants something he doesn't waste time.'

'But it's no way to treat a lady,' Estelle said indignantly.

He grinned and kissed her. 'You didn't seem to mind.'

As they were escorting her off the yacht Petra suddenly had a thought.

'How did he know my cellphone number? I didn't give it to him.'

'He probably paid someone in my household to find out,' Homer said as though it was a matter of course. 'Goodbye, my dear.'

She hurried down the gangplank and into the car. On the journey back to Athens she tried to sort out her thoughts. She was angry, but mostly with herself. So many good resolutions ground to dust because of a certain tone in his voice.

On impulse she took out her phone and dialled the number of Karpos, an Athens contact, an ex-journalist whom she knew to be reliable. When he heard what she wanted he drew a sharp breath.

'Everyone's afraid of him,' he said, speaking quickly. 'In fact they're so afraid that they won't even admit their fear, in case he gets to hear and complains that they've made him look bad.'

'That's paranoid.'

'Sure, but it's the effect he has. Nobody is allowed to see inside his head or his heart—if he has one. Opinion is divided about that.'

'But wasn't there someone, a long time ago—? From the other family?'

'Right. Her name was Brigitta, but I didn't tell you that. She died in circumstances nobody has ever been able to discover. The press were warned off by threats, which is why you'll never see it mentioned now.'

'You mean threats of legal action?'

'There are all kinds of threats,' Karpos said mysteriously. 'One man started asking questions. The next thing he knew, all his debts were called in. He was on the verge of ruin, but it was explained to him that if he "behaved himself" in future, matters could be put right. Of course he gave the promise, turned over all his notes, and everything was miraculously settled.'

'Did anything bad happen to him afterwards?'

'No, he left journalism and went into business. He's very successful, but if you say the name Demetriou, he leaves the room quickly. Anything you know, you have to pretend not to know, like the little apartment he has in Athens, or Priam House in Corfu.'

'Priam House?' she said, startled. 'I've heard of that. People have been trying to explore the cellar for years—there's something there, but nobody's allowed in. Do you mean it's his?'

'So they say. But don't let on that you know about it. In fact, don't tell him you've spoken to me, please.'

She promised and hung up. Sitting there, silent and thoughtful, she knew she was getting into deep water. But deep water had never scared her.

She also knew that there was another aspect to this, something that couldn't be denied.

After fifteen years, she and Lysandros Demetriou had unfinished business.

He'd said he would be waiting for her and, sure enough, he was there by the gate to Homer's estate. As her car slowed he pulled open the door, took her hand and drew her out.

'I won't be long,' she said. 'I just have to go inside and—'

'No. You're fine as you are. Let's go.'

'I was going to change my dress—'

'You don't need to. You're beautiful. You know that, so why are we arguing?'

There was something about this blunt speech that affected her more than a smooth compliment would ever have done. He had no party manners. He said exactly what he thought, and he thought she was beautiful. She felt a smile grow inside her until it possessed her completely.

'You know what?' she said. 'You're right. Why are we arguing?' She indicated for her chauffeur to go on without her and got into Lysandros's car.

She wondered where he would take her, possibly a sophisticated restaurant, but he surprised her by driving out into the countryside for a few miles and stopping at a small restaurant, where he led her to an outside table. Here they were close to the coast and in the distance she could just make out the sea, shimmering beneath the moon.

'This is lovely,' she said. 'It's so peaceful after all the crowds today.'

'That's how I feel too,' he said. 'Normally I only come here alone.'

The food was simple, traditional Greek cooking, just as she liked it. While he concentrated on the order Petra had the chance to consider him, trying to reconcile his reputation as a ruthless tyrant with the suffering boy she'd met years ago.

That boy had been vulnerable and still able to show it, to the extent of telling a total stranger that a betrayal of trust had broken his heart. Now he was a man who inspired fear, who would deny having a heart, who would probably jeer at the idea of trust.

What had really happened all those years ago? And could it ever be put right for him?

She thought again of dancing with him, the other women with their envious, lustful glances as they relived hours spent in bed with that tall, strong body, yielding ecstatically to skills they'd found in no other man.

'Are you all right?' Lysandros asked suddenly.

'Yes—why do you ask?'

'You drew a sharp breath, as though you were in pain.'

'No, I'm not in pain,' she hurried to say.

Unless, she thought, you included the pain of wanting something you'd be wiser not to want. She pretended to search her bag. When she glanced up she found him regarding her with a look of wonder.

'Fifteen years,' he said. 'So much has happened and we've changed, and yet in another way we're still the same people. I would have known you anywhere.'

She smiled. 'But you didn't recognise me.'

'Only on the surface. Inside, there was a part of me that knew you. I never thought we'd meet again, and yet somehow I was always certain that we would.'

She nodded. 'Me too. If we'd waited another fifteen years—or fifty—I'd still have been sure that we would one day talk again before we died.'

The last words seemed to reach right inside him. To talk again before they died. That was it. He knew that normally his own thoughts would have struck him as fanciful. He was a strong man, practical, impatient of anything that he couldn't pin down. Yet what he said was true. She'd been an unseen presence in his life ever since that night.

He wondered how he could tell her this. She'd inspired him with the will to talk freely, but that wasn't enough. He didn't know how.

The food arrived, feta and tomato slices, simple and delicious.

'Mmm,' she said blissfully.

He ate little, spending most of his time watching her.

'Why were you up there?' he asked at last. 'Why not downstairs, enjoying the wedding?'

'I guess I'm a natural cynic.' She smiled. 'My grandfather used to say that I approached life with an attitude of, *Oh, yeah?* And it's true. I think it was already there that night in Las Vegas, and it's got worse since. Given the madhouse I've always lived in, it could hardly be any other way.'

'How do you feel about the madhouse?'

'I enjoy it, as long as I'm not asked to get too deeply involved in it or take it seriously.'

'You've never wanted to be a film actress yourself?'

'Good grief, no! One raving lunatic in the family is enough.'

'Does your mother know you talk like that?'

'Of course. She actually said it first, and we're agreed. She's a sweetie and I adore her, but she lives on the Planet Zog.'

'How old is she really?'

'As old as she needs to be at any one moment. She was seventeen when she had me. My father didn't want any responsibility, so he just dumped her, and she struggled alone for a while. Believe me, anyone who just sees her as a film star should see the back streets of London where we lived in those years.

'Then my father's parents got in touch to say that he'd just died in a road accident. They hadn't even known we existed until he admitted it on his deathbed. They were Greek, with strong ideas about family, and I was all the family they had left. Luckily, they were nice people and we all got on well. They looked after me while Estelle built her career. My grandfather was a scholar who'd originally come to England to run a course in Greek at university. At first I didn't even go to school because he reckoned he could teach me better, and he was right.'

'So you grew up as the one with common sense?'

'Well, one of us had to have some,' she chuckled.

'How did you manage with all those stepfathers?'

'They were OK. Mostly they were lovelorn and a bit dopey, so I had a hard job keeping a straight face.'

'What about the one in Las Vegas?'

'Let's see, he was the—no, that was the other one—or was he? Oh, never mind. They're all the same, anyway. I think he was an aspiring actor who thought Estelle could help his ambitions. When she finally saw through him she tossed him out. She was in love with someone else by then.'

'You're very cool about it all. Doesn't all this "eternal love" affect you?'

'Eternal love?' She seemed to consider this. 'Would that be eternal love as in he tried to take every penny she had, or as in he haunted the set, throwing a fit whenever she had a love scene, or as in—?'

'All right, I get the picture. Evidently the male sex doesn't impress you.'

'However did you guess?'

'But what about your own experience? There must have been one or two brave enough to defy the rockets you fire at them?'

Her lips twitched. 'Of course. I don't look at them unless they're brave enough to do that.'

'That's the first of your requirements, is it? Courage?'

'Among other things. But even that's overrated. The man I married was a professional sportsman, a skier who could do the most death-defying stuff. The trouble was, it was all he could do, so in the end he was boring too.'

'You're married?' he asked slowly.

'Not any more,' she said in a tone of such devout thankfulness that he was forced to smile.

'What happened? Was it very soon after our meeting?'

'No, I went to college and studied hard. It was the same college where my grandfather had been a professor, and it was wonderful because people couldn't care less that I was a film star's daughter, but they were impressed that I was his granddaughter. I had to do him credit. I studied to improve my knowledge of the Greek language, learned the history, passed exams. We were going to come here and explore together, but then he and my grandmother both died. It's not the same without him. I so much wanted to make him proud of me.'

She hesitated, while a shadow crossed her face, making him lean forward.

'What is it?' he asked gently.

'Oh—nothing.'

'Tell me,' he persisted, still gentle.

'I was just remembering how much I loved them and they loved me. They needed me, because I was all that was left to them after their son died. They liked Estelle, but she wasn't part of them as I was.'

'Wasn't your mother jealous of your closeness to them?'

Petra shook her head. 'She's a loving mother, in her way, but I've never been vital to her as I was to them.'

'How sad,' he said slowly.

'Not really. As long as you have someone who needs you, you can cope with the others who don't.'

At that moment all the others who hadn't needed her seemed to be there in the shadows, starting with Estelle, always surrounded by people whose job it was to minister to her—hairdressers, make-up artists, lawyers, psychologists, professional comfort-givers, lovers, husbands. Whatever she wanted, there was always someone paid to provide it.

She was sweet-tempered and had showered her daughter with a genuine, if slightly theatrical affection, but when a heavy cold had forced Petra to miss one of her weddings— Fourth? Fifth?—she'd shrugged, said, "Never mind" and merely saved her an extra large piece of cake.

Petra had soon understood. She was loved, but she wasn't essential. She'd tried to take it lightly, saying that it didn't matter, because she'd found that this was one way to cope. Eventually it had become the way she coped with the whole of life.

But it had mattered. There, always at the back of her mind, had been the little sadness, part of her on the lookout for someone to whom she was vitally necessary. Her. Not the money and glamour with which her mother's life surrounded her, but *her*.

And perhaps that was why a young man's agony and desperation had pierced her heart on a roof in Las Vegas fifteen years ago.

'But your grandparents died,' Lysandros said. 'Who do you have now?'

She pulled herself together. 'Are you kidding? My life is crowded with people. It's like living with a flock of geese.'

'Including your mother's husbands?'

'Well, she didn't bother to marry them all. She said there wasn't enough time.'

'Boyfriends?' he asked carefully.

'Some. But half of them were simply trying to get close to my mother, which didn't do my self-confidence any good. I learnt to keep my feelings to myself until I'd sized them up.' She gave a soft chuckle. 'I got a reputation for being frigid.'

They were mad, he thought. No woman who was frigid had that warmth and resonance in her voice, or that glow on her skin.

'And then I met Derek,' she recalled. 'Estelle was making a film with a winter sports background and he was one of the advisors. He was so handsome, I fell for him hook, line and sinker. I thought it had happened at last. We were happy enough for a couple of years, but then—' she shrugged '—I guess he got bored with me.'

'*He* got bored with *you?*' he asked with an involuntary emphasis.

She chuckled as though her husband's betrayal was the funniest thing that had ever happened to her. He was becoming familiar with that defensive note in her laughter. It touched an echo in himself.

'I don't think I was ever the attraction,' she said. 'He needed money and he thought Estelle Radnor's daughter would have plenty. Anyway, he started sleeping around, I lost my temper and I think it scared him a little.'

'You? A temper?'

'Most people think I don't have one because I only lose it once in a blue moon. Now and then I really let fly. I try not to because what's the point? But it's there, and it can make me say things I wish I hadn't. Anyway, that was five years ago. It's all over. Why are you smiling?'

When had anyone last asked him that? When had anyone had cause to? How often did he smile?

'I didn't know I was smiling,' he said hastily.

'You looked like you'd seen some private joke. Come on. Share.'

Private joke! If his board of directors, his bank manager, his underlings heard that they'd think she was delusional.

But the smile was there, growing larger, happier, being drawn forth by her teasing demand.

'Tell me,' she said. 'What did I say that was so funny?'

'It's not—it's just the way you said "It's all over", as though you'd airbrushed the entire male sex out of your life.'

'Or out of the universe,' she agreed. 'Best thing for them.'

'For them, or for you?'

'Definitely for me. Men no longer exist. Now my world is this country, my work, my investigations.'

'But the ancient Greeks had members of the male sex,' he pointed out. 'Unfortunate, but true.'

'Yes, but I can afford to be tolerant about them. They helped start my career. I wrote a book about Greek heroes just before I left university, and actually got it published. Later I was asked to revise it into a less academic version, for schools, and the royalties have been nice. So I feel fairly charitable about the legendary Greek men.'

'Especially since they're safely dead?'

'You're getting the idea.'

'Let's eat,' he said hastily.

The waiter produced chicken and onion pie, washed down with sparkling wine, and for a while there was no more talking. Watching her eat, relishing every mouthful, he wondered about her assertion that men no longer existed for her. With any other woman he would have said it was a front, a pretence to fool the world while she carried on a life of sensual indulgence. But this woman was different. She inhabited her own universe, one he'd never encountered before.

'So that's how you came to know so much that night in Las Vegas,' he said at last. 'You gave me a shock, lecturing me about Achilles.'

She gave a rueful laugh. 'Lecturing. That just about says it all. I'm afraid I do, and people get fed up. I can't blame them. I remember I made you very cross.'

'I wasn't thrilled to be told I was sulking,' he admitted, 'but I was only twenty-three. And besides—'

'And besides, you were very unhappy, weren't you?' she asked. 'Because of *her*.'

He shrugged. 'I don't remember.'

Her gentle eyes said that she didn't believe him.

'She made you trust her, but then you found you couldn't trust her,' she encouraged. 'You don't forget something like that.'

'Would you like some more wine?' he asked politely.

So he wasn't ready to tell her the things she yearned to know, about the catastrophe that had smashed his life. She let it go, knowing that hurrying him would be fatal.

'So your grandfather taught you Greek,' he said, clearly determined to change the subject.

'Inside me, I feel as much Greek as English. He made sure of that.'

'That's how you knew about Achilles? I thought you'd been learning about him at school.'

'Much more than that. I read about him in Homer's *Iliad*, how he was a hero of the Trojan war. I thought that story was so romantic. There was Helen, the most beautiful woman in the world, and all those men fighting over her. She's married to Menelaus but she falls in love with Paris, who takes her to Troy. But Menelaus won't give up and the Greek troops besiege Troy for ten years, trying to get her back.

'And there were all those handsome Greek heroes, especially Achilles,' she went on, giving him a cheeky smile. 'What made your mother admire Achilles rather than any of the others?'

'She came from Corfu where, as you probably know, his influence is very strong. Her own mother used to take her to the Achilleion Palace, although that was chiefly because she was fascinated by Sisi.'

Petra nodded. 'Sisi' had been Elizabeth of Bavaria, a romantic heroine of the nineteenth century, and reputedly the loveliest woman of her day. Her beauty had caused Franz Joseph, the young Emperor of Austria, to fall madly in love with her and sweep her into marriage when she was only sixteen.

But the marriage had faltered. For years she'd roamed the world, isolated, wandering from place to place, until she'd bought a palace on the island of Corfu.

The greatest tragedy of her life was the death of her son Rudolph, at Mayerling, in an apparent suicide pact with his mistress. A year later Sisi had begun to transform the Palace into a tribute to Achilles, but soon she too was dead, at the hands of an assassin. The Palace had subsequently been sold and turned into a museum, dedicated to honouring Achilles.

'The bravest and the most handsome of them all, yet hiding a secret weakness,' Petra mused.

She was referring to the legend of Achilles' mother, who'd sought to protect her baby son by dipping him in the River Styx, that ran between earth and the underworld. Where the waters of the Styx touched they were held to make a man immortal. But she'd held him by the heel, leaving him mortal in the one place where the waters had not touched him. Down the centuries that story resonated so that the term 'Achilles heel' still meant the place where a strong person was unexpectedly vulnerable.

Of all the statues in the Achilleon, the most notable was the one showing him on the ground, vainly trying to pull the arrow from his heel as his life ebbed away.

'In the end it was the thing that killed him,' Lysandros said. 'His weakness wasn't so well-hidden after all. His assassin knew exactly where to aim an arrow, and to cover the tip with poison so that it would be fatal.'

'Nobody is as safe as they believe they are,' she mused.

'My father's motto was—never let anyone know what you're thinking. That's the real weakness.'

'But that's not true,' she said. 'Sometimes you're stronger because other people understand you.'

His voice hardened. 'I disagree. The wise man trusts nobody with his thoughts.'

'Not even me?' she asked softly.

She could tell the question disconcerted him, but his defences were too firmly riveted in place to come down easily.

'If there was one person I could trust—I think it would be you, because of the past. But I am what I am.' He gave a self-mocking smile. 'I don't think even you can change me.'

She regarded him gently before venturing to touch his hand.

'Beware people you think you can trust?' she whispered.

'Did I say that?' he asked quickly.

'Something like it. In Las Vegas, you came to the edge of saying a lot more.'

'I was in a bad way that night. I don't know what I said.'

A silence came down over him. He stared into his glass,

and she guessed that he was shocked at himself for having relented so far. Now he would retreat again behind walls of caution and suspicion.

Was there any way to get through to this man's damaged heart? she wondered. And, if she tried, might she not do him more harm than good?

CHAPTER FOUR

'I'M SORRY,' Lysandros said quietly. 'This is me; it's who and what I am.'

'You don't let anyone in, do you?' Petra said.

He shook his head with an air of finality. Suddenly then he said, 'But I will tell you one thing. It may only be a coincidence, but it's strange. After I'd taken you back to your room I returned to the tables and suddenly started winning back everything I'd lost. I just couldn't lose, and somehow that was connected with you, as though you'd turned me into a winner. Why are you smiling?'

'You, being superstitious. If I'd said all that you'd make some snooty masculine comment about women having overly vivid imaginations.'

'Yes, I probably would,' he admitted. 'But perhaps you just exercise a more powerful brand of magic.'

'Magic?'

'Don't tell me you've studied the Greek legends without discovering magic?'

'Yes,' she conceded, 'you meet it in the most unexpected places, and the hard part is knowing how to tell it from wishful thinking.'

She spoke the last words so softly that he barely heard

them, but they were enough to give him a strange sensation, part pleasure, part pain, part alarm.

'Wishful thinking,' he echoed slowly. 'The most dangerous thing on earth.'

'Or the most valuable,' she countered quickly. 'All the great ideas started life as wishful thinking. Wasn't there an ancestor of yours who thought, *I wish I could build a boat*? So he built one, then another one, and here you are.'

'You're a very clever woman.' He smiled. 'You can turn anything around, just by the light you throw on it. The light doesn't just illuminate; it transforms all the things that might have served as a warning.'

'But perhaps they should be transformed,' she pointed out. 'Some people become suspicious so quickly that they need to come off-guard and enjoy a bit of wishful thinking.'

'I said you were clever. Talking like that, you almost convince me. Just as you convinced me back then. Maybe it really is magic. Perhaps you have a brand of magic denied to all other women.'

There was a noise behind him, reminding him that they were in a public place. Reluctantly he released her hand, assuming a calm demeanour, although with an effort.

A small buzz came from his inner pocket. He drew out his phone and grimaced at the text message he found there.

'Damn! I was planning to go to Piraeus tomorrow in any case, but now I think I'd better go tonight. I'll be away for a few days.'

Petra drew a long breath, keeping her face averted. Until then she'd told herself that she wasn't quite sure how she wanted the evening to end, but now she had to be honest with herself. An evening spent talking, beginning to open their hearts, should have led to a night in each other's arms, expressing their closeness in another way. And only now that it was being denied to her did she face how badly she wanted to make love with him.

'Will you be here when I get back?' he asked.

'Yes, I'm staying for a while.'

'I'll call you.'

'We'd better go,' she agreed. 'You have to be on your way.'

'I'm sorry—'

'Don't be,' she said cheerfully. 'It's been a long day. I was fighting to stay awake.'

She wondered if he would actually believe that.

When they reached the Lukas villa the great gates swung open for them, almost as though someone had been watching for their arrival. At the house he opened the car door and came up the steps with her. She looked up at him, curious about his next move.

'Do you remember that night?' he asked gently. 'You were such an innocent that I made you go to bed and saw you to the door.'

'And told me to lock it,' she recalled.

Neither of them mentioned the other thing he'd done, the kiss so soft that it had been barely a whisper against her lips— a kiss without passion, only gentle concern and tenderness. It had lingered with her long after that evening, through days and weeks, then through years. Since then she had known desire and love, but nothing had ever quite erased the memory of that moment. Looking at him now, she knew why, and when he bent his head she longed for it to be the same.

He didn't disappoint her. His lips lay against hers for the briefest possible time before retreating, almost as though he'd found something there that disconcerted him.

'Goodnight,' he said quietly.

He left her before she could react, going down to the car and driving away without looking back, moving fast, as though making his escape.

'Goodnight,' she whispered.

It was only when he was out of sight that she remembered she hadn't asked him how he'd known her phone number.

Petra soon found that her hours were full. Her reputation had gone before her, ensuring that several societies contacted her, asking her to join their excursions or talk to them. She accepted as many invitations as possible. They filled the hours that passed without a word from Lysandros.

One invitation that particularly attracted her came from The Cave Society, a collection of English enthusiasts who were set on exploring an island in the Aegean Sea, about twenty miles out. It was a mass of caves, some of which were reputed to contain precious historical relics.

Nikator was scathing about the idea, insisting that the legend had been rubbished years ago, but the idea of a day out in a boat attracted her.

'Mind you, the place I'd really like to see is Priam House, on Corfu,' she told him. 'Is it true that Lysandros owns it?'

He shrugged. 'I think so.'

She was mostly free of Nikator's company. He spent much time away from home, leaving her free to explore Homer's magnificent library. Sometimes she would take out a tiny photograph she kept in her bag and set it on the table to watch over her.

'Like you watched over me when you were alive, Grandpa,' she told the man in the picture, speaking in Greek.

He was elderly, with a thin, kindly face and a hesitant smile. When he was alive that smile had always been there for her.

He had told her about her father, which Estelle hadn't been able to do very fully. And he'd shown her pictures, revealing her own facial likeness to the young man whose life had been cut short.

But there had been another likeness.

'He had a hasty temper,' Grandpa had said sadly. 'He didn't

mean to be unkind, but he spoke first and thought afterwards.' He'd looked at her tenderly. 'And you're just the same.'

It was true. She was naturally easy-going, but without warning a flash of temper would come streaking out of the darkness, making her say things she afterwards regretted. She'd fought to overcome it and had succeeded in dampening it down to the point when few people ever detected its existence. But it was still there, ready to undermine her without warning.

In the final months of her marriage it had made her say things that would have made a reconciliation impossible, even if she'd wanted one. Right now it was probably a good thing that Lysandros wasn't there to hear the thoughts that were bouncing around like Furies in her brain, demanding expression.

One evening Nikator returned home suddenly and locked himself in his room, refusing to open to anyone, even Petra.

'Perhaps Debra will come to see him,' she suggested to Aminta, the housekeeper.

'No, she's gone back to America,' Aminta said hurriedly.

'I thought she was here until next week.'

'She had to leave suddenly. I should be getting on with my work.'

She scuttled away.

It might mean anything or nothing, Petra thought, and she would probably never know. But for a while Aminta avoided her.

Nikator finally emerged, with a slight swelling on his lips which he refused to discuss beyond saying he'd had a fall. Petra didn't feel like pursuing the subject, but she made a mental note to spend as much time out of the house as possible.

Since the evening of the wedding she'd seen Lysandros only once and that was by chance at a grand banquet given by the city authorities. He'd made his way over to her and said courteously that he hoped she was enjoying Athens. He'd mentioned contacting her again in the next few days, but made no specific plans.

He seemed to be alone. No lady had been invited to accompany him to this occasion, just as her own invitation had made no mention of a guest. She was left wondering at whose behest she had been invited.

After their evening together she had been in turmoil. Behind Lysandros's civilised veneer she sensed a man who was frighteningly alone, locked in a prison of isolation, seeking a way out, yet reluctant to take it. It didn't matter that their first meeting had been so long ago. It had left them both with the sense that they knew each other, and under its influence he'd begun the first tentative movements of reaching out to her. Yet he'd been able only to go so far, then no further. Try as he might, the prison bars had always slammed shut at the last moment.

Her heart ached for him. The pain he couldn't fight had affected her, and she would have rescued him if she could. But in the end it was his own nature that stood in the way, and she knew she could never get past that unless he allowed her.

At night she would relive the brief kiss that he'd given her. Any other man would have seized her in his arms and kissed her breathless, which, truth to tell, she'd half hoped he would do. Instead, he'd behaved with an almost Victorian propriety, caressing her lips in a way that called back that other time when he'd thought only of protecting her. And in doing so he'd touched her heart more than passion would ever do.

But there was passion, she knew that. She couldn't be so close to him without reading the promise of his tall, hard body, the easy movements, the power held in check, ready to be unleashed. Nor could she misunderstand the look in his eyes when they rested on her, thinking her unaware. Some day—and that day must come soon—she would break his control and tempt him beyond endurance.

But gradually her despondency gave way to annoyance. Now she could hear the strange woman at the wedding again, warning her that she was one of many and would yield as easily as the others.

'No way,' she muttered. 'If you think that, boy, have you got a shock coming!'

Briskly she informed the household that she would be away for few days, and was in her room packing a light bag when her phone rang and Lysandros's voice said, 'I'd like to see you this evening.'

She took a moment to stop herself exploding at his sheer cheek, and managed to say calmly, 'I'm about to leave for a few days.'

'Can it wait until tomorrow?'

'I'm afraid not. I'm really very busy. It's been a pleasure knowing you. Goodbye.' She hung up.

'Good for you,' Nikator said from the doorway. 'It's about time somebody told him.'

'It's kind of you to worry about me, Nikki, but I promise you there's no need. I'm in charge. I always have been. I always will be.'

The phone rang again.

'I know you're angry,' Lysandros said. 'But am I beyond forgiveness?'

'You misunderstand,' she said coolly. 'I'm not angry, merely busy. I'm a professional with work to do.'

'You mean I really am beyond forgiveness?'

'No, I—there's nothing to forgive.'

'I wish you'd tell me that to my face. I've been inconsiderate, but I didn't…that is…help me, Petra—please.'

It was as though he'd thrown a magic switch. His arrogance she could fight, but his plea for help reached out to touch her own need.

'I suppose I could rearrange my plans,' she said slowly.

'I'm waiting by the gate. Come as you are; that's all I ask.'

'I'm on my way.'

'You're mad,' Nikator said. 'You know that, don't you?'

She sighed. 'Yes, I guess so. But it can't be helped.'

She escaped his furious eyes as soon as she could. Now she could think of nothing but that Lysandros wanted her. The thought of seeing him again made her heart leap.

He was where he'd said he would be. He didn't kiss her or make any public show of affection, but his hand held hers tightly for a moment and he whispered, 'Thank you,' in a fervent voice that wiped out the days of frustrated waiting.

Darkness was falling as Lysandros took her into the heart of town, finally stopping at a small restaurant that spilled out onto the pavement. From here they could look up at the floodlit Parthenon, high on the Acropolis, dominating all of Athens.

The waiter appeared, politely enquiring if they were ready to visit the kitchen. Petra was familiar with this habit of allowing customers to see the food being prepared, and happily followed him in. Delicious aromas assailed them at once, and it took time to go around trying to make a choice. At last they settled on fried calamari followed by lamb fricassee and returned to the table.

For a while the food and wine occupied her. Sometimes she glanced up to find him watching her with an intense expression that told her all she wanted to know about the feelings he couldn't put into words. For her it was enough to know that he had those feelings. The words could wait.

At last he said politely, 'Have you been busy?'

'I've been doing a lot of reading in Homer's library. I've had some invitations to go on expeditions.'

'And you've accepted them?'

'Not all. How has your work been?'

'No different from usual. Problems to be overcome. I tried to keep busy because…because…' his voice changed abruptly '…when I was alone I thought of you.'

'You hid it very well,' she pointed out.

'You mean I didn't call you. I meant to a thousand times, but I always drew back. I think you know why.'

'I'm not sure I do.'

'You're not like other women. Not to me. With you it has to be all or nothing, and I—'

'You're not ready for "all",' she finished for him. Without warning her temper gave a sudden, disconcerting flare. 'That's fine, because neither am I. Are you suggesting that I was chasing you?'

'No, I didn't mean that,' he said hastily. 'I was just trying to apologise.'

'It's all right,' she said.

In fact it wasn't all right. Her contented mood of a moment ago had faded. The strain of the last few days was catching up with her, and she was becoming edgy. She'd wanted him and he'd as good as snubbed her.

Suddenly the evening was on the verge of collapse.

'Can I have a little more wine?' she asked, holding out her glass and smiling in a way that should have warned him.

He took the hint and abandoned the apology, making her feel instantly guilty. He was doing his best, but these were uncharted seas for him. It was she who held the advantage. Resolutely, she worked to lighten the atmosphere.

'Actually,' she said between sips, 'the most exciting thing that's happened to me is an invitation from The Cave Society.'

She told him about the letter. Like Nikator, he was sceptical.

'I'm not swallowing it hook, line and sinker,' she assured him. 'I'm too much of an old hand for that.'

'*Old* hand,' he murmured, regarding her appreciatively.

'Very old. In terms of my reputation, I'm ancient. This—' she pointed to her luxuriant golden mane '—is just dye to hide the fact that I'm white-haired. Any day now I'm going to start walking with a stick.'

'Will you stop talking nonsense?'

'Why?' she asked, genuinely puzzled. 'Nonsense is fun.'

'Yes, but—' He retired, defeated. It wasn't possible to say that the contrast between her words and the young, glorious reality was making him dizzy.

'Oh, all right,' she conceded, 'I don't think there's anything to be found in those caves. On the other hand, I'll usually go anywhere and do anything for a "find", so perhaps I should.'

'But what are you going to find that thousands of others have failed to find?'

'Of course they failed,' she teased, 'because they weren't me. Something is lying there, waiting for me to appear from the mists of time—knowing that the glory of the discovery belongs to me, and only me. Next thing you know, they'll put my statue up in the Parthenon.'

She caught sight of his face and burst out laughing.

'I'm sorry,' she choked, 'but if you could see your expression!'

'You were joking, weren't you?' he asked cautiously.

'Yes, I was joking.'

'I'm afraid I'm a bit—' He shrugged. 'It can be hard to tell.'

'Oh, you poor thing,' she said. 'I know you can laugh. I actually heard you, at the wedding reception, but somehow—'

'It's just—'

'I know,' she said. 'You think too great a sense of humour is a weakness, so you keep yours in protective custody, behind bolts and bars, only to be produced at certain times.'

Lysandros tried to speak, to make some light-hearted remark that would pass the matter off, but inwardly he felt himself retreating from her. Her words, though kindly meant, had been like a lamp shone into his soul, revealing secrets. Not to be tolerated.

'Are you ready for the next course?' he asked politely.

'Yes, please.'

It was definitely a snub, yet she was swept by tenderness and pity for him. He was like a man walking a path strewn with boulders, not knowing they were there until he fell and hurt himself.

And she had a sad feeling that she was the only person in the world who saw him like this, and therefore the only person able to help him.

If only she could, she thought with a qualm of self-doubt. She was still feeling her way tentatively. Suppose she persuaded him to trust her, then faltered and let him down, abandoning him again to mistrust and desolation? Suddenly that seemed like the greatest crime in the world.

As the waiter served them she became aware that a man and a woman were hovering close, trying to get a look at her. When she looked straight at them, they jumped.

'It *is* her,' the woman breathed. 'It *is* you, isn't it?' Then, pulling herself together, she said, 'You really are Petra Radnor?'

'Yes, I am.'

'I saw you on a talk show on television just before we left England, and I've read your books. Oh, this is *such* a thrill.'

There was nothing to do but be polite. Lysandros invited them to sit at the table. His manner was charming, and she wondered if he secretly welcomed the interruption.

'I'm just learning that Miss Radnor is a celebrity,' he said. 'Tell me about her.'

They plunged in, making Petra groan with embarrassment. They were Angela and George, they belonged to The Cave Society and had only just arrived in Athens.

'Our President told us that he'd written to you,' Angela bubbled. 'You will accept our invitation to come to the island, won't you? It would mean so much to us to have a real figure of authority.'

'Please,' Petra said hastily, 'I am not a figure of authority.'

'Oh, but you—'

It went on and on. Petra began to feel trapped. Vaguely she was aware that Lysandros's phone had rung. He answered and his face was instantly full of alarm.

'Of course,' he said sharply. 'We'll come at once.' He hung up. 'I'm afraid there's a crisis. That was my secretary to say I must return immediately, also Miss Radnor, whose presence is essential.'

With a gesture he summoned the waiter, paying not only for his meal and hers but whatever their guests had consumed.

'Good evening,' he said, rising to his feet and drawing her with him. 'It's been a pleasure meeting you.'

They made their escape, running until they were three streets away. Then, under the cover of darkness, he pulled her into his arms.

'Now!' he said.

CHAPTER FIVE

PLEASURE and relief went through her. She had wanted this so much, and now everything in her yearned towards him. Her mouth was ready for him but so was every inch of her body. As he grasped her, so she grasped him, caressing him with hands and lips.

'How did you arrange for the phone to ring?' she gasped.

'It didn't. I simply pressed a button that set the bell off, then I pretended to answer. I had to get you away from there, get you to myself.'

He kissed her again, and his kiss was everything she'd wanted since their meeting. Nothing else in her life had been like it. Nothing else ever would be. It was the kiss she'd secretly longed for since he'd cheated her with a half-kiss all those years ago.

'What have you done to me?' he growled. 'Why can't I stop you doing it?'

'You could if you really wanted to,' she whispered against his mouth. 'Why don't you…why don't you…?'

'Stop tormenting me—'

At that she laughed. Why should she make it easy for him?

'Siren—witch—'

But his lips caressed her even as they hurled names at her.

He was in the grip of a power stronger than himself, and that was just how she wanted him.

From far in the distance an unwelcome sound broke into her joy. It came closer and she realised that a crowd of youngsters had appeared at the end of the street, singing, dancing, chanting up into the sky. Then she recalled that this was European Music Night, when Athens was filled with public celebration.

The crowd passed them, offering good wishes to a couple so profitably engaged. Lysandros grasped her hand and began to run again, but there was no escape. Another crowd appeared from another side street, and another. Seeking an exit, they found themselves in an open square where a rock band was playing on a makeshift stage.

'Where can you get privacy in this place?' Lysandros roared.

'You can't,' Petra cried. She was laughing now, every nerve in her body thrumming with joy. 'There's no privacy; there's only music and laughter—and whatever else you want—'

'It's not funny,' he growled.

'But it is, it is—can't you see—? Oh, darling, please try to understand—please try—'

He relented and touched her face. 'Whatever you say.'

He wasn't quite sure what he meant by that, but he knew they'd come to a place where she was at home, sure-footed, able to lead without faltering. A wise man would accept that and, since he prided himself on his wisdom, he did the sensible thing and let her lead him into the dance.

All about them the other couples swung around, while the band hollered. He knew nothing except that he was looking down at her face and she was laughing, not with amusement but with joy and triumph, inviting him to share. Once, long ago, she'd taken his hand and led him through the tunnel to success. Now she could do it again, except that this success would be different, not a matter of money and crushing foes, but a joyous richness and light, streaming ahead, leading to new life, and whatever that life might bring.

'Let's go,' he cried.

'Where?' she called back in delight.

'Anywhere—wherever you want to take me.'

'Then come.'

She began to run, taking him with her, not knowing where she was heading or why; only knowing that she was with him and that was enough. Now the whole of Athens seemed to be flaming around them.

She stopped at last and they stood, gasping together, their chests heaving. From overhead came the sound of fireworks racing up into the black sky, exploding in an orgy of light, while down below the crowd cried out its pleasure.

'Phew!' she said.

He gave a sigh of agreement and she thumped him lightly.

'You shouldn't be out of breath. I thought you worked out every morning in the gym.'

He did exactly that, and was fully as fit as she expected, but in her company his breathlessness had another cause. He reached for her. Petra saw the firework colours flash across his face, and then his arms were tight about her and his mouth was on hers, teasing, provoking, demanding, imploring.

'Who are you?' he gasped. 'What are you doing in my life? Why can't I—?'

'Hush, it doesn't matter. Nothing matters but this. Kiss me—kiss me.'

She proceeded to show him what she meant, sensing the response go through him, delighting in her power over him and his over her. Soon they must reach the moment that had been inevitable since their meeting, and everything in her yearned towards it.

Lysandros felt as if he were awaking from a dream, or sinking into one. He wasn't sure which. Her plea of 'Kiss me' was entrancing, yet something deep inside him was drawing away. He tried to fight it. He wanted her, but so much that it alarmed him.

Impulse had made him call her tonight. Impulse had made him drag her away from their unwanted companions. Impulse—the thing he'd battled for years—was beginning to rule him.

A puppet dancing on the end of her chain. And she knew it.

'What is it?' she asked, feeling him draw away.

'This place is very public. We should get back to the table; I think I left something there.'

'And then?' she asked slowly, unwilling to believe the thought that was coming into her head.

'Then I think we should both—go home.'

She stared at him, trying to believe what he was doing, feeling the anger rise within her. He hadn't left anything behind and they both knew it. But he was telling her the magic was over. He'd banished it by an act of will, proving that his control was still strong, although he'd brought her to the edge of losing hers.

It was a demonstration of power, and she was going to make him regret it.

'How dare you?' she said in a soft, furious voice. 'Who the hell do you think you are to despise me?'

'I don't—'

'Shut up. I have something to say and you're going to listen. I am not some desperate female who you can pick up and put down when it suits you. And don't pretend you don't know what I mean because you know exactly. They're all standing in line for you, aren't they? But not me.'

'I don't know who gave you such an idea,' he grated.

'Any woman you've ever known could have given it to me. Your reputation went before you.'

His own anger rose.

'I'll bet Nikator had something to say, but are you mad enough to listen to him? Don't tell me he fools you with that "little brother" act!'

'Why shouldn't I believe he's concerned about me?' she demanded.

'Oh, he's concerned all right, but not as a brother. The rumours about him are very interesting at the moment. Why do you think Debra Farley left Athens so suddenly? Because he went too far, wouldn't take no for an answer. Have a look at his face and see what she did to it when she was fighting him off. I gather it took a lot of money to get her to leave quietly.'

'I don't believe it,' she said, ignoring the whispers within her brain.

'I do not tell lies,' Lysandros snapped.

'No, but you can get things wrong. Even the great, infallible Lysandros Demetriou makes mistakes, and you've really made one about me. One minute you say you'll follow "anywhere I want to take you". The next moment it's time to go home. Do you really think I'll tamely accept that sort of behaviour?

'What am I supposed to do now, Lysandros? Sit by the phone, hoping you'll get in touch, like one of those Athens wives? When you called tonight I should have told you to go and jump in the lake—'

'But you didn't, so perhaps we—'

The words were like petrol on flames.

'Well, I'm doing it now,' she seethed. 'You have your work to do, I have mine, and there's no need for us to trouble each other further. Goodnight.'

Turning swiftly away before he could reach out, she hurried back through the streets to the little restaurant. George and Angela were still there, beaming at the sight of Petra.

'We just knew you'd come back,' Angela said. 'You will come to the cave, won't you?'

'Thank you, I look forward to it,' Petra said firmly. 'Why don't we discuss the details now?' She smiled at Lysandros with deadly intent. 'I'll get a taxi home. Don't let us keep you. I'm sure you're busy.'

'You're right,' he said in a forced voice. 'Goodnight. It's been a pleasure meeting you all.'

He inclined his head to them all and was gone. Nor did he look back, which Petra thought was just as well, or he would have seen a look of misery on her face that she wouldn't have admitted for all the world.

Lysandros awoke in a black depression. Now the magical sunshine that had flooded the path ahead had died, replaced by the prosaic everyday light of the city. She wasn't here, and it shamed him to remember how her presence had made him act.

'Wherever you want to take me.' Had he really said that?

He should be glad that she'd hurled the reminder at him, warning him of the danger into which he'd been sleepwalking, saving him in time.

In time?

He rose and went through the process of preparing for the day, moving like an automaton while his brain seethed.

She alarmed him. She mattered too much. Simply by being herself she could lure him out of the armoured cave where he lived, and where he had vowed to stay for the rest of his days.

For years women had come and gone in his life. He'd treated them well in a distant fashion, and seen them depart without regret. But this woman had broken the mould, and he knew that he must cut ties now or risk yielding to weakness, the thing he dreaded most in the world.

He went to his desk, meaning to write a polite letter, accepting her dismissal. That way he wouldn't have to hear her voice with its soft resonance, its memory of pleasure half experienced, still anticipated. He drew paper towards him and prepared to write.

But the pen seemed to have developed a life of its own, and refused to do his bidding. His brain shut down, denying him the necessary words.

This was her doing. She was like one of the sirens of legend, whose voices had lured sailors onto the rocks. How much had they known, those doomed men? Had they gone unknowingly to their death, or had they recognised the truth about the siren-song, yet still been drawn in, unable to help themselves? And when it had been too late, and they sank beneath the waves, had they cursed themselves for yielding, or had their suffering been worth it for the glimpse of heaven?

He would have given anything to know.

At last he gave up trying to write. It was she who had broken it off, and there was nothing more to be said. More business problems made another journey to the port essential, and for several days he had no time to think of anything else. On the journey back to Athens he was able to relax in the feeling of having regained command of his life.

Petra would have replaced him with another eager suitor, and that was best for both of them. He was even glad of it. So he told himself.

On the last mile home he switched on his car radio to hear the latest news. A commentator was describing a search taking place at sea, where a boat had been found overturned. Those aboard had been exploring a cave on an island in the gulf.

'One of those missing is known to be Petra Radnor, daughter of film star Estelle Radnor, who recently married—'

He pulled over sharply to the side of the road and sat in frozen stillness, listening.

She'd said she'd go anywhere and do anything for a 'find', but had she really wanted to go? Hadn't she tried to slide out of it, but then fallen back into the clutches of George and Angela only because of him?

If she hadn't been angry with me she wouldn't have gone on this trip. If she's dead, it's my doing—like last time—like last time—

At last life came back to his limbs. He swung the car round in the direction of the coast, driving as though all the devils in hell were after him.

Night was falling as he reached the sea and headed for the place where the boats were to be found. Outwardly he was calm but he couldn't stop the words thrumming in his head.

She's dead—she's dead—you had your chance and it's gone—again—

A crowd had gathered in the harbour, gazing out to the water and a boat that was heading towards them. Lysandros parked as close as he could and ran to where he could have a better view of the boat.

'They've rescued most of them,' said a man nearby. 'But I heard there was still someone they couldn't find.'

'Does anyone know who?' Lysandros asked sharply.

'Only that it was a woman. I doubt if they'll find her now.'

You killed her—you killed her!

He pressed against the rail, straining his eyes to see the boat coming through the darkness. In the bow stood a woman, huddled in a blanket, as though she'd been rescued from the water. Frantically he strained to see more, but her face was a blur. A passing light suggested that her hair might be light. It could be Petra—if only he could be sure.

His heart was thundering and he gripped the railing so

hard that his hands hurt. It must be her. She couldn't be dead, because if she were—

Shudders racked him.

Suddenly a shout went up, followed by a cheer. The boat was closer now and at last he could see the woman. It was Petra.

He stood there, holding the rail for support, taking deep breaths, trying to bring himself under control.

She would be here in a few moments. He must plan, be organised. A cellphone. That was it! She would have lost hers in the water, but she'd need one to call her mother. He could do that to please her.

Her eyes were searching the harbour until at last she began to wave. Full of joyful relief, Lysandros waved back, but then realised that she wasn't looking at him but at someone closer. Then he saw Nikator dart forward, reaching up to her. She leaned down, smiling and calling to him.

Lysandros stayed deadly still as the boat docked and the passengers streamed off seeking safety. Petra went straight into Nikator's arms and they hugged each other. Then Nikator took out his cellphone, handing it to her, saying things Lysandros couldn't hear, but could guess. Petra dialled, put the phone to her ear and cried, 'Estelle, darling, it's me, I'm safe.'

He didn't hear the rest. He backed hastily into the darkness before hurrying to find his car. Then he departed as quickly as he could.

She never saw him.

Aminta took charge of her as soon as she reached home, making her have a hot bath, eat well and go to bed.

'It was all over the news,' she told Petra. 'We were so worried. Whatever happened?'

'I don't really know. At first it just seemed like an ordinary storm, but suddenly the waves got higher and higher and we overturned. Did you say it was on the news?'

'Oh, yes, about how you were all drowning and they couldn't rescue everyone.'

'There's one woman they're still looking for,' Petra sighed.

She slept badly and awoke in a dark mood. Somewhere in the house she heard the phone ring, and a moment later Aminta brought it in to her.

'It's for you,' she said. 'A man.'

Eagerly she waited to hear Lysandros's voice, full of happiness that she was safe. But it was George, to tell her that the missing woman had been found safe and well. She talked politely for a while, but hung up with relief.

There was no call from Lysandros. The news programmes must have alerted him to her danger, yet the man who had kissed her with such fierce intensity had shown no interest in her fate.

She couldn't blame him after the way she'd ordered him out of her life, yet the hope had persisted that he cared enough to check that she was safe. Apparently not.

She'd been fooling herself. Such interest as he'd ever had in her had been superficial and was now over. He couldn't have said so more clearly.

Nikator was waiting for her when she went downstairs.

'You shouldn't have got up so soon,' he said. 'After what you've been through. Go back to bed and let me look after you.'

She smiled. It had been good to find him on the quay to take her home, and she was feeling friendly towards him. For the next few days he behaved perfectly, showing brotherly kindness without ever crossing the line. It was bliss to relax in his care. Now she was sure that the stories about him weren't true.

If only Lysandros would call her.

* * *

After several days with no sign from Petra, Lysandros called her cellphone, without success. It was still functioning, but it had been switched off. It remained off all the rest of that day, through the night and into the morning.

It made no sense. She could have switched to the answer service; instead, she'd blocked calls completely.

He refused to admit to a twinge of alarm. But at last he yielded and called the Lukas house, getting himself put through to Homer's secretary.

'I need to speak to Miss Radnor,' he said gruffly. 'Be so kind as to ask her to call me.'

'I'm sorry, sir, but Miss Radnor is no longer here. She and Mr Nikator left for England two days ago.'

Silence. When he could manage to speak normally, he said, 'Did she leave any address or contact number?'

'No, sir. She and Mr Nikator said that they didn't want to be disturbed by anyone, for a long time.'

'What happens in an emergency?'

'Mr Nikator said no emergency could matter beside—'

'I see. Thank you.' He hung up abruptly.

At the Lukas mansion the secretary looked around to where Nikator stood in the doorway.

'Did I do all right?' she asked.

'Perfect,' he told her. 'Just keep telling that story if there are any more calls.'

Lysandros sat motionless, his face hard and set.

She's gone—she's not coming back—

The words called to him out of the past, making him shudder.

She's gone—

It meant nothing. She had every right to leave. It was different from the other time.

You'll never see her again—never again—never again—

His fist slammed into the wall with such force that a picture fell to the ground and smashed. A door opened behind him.

'Get out,' he said without looking around.

The door closed hastily. He continued to sit there, staring—staring into the darkness, into the past.

At last he rose like a man in a dream and went up to his room, where he threw a few clothes into a bag. To his secretary he said, 'I'll be away for a few days. Call me on the cellphone if it's urgent. Otherwise, deal with it yourself.'

'Can I tell anyone where you are?'

'*No.*'

He headed for the airport and caught the next flight to the island of Corfu. To have used his private jet would have been to tell the world where he was going, and that was the last thing he wanted.

In Corfu he owned Priam House, a villa that had once belonged to his mother. It was his refuge, the place he came to be alone, even to the extent of having no servants. There he would find peace and isolation, the things he needed to save him from going mad.

The only disturbance might come from students and archaeologists, attracted by the villa's history. It had been built on the ruins of an ancient temple, and rumours abounded of valuable relics that might still be found.

Light was fading as the villa came into sight, silent and shuttered. He left the taxi while there was still a hundred yards to go, so that he might approach unnoticed.

He opened the gate noiselessly and walked around the side of the villa. All seemed quiet and relief flooded him. At last he let himself in at the back and went through the hall to the stairs. But before he could climb he saw something that made him freeze.

The door to the cellar was standing open.

It was no accident. The cellar led directly to the foundations and that door was always kept locked for reasons of safety. Only he had the key.

Rage swept through him at having his solitude destroyed. At that moment he could have done violence. But his fury was cold, enabling him to go down the stairs and approach his quarry noiselessly.

Someone was in the far corner of the cellar with only one small light that they were using to examine the stones, so that the person couldn't be seen.

'Stop right there,' he said harshly. 'You don't understand the danger you're in. I won't tolerate this. I allow nobody in here.'

He heard a gasp as the intruder made a sharp movement. The torch fell to the floor. His hand shot out in the darkness, found a body, seized it, grappled with it, brought it down.

'Now,' he gasped, 'you're going to be sorry you did this. Let's look at you.'

He reached over for the torch that lay on the flagstones and shone it directly into his enemy's face. Then he froze with shock.

'Petra!'

CHAPTER SIX

PETRA lay looking up at him, her eyes wide, her breath coming in short gasps. Hurriedly he got to his feet, drawing her up with him and holding her, for she was shaking.

'You,' he said, appalled. '*You!*'

'Yes, I'm afraid so.'

She swayed as she spoke and he tightened his grip lest she fall. Swiftly he picked her up and carried her out of the cellar and up the stairs to his room, where he laid her gently on the bed and sat beside her.

'Are you mad to do such a thing?' he demanded hoarsely. 'Have you any idea of the danger you were in?'

'Not real danger,' she said shakily.

'I threw you down onto stone slabs. The floor's uneven; you might have hit your head—I was in such a rage—'

'I'm sorry, I know I shouldn't—'

'The hell with that! You could have died. Do you understand that? *You could have died and then I—*' A violent shudder went through him.

'My dear,' she said gently, 'you're making too much of this. I'm a bit breathless from landing so hard, but nothing more.'

'You don't know that. I'm getting you a doctor—'

'You will not,' she said firmly. 'I don't need a doctor. I haven't broken anything, I'm not in pain and I didn't hit my head.'

He didn't reply but looked at her, haggard. She took his face between her hands. 'Don't look like that. It's all right.'

'It isn't,' he said desperately. 'Sometimes I lose control—and do things without thinking. It's so easy to do harm.'

She guessed he was really talking about something else and longed to draw the truth out of him, but instinct warned her to go carefully. He'd given her a clue to his fierce self-control, but she knew by now that he would clam up if she pressed him.

And the time was not right. For the moment she must comfort him and ease his mind.

'You didn't do me any harm,' she insisted.

'If I had I'd never forgive myself.'

'But why? I broke into your house. I'm little more than a common criminal. Why aren't you sending for the police?'

'Shut up!' he said, enfolding her in his arms.

He didn't try to kiss her, just sat holding her tightly against him, as if fearing that she might try to escape.

'That's nice,' she murmured. 'Just hold me.'

She felt his lips against her hair, felt the temptation that ran through him, but sensed wryly that he wasn't going to yield to it. He had something else on his mind.

'How badly bruised are you?' he asked.

'A few knocks, nothing much.'

'Let me see.'

He got to work, opening the buttons of her blouse, drawing it off her, removing her bra, but seemingly unaffected by the sight of her bare breasts.

'Lie down so that I can see your back,' he said.

Wondering, she did so, and lay there while he studied her.

'It's not so bad,' she said.

'I'll get a shirt for you to wear tonight.'

'No need. My things are next door. I've been here several days. Nobody saw me because of the shutters. I brought enough food to manage on and crept about. You see, I'm a really dishonest character.'

He groaned. 'And if something had happened to you? If you'd had a fall and been knocked out? You could have died without anyone knowing and lain here for days, weeks. Are you crazy, woman?'

She twisted around and sat up to face him.

'Yes, I think I am,' she agreed. 'I don't understand anything any more.'

He ground his teeth. 'Do I need to explain to you why the thought of your being in danger wrenches me apart? Are you insensitive as well as crazy and stupid?'

'My danger didn't bother you when I was on that boat that overturned.' A thought struck her. 'Unless you didn't know about it.'

'Of course I knew about it. I went to the harbour in case you needed me. I saw you arrive. After that, I knew you were all right.'

'You—?' she echoed slowly.

'The accident was on the news. Of course I went to see how you were. I saw you get off the boat, straight into Nikator's arms. I didn't want to disturb a touching reunion, so I went home.'

'You were there all the time?' she whispered.

'Where the hell would you expect me to be when you were in danger?' he raged. 'What do you think I am? Made of ice?'

Now she was glad of the understanding that was gradually coming to her, and which saved her from misjudging him. Without it she would have seen only his anger, entirely missing the fear and pain which tortured him more because he had no idea how to express them.

'No,' she said helplessly, holding out her arms to him. 'I'd never think that. Oh, I've been so stupid. I shouldn't have let you fool me.'

'What does that mean?' he asked, going into her arms.

'You hide from people. But I won't let you hide from me.'

He looked down at her naked breasts, just visible in the shadowy light. Slowly, he drew his fingertips down one until they reached the nipple, which was already proud and expectant.

'No more hiding,' he murmured.

'There's nowhere to hide from each other,' she said. 'There never was.'

'No, there never was.'

She began to work on his buttons but he forestalled her, undressing quickly, first his jacket, then his shirt. She leaned towards him so that her breasts touched his bare skin, and felt the tremors that possessed his body, guessed that he would have controlled them if he could, for he was still not yet ready to abandon himself. But that control was beyond him, she was delighted to see.

They removed the rest of their clothes, watching each other with brooding possessiveness, taking their time, for this mattered too much to be rushed. He was still fearful lest he hurt her, caressing her gently, almost tentatively, until the deep motion of her chest told him of her mounting impatience.

For too long she'd dreamed of this moment, and nothing was going to deprive her of it now. She kept her hands against his skin, moving them softly to tease him and make sure he continued with what he was doing.

His touch had made her nipples hard and peaked, so that when she leaned against him he drew a long, shaking breath at the impact.

'This is dangerous,' he whispered.

'Who for?' she challenged. 'Not me.'

'Does nothing scare you?'

'Nothing,' she assured him against his lips, 'nothing.'

She released him briefly to finish removing her clothes, and when he had done the same they returned to each other with new fervour. Now she had what she wanted—the sight of him naked and eager for her—and her blood raced at the thought of meeting his eagerness with her own.

His fingers on her skin made it flame with life.

'Yes—' she whispered. 'Yes—yes—I'm here—come here—'

He pressed her gently back against the pillows and began to caress her everywhere—her neck, her waist, her hips. He was taking his time, arousing her slowly, giving her every chance to think if this was really what she wanted. But thinking was the last thing she could do now. Everything in her was focused on one craving—to enjoy the physical release he could give her and discover if it fulfilled all the wild hopes she'd been building up. It would. It *must*.

She caressed him in return, wherever she could reach, frustrated by her limits. She wanted all of him, and even now that he was loving her in the way she most craved, it mysteriously wasn't enough.

Many times she'd wondered about him as a lover. She knew he could be cool, ironic, distant, but with flashes of intensity through which another, wholly different man could be glimpsed. She'd been intrigued by both men, wondering which of them would finally be tempted to her bed, but none of the pictures that came into her head satisfied her. They were incomplete. As a lover he would have yet another identity and she was eager to meet him.

When he finally moved over her she lay back with a sigh, waiting for him. And he was there, inside her, claiming her, completing and fulfilling her. She clasped her legs around him at once, wanting everything, and heard him give a soft growl, as though, by her gesture, she'd told him something he needed to know.

She gasped, rejoicing at the power in his hips as they released the desire that had overcome him, driving her own desire to new heights and making her thrust back at him, digging her fingers cruelly into his flesh.

'Yes—' she whispered. *'Yes!'*

To her delight he was smiling, as though her pleasure gladdened his heart. She'd known he would be a strong lover but her imagination had fallen short of the reality. He took her with power, never seeming to tire, bringing her to the brink several times before taking her over the edge so that his cry joined with hers as they fell together into a bottomless chasm.

For a long time she lay with her eyes closed, enfolded in the world where only pleasure and satisfaction existed. When she opened them again she found that he was lying with his head on her chest, breathing hard. He lifted it slowly and looked at her.

'Are you all right?' he whispered.

'Everything is fine,' she assured him.

Further words failed her. She knew that what had just happened had transformed her life, not merely because he was the most skilled lover she had ever known, but because her heart reached out to him in a way it had never done for any other man. He could possess her and give to her, but what he claimed in return was something she rejoiced to give. By taking from her, he completed her, and that was beyond all words.

He rose and looked at her. Surveying him in return, she smiled. He still wanted her.

Hooking her arm around his neck, she eased herself up, but then winced.

'Did I hurt you?' he demanded, aghast. 'I forgot—'

'So did I,' she promised him. 'I think I'll get in the shower and see what the rest of me looks like.'

He helped her off the bed, which she needed for her exertions seemed to have weakened her. Clinging to him, she went slowly into the bathroom, switching on the lights so that he could see her clearly for the first time, and turning her to look at her back. She heard him draw a sharp breath.

'Nasty,' he said. 'You must have landed on something sharp. I'm so sorry.'

'I can't feel anything,' she said shakily. 'I guess I have too many other things to feel.'

He started the shower and helped her to get under it, soaping her gently, then laving her with water and dabbing her dry. Then he carried her tenderly back to bed and went to fetch her things from the room where she had been camping.

'You wear cotton pyjamas?' he asked as her nightwear came into view.

'What were you expecting? Slinky lingerie? Not when I'm alone. These are practical.'

'I'll see what I can find us to eat,' he said. 'I may have to go out.'

'There's some food in the kitchen. I brought it with me.'

He made them coffee and sandwiches, tending her like a nanny.

'We ought to have talked before anything happened,' he said. 'I didn't want to hurt you.'

She smiled. 'That's easy to say, but I don't think we could have talked before. We had to get past a certain point.'

He nodded. 'But now it's going to be different. I'm going to look after you until you're better.' Tenderly he helped her into her pyjamas, and a thought seemed to strike him. 'How long have you been here?'

'Three days.'

'When did you get back from England?'

'I haven't been to England. What made you think I had?'

'When I found your phone turned off I called the house and spoke to someone who said you'd gone to England with

Nikator. There was a message that neither of you wanted to be disturbed—for quite a while.'

'And you believed that?' she demanded. 'What are you—dead in the head?'

'How could I not believe it? There was nothing to tell me any different. You'd vanished without a trace. Your phone was switched off.'

'I lost it in the water. I've got a new one.'

'How was I supposed to know? You might have gone with him.'

But he knew that wasn't the real reason for his credulity. Nikator's lie had touched a nerve, and that nerve led back to a lack of self-confidence so rare with him that he couldn't cope with it.

Petra was still indignant.

'It wasn't possible,' she fumed. 'It was never possible, and you should have known that.'

'How could I know it when you weren't there to tell me?' he asked reasonably. 'If I didn't think it through properly, maybe it's your fault.'

'Oh, right, fine. Blame me.'

'You left without a word.'

'*I* didn't say a word? What about you? I don't go pestering a man who's shown he doesn't want me.'

'Don't tell me what I want and don't want,' he said with a faint touch of the old ferocity.

'You were pushing me away, you know you were—'

'No, that's not what I—'

'Sending me different signals that I couldn't work out.'

He tore his hair. 'Maybe I couldn't work them out myself. You told me you'd finished with me—'

'I didn't actually say that—'

'The hell you didn't! Have you forgotten some of the

things you said? I haven't. I'll never forget them. I never wanted you to go away. And then—' he took a shuddering breath '—you could have died on that boat, and you might not have been on it if it weren't for me. I just had to know you were safe, but after that—well, you and he seemed so comfortable together.'

'Except that he took the chance to spread lies,' she seethed. 'I was actually beginning to think he might not be so bad after all. I'll strangle him.'

'Leave it for a while,' he soothed. 'Then we'll do it together. But until then you stay in bed until I say you can get up.'

'I'm not fragile,' she protested. 'I won't break.'

'That's my decision. You're going to be looked after.'

'Yes, sir,' she said meekly, through twitching lips.

He threw her a suspicious glance. She retaliated by saluting him.

'I understand, *sir*. I'll just keep quiet and obey, because I'm gonna be looked after whether I like it or not, *sir*!'

He smiled then. 'Oh, I think you might like it,' he said.

'Yes,' she said happily. 'I think I just might.'

That night she slept better than she'd done for weeks. It might be the effect of snuggling down in Lysandros's comfortable bed, waited on hand and foot and told to think of nothing but getting well. Or perhaps it was the blissful sensation of being beside him all night, ordered to, 'Wake me if you need anything.'

Or the moment when she half-awoke in the early hours to find him sitting by the window, and the way he hurried over, saying, 'What is it? What can I do for you?'

This man would astound those who only knew him in the boardroom. His tenderness was real, and so, to her delighted surprise, was his thoughtfulness. He visibly racked his brains to please her, and succeeded because it seemed to matter to him so much. She slipped back contentedly into sleep.

When she awoke the next morning he was gone and the house was silent. Had she misread him? Had he taken what he wanted, then abandoned her to make her suffer for invading his privacy? But, although that fitted with his reputation, she couldn't make herself believe it of the man who'd cared for her so gently last night.

'Aaaaah,' she gasped slowly, rubbing her back as she eased her way out onto the landing.

Downstairs, the front door opened, revealing him. As soon as he saw her at the top of the stairs he hurried up, demanding, 'What are you doing out of bed?'

'I had to get up for a few minutes,' she protested.

'Well, now you can go right back. Come along.'

But once inside the bedroom he pointed her to a chair, saying brusquely, 'Sit there while I remake the bed.'

Gladly she sat down, watching him pull the sheets straight, until finally he came to help her stand.

'I'm just a bit stiff,' she said, clinging to him gladly and wincing.

'You'll be less stiff when I've given you a good rub. I went out for food and I remembered a pharmacy where they sell a great liniment. Get undressed and lie down.'

She did so, lying on her front and gasping as the cool liniment touched her. But that soon changed to warmth as his hand moved here and there over her bruises.

'They seem more tender now than last night,' she mused.

'You should have rested at once,' he told her. 'It's my fault you didn't.'

'Yes,' she remembered, smiling. 'We did something else instead. It was worth it.'

'I'm glad you think so, but I'm not touching you again until you're better.'

'Aren't you touching me now?'

'This isn't the same thing,' he said firmly.

And it wasn't, she thought, frustrated. His fingers moved here and there, sometimes firm, sometimes soft, but tending her, not loving her. There was just one moment when he seemed on the edge of weakening, when his hand lingered over the swell of her behind, as though he was fighting temptation. But then he won the fight and his hand moved firmly on.

She sighed. It wasn't fair.

Later, in the kitchen, she watched as he made breakfast.

'They wouldn't believe it if they could see you now,' she teased.

He didn't need to ask who 'they' were.

'I'm trusting you not to tell them,' he said. 'If you breathe a word of this I'll say you're delusional.'

'Don't worry. This is one secret I'm going to keep to myself. You don't keep any servants here?'

'I have a cleaning lady who comes in sometimes, but I prefer to be alone. Most of the house is shut up, and I just use a couple of rooms.'

'What made you come here now?'

'I needed to think,' he said, regarding her significantly. 'Since we met…I don't know…everything should have been simple…'

'But it never has been,' she mused. 'I wonder if we can make things simple by wanting it.'

'No,' he said at once. 'But if you have to fight—why not? As long as you know what you're fighting for.'

'Or who you're fighting,' she pointed out.

'I don't think there's any doubt about who we'll be fighting,' he said.

'Each other. Yes, it makes it interesting, doesn't it? Exhausting but interesting.'

He laughed and she pounced on it. 'I love it when you laugh. That's when I can claim a victory.'

'You've had other victories that maybe you don't know about.' He added with a touch of self-mockery, 'Or maybe you do.'

'I think I'll leave you to guess about that.'

'It would be a mistake for me to underestimate you, wouldn't it?'

'Definitely.'

Briefly she thought, if only he were always like this, charming and open to her. But she smothered the thought at once. A man who was always charming was like a musician who could only play one note. Eventually it became tedious. Lysandros was fascinating because she never knew who he was going to be from one moment to the next. And nor did he know with her, which kept them both on alert. Could anything be more delightful?

'I'm sorry about last night,' he said.

'I'm not.'

'I mean I'm sorry I didn't wait until you were better.'

'Listen, if you'd had the self-control to wait I'd have taken it as a personal insult. And then I *would* have made you sorry.'

He gave her a curious look. 'I think you will one day, in any case,' he said.

'Perhaps we should both look forward to that.'

She rose, reaching out to take some plates to the sink, but he forestalled her. 'Leave it to me.'

'There's no need to fuss me like an invalid.' She laughed. 'I really can do things for myself.'

His reply was a look of sadness. 'All right,' he said after a moment.

'Lysandros, honestly—'

'I just wish you'd let me give you something—do things for you—'

Heart-stricken, she touched his face, blaming herself for being insensitive.

'I didn't want to be a nuisance,' she whispered. 'You have so many really important things to do.'

He put his arms right around her and drew her close against him.

'There's nothing more important than you,' he said simply.

Later she was to remember the way he'd held her and wonder at it. It hadn't been the embrace of a lover, more the clasp of a refugee clinging onto safety for dear life. He couldn't have told her more clearly that she'd brought something into his life that was more than passion—more life-enhancing while he had it, more soul-destroying if he lost it.

CHAPTER SEVEN

When the washing-up was done Petra asked, 'What are we going to do today?'

'You're going to rest.'

'I think a little gentle exercise will be better for me. I could continue exploring the cellar—'

'No!' This time there was no doubt that he meant it. 'We can have a short outing, an hour on the beach, and lunch, then back here for you to rest.'

'Anything you say.'

Lysandros regarded her cynically.

There was a small car in the garage and he drove them the short distance to the shore, where they found a tiny beach, cut off from the main one and deserted.

'It's private,' Lysandros explained. 'It belongs to a friend of mine. Don't stretch out in this burning sun, not with your fair skin. Do you want to get ill?'

He led her to the rocks, where there was some shade and a small cave that she used for changing. Now she was glad she'd had the forethought to bring a bathing costume when she came to Corfu, meaning to enjoy some swimming while she investigated his house. No chance had occured, but now she changed gladly, longing to feel the sun on her skin, and emerged to find that he'd laid out a large towel for her to lie on. There was even a pillow, making it blissful to lie down, although she hadn't been awake long.

He'd brought some sun lotion to rub in, but was doubtful.

'You shouldn't have this as well as liniment,' he explained. 'We'll leave it for a while, but you stay in the shade. No, don't try to move the towel. Leave it where I put it.'

'Yes, sir. Three bags full, sir.'

He frowned. 'This is something I sometimes hear English people say, but I don't understand it.'

She explained that the words occurred in a nursery rhyme, but he only looked worried.

'You say it to make fun of someone?' he ventured.

'Only of myself,' she said tenderly. 'The mockery is aimed at me, and the way I'm tamely letting you give me orders.'

This genuinely puzzled him. 'But why shouldn't I—?'

'Hush.' She laid a finger over his lips. He immediately kissed it.

'It's for your own good,' he protested. 'To care for you.'

'I know. The joke is that part of me is as much of a sergeant major as you are. I give orders too. But I let you say, "Do this, do that" without kicking your shins as I would with any other man. It's like discovering that inside me is someone else that I've never met before.'

He nodded. 'Yes, that's how it is.'

To complete her protection he'd hired a large parasol. Now he put it up and made sure that she was well covered.

'What about you?' she said. 'You might catch the sun, unless I rub some of that lotion into you.'

Unlike her, he was dark and at less danger from sunburn, but the thought of caressing him under the guise of sun care was irresistible.

'You think I need it?' he asked.

'Definitely.'

He gave her a brief look and lay back beside her so that she could begin work on his chest. He said nothing for a while, just lay still while her fingers worked across his skin, curving to shape the muscles, enjoying herself.

'How did we get here?' he murmured.

'I don't know. We seem to have missed each other so many times. You'd come just so far towards me, then clam up. Everything would be fine between us, then you'd act as though I was an enemy you had to fight off. That night in Athens—'

'I know. I'm sorry about that. I hated myself at the time, but I couldn't stop. You were right to reject me.'

He wasn't fighting her any more and suddenly there was a vulnerable look on his face that she couldn't bear to see. He was powerful and belligerent, but this was her territory where her skills were greater than his, and it was dangerously easy to hurt him.

'We've never understood each other well,' she said gently. 'Perhaps now we have a chance to do that.'

His brow darkened. 'Are you sure you want to try? It might be better not to. I'm bad news. I hurt people. I don't mean to, but often I'm so cut off that I don't realise I'm doing it.'

'You wouldn't be trying to scare me, would you?'

'Warn you. I doubt I could scare you.'

'I'm glad you realise that.'

'So listen to me. Be wise and go now. I'm bad for you.'

'That's all right; I'll just retaliate in kind. When it comes to being bad, you are dealing with an expert.' He started to reply but she silenced him. 'No, I talk, you listen. I've heard what you have to say and I'm not impressed by it. I'm a match for you any day. If we fight, we fight, and you'll come off worst.'

'Oh, will I?' Now his interest was aroused.

'You'd better believe it,' she chuckled. 'Won't that be a new experience for you?'

'A man should be prepared for new experiences. That's how he gets strong and able to achieve victory every time.'

'Every time, hmm?'

'Every time,' he assured her.

'We'll put that to the test. Right now—' she drew back and got to her feet '—I'm going for a swim.'

She was off down the beach before he could get to his feet. By the time he caught her she'd reached the water and hurled herself in. He followed, keeping up with her as she swam out to sea, then getting ahead and stretching out his hands to her. She clasped them, looking up, laughing, rejoicing in the sunlight.

'Steady,' he said, supporting her as she leaned over backwards.

They swam for a while, but she was stiff and as soon as he saw her wince slightly he said, 'Now we're going ashore to have something to eat.'

As they walked up the beach she took the chance to study him. Last night she'd lain with this man, welcomed him inside her, felt a pleasure that only he had ever been able to give, but in the poor light she hadn't seen him properly. Now she looked her fill at his tall muscular body that might have belonged to an athlete instead of a businessman.

Certain moments from their lovemaking came back to her, making her tremble. How easily he'd driven her to new heights, how fierce was the craving he could make her feel, how inspired were the movements of his hands, knowing just where and how to touch her. If she could have had her way she would have pulled him down onto the sand right then. Instead, she promised herself that the wait would not be long.

They found a small restaurant by the sea, and sat where they could watch the waves.

'What happened with the boat?' he asked.

'I don't know really. The weather was fine at first. We went to several caves, didn't find anything. I should never have gone—'

'And you wouldn't have done but for me. If you'd died—'

'That's enough of that.' She stopped him firmly. 'I didn't die. End of story.'

'No,' he said softly. 'It's not the end of the story. We both know that.'

She nodded but said no more.

'After we quarrelled I was sure that we had nothing further to say to each other, but then I heard of your danger and—' he made an agitated gesture '—nothing's been the same since. When I saw you safe the world became bright again, but then there was Nikator. When I heard you'd gone away with him—'

'You should have known better than to believe it.'

'But how could I? You wouldn't believe me when I warned you about him and when I saw you together I thought you'd chosen him over me. I don't really know you at all, except that something here—' he touched his heart '—has always known you.'

'Yes, but that isn't going to make it easy,' she reflected. 'The path led in so many directions that it was confusing, and in the end we stumbled against each other by accident.'

'This meeting was hardly an accident,' he observed lightly. 'You broke into my house.'

'True. I committed a criminal act,' she said, smiling. 'I didn't actually want to. I had planned to ask you to let me explore, but then we quarrelled and—' She gave an eloquent shrug.

He nodded. 'Yes, when you've told a man to go and jump in the lake it would be hard to ask him a favour in the next breath.'

'I'm glad you understand my difficulty. And I couldn't just go tamely away without investigating, could I? Breaking and entering was my only option.'

'But how did you get in? My locks are the most up-to-date.'

Her smile told him that these were minor difficulties, made to be overcome.

'Estelle made a film about organised crime a few years back,' she recalled. 'One of the advisers was a locksmith. I learned a lot from him. He said there was no such thing as a lock that couldn't be picked, even a digital one.'

He regarded her cautiously, not sure whether to believe her. At last he ran a finger gently down her cheek, murmuring, 'So you wouldn't call yourself an honest woman?'

'Honest? Lysandros, haven't you understood yet? I'm a historian. We don't *do* honest, not if it gets in the way. If we want to investigate something, we just go ahead. We break in, we forge papers, we tell lies, we cheat, we do whatever is needed to find out what we need to know. Of course we sometimes get permission as a matter of convenience, but it's not important.'

He grinned. 'I see. And if the owner objects—?'

She regarded him from dancing eyes and leaned forward so that her breath brushed his face.

'Then the owner can take his silly objections and stuff them where the sun doesn't shine,' she murmured.

'I'm shocked.'

'No, you're not. I'll bet it's what you do yourself every day of the week.'

'And I would bet that you could teach me a few new tricks.'

'Any time you like,' she murmured against his lips.

'I was talking about business.'

'I wasn't. Let's go home.'

On the way he stopped off to buy food in quantity, and

Petra realised that he was stocking up for several days. She smiled. That suited her exactly.

The sun was setting as they entered the house and locked the world out. In the shadowy hall he took her into his arms for a long kiss. The feel of his mouth on hers was comforting and thrilling together. He was partly hers and she was going to make him completely hers, as she was already his.

He kissed her neck, moving his lips gently, then resting with his face against her, as though seeking refuge. She stroked his hair until he looked up, meeting her eyes, and together they climbed the stairs to the bedroom.

Last night they had claimed each other with frantic urgency. Tonight they could afford to take their time, confident in each other and their new knowledge of their hearts and what they shared.

At first he moved slowly, cautiously, and she loved him for his care for her. As every garment slipped away he touched her bare flesh as though doubtful that he could take the next step. She undressed him in the same way, eager to discover the body she'd admired on the beach that day.

It didn't disappoint her. He was hard and fit, reminding her of what she'd enjoyed once, making her tremble with the thought of what was to come.

He laid her on the bed and sat for a moment, watching her with possessive eyes.

'Let me look at you,' he whispered.

She was happy for him to do so, knowing that she would please him. A man who'd discovered unexpected treasure might have worn the look she saw on his face. She raised her arms over her head, revelling in flaunting her nakedness for him, knowing that it was worth flaunting.

At last he laid a gentle hand on one breast, relishing the movement as it rose and fell with her mounting desire, then leaning down to circle the nipple with his lips and begin a soft assault. She took a long shuddering breath and immediately arched against him.

'Yes,' she murmured, 'yes—'

'Hush, we don't have to rush.'

How could he say that? she wondered. Already his arousal was fierce and strong, making her reach out with eager exploring fingers. But he was in command of himself, with the power to take his time while he teased and incited her.

'You're a devil,' she whispered.

He didn't reply in words, but he raised his head long enough for his eyes to flash a humorous message, saying, clearer than words, that a devil was what he knew she wanted, and he was going to fulfil her desire.

He increased his devilment, turning up the tension as he got to work on the other breast, moving even more slowly now, making sure she was ready, but she was ahead of him, more than ready, eager and impatient.

'Now,' she breathed. *'Now!'*

He was over her before the words were out, finding the place that was clamouring for him, claiming it with a swift movement that sent her into a frenzy of pleasure.

This was unlike anything that had happened to her before. No man had ever filled her so completely, while still leaving her with a feeling of freedom. She thrust back against him, needing more of him, demanding everything, receiving it again and again.

When it was over she held him tightly, as though needing him for safety in this new world that had opened. But then she realised that there was no safety, for either of them. That was the glory of it.

He raised his head and there was a kind of bafflement in his eyes.

'You—' he said softly, 'you—'

'I know,' she whispered. 'It's the same with me.'

It was as though her words had touched a spring within him, releasing something that brought him peace. He laid his head down on her again, and in a moment he was asleep.

Petra didn't sleep at once. Instead, she lay savouring her joy and triumph, kissing him tenderly, silently promising him everything. Only gradually did she slip away into the happy darkness.

They spent most of the next day in bed, not making love, but cuddling, talking, then cuddling some more in a way that would have been impossible only a short time ago. His body, so perfectly formed and skilled for giving her sexual pleasure, was mysteriously also formed for things cosy, domestic and comforting. It was a mystery, and one she would enjoy solving later.

'I don't know what I'd have done if I'd lost you,' he murmured as they lay curled against each other. 'It felt like being in prison, except that somehow you had the key, and you could help me break out.'

'You kept coming to the edge of escape,' she remembered, 'but then you'd back off again and slam the door.'

'I lost my nerve,' he said with self-contempt. 'I wasn't sure if I could manage, so I'd retreat and lock the doors again. But I couldn't stay in there, knowing you were outside, calling to me that the world was a wonderful place. You saved me the first time; I knew you could save me again.'

'How did I save you?'

His only reply was a long silence, and she felt her heart sink. So often they'd come to the point where he might confide in her, but always his demons had driven him back. This time she'd hoped it might be different, that their loving had given him confidence in her. But it seemed not. Perhaps, after all, nothing had changed.

She'd almost given up hope when Lysandros said in a low voice, 'I never told you why I was in Las Vegas. The fact is

I'd quarrelled with my family. Suddenly it seemed hateful to me that we were always at war about so much. I wanted no more of it. I left home and went out to "live my own life", as I put it. But I got into bad ways. The night we met I'd been like that for two years, and I was headed for disaster if something didn't happen to save me. But something did. I met you.'

'And quarrelled with me,' she said with just a hint of teasing.

'We didn't quarrel,' he said quickly. 'Hell, yes, I suppose we came to the edge of it because I wasn't used to being told a truth I didn't want to hear—that dig about Achilles sulking in his tent.'

'But it wasn't a dig. I was just running over the legend in my usual thoughtless way.'

'I know. You may even have done me a favour.'

Another silence while he fought his inner battle.

'It's all right,' she said. 'Don't tell me anything you don't want to.'

'But I do want to,' he said slowly. 'If you only knew how much.'

She touched his hand again, and felt him squeeze her fingers gratefully.

'That remark got to me,' he said at last. 'I was twenty-three and…I guess, not very mature. I'd left my father to cope alone. You showed me the truth about myself. I did a lot of thinking, and next day I came home and told my father I was ready to take my place in the business. We became a partnership and when he died ten years ago I was able to take over. Thanks to you.'

'Should I be proud of my creation?'

'Do you think so?'

'Not entirely. You're not a happy man.'

He shrugged. 'Happiness isn't part of the bargain.'

'I wonder who you struck that bargain with,' she mused. 'Perhaps it was the Furies.'

'No, the Furies are my advance troops that I send into battle. This isn't about my feelings. I do my job. I keep people in work.'

'And so you benefit them. But what about you, yourself, the man?'

His eyes darkened and he seemed to stare into space. 'Sometimes,' he said at last, 'I've felt he hardly exists.'

She nodded. '*He's* an automaton that walks and talks and does what's necessary,' she said. 'But what about *you*?' She laid a soft hand over his heart. 'Somewhere in there, you must exist.'

'Perhaps it's better if I don't,' he said heavily.

'Better for whom? Not you. How can you live in the world and not be part of it?'

He grimaced. 'That's easier than you think. And safer.'

'Safer? You? The man who's supposed to be immortal?'

'*Supposed* to be—'

'Except for that one tiny place on the heel? Shame on you, Achilles. Do you want me to think you're afraid to take the risks that we less glorious mortals take every day?'

He drew a sharp breath and grasped her. 'Oh, you're good,' he said. 'You're clever, cunning, sharp; you know how to pierce a man's heart—'

'You have no heart,' she challenged him. 'At least, not one you care to listen to.'

'And if I listened to it, what do you think it would say to me—about you?'

'I can't tell you that. Only you can know.'

'It will speak in answer to your heart,' he riposted cunningly. 'If I knew what that was saying—'

'Can't you read it?' she whispered.

'Some of it. It laughs at me, almost like an enemy, and yet—'

'Friends laugh too. My heart is your friend, but perhaps an annoying friend. You'll have to be prepared for that.'

'I am, I promise you. Petra—Petra—say you want me.'

'If you haven't worked that out for yourself by now—'

His hands seemed to touch her everywhere at once.

'I hope that means what I think it means,' he growled. 'Because it's too late now.'

She put her arms around his neck. 'Whatever took you so long?'

When she awoke it was early morning and she was alone. Beside her the bed was empty, but the rumpled sheet and pillow showed where he had been. Touching the place, she found that it was still warm.

She sat up listening, but there was only silence. Slipping out of bed, she went to the door, but when she opened it she saw that there was no light on in the bathroom, and some instinct told her that he was in trouble.

She thought she could hear a faint sound from the far end of the corridor. Moving quietly, she followed it to the end, where it turned into another corridor. There she heard the sound again, and this time it sounded like soft footsteps, back and forth. She followed it to the end and waited a moment, her heart beating, before turning the corner.

A short flight of stairs rose before her. At the top stood Lysandros, by the window, looking out onto the world below. He turned, walked back and forth like a man seeing his way in unfamiliar territory, finally coming to a halt in front of a door.

She waited for him to enter the room. Perhaps she could follow him quietly, and so gain a clue to his trouble. But instead he remained motionless for what seemed like an age. Then he leaned against the door, his shoulders sagging in an attitude that suggested he was on the point of collapse. She was about to go to him, offering comfort, when he straightened up and turned around in her direction.

Hurriedly she retreated, and vanished before he could see her. She managed to reach the bedroom without being discovered and was huddled down with her back to him when he came in. She sensed him get in beside her and lean over her, apparently trying to check if she was asleep. She decided to chance it and opened her eyes.

'Hello,' she said, opening her arms to him.

Now, surely, he would come into them and tell her what had happened, because now they were close in hearts and minds and he didn't need to hide things from her.

But, instead, he drew back.

'I'm sorry if I disturbed you,' he said. 'I was just thinking of getting up.'

'You're going to get up now?' she asked slowly.

'Yes, I get stiff lying here all night, but you stay. I'll bring you some coffee later.'

He left the room quickly, leaving her wanting to scream out a protest.

No matter what happiness they seemed to share, beneath it was a torment that hounded him, and which he could not bring himself to share with her. Everything she'd longed for was an illusion. She was still shut out from his deepest heart. She buried her face, and the pillow was wet with her tears.

CHAPTER EIGHT

PETRA wondered how Lysandros would be when they met again at breakfast, whether he would show any awareness of what had happened. But he greeted her cheerfully, with a kiss on the cheek. They might have been any couple enjoying a few days vacation without a care in the world.

'Is there anything you'd like to do?' he asked.

'I'd love to go to Gastouri.'

She was referring to the tiny village where the Achilleion Palace had been built.

'Have you never been before?' he asked in surprise.

'Yes, but it was a hurried visit to get material. Now I'll have time to explore properly.'

And perhaps, she thought, it would help her cope with the sadness of being rejected again.

The village lay about seven miles to the south, built on a slope, with the Palace at the top, overlooking the sea. This was the place that the Empress Elizabeth had built to indulge her passion for the Greek hero, who seemed to have reached out to her over thousands of years. His courage, his complex character, his terrible fate, all were remembered here.

As soon as they entered the gates Petra was aware of the

atmosphere—powerful, vital, yet melancholy, much as Achilles himself must have been.

Just outside the house was the statue of the Empress herself, a tiny figure, looking down with a sad expression, as though all hope had left her.

'She used to annoy my father,' Lysandros said. 'He said she was a silly woman who couldn't pull herself together.'

'Charming.'

'When my mother brought me here he'd insist on coming too, and showing me the things *he* wanted me to remember, like this one.'

He led the way to a tall bronze statue showing Achilles as a magnificent young warrior, wearing a metal helmet mounted with a great feathered crest. On his lower legs was armour, embossed at the kneecaps with snarling lions.

From one arm hung a shield while the other hand held a spear. He stood on a sixteen-foot plinth, looming over all-comers, staring out into the distance.

'Disdainful,' Petra said thoughtfully. 'Standing so far above, he'd never notice ordinary mortals like us, coming and going down here.'

'Perhaps that's how Sisi liked to picture him,' Lysandros suggested with a touch of mischief.

'Sisi knew nothing about it,' Petra said at once. 'After her death the Palace was sold to a man, and *he* put this statue here.'

He grinned. 'I might have guessed you'd know that.'

'So that's who your father wanted you to be,' she reflected, straining her head back to look up high to Achilles' face.

'Nothing less would do for him. There's also the picture inside which he admired.'

The main hall was dominated by a great staircase, at the top of which was a gigantic painting depicting a man in a racing chariot, galloping at full speed, dragging the lifeless body of his enemy in the dirt behind.

'Achilles in triumph,' Petra said, 'parading his defeated enemy around the walls of Troy.'

'That was how a man ought to be,' Lysandros mused. 'Because if you didn't do it to them, they would do it to you. So I was raised being taught how to do it to them.'

'And do you?'

'Yes,' he replied simply. 'If I have to, otherwise I wouldn't survive, and nor would the people who work for me.'

'Parading lifeless bodies?' she queried.

'Not literally. My enemies are still walking about on earth, trying to destroy me. But if you've won, people have to know you've won, and the lengths you were prepared to go to. That way they learn the lesson.'

For a moment his face frightened her, not because it displayed harshness or cruelty, but because it displayed nothing at all. He was simply stating a fact. Victory had to be flaunted or it was less effective, and she could see that he didn't really understand why this troubled her.

They moved on through the building, looking at the friezes and murals, the paintings and statues all telling of another world, yet one that still reached out to touch this one. Lysandros might speak wryly of his mother's fascination with the legendary Achilles, yet even he felt the story's power over him.

Heroism was no longer simple as in those days, but he'd been born into a society that expected him to conquer his enemies and drag them behind his chariot wheels. The past laid its weight on him, almost expecting him to live two lives at once, and he knew it. Fight it as he might, there were times when the expectations almost crushed him.

If she'd doubted that, she had the proof when they moved

back into the garden and went to stand before the great statue depicting Achilles' last moments. He lay on the ground, trying to draw the arrow from his heel, although in his heart he knew it was hopeless. His head was raised to the heavens and on his face was a look of despair.

'He's resigned,' Lysandros said. 'He knows there's no escaping his destiny.'

'Then perhaps he shouldn't be so resigned,' Petra said at once. 'You should never accept bad luck as inevitable. That's just giving in.'

'How could he help it? He knew his fate was written on the day he was born. It was always there on his mind, the hidden vulnerability. Except that in the end it wasn't hidden, because someone had known all the time. None of us hide our weaknesses as well as we think we do.'

'But perhaps,' she began tentatively, 'if the other person was someone we didn't have to be afraid of, someone who wouldn't use it against us—'

'That would be paradise indeed,' Lysandros agreed. 'But how would you know, until it was too late?'

They strolled for a while in the grounds before he said, 'Is there any more you need to see here, or shall we go?'

On the way home his mood seemed to lighten. They had a cheerful supper, enlivened by an argument about a trivial point that he seemed unable to let go of, until he covered his eyes with his hands, in despair at himself.

'It doesn't matter, does it?' he groaned. 'I know it doesn't matter and yet—'

'You're a mess,' she said tenderly. 'You don't know how to deal with people—unless they're enemies. You deal with *them* well enough, but anyone else—you're left floundering. You know what you need?'

'What's that?'

'Me. To put you on a straight line and keep you there.'

'Where does this line lead?'

'Back to me, every time. So make up your mind to it; I'm taking charge.'

He regarded her for a moment, frowning, and she wondered if she'd pushed his dictatorial nature too far. But then the frown vanished, replaced by a tender smile.

'That's all right, then,' he said.

She smiled in a way that she could see he found mystifying. Good. That suited her perfectly.

Quickly she reached into her pocket, drew out a small notebook and pencil that never left her, then began counting on her fingers and making notes.

'What are you doing?' he demanded.

'Calculating. Do you know it's exactly eighteen hours and twenty-three minutes since you made love to me?' She sighed theatrically. 'I don't know. Some men are all talk.'

Before he could think of an answer, she rose and darted away.

'Hey, where are you going?'

'Where do you think?' she called back over her shoulder from halfway up the stairs.

He managed to pass her on the stairs and reach the bedroom first.

'Come here,' he said, yanking her close and holding her tightly, without gentleness. *'Come here.'*

It was less a kiss than an act of desperation. She knew that as soon as his lips touched hers, not tenderly but with a ferocity that mirrored her own. They had shared kisses before, but this was a step further. In the past she'd been struggling with her own reaction, and doubtful of his. But the previous two times they'd made love had told each of them something about the other, and where they were going together.

Now there were no doubts on either side, no room for

thoughts or even emotions. They wanted each other as a simple physical act, free of everything but the need for satisfaction.

His mouth seemed to burn hers while his tongue invaded her, demanding, asking no quarter and giving none. His urgency thrilled her for it matched her own, but she wouldn't let him know that just yet. She had another plan in mind.

'Mmm, just as I hoped,' she murmured.

He ground his teeth. 'You pulled my strings and I jumped, didn't I?'

''Fraid so. And you have another problem now.'

'Surprise me.'

'I'm a horrible person. In fact I'm just horrible enough to get up and walk away right now.'

His hands tightened on her in a grip of steel. *'Don't even think about it.'*

She began to laugh with delight, revelling in the ruthless determination with which he held her, threw her onto her back and invaded her like a conqueror. She was still laughing when her explosion of pleasure sent the world into a spin.

Afterwards he looked down at her, gasping and frenzied.

'You little—*it's not funny!'*

'But it is funny. Oh, my darling, you're so easily fooled.'

He began to move inside her again, slowly, making her wait but leaving her in no doubt that he had the strength and control to prolong the moment.

'Were you expecting this too?' he whispered.

'Not exactly expecting, but I was hoping—oh, yes, I was hoping you'd do just what you're doing now—and again—and again—oh, darling, *don't stop!'*

She ceased to be aware of time, losing track of how often he brought her to climax. It didn't matter. All that mattered was that he'd transported her to another world, while giving her the vital feeling that she too had transported him. Whatever happened to them happened together, and she cared about nothing else.

When he finally managed to speak it was with ironic humour.

'I did it again, didn't I? Danced to your tune. Is there any way I can get one step ahead of you?'

She seemed to consider this. 'Probably not. But I'd hate you to stop trying.'

Now it was his turn to laugh. She felt it against her before she heard it, and her soul rejoiced because it was through laughter that she could reach him.

The next few days were hazy. They spent much of the time out, wandering the island or lazing on the beach, their evenings indoors, talking with a freedom which once would have been impossible. They spent the nights in each other's arms.

She knew it couldn't last for ever. For now they were living in a world apart, where each of them could yield to the new personality the other could evoke. He could doff his harsh exterior, emerge from the prison cell where his heart normally lived, and let her see the side of him that was charming and outgoing.

But it was unreal. Such perfect happiness could never last unchallenged. Sooner or later she must face the part of him that remained hidden from her, or retire in defeat because he wouldn't allow her in.

She'd never told him of the night she'd followed him to the distant room. Once she slipped upstairs to try the door and, as she'd expected, found it locked. In her mind it came to symbolise the fact that she still hadn't gained entry into the deepest heart of him. Despite their happiness, she wondered if she ever would.

One night she awoke to find herself alone again. The door was open and from a distance she thought she could hear sounds. Quickly she scrambled out into the corridor and was just in time to see Lysandros turning the corner. He walked in a slow, dazed manner, as though he was sleepwalking.

When she reached the little staircase he was just standing at the top. He approached the door slowly, then, before her horrified eyes, he began to ram his head against it again and again, as though by seeking pain he could blot out unbearable memories.

Suddenly she was back on the roof all those years ago and he was in her arms, banging his head against her, seeking oblivion from misery too great to be borne. And she knew that fifteen years had changed nothing. In his heart he was the same young man now as then.

She would have run to him, but he stopped suddenly and turned, leaning back against the door. Through the window the moonlight fell on his face, showing her a depth of agony that shocked her.

He didn't move. His eyes were closed, his head pressed back against the door, his face raised as though something hovered in the darkness above him. As she watched, he lifted his hands and laid them over his face, pressing them close as though he could use them as a shield against the Furies that pursued him. But the Furies were inside him. There was no escape.

Wisdom told her to retreat and never let him know that she'd seen him like this, but she couldn't be wise now. He might try to reject her, but she must at least offer him her comfort.

She moved the rest of the way quickly and quietly, then reached up to draw his hands away. He started, gazing at her with haggard eyes that saw a stranger.

'It's all right; it's only me,' she whispered.

'What are you doing here?'

'I came because you need me—yes, you do,' she added quickly before he could speak. 'You think you don't need anyone, but you need me because I understand. I know things that no one else knows, because you shared them with me long ago.'

'You don't know the half of it,' he whispered.

'Then tell me. What's in that room, Lysandros? What draws you here? What do you see when you go inside?'

His reply startled her. 'I never go inside.'

'But…then why…?'

'I don't go in because I can't bear to. Each time I come here, hoping to find the courage to enter, but that never happens.' He gave a mirthless snort of laughter. 'Now you know. *I'm a coward.*'

'Don't—'

'I'm a coward because I can't face her again.'

'Is she in there?' Petra asked.

'She always will be. You think I'm mad? Well, perhaps. Let's see.'

He opened his hand, revealing the key, allowing her to take it and put it in the lock. Turning it slowly, she pushed on the door. It stuck as though protesting after being closed for so long, but then a nudge opened it and she stood on the threshold, holding her breath, wondering fearfully what she would find.

At first she could see very little. Outside the dawn was breaking, but the shutters were still closed and only thin slivers of light managed to creep in. By their faint glow she realised that this room had been designed as a celebration of love.

The walls were covered in paintings depicting gods, goddesses and various Greek legends. Incredibly, Petra thought she recognised some of them.

'These pictures are famous,' she murmured. 'Botticelli, Titian—'

'Don't worry, we didn't steal them,' Lysandros said. 'They're all copies. One of my mother's ancestors wanted to "make a figure" in the world. So he hired forgers to go all over Europe and copy the works of great artists—paintings, statues. You'll probably recognise the statues of Eros and Aphrodite as well.'

'The gods of love,' she whispered.

'His wife directed matters, and had this room turned into a kind of temple.'

'It's charming,' Petra said. 'Had they made a great love match?'

'No, he married the poor woman for her money, and this was her way of trying to deny it.'

'How sad.'

'Love often is sad when you get past the pretty lies and down to the ugly truth,' he said in a flat voice.

But now she scarcely heard him. Disturbing impressions were reaching her. Something was badly wrong, but she wasn't sure what. Then she drew closer to a statue of Eros, the little god of love, and a chill went through her.

'His face,' she murmured. 'I can't see, but surely—'

With a crash Lysandros threw open the shutters, filling the room with pale light. Petra drew a sharp, horrified breath.

Eros had no face. It looked as if it had been smashed off by a hammer. His wings, too, lay on the floor.

Now she could look around at the others and see that they were all damaged in a similar way. Every statue had been attacked, every painting defaced.

But the worst of all was what had happened to the bed. It had been designed as a four-poster but the posts too had been smashed, so that the great canopy had collapsed onto the bed, where it lay.

Someone had attacked this temple to love in a frenzy, and then left the devastation as it was, making no attempt to clear up. Now she could see the thick dust. It had been like this, untouched, for a long, long time. That was as terrible as the damage with its message of soul-destroying bitterness.

'You asked if she were in here,' Lysandros said. 'She's been here since the night I brought her to this house, to this room, and we made love. She'll always be here.'

'Was she here when—?'

'When I did this? When I took an axe and defaced the statues and the pictures, smashed the bed where we'd slept, wanting to wipe out every trace of what I'd once thought was love? No, she wasn't here. She'd gone. I didn't know where she was and after that—I didn't find her until she died, far away.'

He turned to the wrecked bed, gazing at it bleakly as though it held him transfixed. Shivers went through Petra as she realised that he'd spoken no more than the truth. His dead love was still present, and she always would be. She followed him through every step of his life, but she was always here, in this house, in this room, in his heart, in his nightmares.

'Come away,' she said, 'There's nothing here any more.'

It wasn't true. In this room was everything that was terrible, but she wouldn't admit that to him, lest her admission crush him further. She drew him to the door and locked it after them. She knew it would take more than a locked door to banish this ghost from his dark dreams, but she was determined to do it.

He's got me now, she told the lurking presence in her mind. *And I won't let you hurt him any more.*

She didn't speak to Lysandros again, just led him back to their bed and held him in her arms.

At last some life seemed to return to Lysandros and he roused himself to speak.

'Since we've been here together, I've found myself going more and more to that room, hoping that I could make myself enter and drive the ghost away.'

'Perhaps I can help you do that,' she suggested.

'Perhaps. I've resisted it too long.'

'Am I something you need to resist?' she whispered.

He took so long to reply that she thought he wasn't going to say anything, but at last he spoke as though the words were dragged out of him by pincers.

'From the first evening you have filled me with dread,' he said slowly. 'With dread—with fear. There! That's the truth. Despise me if you will.'

'I could never despise you,' she hastened to say. 'I just can't think of any reason why you should be afraid of me.'

'Not of you, but of the way you made me feel. In your presence my defences seemed to melt away. I felt it when we met at the wedding. When I discovered that you were the girl on the roof in Las Vegas I was glad, because it seemed to explain why I was drawn to you. We'd been practically childhood friends so naturally there was a bond. That's what I told myself.

'But then we danced, and I knew that the bond was something far more. I left the wedding early to escape you, but I called you later that day because I had to. Even then I couldn't stay away from you because you had an alarming power, one I shied away from because I'd never met it before and I knew I couldn't struggle against it.

'Do you remember the statue we saw in the Achilleion Palace? Not the first one where Achilles was in all his glory, but the second one, where he was on the ground, trying to remove the arrow, knowing that he couldn't? Did you see his face, upturned to the sky, begging help from the gods because he knew that this was stronger than him and only divine intervention could save him from its power?'

'But he was fighting death,' Petra reminded him. 'Do I represent death?'

He smiled faintly and shook his head.

'No, but you represent the defeat of everything I believed was necessary to keep me strong. The armour that kept me at a cautious distance from other people, the watchfulness that never let me relax, so that I was always ahead of the game and all the other players. In your presence, all of that vanished. I implored the gods to return my strength so that I could be as safe against you as I was against everyone else, but they didn't listen—possibly because they knew I didn't really mean it.

'Your power over me came from something I'd never considered before. It wasn't sex, although there was that too. Lord, how I wanted to sleep with you, possess you! It drove me half demented, but I could cope with that. It was something else, much more alarming.'

'I know,' she said. 'I could make you laugh. I've always loved doing that, not because it gave me power but because I hoped it might make you happy.'

'It did, but it also alarmed me because it meant I was vulnerable to you as to nobody else in the world, man or woman. So I departed again. This time I went away for days, but then I began to worry that you might have returned to England, and I discovered I didn't want that after all. I was acting like a man with no sense, wanting this, wanting the opposite, not knowing what I wanted—like a man in love, in fact. So I called you.'

'I was with Nikator,' she remembered. 'He guessed it was you and warned me against you.'

'He was right.'

'I know he was. I never doubted that for a moment. Do you think I care what that silly infant thinks, as long as you come back to me?'

'When I saw you again I knew I couldn't have stayed away any longer,' he said, 'but I also knew I'd come back to danger. I was no longer master of myself, and that control—that mastery—has been the object of my life. I understood even then that I couldn't have both it and you, but it's not until now—'

It was only now that he'd brought himself to face the final

decision, and for a moment she still wasn't sure which way it would go. There was some terrifying secret that haunted him, and everything would depend on what happened in the next few minutes.

Suddenly she was afraid.

CHAPTER NINE

AT LAST he began to speak.

'It started in my childhood with my mother's fantasies about Achilles and his hidden vulnerability. I understood the point about keeping your secrets to yourself, but in those days it was only theory, little more than a game. I was young, I had more money than was good for me, I felt I could rule the world. I fancied myself strong and armoured, but in truth I was wide open to a shrewd manipulator.'

'Is that what *she* was?' Petra asked.

'Yes, although it wasn't so much her as the men behind her. Her name was Brigitta. She was a great-niece of Homer, not that I knew that until later. We met by chance—or so I thought—on a skiing holiday. In fact she was an excellent skier, but she concealed that, just kept falling over, so I began to teach her and somehow we fell over a lot together.

'Then we abandoned skiing and went away to be by ourselves. I was in heaven. I didn't know any girl could be so lovely, so sweet, so honest—'

He drew a ragged breath and dropped his head down onto his chest. He was shaking, and she wondered with dismay if this was only memory. After all these years, did some part of his love still survive to torment him?

She reached out to touch him but stopped at the last minute and let her hand fall away. He didn't seem to notice.

After a while he began to speak again.

'Of course I was deceiving myself. It had all been a clever trap. She was thrown into my path on purpose so that I could make a fool of myself over her. Even when I discovered who she was I didn't have the wit to see the plot. I believed her when she said she'd concealed her background because she was truly in love with me and didn't want me to be suspicious. Can you imagine anything so stupid?'

'It's not stupid,' Petra protested. 'If you really loved her, of course you wanted to think well of her. And you must have been so young—'

'Twenty-one, and I thought I knew it all,' he said bitterly.

'How old was she?'

'Nineteen. So young; how could I possibly suspect her? Even when I found out she was using a false name, that she'd engineered our meeting—even then I believed that she was basically innocent. I *had* to believe it. She was the most beautiful thing that had ever happened to me.'

She could have wept for the boy he'd been then. To cling to his trust in the face of the evidence suggested a naïvety that nobody meeting him now would ever believe.

'What happened?' she asked.

'We planned to marry. Everyone went wild—the two foes putting their enmity aside to join forces and present a united front to the world. My father advised me to delay; he was uneasy. I wouldn't listen. We came here to be alone together and spent the summer living in this house. I wouldn't have thought that anyone could be as happy as I was in those weeks.'

His mouth twisted in a wry smile.

'And I'd have been right not to believe it. It was all an illusion, created by my own cowardly refusal to face the fact that she was a spy. She didn't learn much, but enough for the Lukas family to pip us to the post on a lucrative contract. It was obvious that the information must have come from her, and that she'd listened in to a telephone conversation I'd had and managed to see some papers. She denied it at first, but there was simply no other way. I turned on her.'

'Well, naturally, if you felt betrayed—'

'No, it was worse than that. I was cruel, brutal. I said such things—she begged my forgiveness, said she'd started as a spy but regretted it in the end because she came to love me truly.'

'Did you believe her?' Petra asked.

'I didn't dare. I sneered at her. If she truly regretted what she'd done, why hadn't she warned me? She said she tried to back out but Nikator threatened to tell me everything. But he promised to let her off if she did one last job, so that's what she did.'

'But Nikator must have been little more than an child in those days,' Petra protested.

'He was twenty. Old enough to be vicious.'

'But could he have organised it? Would he have known enough?'

'No. There was another man, a distant cousin called Cronos, who hadn't been in the firm more than a couple of years and was still trying to make his mark. Apparently he was a nasty piece of work, and he and Nikator hit it off well, right from the start. People who knew them said they moved in the same slime. Cronos set it up and used Nikator as front man.'

'Cronos set it up?' she echoed. 'Not Homer?'

'No, to do him justice, he's a fairly decent man, a lot better than many in this business. The story is that after the whole thing exploded Homer tore a strip off Cronos and told him to get out if he knew what was good for him. At any rate Cronos vanished.

'Obviously, I don't know the details of any family rows, but my impression is that Homer was shocked by Nikator's behaviour. Being ruthless in business is one thing, but you don't involve innocent young girls. But Nikator had come down hard on Brigitta when she tried to get free. He bullied her into "one last effort", and she thought if she did that it would be over.'

'No way,' Petra said at once. 'Once he had a blackmail hold over her he'd never have let it go.'

'That's what I think too. She was in his power; I should have seen that and helped her. Instead, I turned on her. You can't imagine how cruelly I treated her.'

But she could, Petra thought. Raised with suspicion as his constant companion, thinking he'd found the love and trust that could make his life beautiful, he'd been plunged back into despair and it had almost destroyed him. He'd lashed out with all the vigour of a young man, and in the process he'd hurt the one person he still loved.

'I said such things,' he whispered. 'I can't tell you the things I said, or what they did to her—'

'She'd deceived you.'

'She was a child.'

'So were you,' she said firmly. 'Whatever happened to her, *they* were responsible, the people who manipulated her. Not you.'

'But I should have saved her from them,' he said bleakly. 'And I didn't. We had a terrible scene. I stormed out of the house, saying I hated the sight of her and when I returned she'd vanished. She left me a letter in which she said that she loved me and begged my forgiveness, but there was nothing to tell me where she'd gone.'

Petra made no sound, but her clasp on him tightened.

'I couldn't—wouldn't believe it at first,' he went on in a voice that was low and hoarse. 'I went through the house calling her name. I was sure she had to be hiding somewhere, waiting for a sign from me. I cried out that we would find our way somehow, our love was worth fighting for.'

And after each call he'd stood and listened in the silence. Petra could see it as clearly as if she'd walked the house with that devastated young man. She heard him cry, *'Brigitta!'* again and again, waited while he realised that there would be no answering call, and felt her heart break with his as the truth was forced on him.

And she saw something else that he would never speak of—the moment when the boy collapsed in sobs of despair.

'What did you do after that?' she asked, stroking his hair.

'I believed I could find her and still make it right. I set detectives on her trail. They were the best, but even they couldn't find her. She'd covered her tracks too well. I tried the few who remained of her family in another country, but they weren't close and she hadn't been in touch with them. I tried Nikator. There was just a chance that he knew something, but I'm convinced he didn't. I scared him so badly that he'd have told me if he could.

'In the end I faced facts. A woman who could escape so completely must have been very, very determined to get well away from me. But I didn't stop. Months passed, but I told them to keep looking because I couldn't face the prospect of never seeing or talking to her again. I had to ask her forgiveness, do what I could to make it right.

'At last I got a message from a man who said he thought he might have found her, but it was hard to be sure because she couldn't talk and just sat staring into space all the time. I went to see her and found—' He shuddered.

Petra didn't make the mistake of speaking. She simply sat with him in her arms, praying that her love would reach him and make it possible for him to confront the monster.

'I found her in a shabby room in a back street, miles away,' he managed to say at last. 'The door was locked. The last time anyone had gone in there she'd been so frightened that she'd locked it after them. I kicked it open and went in.

'She was sitting up on a bed in the corner, clutching something in her arms as though she had to protect it. She screamed at the sight of me and backed away as though I was an enemy. Maybe that's how I looked to her then. Or maybe she just didn't know me.'

Another silence, in which she felt his fingers tighten on her arm, release her and tighten again.

'At last all the fight seemed to go out of her. She sagged against the wall and I managed to get close and look at what she was holding.'

His grip was agonisingly tight. Petra closed her eyes, guessing what the bundle had been, and praying to be wrong.

'It was a dead baby,' Lysandros said at last.

'Oh, no,' Petra whispered, dropping her head so that her lips lay against his hair.

'It was premature. She'd hidden her pregnancy and had no proper medical attention, so she gave birth alone. Then she just sat clutching the child and not letting anyone near her. She'd been like that for days, shivering, starving, weeping.

'I begged her to calm down, told her it was me, that I loved her, I'd never harm her, but she told me to go away because she had to feed the baby. By that time he must have been dead for days. He was cold in her arms.

'The people who owned the house were decent and kindly, but they couldn't cope. I had her moved to hospital, ordered the best attention for her, said I'd pay for everything— whatever money could buy, I'd give her.' He said the last words with bitter self-condemnation.

'I went to see her every day in the hospital, always thinking that the care she was receiving would soon take effect, she would become herself again, and we could talk. But it didn't happen. As she became physically stronger her mind seemed to retreat further into a place where I couldn't follow, and I understood that she wanted it that way. But still I waited, hoping she'd recover and we could find each other again.

'Then she had a heart attack, apparently an adverse reaction to a drug she'd been given, but the doctors told me that she wasn't fighting for life. Her will had gone, and it was only a matter of time. I sat beside her, holding her hand, praying for her to awaken. When she did I told her that I loved her and begged her forgiveness.'

'Did she forgive you?' Petra asked quietly.

'I don't know. She only said one thing. By that time she'd accepted that the child was dead and she begged me to make sure he was buried with her. I gave her my word and, when the time came, I kept it. She's buried with our baby in her arms.'

'She must have recognised you to ask such a thing,' Petra said.

'I've told myself that a thousand times, but the truth is that she might have said it to anyone she thought had the power to ensure that it happened. I've tried to believe that she forgave me, but why should I? What right do I have after what I did? I terrified her into running away and hiding from the world when she desperately needed help.

'What kind of life did she have? The doctors told me she was severely undernourished, which had damaged the child, hence the premature birth—and death—of my son.'

'You have no doubt that—?'

'That he was mine? None. She must have been about a month pregnant when we parted. They were very tactful. They offered me a test, to be sure, but I refused. Such a test implied a doubt that dishonoured her. She was carrying my son when I abandoned her.'

'But you didn't throw her out,' Petra protested.

'No, I wanted her to stay here until I could arrange our breakup to look civilised in the eyes of the world,' he said savagely. 'And then, fool that I was, I was surprised when I came back and found her gone. Of course she fled. She looked into the future I'd mapped out and shuddered. I didn't throw her out, but I drove her out with coldness and cruelty.

'If I'd known—everything would have been different, but I made her feel that she had no choice but to run away from me. So there was nobody to help her when she knew about her condition. She faced everything alone, and they both died.

'I was with her to the last. She died in my arms, while I prayed for a word or a look to suggest that she knew me. But there was nothing. She'd gone beyond my reach and all I could do was hold her while she slipped away, never knowing that I was begging her forgiveness. I destroyed her life, I destroyed her last moment, I destroyed our child—'

'But it wasn't—'

'It's my fault—don't you understand? *I killed them, both of them.* I killed them as surely as if I'd—'

'No,' she said fiercely. 'You mustn't be so hard on yourself.'

'But I must,' he said bleakly. 'If I'm not hard on myself, who will be? How many times since then have I gone to her tomb and stood there, watching and waiting for something that's never going to happen?'

'Where is her tomb?'

'Here, in the garden. I had the ground consecrated and got the priest to come and bury them both at the dead of night. Then I covered the place so that nobody can find it by accident.

'Then I had to decide what to do with myself. I looked at what this kind of life had made of me, and I hated it. I told my father I was finished with it all, and took the next plane out of Greece, trying to escape what I'd done, what I'd turned into.

'When you and I met, I'd been on the run for two years.' He gave a brief bark of laughter. 'On the run. Like a criminal. That's how I felt. I went to Monte Carlo, to New York, Los Angeles, London, Las Vegas—anywhere I could live what they call "the high life", which is another way of saying I indulged myself in every despicable way. I drank too much, gambled too much, slept around too much, all because I was trying to escape myself. But at the end, there was always a menacing figure waiting for me at the end of the road. And it was me.

'Then, one night in Las Vegas—well, you know the rest. You showed me to myself in a light I couldn't bear, and I returned to Greece the next day.'

'It wasn't just me,' Petra said. 'You were ready to see things differently or I couldn't have had any effect.'

'Maybe. I don't know.' He gave her a faint smile. 'Part of me prefers to give you the credit—my good angel, who stopped me going even further astray the first time and now—'

'Now?' she asked cautiously.

'I'm not blind, Petra. I know about myself. I'm not a man anyone in their right mind could want to meet. I scare people, and that's been fine up to now. It suited me. But you showed me the truth then, and somehow you've done it again. For years I've sheltered deep inside myself because that way I felt safer. I keep people at a distance because if you don't let yourself need anyone, nobody can hurt you.

'But I can't keep you at a distance because you've been in there—' he touched his heart '—for a long time. I've never told anyone else what I've told you tonight, and I never will. Now you know all my secrets and I'm glad of it, for a burden is gone from me.'

He rested his face against her and she dropped her head, while her tears fell on him.

They slept for a while and awoke in each others' arms, to

find daylight flooding into the room. Anxiously, Petra looked at his face but was reassured. He was smiling, relaxed.

'No regrets?' she asked softly.

He shook his head. 'None with you. Never. Come with me.'

They dressed and he took her hand, leading her downstairs and out of the house.

She'd briefly glimpsed the garden from an upstairs window and seen that it was mainly a wilderness. Everything was overgrown, and now she thought she knew why.

He led her to a distant place under the trees and removed some branches and leaves. Beneath them was a stone in which were carved a few simple words and dates. He had hidden Brigitta and her child away from the world, protecting them as best he could. Without asking, Petra knew that nobody else had ever seen this place.

'So many times I've stood here and begged her forgiveness,' he said. 'What should I tell her about you?'

Her grandfather had once told her that no true Greek was ever completely free of the past. Now Lysandros, this modern man, at home in the harsh world of multibillion dollar business, spoke like an ancient Greek who felt the River Styx swirl around his feet and, beyond it, Hades, the other world, where souls still suffered and communicated with the living.

Could it be true? Was Brigitta there now, gazing at him across the waters, drawing him back, crying that he was hers alone and they should be together for all eternity?

No! She wouldn't allow it.

'You don't have to tell her anything about me,' she said. 'She knows that I love you, just as she does. And, because of that love, she forgives you. Don't forget that where she is now, she understands everything she didn't understand before and she wants your suffering to end.'

It touched her heart to see the relief that came into his face, as though anything said by herself could be trusted, however strange or outrageous it might sound to anyone else.

They walked slowly back into the house and upstairs. Now he kissed her softly, almost tentatively, letting her know that this was different from any other time. They had crossed a boundary of love and trust, and the way ahead was changed for ever.

'Mine,' he whispered, 'all mine.'

'Yours as long as you want me,' she whispered back.

'That will be for ever.'

'And are you mine?' she asked.

'I think I've been yours since the first moment. In my heart I always knew. It just took this long to admit it.'

They lay down, holding each other, touching gently, eager to explore yet unwilling to hurry. Taking their time was a tribute that they owed to each other and they paid it in full. He sought the places where her bruises had been worst, laying his lips over them in care and comfort.

'I'm fine now,' she said. 'You've looked after me so well.'

'And I always will,' he vowed.

His fingers played in a leisurely way over her breasts, first one, then the other, almost as if he were discovering them for the first time, wondering at their beauty. At last he laid his face against them and she felt his tongue, softly caressing. Tremors went through her. New life invaded her body.

She began to run her own hands over him, exploring and teasing him, rejoicing at the suppressed groan that came from him.

'You do your magic,' he breathed. 'Where does it come from? Are you one of the sirens?'

'Do you want me to be?'

'Only for me. No other man must hear that siren-song. And I must hear it for ever.'

She turned, pressing him gently onto his back and lying across him so that her peaked nipples brushed him lightly.

'But they did hear it for ever,' she said, inviting him further into the fantasy. 'Those doomed sailors knew it would be the last sound they ever heard. Did they follow it willingly?'

This was the question he'd asked himself many times but always in solitude. Now, in her arms, he knew the answer.

'Willingly,' he agreed, 'because at the last nothing else mattered. Nothing else—ever—but to follow that song wherever it led.'

She smiled down at him. 'An adventurous man,' she mused. 'That's what I like. I'm going to take you to such places— where no one's ever been before—'

'Wherever it leads,' he murmured. 'As long as it leads us together.'

When he turned again to bring her beneath him she went gladly, opening for him in warmth and welcome, feeling herself become complete, and then complete again as they climaxed together.

'No,' she begged as it ended. 'Don't leave me.'

'I shall never leave you,' he said, changing her meaning. 'My body will never leave you and nor will my heart. I'm yours. Do you understand that? Yours for always.'

'My darling—'

'I wish I could find the words to tell you what it means to me to have found someone I need never doubt. It's more than happiness. It's like being set free.'

'Dearest, be careful,' she said worriedly. 'I'm human, not perfect.'

'Rubbish, you *are* perfect,' he said, laughing.

'I'll never knowingly betray you, but I might make some silly human mistake. Please, please don't think me better than I am, in case you end up thinking me worse than I am.'

'It wouldn't be possible to think you better than you are,' he said. 'You are perfect. You are honest and true, and divinely inspired to be the one person on earth who can keep me safe and happy.'

There was no middle way with this man, she realised. It was all or nothing, with no reservations. The heartfelt simplicity with which he placed himself and his fate in her hands made her want to weep. And silently she prayed that he might never be disappointed in her, for she knew it would destroy him.

CHAPTER TEN

LYSANDROS awoke in the darkness to find Petra watching him.

'What is it?' he asked. 'Something on your mind? Tell me.' When she still hesitated he sat up and slipped an arm around her. 'Tell me,' he repeated. 'You've always wanted me to talk, but how often do you confide in me?'

When she didn't answer he said, 'It has to work each way, you know. If you don't honour me with your confidence, what am I to think?'

'All right, I will,' she said slowly.

'But it's hard, isn't it?'

'Yes, because I've never really explained it before. There was nobody to explain to. You asked me if I was yours. In fact I'm yours more than you know.'

He thought for a moment. 'You mean something special by that, don't you?'

'Yes. There are things I couldn't tell you because they might have been a burden on you.'

'You? A burden? That isn't possible.'

'If you knew how much I depend on you, you might find it a weight.'

'Now you're humouring me. Isn't it me clinging to you because I find in you what I can find in nobody else?'

'I hope you do, but it's mutual and I couldn't admit that before. But, since we've found each other, maybe I can.'

He touched her chin, turning it gently towards him so that he could regard her intently. Now she had all his attention. Something in her voice told him this was vital.

'You're the first person I've ever really mattered to,' she said simply.

'Your mother—'

'Estelle's a darling but I've never figured high on her list of priorities. She'd have loved a pet cat just as much. She's always been dashing off here and there, leaving me with other people, and I didn't mind because the other people were my grandparents and I loved them. But that was pure luck. If we hadn't been lucky enough to have found them, I sometimes wonder what she'd have done.

'My grandparents loved me, but each came first with the other. That's as it should be, but when she died I knew he wouldn't be long following.'

'There must have been men who wanted you,' he observed.

'Well, they wanted something. Maybe it was me, maybe it was what I brought with me—money, a glamorous background. It left me rather cynical, and I kind of hoisted the cynicism into place as a defence, rather like Achilles kept his shield at the ready.'

He nodded. 'And when you do that, there are always some people who only see the shield.'

'Yes, you know about that, don't you?' She gave a wry smile. 'We're not so different, you and I. Your defence is glaring at people, mine is laughter and pretending never to mind about anything.'

'I had begun to understand that,' he said. 'But I didn't really see behind it until now. Your shield is more skilful than mine.'

'Nobody sees behind it unless I show them. But I can show you because of what you give me.'

'I need you more than any man has ever needed a woman since the dawn of time,' he said slowly.

'You need me as nobody else ever has or ever will, and that's the greatest gift in the world. Nobody has ever given it to me before, and I don't want it from anyone else. You've made me complete. I was afraid I'd go through life without ever having that feeling.'

He laid his forehead against her.

'And I was afraid you'd find me too demanding,' he said.

'You could never be demanding enough,' she assured him. 'The more you demand, the more you fulfil me. You've given me life, as though my real self had only just been born. I don't think you really understand that yet, but you will, my love. It will take time.'

'And we have all the time in the world,' he said, taking her into his arms.

Now their lovemaking was different, infused with the knowledge of each other's heart that they had just discovered. To Petra it was more like a wedding night than the real one she'd known years ago.

At some time in the dawn he murmured, 'There's a story of how, after Achilles' death, he was honoured as a great lord among the other dead souls. But he longed only to be alive and said he would rather return to live on earth as a servant than stay among the dead as a lord. I never understood that story until now.'

'You mean,' she mused, 'that if I were to treat you like a servant, that would be fine as long as you were with me?'

He considered. 'Can I think about that some more?'

He felt her shaking against him and joined in her laughter. She watched him with delight and saw an answering delight in his eyes. He touched her face and spoke softly.

'Love me,' he said in a voice that almost pleaded. 'Love me.'

She knew a surge of joy and reached out to caress him, draw him back into her arms and show him that he belonged there. They made love slowly, yet with a subtle intensity that said more than a million words.

It was much later that it occurred to her that he'd said not, *Make love to me*, but 'Love me.' And only when it was too late did she understand the distinction.

Next day he swept her out into the car and drove down to the shore.

'But not the same as last time,' he said. 'This is a fishing village—at least it was when this island still had a thriving fishing industry. Now they cater for tourists who are interested in fishing. It's time you met my friends.'

His friends turned out to be a family of one-time fishermen, who greeted Lysandros like a long-lost brother and drew Petra into the warmth.

There seemed to be dozens of them. She lost track of the husbands, wives, sons, daughters, cousins, nieces and nephews. She only knew that they all smiled and treated Lysandros as one of the family.

'My mother brought me here for a holiday when I was a kid,' he explained. 'I ran off to go exploring, got lost and the family rescued me. We've been the best of friends ever since.'

She guessed that they'd been well rewarded. The fishing boat on which they now ran tourist expeditions was top of the range. But it was hard to be cynical about these people and when Kyros, the patriarch, said that the nicest thing about Lysandros was not his generosity but the days when he could find time to visit she felt inclined to believe it.

He seemed to size her up, finally deciding that he could trust her with further confidences.

'One day, years ago,' he told her, 'we found him wandering alone on the beach. We hadn't known that he was coming here. He hadn't let us know, or come to the house. Later he said he'd meant to visit us but he arrived in the early morning when the beach was deserted and he thought he'd take a walk. He walked there for hours. A friend saw him and told us. I went down there and walked with him for a while, but he wouldn't come home with me.

'Then my sons took over and they walked with him all night, up and down, up and down, the length of the beach. He was like a machine, talking only in grunts. At last he began to slow down and we managed to persuade him to come with us. We put him to bed and he slept for two days.'

'Did he ever tell you what made him like that?' Petra asked.

'I don't think he knew a lot about it. He just seemed to have been lost in another world, one he couldn't remember or didn't want to remember. We didn't press him. He was our friend, in trouble, and that's all we needed to know. We did suggest that he should see a doctor, but he said we had been his doctors and he wanted no other. I've never seen him like that again so perhaps we were able to make him a little better. I hope so, anyway. He's such a nice guy.'

It was obvious that he knew nothing of the reality of Lysandros's life. The well-known name Demetriou told him that this was a businessman, rich enough to buy them the boat, but they had no conception of the full extent of his fortune and power.

And that was why they mattered to him so much, Petra realised. They were the close-knit, loving, knockabout family he'd never had and would have loved to have. To them he was 'a nice guy', a little removed by his money, but not enough to stop him being one of them.

Unlike virtually everyone else, they neither feared him nor

showed exaggerated respect, which was a relief to him. Instead, they ribbed him mercilessly, yelled cheerful insults, challenged him to races along the sand and rioted when they beat him.

The girls cast soulful eyes at his handsome face and powerful, elegant movements, but their husbands and boyfriends pulled them firmly aside, glaring possessively, daring Lysandros to try to take advantage, forgiving when he didn't.

How different from the Athens husbands who would pimp their wives into his bed in exchange for a contract. No wonder Lysandros loved coming here. It was his only contact with normal life, and the sight of him relishing it was as much a revelation as anything she'd learned in the last few days. He even helped Kyros's wife, Eudora, with the cooking.

Later Eudora whispered in her ear, 'You're the only woman he's ever brought here. That's why everyone's looking at you. Don't tell him I told you.'

She gave a satisfied nod, as though she personally had brought about the miracle, and scurried away.

Afterwards they went out in the boat. Dressed in a swimsuit, Petra sat in the prow, wondering if life could get any better than this.

She drew a deep contented breath, looking up at the sky, then around her at the sea and the horizon. There, a little distance away in the boat, were Lysandros and Kyros chatting casually, laughing in the easy way of friends.

Then she blinked, uncertain whether she'd seen what she thought she'd seen.

Was she going mad, or had Kyros cocked his head significantly in her direction, mouthing the words, 'Is she—the one?'

And had Lysandros nodded?

I'm fantasising, she told herself hastily. *I can't have read Kyros's lips at this distance. Can I?*

But when she looked again they were both regarding her

with interest. To save her blushes she dived overboard and Lysandros joined her.

'Careful, it's deep out here,' he said, holding out his hands to steady her.

She took them and he trod water, drawing her closer, closer against his bare chest, until he could slip his arms right around her, kissing her while treading water madly. Behind them they could hear cheers and yells from the boat.

When they climbed back on board Kyros hinted slyly that there was a cabin below if they wished. More cheers and yells while his wife told him to behave himself and he silenced her with a kiss. It was that sort of day.

Returning home, they ate their fill before going out into the village square where there was dancing. Lysandros could dance as well as any of them. The girls knew it and queued up for their turn. Petra was untroubled. She had all the male attention she could possibly want, and she was enjoying the sight of him unselfconscious and actually seeming happy.

He saw her watching him and waved before being drawn back into the dance by three young females at once, while their menfolk looked on wryly. At the end he blew each of them a kiss before holding out his hands to Petra and drawing her onto the floor.

'Dance with me,' he murmured. 'And save me from getting my throat cut.'

He was showing her off in public, but why? To make a point to the others, or simply because he was more than a little tipsy? Joyfully she decided that she didn't care. This was the man nature had meant him to be before the demons got their destructive hands on him, and if it was the last thing she did she would open the door that led back to that world and lead him through it.

'We ought to be going,' he gasped at last. 'The trouble is, that wine Kyros serves is…well…' He sat down suddenly.

'And everyone else is as woozy as you,' she said. 'Even me.'

'I'm not.' The young man who spoke was the eldest son of the house, wore a priest's garb and was stone cold sober. 'I'll drive you home.'

'And I'll pay for your taxi back,' Lysandros said sleepily. 'Done.'

On the way home they sat in the back, with his head on her shoulder, his eyes closed. As the car came to a halt the priest looked back and grinned.

'I've never seen him let go like that before,' he said. 'I congratulate you.'

She didn't ask what he meant. She didn't need to. Her spirits were soaring.

Lysandros awoke long enough to hand over a bundle of notes. 'That'll pay for the taxi. Anything over, put it in the collection box.'

The priest's eyes popped as he saw the amount.

'But do you know how much you've given—?'

'Goodnight!' Lysandros was halfway up the path.

She undressed him while he lay back and let her do all the work.

'You think you're a sultan being attended by the harem,' she observed as she finished.

He opened one eye. 'It seemed only fair to show you that I can behave as badly as any other man who dances with a dozen women, gets smashed out of his mind and lets his wife wait on him. Goodnight.'

He rolled over and went to sleep on his front, leaving her with the view of the most perfectly shaped male behind she'd ever seen, and wondering if he knew he'd called her his wife.

He slept late next morning, unusual for him. She rose and

made coffee, returning to find him leaning back against the pillow, one arm behind his head and a wicked look in his eyes. Nor was the wickedness confined to his eyes. A glance at the rest of him told her that he was ready to make up for the deficiencies of the night before.

But she decided not to indulge him at once. They drank coffee sedately, although the look in his eyes was far from sedate. She showed no sign of noticing this, but after a while she slipped off her flimsy silk nightdress and began to find small jobs to do about the room, knowing that they gave him a perfect view of her from various angles.

'Do you have to do that?' he asked in a strained voice.

'Well, I thought one of us should do some tidying up,' she said innocently.

'*Come here!*'

Wasting no further time, she raced to the bed and took him in her arms.

'Just let me love you,' she said.

'As long as you do love me,' he said heavily.

'I do. I always will.'

He would have spoken again but she silenced him by laying her mouth against his, taking his attention so that at first he didn't notice her softly wandering hands until the excitement building with her caresses overtook him totally and he drew a long shuddering breath.

'I have ruthless ways of making my wishes known,' she whispered against his mouth.

'I believe you,' he groaned.

'You think you know me, but you haven't begun to discover what I'm capable of.'

'Why don't you—show me?'

She let her fingers explore a little further, reaching the

place between his legs where his response was rapidly growing out of control. 'Like that?'

'Just like that.'

Now her fingers were enclosing their object, revelling in its size and the thought of having it inside her. Then she moved over him so that she could fit her legs astride him and make him hers in her own way.

She had the glorious sense of being able to do anything she wanted. Everything was right because they were together and did everything together. It was right to celebrate their hearts but also right to celebrate their bodies as they were doing now. So she did as she pleased, confident of pleasing him at the same time, and knew by his expression that she'd outdone herself.

'That was very nice,' she said, luxuriating in his arms afterwards.

'Very nice?' he growled. 'Is that the best you can say?'

'Do you have anything else to suggest?'

'Oh, yes,' he said. 'I have plenty more to suggest. Come here—'

'Suppose I don't want to?'

'You've left it much too late to say that. *Now, come here.*'

Carolling with laughter, she raised her arms over her head and cried, 'Shan't!'

'Oh, yes, you will.'

So she did.

When Lysandros's cellphone began to ring he regarded it for a long time before saying reluctantly, 'I suppose I ought to answer that.'

'I'm amazed you haven't been on the phone more often,' she said. 'In fact I'm amazed it hasn't rung more often.'

'I gave strict instructions to my staff not to disturb me unless it was vital. Linos, my assistant, is pretty good that way.

He's called a couple of times, I've given him instructions for managing without me and so far he's not done too badly. But I suppose—' He sighed.

'We have to get back to the real world.'

He kissed her. 'After this, the real world will be different.' He answered the phone. 'Yes, Linos? Oh, no, what's happened? All right, all right, one thing at a time.'

Sad but resigned, Petra made her way upstairs to start packing. The dream life couldn't last for ever, and now was the time to see if it could be carried into reality. The omens were good.

'I've called the airport,' she said when Lysandros appeared. 'There's a flight to Athens in a couple of hours.'

He sighed and put his arms around her. 'I wish you'd said a couple of years, but I suppose we have to take it. There's a big meeting coming up that Linos says he can't manage without me.'

'It had to happen some time,' she said. 'The sound of battle, summoning you to the fray.'

'It's funny how that doesn't sound so good any more. But you'll be with me, and we can start making plans.'

Her lips twitched. 'Plans for what?'

He rested his forehead against hers. 'Plans for the future, and if I have to explain that to you, then I've been wasting my time recently. Unfortunately, this isn't the moment to make the point. But I think you know what I'm talking about.'

Marriage. He hadn't posed a formal question but he acted as though matters were already settled between them, and she knew it was a sign of their closeness that he felt free to do so.

She went with him upstairs to take a last look at the smashed room he'd shared with Brigitta, but she refused to go with him to the grave.

'You need to say goodbye to her alone,' she said gently. 'If I'm there it will spoil it for her.'

'How can you speak so?' he asked in wonder. 'As though she was real to you, as if you'd met her and talked to her.'

'They say that nobody ever comes back across the River Styx,' she mused, speaking of the river that ran between earth and Hades, as the underworld was often known. 'But I wonder. If someone has something important enough, a message that they simply must deliver—well, let's just say that I think some part of her might still be there. But she wants you to talk to her alone. I don't really belong here.'

He frowned. 'Do you mean not to come back to this house with me?'

'I don't think she wants me to. This is her place. You and I can have somewhere else. Keep this for her, to honour her.'

Her words fell like blessed balm on his soul. He'd been wondering how to solve this conundrum, fearing that the part of his heart that remained loyal to the past might offend her. But she'd understood, as she understood everything about him. He kissed her and walked out into the grounds, offering thanks as he went.

Petra watched him until he disappeared.

The grave lay quiet in the afternoon sun, with only the faintest breeze disturbing the branches of the trees overhead. Lysandros stood there for a long time, listening, but there was only silence.

'Perhaps she imagined it,' he whispered at last, 'or perhaps you really can talk to her and not to me. We never could open our hearts to each other, could we?'

Overhead, the leaves rustled.

'I tried my best. Do you remember how desperately I talked to you as you prepared to cross the eternal river with our child in your arms? But you never looked back, and I knew I'd failed you yet again. That failure will be with me always.

'Petra was right to say that I honour you still, and that will last for ever. This place will always be yours and no other woman's. Nothing can change that.

'But there has been a change in me—can you forgive that, if nothing else? It seems almost wrong to find happiness with her after so much that we could have had, and lost, but I can't help myself. She is everything to me, yet I still—*honour* you.'

He couldn't have said what he was hoping for, but nothing came—no sign, no message, no absolution. Only the wind became stronger until it was gusting fiercely in the trees, shaking the branches. Autumn was still some way off, yet the leaves were falling, seeming to bring the darkness closer.

Suddenly he couldn't bear to stay here. Turning, he hurried back to the light.

At the Villa Lukas the air was buzzing with the news that the bride and groom would soon be home from their honeymoon.

'Such a party there's going to be!' Aminta carolled. '*Everyone* is coming—the press, the television cameras—'

'Any guests?' teased Petra.

'All the most important people,' Aminta said blissfully.

'No, I mean real guests—friends, people the host would want anyway, even if the press have never heard of them.'

Aminta stared at her, baffled. It was clear that after years of working for a billionaire shipping magnate she barely understood the concept of friendship for its own sake, so Petra laughed and went on her way. After all this time as part of a film star's retinue, why was she surprised? Perhaps because her time alone with Lysandros had caused a seismic shift in her perceptions.

As soon as she reached her bedroom there was a call from Estelle, full of excitement at the rumours.

'You and Lysandros were seen together on Corfu, going out in a boat and driving through the streets. Come on, tell!'

'There's nothing to tell,' Petra said primly.

'Hmm! As good as that, eh? We'll invite him to our party and take a good look at you two together.'

'I shall warn him not to come.'

'You won't, you know.' Chuckling, she hung up.

The next call was from Lysandros to say he had to return to Piraeus. 'So it'll be several days before we see each other,' he said with a sigh.

'Just be back for the big party next week. Then it's all going to descend on us.'

He laughed. 'I promise to be there. I don't know how I'm going to manage being away from you.'

'Just come back to me,' she said tenderly.

When the call was over she sat smiling. Looking up, she caught a glimpse of herself in the mirror and laughed.

'I look like an idiot. I feel like an idiot. So I guess that makes me an idiot. I don't care. I didn't know there was this much happiness on earth.'

From the corridor outside came the sound of footsteps. Then the door was flung open and Nikator stood on the threshold. His eyes were bright, his face flushed, his chest heaving, and Petra knew there was going to be trouble.

'Hello, brother, dear,' she said brightly, slightly emphasising 'brother'. But it was useless and she knew it.

'Don't say that,' Nikator hurled at her. 'Oh, Petra, don't say that!'

He dropped to his knees beside her, reaching out to clasp her around the waist, and she had to fight not to recoil. Their last meeting had been two weeks ago, just before she'd gone to Corfu. Nikator had implored her to stay, upset when she refused, desperate when she wouldn't tell him where she was going.

The same exaggerated look was on his face now, making her say soothingly, 'You don't want me to call you "dear"?

All right, I won't, especially as I'm angry with you. How dare you let Lysandros think we'd gone to England together?'

He reached up to seize her in a fumbling grip. She tried to free herself but found there was unexpected steel behind the childish movements.

'I couldn't help it. I love you so much I'm not responsible for my actions. I wanted to save you from Demetriou—'

'But I didn't want to be saved,' she said, trying to introduce a note of common sense. 'I love him. Try to understand that. I love *him*, not you.'

'That's because you don't know what he's like. You think you do. You believe what he told you about Brigitta, but there was no need for her to die. If he hadn't bullied her mercilessly she wouldn't have been alone when—'

He pulled himself up far enough to sit on the bed beside her, his hands gripping her shoulders.

'He's fooled you,' he gasped. 'He only wants you because you're mine. He has to take everything that's mine. It's been that way all my life.'

'Nikki—'

'You don't know what it's been like, always being told that the Demetriou family were lucky because they had a worthy son to take over, but my father only had me. Everyone admires him because he brutalises people into submission. But not me. I can't be brutal.'

'But you can be sneaky, can't you? Grow up, little boy!'

'Don't call me that,' he screamed. 'I'm not a child; I'll show you.'

She tried to push him off but his grip tightened. He rose to his feet, thrusting her back against the bed and hurling himself on top of her. Next thing, his mouth was over hers and he was trying to thrust his tongue between her lips.

Frantically she twisted her head away, trying to put up a hand to protect her mouth and writhing this way and that to avoid him.

'Get off me,' she gasped. 'Nikki, do you hear? *Get off me!*'

'Don't fight me. Let me love you—let me save you—'

With a last heave she managed to get out from under him, shoving him so hard that he fell to the floor. In a flash she was on her feet, dashing to the door, yanking it open.

'Clear out and don't come back!' she snapped.

But he made another lunge, forcing her to take drastic action with her knee. A yowl broke from him and he clutched himself between the legs, stumbling out into the corridor under the interested eyes of several maids.

He got to his feet, his eyes burning.

'You'll regret that,' he said softly.

'Not half as much as you'll regret it if you bother me again,' she snapped.

He threw a look of pure hatred at the servants and hurried away.

'Thanks, miss,' one of the maids said.

From which Petra deduced that several of them had been longing to do the very same thing.

Returning to her room, she tried to calm down. She'd known Nikator could be unpleasant but he was worse than she'd imagined.

In her agitation she forgot to wonder how he knew that Lysandros had told her about Brigitta.

CHAPTER ELEVEN

Two days later Homer and Estelle made a grand and glorious return, under the gaze of carefully arranged cameras. Plans for the party started at once, although first Aminta had a servant problem to deal with. Nikator had made certain accusations against the maids, who pleaded with Petra for help, which she gave.

'I'm sorry, Homer, I don't want to quarrel with you or your son,' she said, 'but Nikator was limping when he left and I'm afraid the maids saw. So now he has a grudge against them.'

Homer was a wise man and he knew his son's bad side. He believed her, thanked her, told Nikator to stop talking nonsense and made him apologise to Petra. Instead of the explosion of temper she'd feared, Nikator seemed to be in a chastened mood.

'Which means he's more dangerous than ever,' Lysandros said as they dined together. 'The sooner you're out of there the better. In the meantime I'll have a quiet word with him.'

'No, don't,' she begged. 'I'm quite capable of having my own quiet word, as he's already discovered. I'm only afraid he'll spin you some silly story about him and me—'

'Which you think I'll be stupid enough to believe?' Lysandros queried wryly. 'Credit me with more intelligence than that.'

Nikator seemed to be making an effort. She went downstairs once to find him with a large painting that he'd bought as a gift for his father. It depicted the Furies, terrifying creatures with snakes for hair and blood dripping from their eyes. Petra studied the picture with interest. She'd been conscious of the Furies recently, but now she felt free from them.

'The point was, they never let up,' Nikator said. 'Once they started on you, they'd hound you for ever.'

She wondered if he was sending a message that he would never forgive her for offending him. He would harm her or Lysandros if he could, she was sure of it. But they were both on the watch for him, and surely there was nothing in his power.

The party was going to be the society event of the season. Fellow film stars from Hollywood were flying in to dance, sing and raise their glasses in the fake Parthenon. Every businessman in Athens would be there, hoping to meet a film star, plus some film makers hoping to secure backing from rich men.

When the night came there was no sign of Nikator. Homer grumbled about the disrespect to his bride, but Petra also thought she detected a note of relief.

'Maybe when you and Lysandros are formally engaged it might be easier,' her mother said quietly. 'He'll have to accept it then. Just don't take too long about it. It might be the best thing for everyone.'

'But surely Lysandros is the foe?'

'A rival, not a foe. If the two families could come together Homer thinks it might be wonderful.'

'What about Nikator? Surely Homer wouldn't cut his son out?'

'Not out of his life or his heart, but out of the shipping business, yes. He could buy him a gaming house, or something else that would give him a good life without threatening people's jobs in the shipyard.'

It seemed the perfect solution, but Petra wondered if it would offend Nikator's pride and increase his hatred of Lysandros. Mentally she put it aside to be worried about later. For now all she cared about was the coming evening, when she would see her lover again and dance in his arms.

She'd chosen a dress of blue satin, so dark that it was almost black. It was a tight fit, emphasising her perfect shape, but with a modest neckline, to please Lysandros.

How handsome he was, she thought, watching him approach. Homer greeted him enthusiastically; he replied with smiles and expressions of civility. Petra remembered how Lysandros had cleared Homer of any involvement in Brigitta's tragedy, saying, 'To do him justice, he's a fairly decent man, a lot better than many in this business.'

So it was true what Estelle had suggested. Her marriage to Lysandros might signal a new dawn in the Greek shipping business, and everyone knew it. Including Nikator.

Lysandros did the usual networking with Petra on his arm, and everyone had the chance to study them as a couple.

'Has anyone told you what they're all thinking?' he murmured as they danced.

'They were lining up to tell me,' she said with a laugh. 'We were watched in Corfu. Estelle says we were seen together, driving through the streets and on the boat.'

He shrugged. 'They're public places. People were bound to see us. When we marry, I suppose that will be in public as well—' He smiled and added softly, 'At least, the first part of it will.'

'Oh, really?' she murmured. 'I don't remember getting a proposal.'

'You've had a proposal every minute of the last few days and you know it,' he said firmly. He rather spoilt the autocratic sound of this by murmuring, 'Siren,' so softly that his breath on her cheek was almost all she knew.

'Don't I get an answer?' he asked.

'You had your answer the first time we made love,' she said. 'And you hadn't even asked me.'

'But now I've asked and you've answered, we might tell them,' he suggested.

'Tell this crowd? I thought you'd hate to be stared at.'

'As long as they see what I want them to see, that's all right. If they watch me walking off with the most beautiful woman in the room, I can live with that.'

He tightened his arm around her waist, swirling her around and around while everyone laughed and applauded. Petra remembered that later because it was almost her last moment of unclouded joy.

As they came out of the swirl and her head began to clear she saw something that made her sigh. Even so, she didn't realise that disaster had walked in. Disaster was called Nikator, and he had a smile on his face. It was a cold, tense smile, but even so it gave no sign of what was about to crash down on her.

'What's he up to?' she asked as he embraced Homer and Estelle.

'Trying to win forgiveness for turning up late,' Lysandros remarked. 'Pretend he doesn't exist, as I'm doing.'

His words reminded her of how hard it must be for him to appear at ease in Nikator's presence, and she smiled at him in reassurance.

'Better still,' Lysandros said, 'let's show him exactly where he stands.'

Before she knew what he meant to do, he'd pulled her closer and laid his mouth on hers in a long kiss, whose meaning left nothing to the imagination.

Now he'd made his declaration to the world. This man, who'd spent so long hiding his true self behind protective bolts and bars, had finally managed to throw them aside and break out to freedom because the one special woman had given him the key. He no longer cared who could look into his soul because her love had made him invincible.

As the kiss ended and he raised his head, his manner was that of a victor. A hero, driving his chariot across the battlefield where his enemies lay defeated, might have worn that air of triumph.

'Let him do what he likes,' he murmured to her. 'Nothing can touch us now.'

She was to remember those words long after.

'Ah!' cried Nikator. 'Isn't love charming?'

His caustic voice shattered her dream and made her shudder. Nikator had marched across the floor and stood regarding them sardonically, while Homer hurried behind and laid an urgent hand on his son's arm. Nikator threw it off.

'Leave me, Father; there are things that have to be said and I'm going to enjoy saying them.' He grinned straight at Lysandros. 'I never thought the day would come when I'd have a good laugh at you. You, of all men, to be taken in by a designing woman!'

'Give up,' Lysandros advised him gently. 'It's no use, Nikator.'

'But that's what's so funny,' Nikator yelped. 'How easily you were fooled when you fancied yourself so armoured. *But the armour doesn't cover the heel, does it?*'

Even this jibe didn't seem to affect Lysandros, who continued to regard Nikator with pity and contempt.

'And your "heel" was that you believed in her,' Nikator said, jabbing a finger at Petra. 'You're too stupid to realise that she's been playing you for a sucker because there's something she wanted.'

'Hey, you!' Estelle thumped him hard on the shoulder. 'If you're suggesting my daughter has to marry for money, let me tell you—'

'Not money!' Nikator spat. 'Glory. Anything for a good story, eh?'

'What the hell are you talking about?' Lysandros demanded. 'There's no story.'

'Of course there is. It's what she lives by, her reputation, getting a new angle on things that nobody else can get. And, oh, boy, did she get it this time!'

Even then they didn't see the danger. Lysandros sighed, shaking his head as if being patient with a tiresome infant.

'You won't laugh when you know what she's been doing,' Nikator jeered. 'Getting onto the press, telling them your secrets, repeating what you said to her—'

'That's a lie!' Petra cried.

'Of course it's a lie,' Lysandros said.

The smiling confidence had vanished from his face and his voice had the deadly quiet of a man who was fighting shock, but he was still uttering the right words.

'Be careful what you say,' he told Nikator coldly. 'I won't have her slandered.'

'Oh, you think it's a slander, do you? Then how does the press know what you said to her at the Achilleion? How do they know you showed her Brigitta's grave and told her how often you'd stood there and begged Brigitta's forgiveness? Have you ever repeated that? No, I thought not. But someone has.'

'Not me,' Petra said, aghast. 'I would never—you can't believe that!'

She flung the last words at Lysandros, who turned and said quickly, 'Of course not.'

But his manner was strained. Gone was the relaxed joy of only a few minutes ago. Only two of them knew what he had said to her at that grave.

'It's about time you saw this,' Nikator said.

Nobody had noticed the bag he'd brought with him and dropped at his feet. Now he leaned down and began to pull out the contents, distributing them to the fascinated crowd.

They were newspapers, carrying the banner headline, *The Truth About Achilles: How She Made Him Talk*, and telling the story of the well-known historian Petra Radnor, who'd first come to prominence when, little more than a girl, she'd published *Greek Heroes of the Past*.

The book had been such a success that it had been revised for a school edition and was now being considered for a further revision. This time the angle would be more glamorous and romantic, as Ms Radnor considered Greek men today and whether they really lived up to their classical reputation. For the moment she was working on Achilles.

There followed a detailed description of the last few weeks—their first meeting at the wedding, at which *Ms Radnor exerted all her charms to entice her prey*, the evening they had spent together dancing in the streets, and finally their time on Corfu in the villa where 'Achilles' had once lived with his other lover, who was buried there.

> *Together they visited the Archilleion, where they stood before the great picture of the first Achilles dragging the lifeless body of his enemy behind his chariot, and the modern Achilles explained that he was raised to do it to them before they did it to him.*

Which was exactly what he'd said, Petra thought in numb horror.

It went on and on. Somehow the people behind this had learned every private detail of their time together at the villa, and were parading it for amusement. 'Achilles' had been trapped, deluded, made a fool of by a woman who was always one step ahead of him. That was the message, and those who secretly feared and hated him would love every moment of it.

All around she could see people trying to smother their amusement. Homer was scowling and the older guests feared him too much to laugh aloud, but they were covering their mouths, turning their heads away. The younger ones were less cautious.

'Even you,' Nikator jeered at Lysandros. 'Even you weren't as clever as you reckoned. You thought you had it all sussed, didn't you? But she saw through you, and oh, what a story she's going to get out of it, *Achilles!*'

Lysandros didn't move. He seemed to have been turned to stone.

Nikator swung his attention around to Petra.

'Not that you've been so clever yourself, *my dear deluded sister.*'

Estelle gave a little shriek and Homer grabbed his son.

'That's enough,' he snapped. 'Leave here at once.'

But Nikator threw him off again. Possessed by bitter fury, he could defy even his father. He went closer to Petra, almost hissing in her face.

'He's a fool if he believed you, but you're a fool if you believed him. There are a hundred women in this room right now who trusted him and discovered their mistake too late. You're just another.'

Somehow she forced herself to speak.

'No, Nikator, that's not true. I know you want to believe it, but it's not true.'

'You're deluded,' he said contemptuously.

'No, it's you who are deluded,' she retorted at once.

'Have you no eyes?'

'Yes, I have eyes, but eyes can deceive you. What matters

isn't what your eyes tell you, but what your heart tells you. And my heart says that this is the man I trust with all of me.' She lifted her head and spoke loudly. 'Whatever Lysandros tells me, that is the truth.'

She stepped close to him and took his hand. It was cold as ice.

'Let's go, my dearest,' she said. 'We don't belong here.'

The crowd parted for them as they walked away together into the starry night. Now the onlookers were almost silent, but it was a terrible silence, full of horror and derision.

On and on they walked, into the dark part of the grounds. Here there were only a few stragglers and they fell away when they saw them coming, awed, or perhaps made fearful, by the sight of two faces that seemed to be looking into a different world.

At last they came to a small wooden bridge over a river and went to stand in the centre, gazing out over the water. Still he didn't look at her, but at last he spoke in a low, almost despairing voice.

'Thank you for what you said about always believing me.'

'It was only what you said to me first,' she said fervently. 'I was glad to return it. I meant it every bit as much as you did. Nikator is lying. Yes, there was a book, years ago, but I told you about that myself, and about the reissue.'

'And the new version?'

'I knew they were thinking of bringing it out again, but not in detail. And it certainly isn't going to be anything like Nikator said. Lysandros, you can't believe all that stuff about my "working on Achilles" and pursuing you to make use of you. It isn't true. I swear it isn't.'

'Of course it isn't,' he said quietly. 'But—'

The silence was almost tangible, full of jagged pain.

'But what?' she asked, not daring to believe the suspicions rioting in her brain.

'How did they discover what we said?' he asked in a rasping, tortured voice. 'That's all I want to know.'

'And I can't tell you because I don't know. It wasn't me. Maybe someone was standing behind us at the Achilleion—'

'Someone who knew who we were? And the grave? How do they know about that?'

'I don't know,' she whispered. 'I don't know. I never repeated anything to anybody. *Lysandros, you have got to believe me.*'

She looked up into his face and spoke with all the passion at her command.

'Can't you see that we've come to the crossroads? This is it. This is where we find out if it all meant anything. I am telling you the truth. Nobody in the world matters more to me than you, and I would never, ever lie to you. For pity's sake, say that you believe me, *please.*'

The terrible silence was a thousand fathoms deep. Then he stammered, 'Of course…I do believe you…' But there was agony in his voice and she could hear the effort he put into forcing himself.

'You don't,' she said explosively as the shattering truth hit her. 'All that about trusting me—it was just words.'

'No, I—*no!*'

'Yes!'

'I tried to mean them, I wanted to, but—'

Her heart almost failed her, for there on his face was the look she'd seen before, on the statue at the Achilleion, when Achilles tried to draw the arrow from his foot, his expression full of despair as he realised there was no way to escape his fate.

'Yes—*but,*' she said bitterly. 'I should have known there'd be a "but".'

'Nobody else knows about that grave,' he said hoarsely. 'I can't get past that.'

'Perhaps Nikator does know. Perhaps he had someone following us—'

'That wouldn't help them find the grave. It's deep in the grounds; you can't see it from outside. I've never told anyone else. You're the one person I've ever trusted enough to…to…'

As the words died he groaned and reached for her. It would have been simple to go into his arms and try to rediscover each other that way, but a spurt of anger made her step back, staring at him with hard eyes.

'And that's the worst thing you can do to anyone,' she said emphatically. 'The more you trust someone, the worse it is when they betray you.'

He stared at her like a man lost in a mist, vainly trying to understand distant echoes. 'What did you say?' he whispered.

'Don't you recognise your own words, Lysandros? Words you said to me in Las Vegas. I'll remind you of some more. "Nobody is ever as good as you think they are, and sooner or later the truth is always there. Better to have no illusions, and be strong." You really meant that, didn't you? I didn't realise until now just how much you meant it.'

'Don't remind me of that time,' he shouted. 'It's over.'

'It'll never be over because you carry it with you, and all the hatred and suspicion that was in you then is there still. You just hide it better, but then something happens and it speaks, telling you to play safe and think the worst of everyone. Even me. Look into your heart and be honest. Suddenly I look just like all the others, don't I? Lying, scheming—'

'Shut up!' he roared. 'Don't talk like that. I forbid it.'

'Why, because it comes too close to the truth? And who are you to forbid me?'

If his mind had been clearer he could have told her that he was the man whose fate she held in her hands, but the clearheadedness for which he was famed seemed to have deserted him now and everything was in a whirl of confusion.

'I *want* to believe you; can't you understand that?' He gripped her shoulders tightly, almost shaking her. 'But tell me how. Show me a way. *Tell me!*'

His misery was desperate. If her own heart hadn't been breaking, she would have been filled with pity for him.

'I can't tell you,' she said. 'That's one thing you must find for yourself.'

'Petra—please—try to understand—'

'But I do. I only wish I didn't. I understand that nothing has changed. We thought things could be different now. I love you and I hoped you loved me—'

'But I do, you know that—'

'No, even *you* don't know that. The barriers are still there, shutting you off from the world, from me. I thought I could break them down, but I can't.'

'If you can't, nobody can,' he said despairingly. Then something seemed to happen to him. His hands fell, he stepped back, and when he spoke again it was with the calm of despair. 'And perhaps that's all there is to be said.'

There was a noise from the distance, lights; the party was breaking up. People streamed out into the garden and now the laughter could be clearly heard, rising on the night air.

And the derision would torture him as well as the loss of his faith in her. Bleakly she wondered which one troubled him more.

'I'll be in touch,' he told her. 'There are ways of getting to the bottom of this.'

'Of course,' she said formally, waiting for his kiss.

Briefly he rested his fingertips against her cheek, but apart from that he departed without touching her.

* * *

The detective work was relatively easy. It didn't take long to establish that the 'newspaper copies' were forgeries, specially printed at Nikator's orders, the text written to Nikator's dictation.

But that helped little. It was the overheard conversations that were really damaging, the fact that they couldn't be explained, and the fact that hundreds of people at the party had read them.

Calling her publishers, Petra told them to abandon plans for a reissue of her book. They were dismayed.

'But we've heard such exciting stories—'

'None of them are true,' she snapped. 'Forget it.'

She and Lysandros were still in touch, but only just. They exchanged polite text messages, and she understood. He was avoiding her and she knew why. If they had met face to face he wouldn't have known what to say to her. He was back stranded again in the sea of desolation, unable to reach out to the one person who'd helped him in the past.

Or perhaps he just didn't know how to tell her that the break was coming and there was no escape.

It might have been different, she knew. By quarrelling, they had done exactly what Nikator had wanted.

But it went deeper than that. However it looked, Nikator hadn't really caused the chasm between them; he'd merely revealed its existence. Sooner or later the crack in their relationship would have come to light.

Sometimes she blamed herself for the anger that had made her attack him when he was wretched, but in her heart she knew it changed nothing. He was the man he was, and the hope she'd briefly glimpsed was no more than an illusion.

In her present bitter mood she wondered how much of her view of him had been real, and how much she'd shaped him to fit her own desires. Had he really needed her so much, or had she just refused to see that he was self-contained, needing neither her nor anyone else? It was suddenly easy to believe that, and to feel alone and unwanted as never before in her life.

'Surplus to requirements,' she thought angrily as she lay in bed one night. 'A silly woman who reshaped her image of a man to suit herself. And got her just deserts.'

In a fury of despair and frustration, she began to bang her head on the pillow and only stopped when she realised that she was mirroring his movements. She wished he were there so that she could share it with him.

But would he ever be with her again?

In Homer's library she found her own volume, the one on which Nikator had built his attacks.

'Now I know where he got the idea,' she thought wryly, turning to the Achilles section and reading her own text.

His name had been linked with many women, but the one for whose love he'd given his life was Polyxena, daughter of King Priam of Troy. His love for her had held out the hope of a peace treaty between the Greeks and the Trojans, and an end to the war. But Paris was enraged. Such a treaty would have meant he had to return Helen to her husband, and that he was determined not to do.

Through his spies he knew that Achilles could only be destroyed through his heel and he haunted the temple, waiting for the wedding. When Achilles appeared Paris shot him in the heel with a poisoned arrow.

In a further twist to the tale, Achilles' ghost was reputed to have spoken from the grave, demanding that Polyxena be sacrificed and forced to join him in death. Whereupon she was dragged to the altar and slain.

And what happened after that? Petra wondered. Had he met

her in a boat on the River Styx, ready to convey her to the underworld? Had she told him that he couldn't really have loved her or he would have behaved more generously? Or had he accused her of betraying him, giving that as his reason for condemning her to death? One way or another, it had ended badly, as many love affairs did.

Or was the story wrong? Had he not forced her to join him in death, but merely implored her, knowing that she would be glad to join him? When they met at the Styx had he held out his arms to her, and had she run to him?

I'm going crazy, she thought. I've got to stop thinking like this.

Stop thinking about him. That was all it would take.

It would never happen unless they could find some point of closure. And she could think of nothing that would provide a definite answer.

Unless…

Slowly she straightened up in her seat, staring into the distance, seeing nothing but the inspiration that had come to her.

That's what it needs, she thought. Of course! *Why didn't I think of that before?*

CHAPTER TWELVE

THE text message was simple and heartfelt.

I need to talk to you. Why have you stopped replying? L

He hesitated before sending it, afflicted by a feeling that the world had turned on its head. He'd received so many texts like this, but never before had he sent one. Would she reply to him as he had so often replied to the others? The thought sent him cold with alarm. But he must do this. He could no longer endure the silence between them. He pressed the button.

Her reply was quick.

I'm sorry. I needed to be alone to think. P

He answered, *I thought that, but it's a mistake. We must do our thinking together. L*

She texted back, *We only hurt each other.*

This time he sent her only one word. *Please.*

She called back and he heard her voice.

'Please, Lysandros, it's better if we don't talk for a while.'

'No,' he said stubbornly. 'It isn't. There's a way out of this—'

'Not if you don't believe me. And in your heart you don't. Goodbye—my dearest.'

As she hung up he passed a hand over his eyes, troubled

by something he'd heard in the background, something he couldn't quite place—something—

He bounded to his feet, swearing. A tannoy announcement. That was what he'd heard. She was at the airport.

Frantically he called back, but she'd switched off. Neither speech nor text could reach her now. She was on her way back to England.

The world was coming down about his ears. Once she was gone he'd lose her for ever; he knew that well. And then everything would end.

He moved like lightning, calling his private pilot. A moment later he was rushing through the grounds to the landing stage where his helicopter waited, and a few minutes after that they were in the air.

While the pilot radioed ahead to the airport, arranging for a landing and a car to meet them, he called Information to check the next flight to England. It would take off in half an hour. He groaned.

The pilot was skilful and made Athens Airport in the fastest possible time. The car was waiting, taking him to the main building. As he stared out of the window he prayed for a delay, something that would give him the chance to get her off the plane. But then he saw it, rising into the sky, higher and higher, taking his life with it.

Even so, he clung to hope until the last minute. Only the word *Departed* on the board forced him to accept the brutal truth. She had gone. He'd lost her. His life was over. He almost reeled away from the desk, blinded by misery, wanting to howl up to heaven.

He was pulled up short by a collision. Two arms went around him, supporting him as they had so often done before. He tried to pull himself together.

'I'm sorry, I—*Petra*!'

She was clinging to him, staring up into his face, hardly able to believe what was happening.

'What's the matter?' she asked quickly. 'Why are you here?'

'To stop you leaving. I thought you'd be on that plane for England that just took off. You can't go like this.'

'Like this?' she asked hopefully.

'Not until we've settled things.'

She didn't know what to make of that. It might almost have been business-speak, but he was trembling in her arms.

'I'm not going back to England,' she said. 'That's not why I'm here. Please calm down. You worry me.'

He was taking huge gulps of air as relief shuddered through him.

'Let's find somewhere to sit,' she said, 'and I'll explain.'

Over a drink she said quietly, 'I was going to Corfu. I've been thinking a lot about how Nikator knew what we said, and it seems to me that he must have known a lot more about Priam House than he's ever let anyone know; enough to have bugged the place, even long ago. So I was going to see what I could find.'

'Yes,' he said. 'That's it. We'll find the answer. But why didn't you tell me?'

'I wasn't sure how you'd—well, anyway, I meant to go alone, but when I got here I realised I should tell you first. Because if I find bugs, I need you to be there, don't I? Otherwise—' she gave a wan smile '—otherwise, how will you know I didn't plant them, to clear myself?'

'Don't,' he whispered.

'Anyway, I was just about to leave the airport. I was going to come to you and tell you what I was thinking, but here you are. What brought you here?'

'You. I heard an announcement in the background and I thought you were leaving the country. I had to come and stop you. Look, it doesn't matter about all the other things. I can't let you go.'

'Even though you still doubt me?' she asked wryly. 'No, never mind. We'll worry later. We can't tell how this is going to work out.'

'My helicopter's here. It can take us straight on to Corfu, and we'll find all the answers we need there.'

Petra didn't reply. She knew that everything was far more complicated than he'd understood. They might find some answers, but not all and there were still obstacles to overcome. But this wasn't the time to say so.

For the moment she would enjoy the happiness of seeing him again, even though that happiness was tinged with bitterness and the threat of future misery.

An hour later the helicopter set them down on Corfu. As they covered the last few miles she wondered if this was just a forlorn hope and they were chasing it to avoid facing the truth.

'Does anyone know where Nikator is?' he asked suddenly. 'I've been looking for him, but he seems to have vanished.'

'Nobody's seen him for days.'

'How wise of him to avoid me. It was always the way when he was in trouble,' Lysandros said. 'He never did stick around to face things.'

'You do know that he did this, don't you?'

'I've been finding out. And when we know this last thing—'

Then you'll trust me, she thought. But not until then.

Was she making too much of it? she wondered. He'd come looking for her, desperate to stop her leaving him. Wasn't that enough?

But it wasn't. What still lived in her mind was the look that had fleetingly been on his face when disaster had struck. It had been a look of appalled betrayal, saying that she was no different from all the others. Now something must happen to wipe it out, but she had a terrible fear that nothing ever could.

The house was as they had left it, except that then it had been infused with joy. That had vanished now and its silence was the deadly silence of fear.

Lysandros wasted no time. Gathering tools from the shed, he strode out, through the grounds, under the trees, to the place where Brigitta and her child lay, incongruously at peace. Somehow Brigitta seemed a very real presence now, crying out to Lysandros to remember only her love and forget all else.

In the end he'd managed to do that. But too late.

'Why is he doing this?' Petra asked her spirit. 'Can he really only love and trust me when he has something tangible to hold? Isn't there anything deep inside him that tells him the truth? Those times when our hearts were so close that we were like one, do they count for nothing now?'

She thought she could hear Brigitta's melancholy cry, echoing from Hades, the underworld, across the River Styx and down the centuries. There was no hope in that sound.

'That's it!'

Lysandros's shout broke into her thoughts. He'd been hard at work, digging, scrabbling around the grave. Now there was a look of triumph in his eyes.

'Got them,' he said, holding something up.

'What have you found?' she asked.

'Bugs. Tiny microphones powerful enough to pick up anything, including what we said to each other.'

So she was cleared. She waited for the surge of joy that this should have brought her, but nothing happened.

'So this place was bugged,' she said.

But her heart was still waiting for him to say that he would have believed in her anyway, even if he'd found nothing. Desperately hoping, she nudged him in the right direction.

'But how do you know that I didn't come here earlier and put them there?'

If only he would say, *Because I know you wouldn't do that.*

Instead, beaming and oblivious to the undercurrents, he said, 'Of course you didn't. Look at them, they're old. They've been here for years. Nikator must have had spies that told him about this place and bugged it long ago. He's just been waiting for his moment.'

'Ah, I see. So the evidence clears me.'

'Of course it does.'

He scrambled up out of the grave and seized her shoulders.

'Darling, can't you see how wonderful this is? It makes everything right.'

'Does it?' she whispered.

He barely heard her words and totally missed her meaning.

'Come here,' he said, pulling her to him, kissing her fiercely. 'Now nothing can part us again.'

He seized her hand and began to run back to the house, his face shining with happiness. Upstairs, he kicked in the door of his bedroom and drew her swiftly down on the bed. She had a split second to make up her mind, whether or not to go through with this, for she knew that they were coming to the end. But for that very reason she would allow herself this one last time.

She made love to him as never before, giving him not just her body, but a heart infused with sorrow. Everything in her belonged to him. Soul and spirit were his, and there would never be anyone else. He had spoiled all other men for her, and she would live with that. But she could no longer live with him.

With every tender gesture, every whispered word, she bid him farewell. Each caress was a plea for him to remember always that she had loved him utterly and always would, even though their ways must now lie apart.

They reached their moment together and she saw him smiling down at her in triumph and relief, something that had always been her peak of joy. Afterwards he held her tenderly, protectively, and she had to struggle not to weep.

'Thank goodness,' he said fervently. 'We so nearly lost each other.'

To him it was all so simple. He hadn't faced the inevitable yet, but she must face it for both of them.

'Lysandros—'

'What is it, my darling?'

'Don't you realise that we *have* lost each other?'

'No, how can we? We know how it was all done now. The whole newspaper thing was fake, he had us followed to the Achilleion by someone who eavesdropped on what we said, and now we've found the evidence that clears you.'

As soon as he said the last words he knew what he'd done. She saw it in the sudden dismay that swept over his face.

'Yes,' she said sadly, 'you needed evidence to clear me because my word alone wasn't enough.'

'Don't,' he interrupted her hurriedly. 'Don't say it.'

'I have to. I'm going away—at least for a little while.'

'No. I won't let you go. I'll make you stay until you see sense—' He heard himself and screwed up his eyes in dismay. 'I didn't mean it like that.'

'It's all right. I love it that you want me, but perhaps it isn't right for us. If you only knew how much I've longed for you to believe in me anyway, in the face of all the evidence. Now it's too late.'

'But we've just made everything right.'

'My dearest, we've made nothing right. Can't you see that? We made love, and it was beautiful, but real love is so much more than passion. I know what to do when I'm in your arms. I know the caresses you can't resist, just as you know the ones that affect me. We know how to tempt each other on and on until we explode with desire, and for a while that seems enough. But it soon passes, and then we have to see the distance between us.'

'It doesn't have to be there,' he said harshly. 'We can overcome it.'

She loved him for his stubborn belief. She would have given anything to yield to it and it broke her heart to refuse, knowing that she was breaking his heart in the process.

She remembered how he'd raced to the airport to stop her leaving, caring nothing for her guilt or innocence as long as he kept her with him. Surely that was enough? But he was an acquisitive man. What was his had to remain his. There might be no more in his possessiveness than that. It wasn't enough to build on.

If only, she thought desperately, there was still something that could happen—something that could give them hope for the future—but the last chance had gone. He had the evidence in his hands now, and evidence made blind trust unnecessary.

It was too late. Nothing could happen now.

'You're saying that I've failed you,' he grated. 'You can't forgive me.'

'There's nothing to forgive,' she said passionately. 'What was done to you was terrible, and it's not your fault that it's scarred you. But it has. You can't really believe in anyone now, even me. I thought I could help you but I can't. Please try to understand.'

A dead look came into his eyes.

'Yes,' he said at last. 'Of course you must go, because I let you down, didn't I? Get out while you can. Get out before I destroy you as I did her.'

He dressed hurriedly and walked out without looking back.

Shattered, she stared after him. This was what she'd planned, but now it was here it was terrible. Throwing on her clothes, she hurried out after him.

As soon as she reached the head of the stairs she knew that something had happened. The door to the cellar stood open. Through it she could see a light and hear voices.

She knew who would be there before she entered. Lysandros stood by the far wall, his eyes fixed on Nikator, who aimed a small pistol at him.

'Get out,' Lysandros shouted to her. 'Go now.'

'Oh, I don't think so,' Nikator said, pointing the pistol at her. 'I've waited so long to get you both together. Come down, my dear, and let's all three have a talk.'

She'd thought she knew the worst of Nikator. But now his eyes were bright as if he was high on something and his most dreadful side was on display. This man could kill, she was sure of it. And now only one thing mattered.

'How do you come to be here, Nikki?' she asked, trying to sound casual.

'It wasn't hard. I knew you'd both arrive soon.'

'Let her go,' Lysandros said. 'I'm the one you want.'

'But she's also the one I want. She always has been. And now I'm tired of waiting. If not one way, then another. Isn't that so?'

'Then you can have me,' Petra said. 'Let Lysandros go and I'm all yours, Nikki.'

'*No!*' Lysandros's howl of rage and despair seemed to hit the ceiling, causing some dust and wood flakes to float down.

'It makes no difference to you,' she told him, smiling. 'We'd decided to part anyway. I never stay with any man for long. What do you say, Nikki?'

She was still on the stairs and he reached up to take her hand and draw her down beside him.

'You mean you'd stay with me—?'

'If you let Lysandros go.'

Nikator laughed softly, horribly.

'Oh, darling, I so much want to believe you, but you're lying. You're still in love with him. After all the things I've heard you say to him—'

'You mean—?'

'Yes, I heard it all. It's not just the gardens that are bugged. Everywhere. I bugged it years ago. Years and years I've been waiting. I've been with the two of you all the time.'

Lysandros's roar filled the air. The next moment he'd launched himself onto Nikator. There was an explosion as the pistol went off and the next moment the whole place was shaking as the bullet hit the old ceiling, which began to disintegrate.

'It's coming down,' Lysandros said hoarsely. 'Get out fast.'

But the wooden stairs were collapsing and the next moment the ceiling began to descend on them. She saw it getting closer, then it was blocked out by Lysandros's head, and then there was darkness.

He was in the place that had always been waiting for him. Before him stretched the Styx, the river that ran between the living and the dead. He'd known in his heart that the final choice was out of his hands, and now that he was here he would go wherever the river took him.

Had there ever been a choice? He'd seen the roof coming down on the woman he loved, and he'd lunged forward to put himself between her and danger. There had been no time to think, only the knowledge that without her life was unbearable. He would die with her, or instead of her. Either way, he was content.

He ached all over from the weight of the ceiling on his

back, pinning him against her as she lay beneath him, so frighteningly still that he feared the worst.

'Not yet,' he whispered. 'Wait for me, and we'll cross the river together.'

Incredibly, he sensed a tremor beneath him. Then a soft breath broke from her.

'Petra, Petra,' he said urgently. 'Are you alive? Speak to me.'

'Aaaah—' The word was so soft he hardly heard it.

'Can you hear me?'

Her eyes opened a little way, fixed on him. 'What happened?'

'The roof fell on us. We're trapped here. There's no way out unless someone up there sees what's happened.'

And nobody would, they both realised. They were underground, in a part of the house not visible from the road. They could stay here, undiscovered, for days, perhaps longer.

'You saved me,' she murmured.

'I only wish I had.'

'You took the weight of the rafters to protect me. You could have got out—'

'And live without you? Do you think I want that? It's together or nothing.'

She managed to turn her head. There were tears in her eyes. 'Darling, are you very much hurt?'

'No, but I can't move, and I can't get you out.'

They both knew that if he tried to move he would bring the rest of the place down on them both.

'Together or nothing,' she murmured.

'There's just one thing I could try,' he said.

Taking a deep breath, he gave a shout, but immediately there was an ominous sound overhead and plaster began to pour down. They clung together, seeking refuge in each other.

'Dear God!' he said. 'I neglected this place and let it get in such bad condition. This is my fault.'

'Or maybe it's my fault,' she said softly. 'I came excavating here without thinking of safety. Who knows what damage I might have done?'

'Don't try to spare me,' he said savagely. '*I* did this. *I* harmed you. *I killed you.*'

'Darling, it doesn't matter now. Just hold me.'

'For ever,' he said fiercely, managing to get his arms about her. 'And perhaps help will come in time. We must hold on to that, Petra—Petra?'

Her eyes had closed and her breathing had become faint.

'Petra! Listen to me. For pity's sake, wake up.'

But she didn't open her eyes, and he knew that the boat was waiting for her; she was embarking on the last journey, leaving him behind.

'Not yet,' he begged. 'Not until you've heard me—forgiven me. I shouldn't have doubted you—say that you understand— that it won't part us for ever—'

Once before he'd implored forgiveness from a woman as she'd begun the journey across the river, but she hadn't heard him. Her face had been implacable as she'd climbed into the boat with her child in her arms, not seeing or hearing him, never knowing of his grief and contrition.

Now it was happening a second time, unless he could find a way to prevent it.

'Forgive me,' he whispered. 'Make some sign that you forgive me—'

For he knew that without her forgiveness they could not make the final journey together. He'd betrayed their love with his mistrust; a crime that would keep them apart for all eternity and only her blessing could wipe that out.

But she was drifting beyond him, to a place he couldn't follow.

Now he understood the face of the statue, raised in despair,

calling on the gods of Olympus to grant his last request, helpless, hopeless.

'Wake up,' he begged. 'Just for a moment, *please*.'

But there was only stillness and the sound of her breathing, growing fainter.

As he saw her slipping away Achilles lifted his face to the
heavens, silently imploring,

'Take me, not her! Let her live! Take me!'

She was in another world. There was the Styx, the river that
led to the underworld and from which there was no return,
save as a spirit. She looked back at the earth from which she'd
come, but it was too late. She had left it for ever.

Then, coming towards her across the water, she saw a boat,
with a man standing in the prow. He was tall and magnificent
and all the lesser creatures fell away before him, but he had no
eyes for them. He was searching for something, and when he saw
her his eyes brightened and his hands reached out, imploring.

Now she knew him. He was the man who had chosen to
die for her, and was asking if she was ready to follow him.

'I wasn't sure you'd come,' he said. 'It could only happen
if you were willing.'

'How could I be unwilling to spend my eternity with
you?' she asked.

She went towards him and he lifted her into the boat.

'Eternity,' he whispered.

The boat turned and began to make its way back across the
water, until it vanished.

'My darling, wake up, please!'

Slowly she opened her eyes, frowning a little. The underworld didn't look as she'd expected. It looked more like a
hospital room.

'How did I get here?'

'They came in time,' Lysandros said from where he was seated beside her bed. 'Somebody heard the gun go off and raised the alarm. Rescuers got us out.'

Now she could see him more clearly. His head was bandaged and his arm was in a sling.

'How badly are you hurt?' she asked.

'Not much; it looks worse than it is. The doctor says we're both badly bruised, but no worse.'

'What about Nikator?'

'He's alive. I got a message to Homer, and he's taking him away to a special hospital where I think he'll need to stay for some time. I've told everyone it was an accident. Nobody else needs to know the truth. Never mind him. I was afraid you weren't going to come round.'

Now she remembered. He had thrown himself between her and the descending roof.

'You saved my life,' she murmured. 'You could have been killed.'

'And so could you. Do you think I'd let you go on alone? I'd have followed, wherever you went, whether you wanted me or not.'

'Of course I'd have wanted you,' she murmured. 'How could I be unwilling to spend my eternity with you?'

'Do you mean that?' he asked anxiously. 'You spoke as though it was all over between us, and I don't blame you, but then—'

But then he had chosen to die rather than live without her. It was the sign she had longed for, his offering on the sacrificial altar. Now she belonged to him in every way, in his way, and in her own.

She had no illusions about their life together. He would

always be a troubled man, but his very troubles called on something in her that yearned to be vitally necessary to him. It would never be easy, but they belonged together.

'I'll never let you go again,' he said, 'not after that time I spent holding you down there, wondering if you were ever going to wake, whether you were going to live or die, whether you'd allow me to go with you.'

'Allow?'

'It was always up to you. You could have gone on ahead without me, or sent me on without you. I could only beg you to show me mercy. While you were unconscious I listened to the things you said, longing to hear something that gave me hope. But your words were strange and confusing.'

'Tell me about them.'

'Once you said, "The story is wrong." What did you mean?'

'The story about Achilles forcing Polyxena to die. He didn't force her. He only asked her to follow him if she was willing. And she was.'

'How do you know?'

'Never mind. I know.'

'Is this another triumphant "find" that will boost your reputation?' he asked tenderly.

'No, I'll never tell anyone else but you. This is our secret.'

He reached out a hand to touch her face with tentative fingers.

'Never leave me,' he said. 'You are my life. I can have no other and I want no other.'

'I'm yours for as long as you need me,' she vowed.

It was a few days before they were both well enough to leave the hospital. They paid a final visit to the villa and wandered through the grounds.

'I'm having it demolished,' he said. 'I could never come here again. We'll make our home somewhere else.'

'What about Brigitta, and your child? We can't leave them here. Let's take them back to Athens and let them rest in the grounds there.'

'You wouldn't mind that?' he asked.

She shook her head. 'She's part of your life, and but for her we might never have met.'

'And if we hadn't met my life would have gone on in the old dead, hopeless way. I have so much to be grateful for. I feared love as a weakness, but I was wrong. Love is strength, and the true weakling is the man who can't love, or the one who fears to let himself love.

'For years I've held myself behind doors that were bolted and barred, refusing to allow anyone through. I thought I was safe from invasion, but in truth I was destroying myself from within. Now I know that there's no true strength except what you give me in your arms, and in your heart.'

She took his face between her hands.

'You're right,' she said. 'It's not a weakness to need people. It's only a weakness if you don't know that you need them, so you don't reach out to them, and you're left floundering alone. But if you reach out, and they reach back, then your strength can defeat worlds.'

'And you did reach back, didn't you?' he asked. 'It wasn't just chance that we met again after so many years.'

'True. I think the ancient gods gave their orders from Mount Olympus.'

'And that's why it's been inevitable between us from the start—if you really feel you can put up with me.'

'How could I disobey the orders of the gods?' she asked him tenderly.

And what the gods ordered, they would protect. Their life together had been ordained, and so it must be. It would be a life of passion and pain, quarrels, reconciliations, heartbreak and joy. But never for one moment would they doubt that they were treading the path that had been preordained for them.

One day the River Styx would be waiting to carry them on, to Eternity.

But that day was not yet.

MILLS & BOON

MODERN

Power and Passion

Prepare to be swept off your feet by sophisticated, sexy and seductive heroes, in some of the world's most glamourous and romantic locations, where power and passion collide.

MILLS & BOON
Desire

Indulge in secrets and scandal, intense drama and plenty of sizzling hot action with powerful and passionate heroes who have it all: wealth, status, good looks... everything but the right woman.

JOIN US ON SOCIAL MEDIA!

Stay up to date with our latest releases, author news and gossip, special offers and discounts, and all the behind-the-scenes action from Mills & Boon...

 millsandboon

 millsandboonuk

 millsandboon

It might just be true love...